Praise for Laura Marie Altom

"Altom's quirky characters, innovative _____ and humorous storyte_____ _____rable read."

—_____ _____ _Bride_

"Action-packed, y_____ _____g Joe_

"An extremely emotional story about love and loss. Have a tissue on hand—Altom will tug at your heart."

—*RT Book Reviews* on *Daddy Daycare*

Praise for Marin Thomas

"Thomas slowly and skillfully unveils the personal secrets that affect the moves of each character and presents two people riddled with guilt over a loved one's death with emotional dexterity."

—*RT Book Reviews* on *No Ordinary Cowboy*

"If you want a sweet and heartwarming read, don't miss *True Blue Cowboy* by Marin Thomas."

—*HarlequinJunkie.com*

"Though Riley's charming and Maria sincere, and their romance is sweetly electric, it's the tribulations and triumph of the three delinquent teens in this story that will steal readers' hearts."

—*RT Book Reviews* on *A Rodeo Man's Promise*

His Christmas Baby

Laura Marie Altom & Marin Thomas

Previously published as *The Cowboy SEAL's Jingle Bell Baby*
and *The Surgeon's Christmas Baby*

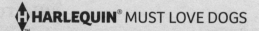

H HARLEQUIN® MUST LOVE DOGS

If you purchased this book without a cover you should be aware that this book is stolen property. It was reported as "unsold and destroyed" to the publisher, and neither the author nor the publisher has received any payment for this "stripped book."

ISBN-13: 978-1-335-69089-0

His Christmas Baby

Copyright © 2018 by Harlequin Books S.A.

First published as The Cowboy SEAL's Jingle Bell Baby
by Harlequin Books in 2016 and
The Surgeon's Christmas Baby by Harlequin Books in 2015.

The publisher acknowledges the copyright holders
of the individual works as follows:

The Cowboy SEAL's Jingle Bell Baby
Copyright © 2016 by Laura Marie Altom

The Surgeon's Christmas Baby
Copyright © 2015 by Brenda Smith-Beagley

Recycling programs
for this product may
not exist in your area.

All rights reserved. Except for use in any review, the reproduction or utilization of this work in whole or in part in any form by any electronic, mechanical or other means, now known or hereafter invented, including xerography, photocopying and recording, or in any information storage or retrieval system, is forbidden without the written permission of the publisher, Harlequin Enterprises Limited, 22 Adelaide St. West, 40th Floor, Toronto, Ontario M5H 4E3, Canada.

This is a work of fiction. Names, characters, places and incidents are either the product of the author's imagination or are used fictitiously, and any resemblance to actual persons, living or dead, business establishments, events or locales is entirely coincidental.

This edition published by arrangement with Harlequin Books S.A.

For questions and comments about the quality of this book, please contact us at CustomerService@Harlequin.com.

® and TM are trademarks of Harlequin Enterprises Limited or its corporate affiliates. Trademarks indicated with ® are registered in the United States Patent and Trademark Office, the Canadian Intellectual Property Office and in other countries.

HARLEQUIN®
™ www.Harlequin.com

Printed in U.S.A.

CONTENTS

Laura Marie Altom is a bestselling and award-winning author who has penned nearly fifty books. After college (go, Hogs!), Laura Marie did a brief stint as an interior designer before becoming a stay-at-home mom to boy-girl twins and a bonus son. Always an avid romance reader, she knew it was time to try her hand at writing when she found herself replotting the afternoon soaps.

When not immersed in her next story, Laura plays video games, tackles Mount Laundry and, of course, reads romance!

Laura loves hearing from readers at either PO Box 2074, Tulsa, OK 74101, or by email, balipalm@aol.com.

Love winning fun stuff? Check out lauramariealtom.com.

Books by Laura Marie Altom

Harlequin Western Romance

Cowboy SEALs

The SEAL's Miracle Baby
The Baby and the Cowboy SEAL
The SEAL's Second Chance Baby
The Cowboy SEAL's Jingle Bell Baby
The Cowboy SEAL's Christmas Baby

Visit the Author Profile page
at Harlequin.com for more titles.

THE COWBOY SEAL'S
JINGLE BELL BABY

Laura Marie Altom

When I asked my daughter who this book should be dedicated to, she smiled and said, "Duh—me and Yeti." Yeti's her big, doofus black Lab who's so naughty that he actually takes time away from my writing. He doesn't in any way deserve a book dedication, but since he's so cute, I'll cave... :-)

For Hannah & Yeti

Prologue

'Twas the night before Easter...

"How about letting a cowboy buy you a drink?" Navy SEAL Rowdy Jones slurred his words, but the evening's libations bolstered his courage. As such, he'd moseyed over to the gorgeous little hottie who'd stolen his last rational thought.

She appraised him as if he were a stud sire up for auction.

"Want me to spin around so you get the full force of my magnetic attraction?" he asked with a grin.

In a dive bar filled with boot-wearing, beer-guzzling cowboys, she sipped a martini. Her white dress clung tight enough to have been painted on. She had the face of an angel, with cherry-red lips and a sleek wave of blond hair his fingertips knew would feel silky.

Instead of speaking, she downed more of her drink, then raised her hand, motioning for him to twirl.

More than a little turned on by her silent take-charge demeanor, he raised his longneck beer high, gyrating his ass in time with George Strait's "All My Ex's Live in Texas."

He didn't just want this gal; he *had* to have her— all of her. Down and dirty and every way in between.

In his thirty-odd years, he'd gotten pretty good at sizing up a man's or woman's character. The woman's exterior screamed iceberg dead ahead. But a sadness in her eyes made him wonder if her carefully applied outer persona was eggshell fragile.

"Like what you see?" he asked on the turn around.

Without a trace of a smile, she nodded.

"Wanna get a room?"

She nodded again.

She set her drink on the bar, then held out her hand as if she were a princess and he her loyal subject.

His brain couldn't quite compute the fact that she was taking him up on his offer, but he wasn't complaining. He paid their bar tabs, then led her through the maze of Saturday-night heroes, all striving to outshine one another with their tall tales.

Though the next morning would ring in Easter, their miserable portion of North Dakota hadn't gotten the memo. Earlier that night at the annual rodeo, the temperature had been pleasant enough, but a front must've moved in and cold wind whipped his mystery gal's formerly smooth hair into a wild, sexy tangle.

Given the nasty weather, the bar's exterior was lonely. Neon beer signs glowed through dusty windows.

The parking lot's one light didn't do much to show their way to the adjoining motel.

Giddy Up Inn wasn't fancy, but he'd heard from temporary cowboys hired to move cattle from seasonal ranges that it was clean.

The lobby was plain.

A single red Formica counter held a cash register and a few struggling plants. The air smelled of Lysol and the coffee brewing on a corner stand.

Rowdy paid cash for the room, and the weary-looking clerk handed over an actual key attached to a plastic horseshoe.

Back outside, Rowdy sheltered his dream girl from the worst of the wind. He found room twenty-one and slipped the key into the lock.

The room was cold, so he quickly shut the door and turned on the heat.

The woman stood just inside the door.

She hugged herself and looked on the verge of crying.

"Look," he said, "if you'd rather call this off, I'd understand." He hooked his thumbs in his Wranglers' back pockets. "I mean, I'd be lying if I said I wouldn't be disappointed, but my momma raised me to be a gentleman and—"

"You always talk this much?"

She flew at him like a summer wind—wild and hot.

She braced her hands to his stubbled cheeks, slanting her lips across his with what he could describe only as an angry, frenzied need. He met the sweep of her tongue and groaned.

When she reached for his belt buckle, he was all

too happy to help her along. She jerked his denim shirt open with enough force to rain buttons onto the carpeted floor. She pressed her small, nimble hands to his chest, kneading his pecs, skimming his abs. She trailed her lips over his bare skin, nipping his left biceps, sucking the hollow at the base of his neck.

Her every action screamed desperation.

The gentleman in him wondered why.

The horny bastard only wanted more.

He spun her around, jerking down the zipper on her dress. It might be white, but her attitude was bad-girl red. He let the garment drop to the floor, and with her back to him, he kissed her neck, cupping his hand to her belly to press her against his obvious need.

Her bra and panties weren't from around these parts. White lace fine enough for him to rip off her with his teeth yet fancy to the degree he wasn't ashamed to admit he felt damn near intimidated.

As if her curves weren't tough enough to handle, there was her scent—once again at odds with her outer ice queen. How could she look so cold, and yet, when he breathed her in, smell like sunshine and lemonade or wildflowers swaying in a gentle breeze.

His physical ache to be inside her had grown to a near-frantic need. A nagging voice told him to at least dig a condom from his wallet. After a few tries in between kisses, he finally managed to roll one on. But too many beers and two hands filled with her ample breasts made him not much interested in anything beyond unlatching her bra and then dragging down the sheer panties.

She dropped his jeans and he was damned glad to have gone commando.

They were kissing again, and he found her hot and ready. Without thinking, he hefted her onto the dresser, then rammed all the way home. She cried out but then dug her fingers into his back, urging him faster and harder.

He didn't know her name or job or where she could possibly be from, but none of that mattered. She was his every wicked fantasy. His whole world encapsulated in a lemonade-scented dream.

He thrust until he couldn't think or breathe.

Until raw sensation struck him temporarily blind.

Mere moments after spilling his seed, he had to have her again…

Chapter 1

'Twas almost the night before Halloween...

"Just shoot me..." Rowdy stared at his cell phone as if it had bit him.

"What's wrong?" His roommate and fellow navy SEAL, Logan, slurped from his milkshake.

"What do you think?" He glared at his friend, who was a genius with plastic explosives but apparently couldn't manage setting up auto-pay for their damn utility bills. "Try dropping your cell down an Afghanistan well, then slogging through six months' worth of voice mail. I'd delete it all but turns out some of this crap is important—like when the gas company calls with a recorded message explaining our service got turned off for nonpayment."

"Oops. Yeah, I meant to look into that. No wonder we've been stuck with cold showers." Logan shrugged and took another sip.

Rowdy rolled his eyes and moved on to the next message.

While his friends worked their way around Virginia Beach's Lynnhaven Mall's food court, sampling all the fast food they'd missed while overseas, Rowdy had been trapped at his cell phone provider's store, buying a new phone. He'd bummed Logan's for occasional chats with his parents, but since he'd been with the only other people he ever called, he figured there was no point in replacing it till now.

Just as Rowdy played the last message, Logan signaled that he was headed to the Corn Dog Factory.

Paul Jameson—nicknamed Duck on account of his giant paddle feet—stood in line at Sbarro.

"Um, hello?" a woman said in a tentative tone. "Hope I have the right man? I'm trying to reach Rowdy? Gosh, I'm sorry. I just realized that though you gave me this number, I don't even know your last name. You might not remember me, but we shared a, um… Let's just say we were together—the night before Easter, and… I don't know any easy way to say this, so here goes. I'm pregnant. You're the father. But no worries—I'm putting the baby up for adoption, so you're off the hook. I already found an amazing family, and our son is g-going to lead a g-great life." Wait, what? *His son?* Her voice broke up. Was she crying? "Anyway, if I don't hear back from you soon, I'll assume this plan works for you, too. Bye." Click.

Stunned, Rowdy stood in the food court's center for

what felt like an eternity while throngs of shoppers walked around him. How could an accidental pregnancy happen to him *twice*?

"Dude…" Logan slapped him on the back. "You look like hell. I didn't forget any other payments, did I?"

Rowdy stumbled into the nearest chair at the nearest table, then cued up the message again on his phone. "Listen."

Duck wandered up with a slice of pepperoni that was almost as big as his feet. He leaned in.

Logan sat, setting his corn-dog tray with about eighteen mustard packets in front of him. By the time the message had ended, he'd paled, too. "Dude… What the hell? Didn't you learn back in high school to always wear a raincoat?"

"I always do—did. This has to be another mistake." His mind flashed on that one brief doubt he'd had about his condom before plunging inside the woman who'd made him care about nothing other than giving her as much pleasure as she was giving him. Was it possible the condom broke?

"Then this chick must be like the other one who tried scamming you?"

"Exactly." Only that time, Logan knew for a fact his protection had been fully in force.

Duck said, "No wonder Ginny never lets me off my leash to play with you. Rowdy, you're a freakin' mess."

Rowdy glared at his supposed friend. The guy was married with four kids. His leash was a choke chain with links made of emotional steel. Poor guy hardly got out at all. But he seemed happy. Aside from their SEAL team, Duck's wife and kids were his world.

As for Rowdy? Being a SEAL was his world. Period. End of story. But what if this woman was telling the truth…

He winced.

"When did she call?" Logan asked.

"Six months ago."

"Damn. So, like, your bun's almost ready to pop out of the oven?" Logan bit into his first of three corn dogs.

Rowdy pressed the heels of his hands to his throbbing forehead. "What am I going to do? Because one thing's for sure—there's no way in hell she's giving away my son. On the flip side, I'll be the first to admit I'm not marriage material."

"Great attitude, man." Duck smacked the back of Rowdy's head. He'd have considered popping him back, but Duck outweighed him by fifty pounds of pure muscle. "Get your head out of your ass and get a clue. Family life is great. You, me, Ginny and your new bride can all have cookouts on the beach. My kids will love playing with yours."

"See?" Logan stole a pepperoni from Duck's slice. "No worries. Already, we've downgraded this situation from a DEFCON 2 paternity emergency down to a nice, steady DEFCON 5 beach barbecue. We've got your back. Plus, I'll make a great uncle."

Some days Rowdy wished he had better friends.

Ex-rodeo queen, ex-wife and ex-debutante Tiffany Lawson was seven months pregnant and determined to squeeze her formerly size-six feet into a pair of her favorite Jimmy Choos. It was a given no clothes in her closet fit, but now her shoes wouldn't, either?

As for the no-good, rotten dirt clod of a cowboy who'd landed her in this position and hadn't even had the decency to call? He could go straight to Hades for all she cared. Rowdy was low-life pond scum—*lower*. She didn't even know his last name! Which, granted, didn't say a heckuva lot about her decision-making skills, but still…

The less time spent dwelling on him, the better.

"Honey, no matter how hard you try cramming your toes into those darlings, they're not going to fit." Her mother, former Dallas society maven Gigi Hastings-Lawson, didn't even bother looking up from the same copy of *Town & Country* she'd been reading for three months. Thanks to Big Daddy Lawson's slight issues with the law, she couldn't afford a new one. Since he'd be away for a nice long while and their Dallas mansion had been seized, Tiffany and her mother now lived in the godforsaken speck on the map known as Maple Springs, North Dakota.

Making matters worse—if that were even possible— was the fact that Tiffany didn't earn enough money in real estate to have her own place. She and her mom lived with her paternal grandmother, Pearl. Since Big Daddy had paid off her house long before his trouble with the law, authorities allowed her to keep it.

"You did hear it's supposed to snow?" Her mother lounged on the white velvet chaise Tiffany had salvaged from their former home by strapping it to the roof of the secondhand red Jeep Cherokee she'd bought from their former housekeeper.

Mr. Bojangles—her spoiled teacup Chihuahua— slept on her mother's lap. He wore a black sweater and rhinestone collar. It had become her own special ironic hell that her dog now dressed better than her.

"When is it not supposed to snow?" Tiffany peered out her bedroom window to find another gloomy day in her equally gloomy life.

Blustery wind shook Pearl's century-old home like a dog with a bone.

For comfort, she cupped her hands to her baby bump, but even that wasn't satisfying, knowing she'd soon give her son to the Parkers. They were an amazing couple—both attorneys. Jeb Parker was considering a gubernatorial campaign. Susie Parker promised as soon as the baby was born, she'd resign to stay home with their new son.

In her former life, Tiffany had much the same plans, but then her father's legal woes had been too much for her ex, Crawford, to deal with, and that had been that. He'd filed for a quiet divorce and was now married to one of her best friends—a former Miss Texas. *C'est la vie.*

Tiffany did learn one valuable lesson from her pain—men were as flighty as trash in the wind. Never to be trusted. They made you love them and then broke your heart. Okay, maybe that was more than one lesson, but bottom line, she would never, ever, *ever* give her heart to another man.

A twinge of guilt for her infant son made her hug her tummy. *You're excluded, little fella. You'll be the one man on the planet who's perfect in every way. I might not be physically with you while you're growing up, but I'll be with you every day in spirit.*

Tiffany reached for her hot-pink sequined Uggs,

cramming them over the navy tights she wore with the only fashionable maternity dress she owned that still fit—she'd change into her navy pumps at the office. Early on in her pregnancy, she'd found cute, cheap dresses at thrift shops, but now that she was huge, secondhand maternity wear was as elusive as late-October real estate sales.

"Maybe you should stay in?" Gigi had moved on to a more current *Vanity Fair*.

Mr. Bojangles glared at the imposition of waking when she moved.

"Mom, stop." Tiffany added a pale pink cardigan over the dress, then a floral scarf and pearls. At this point, accessorizing was her only hope of maintaining a businesslike appearance at Hearth and Home Realty, where she worked twice as hard as her coworker Lyle, yet because he was the boss's nephew, he had a knack for landing the best listings. "We can't live in Maple Springs forever. Don't you want to get back to Dallas?"

"Honestly?" Gigi sighed. "I'd rather continue hiding. As long as Big Daddy's *away*, I'm not setting foot in polite society."

To this day—months after her husband's formal sentencing—Gigi refused to state out loud that her husband was in prison. She much preferred genteel euphemisms that sidestepped the harsh reality that it could be a year before she had a true marriage again.

Tiffany had visited her father only twice but regularly called.

Gigi preferred old-fashioned paper correspondence.

"I've got to get to a showing by nine. Try helping Grammy with some housework, okay?" Tiffany kissed her mother's cheek—already fully made up and smelling of pricey lotion and cream. To show how much she adored her mom, Tiffany picked up sample-sized expensive-brand cosmetics at Bismarck department stores or online at discount wholesalers. There was no need for Gigi to ever learn the true extent of just how bad things were financially.

"I'll try, dear, but you know how dust makes me sneeze."

"I know. Just do your best." Tiffany rubbed Mr. Bojangles between his ears, then made it down the two-story home's creaky front stairs and almost to the door before getting busted by her grandmother.

"Don't even think of dashing out of here without a proper breakfast."

"Grammy, I'm starving and would love to eat but have to meet a client by nine."

"What if I made you an egg-and-cheese sandwich to go?"

Tiffany's tummy growled. That did sound awfully tempting.

"See?" Grammy smiled. "Your boy's already got an appetite."

"Okay, I'll eat. But I'm meeting Mr. Jones at the office at nine, so I can't be late. And, Grammy, you know I can't keep the baby."

"Nonsense." Pearl guided Tiffany into the kitchen and parked her in a comfy chair at the table her ancestors had reportedly hauled west in a covered wagon.

She happily sighed when her grandmother handed her a steaming mug of homemade cocoa with whipped cream on top.

"Mmm... I love you," Tiffany said.

"I know," Pearl said.

When the first piece of bacon hit the skillet, Mr. Bojangles scurried into the kitchen. Of course, Grammy fed him part of a still-warm buttermilk biscuit.

The eggs frying in butter in her grandmother's favorite cast-iron skillet smelled so good that Tiffany didn't even get too terribly upset when an extra-hard wind gust rattled the paned windows. She just glanced that way to note that it had indeed started to snow.

The flakes were huge—like designer gumballs falling topsy-turvy, covering ugly brown grass with a tidy blanket of white.

Would her son love playing in the snow as much as she used to when visiting her grandmother over the holidays?

Along with the realization that she'd never know, pain knotted the back of her throat. She squashed it.

Giving up her son was the hardest thing she'd ever do, but it was hands down the best decision for *him*. For his future life. What she wanted didn't matter. If it did...

Well, she squashed that thought, too.

Rowdy loved staying with his folks, but having spent the bulk of the past ten years in warm—if not downright hot—climates, he much preferred the family traveling to Virginia to see him. A few times a year, they packed up his brother, Carl, sister-in-law, Justine, and their two rug rats, six-year-old Ingrid and eight-year-old Isobel, to come to the beach.

Clearly, the last time he'd been in Maple Springs had

been a disaster. He'd always had a thing for cowgirls and Tiffany had been as hot as they come.

Last Easter had been unseasonably warm, and after the annual rodeo he'd attended, he and a few friends had headed to the town's only bar. He'd met Tiffany in one of those twists of fate you might see in movies but think never actually happen.

Rowdy had tried calling her, but the number had been disconnected. He'd next gotten on the phone with his mom and had her make a few discreet inquiries.

Rowdy had been under the impression that Tiffany lived in Dallas, but turned out a very pregnant girl named Tiffany Lawson currently resided with Pearl Lawson, who used to run the town's only grocery before selling it to the Dewitt brothers—all of which was a roundabout way of explaining why he was now headed down Buckhead Road to meet with Tiffany at her place of business at Hearth and Home Realty. If his mom ever gave up ranch life, she ought to consider signing on with the CIA. No spook Rowdy had met came close to solving a mystery like his mom.

That said, she was currently none too happy with him.

For quite a few years, she'd expected him to marry and give her more grandkids. The news that she might already have a grandson on the way had been far more agreeable to her than him. It hadn't been that long since he'd been through a similar scenario, and he couldn't handle that brand of stress again.

Regardless, he had plenty of leave time coming, so he'd let his CO know he'd be gone a few weeks, then hopped the earliest flight to Bismarck. His family had been thrilled to pick him up from there. That had been yesterday.

First on this morning's agenda was meeting with the mother of his child and hopefully having a rational, adult conversation about a number of topics. First, he needed to be 100 percent sure the baby was his. Second, he'd inform her that she had no right in hell to give his son away to strangers—or anyone else. That said, he wasn't sure what might happen next, but he was an honorable man.

He and Tiffany would find a mutually amenable arrangement.

His folks felt Rowdy should have at least given the woman a courtesy call that he was in town, but when it came to the topic of signing away his kid, he wasn't in a courteous mood.

In a businesslike setting, everyone would be on their best behavior.

The twenty-minute drive from the ranch to town gave him too much time to think.

Maple Springs was nice enough in the summer, but once winter set in, the place could best be described as gray. A half-mile, single-sided stretch of old-as-dirt grayish brick buildings housed antiques stores, insurance agents, the drugstore, the diner and café, three clothing stores, and a day care. A few years back, his mom told him the mayor's wife decreed the windows of each business be fitted with red-striped canvas awnings. In warmer months, they were okay, but the rest of the year, they resembled soggy ice-and snow-crusted circus popcorn boxes.

Judging by how fast the snow was falling, this might

be one of the last weeks of the year when both sides of Richard L. Fulmer Avenue were available for parking. The usual snowplow drift grew on the same side of the road as the railroad tracks. That side also happened to not have any businesses—at least not until a good two miles outside town, where the Robert T. Fulmer Tavern had moved into the former feed store's building. Mayor Richard L. Fulmer was less than pleased about his twin brother serving spirits, which was why the establishment had to be outside city limits.

As long as the beer was cold, nobody in town gave two hoots. As an added bonus, Robert had been kind enough to restore the long-abandoned roadside motel just next door. Much to his brother's dismay, he'd been voted Maple Springs' Man of the Year in 1998 for giving free rooms to patrons too tanked to drive.

Rowdy recalled that at the time of his son's conception, he was awfully thankful for the motel's close proximity.

He pulled his dad's truck into an empty space just down from Hearth and Home's office. When he wasn't in town, Rowdy stored his truck in one of the ranch's outbuildings. As his lousy luck would have it, this morning, the damned thing hadn't started.

In an attempt to hold off winter's fast-approaching gloom, pumpkin lights hung from the office's awning. Skeletons danced from gaslight sconces on either side of the mirrored-glass double doors.

Rowdy turned off the engine, then sat a spell to compose his thoughts. He'd made his appointment with Tiffany through her secretary. Would Tiffany even remember who he was? For that matter, was she mistaking him for another man? There was also an off chance this gal wasn't even the same woman with whom he'd had relations. If she wasn't, he'd be free to return to his normally kick-ass life.

Forcing a deep breath, he dove from the balmy truck cab to the miserable white mess outside.

Sleet mixed with the snow.

Wind pitched it like darts against his forehead and cheeks. He tugged his battered brown leather cowboy hat lower and raised his long duster coat's collar higher.

Hell's bells, what he wouldn't give to be back in Virginia.

Everyone on the bustling street walked with their heads down. It was a downright miracle there weren't more pedestrian collisions.

He yanked open the door to find wondrous heat. It took a few seconds for his eyes to adjust to the sudden lack of sleet in them. When they did, he found a cozy seating area that had a sofa and two armchairs facing a coffee table and electric fireplace.

"Mr. Jones?" A woman with curly brown hair that was almost as big as her bosom rose from her desk to extend her hand. "Our Tiffany will be glad you made it through this storm. Sometimes newcomers take a while to adjust to our weather, don'tcha know."

"True. But I grew up here, so I'm used to it." Her thick accent had him working to hide a smile. When he'd lived in town, he hadn't noticed, but now that he'd been away, he heard how pronounced it was in some Maple Springs residents.

"You did? Well, why didn't you say so? Who are your people?"

"Patsy and James Jones. Know them?"

"As I live and breathe. *Rowdy?*"

"Yes, ma'am. Have we met?"

"Boy—you're breaking my heart." She pressed her hand to her impressive rack. "I'm Doris Mills. Well, used to be Doris Patrick, but that was before I went and married Skeeter. I used to be your fourth-, fifth- and sixth-grade Sunday-school teacher. Don't you remember?"

"Sure. Sorry. It's been a while."

"I'll say." She looked him up and down, then whistled. "You've grown into a cool drink of water. Bet your momma's pleased as punch 'bout you moving home."

To avoid getting into the whole messy business of why he was actually in town, Rowdy said, "I, ah, really need to talk with Tiffany and figured having her show me a house or two would be the best way to connect."

"You two sweet on each other? You always did have the kindest heart. It's adorable that you don't mind her being…" she reddened and patted her own robust belly "…you know… By another man."

Ouch. "Would you mind pointing me to her office?"

"Oh—sure, sure." She waved toward a short hall. "Two doors down on your left."

"Perfect. Thanks."

Rowdy stood outside the partially closed office door for a good thirty seconds. He'd have felt more comfortable pulling all-night surveillance in croc-infested waters. This whole thing raised an uncomfortable number of similarities to a not-so-distant situation he'd just as soon forget. Besides, aside from what his brother had told him about the crap he'd gone through with Justine's cravings, mood swings and general crankiness, Rowdy knew nothing about pregnant women. That said, he did know a fair bit about charming the normal variety of gal and planned on using the same general logic.

"Thank you, Susie. Promise, as soon as I have my next sonogram, I'll email the pictures."

Eavesdropping on Tiffany's call, Rowdy narrowed his gaze.

"Susie, I'm expecting a client any second, but promise, I'll sign all of your attorney's documents this afternoon." There was a long pause. "Please stop worrying. I have no intention of backing out of the adoption. This baby boy will soon be yours."

"The hell he will." So much for adult professionalism or laying on the charm. Rowdy stormed Tiffany's office like an enemy camp—only instead of rescuing hostages or liberating territory, he was claiming his unborn son.

Chapter 2

"Susie, I've gotta go." After hanging up the phone, Tiffany's eyes widened in shock and maybe even a little horror to find her baby's daddy standing a mere five feet away. "You…"

The man she hadn't shared a room with since she could see her own toes closed the door.

"What are you doing here? How did you even find me?" Flustered, she couldn't decide what to do with her hands. She skimmed her no-doubt-messy hair, then tried crossing her arms, but that didn't feel quite right, because she'd grown so top-heavy that her arms were practically under her chin —yet one more reason to despise the man standing before her.

"Got your message." He wagged a silver-toned cell phone.

"Little late, aren't you?"

He shrugged. "Been out of town. Unavoidable delay."

"Uh-huh…" She returned to her email. "Whatever you've got to say, you're not just a *little* late, but *all-the-way* late. Adoption plans are already in place."

"About that…" He stepped forward, bracing his hands on either side of her small desk. In a quiet, down-right lethal tone, he said, "There's no way in hell you're signing away my son."

Tiffany gulped. The last time she'd seen him he'd been handsome, but she'd also been wearing martini goggles and in hindsight had figured it was an impossibility for him to look half as good as she remembered. Wrong. He looked even better. He smelled amazing, too—like a day at the beach. Warm sun and sand and a hint of sexy sweat. She sneaked a peek at whisker-stubbled cheeks and eyes green enough to remind her of her former Dallas mansion's lawn.

Straightening in her chair, she retorted, "As a matter of fact, I am giving him up. We might have discussed the matter had you been courteous enough to call within hours—or even days—of my message. But when you failed to share so much as an opinion after months, what did you expect? As much as I'd love being a mom, I can barely afford being me—which reminds me, I have an appointment for a showing, so you'll need to leave."

He not only didn't leave but set his battered brown leather cowboy hat in one guest chair, then proceeded to help himself to the other. His legs were so long they didn't fold right given the cramped space, so he stretched them out. Beneath her desk, the toes of his cowboy boots touched the toes of her pumps.

She lurched backward as if she'd been struck by a rattler.

"Let me guess?" he asked with a lopsided, white-toothed grin. "This client is a Mr. Jones?"

"Yes. You know him?"

"I am him." He chuckled.

"No, no, no…" She massaged her forehead.

"Oh, yes."

"But I needed that commission." Her stinging eyes and tight throat might mean she was ready to cry, but she refused to give him the satisfaction.

"Relax. I'll help you raise the baby. Financially, and you know . . ." He waved his hands. "With all the other stuff kids need."

"Great—only you won't be raising him at all. Susie and Jeb Parker will. They're amazing people, and both have real jobs—as opposed to you. I'm assuming you're a low-life seasonal cowboy? Now that you've earned enough cash to buy beer through the long, cold winter, you're back in town to raise a little hell?"

"First, cut the attitude and sass. Second, how about trying to act like a civilized adult. Third, I'm a freaking navy SEAL—it doesn't get much more *real* than that, sweetheart."

"You're in the navy? In the middle of North Dakota? The night we were together, you told me you were a bull rider. But now I see you meant to say you're just full of bull." She primly folded her hands atop her desk. What she wouldn't give to have one of her father's former legal team make mincemeat of this loser—although they hadn't been all that successful with her dad.

"Okay…" He sighed, then leaned back in his chair,

opening his long duster coat just enough for her to see how well his brown sweater clung to his broad chest. "I get that the night we met, I wasn't exactly on my best behavior, but then, neither were you."

True.

"But here's the deal. I really am in the navy, and I was in town for the annual rodeo and to visit my family for Easter. They were supposed to join me in Virginia Beach, but Dad tripped during the last big snow and hurt his back. The reason I never got your message is because I was in Afghanistan and dropped my damned phone down a well."

"Show me pics or it didn't happen." What kind of drugs was this guy on? "Oh—but since your phone is at the bottom of a well, guess that won't happen, either."

"Ever heard of the *cloud*?" His expression brightened when he pulled out his phone to start flipping through photos of a guy wearing desert camo, mirrored Ray-Bans and a similar cowboy hat, only with a full beard and shaggy hair. "Here I am with a donkey, and playing soccer with village kids—that's the phone-eating well in the background..." He pointed. "There's me driving a tank, and me in a cave— Oh, here I am with a cheetah. You find the damnedest things in terrorist camps."

"Okay, okay, so you proved you've been somewhere in the Middle East, but as for you being a SEAL? Let's get real. If I had a dollar for every time some guy in a bar told me he was a fighter pilot or spy—or in your case, bull rider—I sure wouldn't be selling real estate in the middle of nowhere, North Dakota."

"Case in point." He stashed his phone in his back pocket, then winked. "You sure didn't have a problem with my line the night we made our son—*if* he even is mine." He said the words, but Logan's churning stomach recalled that split second of condom doubt. He could deny it all he wanted, but in all probability, this baby was his.

She rolled her eyes.

"Ready to reach an amicable arrangement?"

"No. Because not only do I not believe you're from Maple Springs, but I think you're lying about the navy and your rodeo glory days and probably damn near everything else you've ever told me."

"That's it." Jaw clenched, he leaped to his feet, planted his hat on his head, then rounded to her side of the desk. Hand on her upper arm, he barked, "Get up. There's someone you need to meet."

"I'm not going anywhere with you."

"Oh, yes, you are."

"*No*, I'm not."

"Look…" Even though he'd released her, she could have sworn his each individual fingertip scorched her skin through her dress. He knelt so his gaze landed dead even with hers. He was close enough for his warm, coffee-laced breath to flare her nostrils and raise achingly familiar goose bumps up and down the length of her arms. To compensate for the fact that her lungs forgot how to breathe, she gasped—unfortunately making her sound like a flopping fish. Good God, he was a fine-looking man. "I understand why my showing up like this would catch you off guard, but promise, I have nothing but you and our baby's best interests at heart. If you want to share custody, I'll happily pay child support. If you want to go the old-fashioned route and get hitched, I'd hardly say I'm thrilled with the idea, but we could work something out. Come back to Virginia with me. I'm damned good-looking and you're a stone-cold fox. This baby's gonna be a heartbreaker. We'll make things legal. You stay home with the rug rat and I'll provide you both with a decent living. I get why you might not trust me, but since we already have an appointment, at least come with me to my parents' ranch. Meet my mom and dad—they'll vouch for me. Give me a chance to prove I'm a stand-up guy."

His speech made Tiffany more than a little miffed.

Their looks were irrelevant.

Besides, she had a plan. A good plan. He'd been out of her picture for months. How dare he barge in here and act like he was now in charge?

"What do you say? It's nasty outside, but Dad's got a fire going and Mom makes crazy-good hot chocolate. Toss in one of her homemade cinnamon rolls and I promise, you won't be disappointed."

What if I already am? Not by any of what he'd just proposed, but by the fact that it was far too late to put on the brakes and start over with their relationship. She never would have slept with the guy if something about him hadn't drawn her in. He was smart-mouthed and cocky and no doubt a pain in the ass to deal with in everyday life. But his green eyes made her feel as warm as if she were back home in Dallas, relaxed and happy, strolling hand in hand barefoot across a sumptuous grass lawn she hadn't had to mow.

"Tiff?"

"What happened to you thinking I'm lying about

you being my baby's father? Plus, I don't even know your full name."

"Sorry. Now that I've seen you, I remember how we both went more than a little crazy that night. As for my name, it's Rowdy Jones. Right there on your appointment sheet." He nodded to the memo on her desk. Mr. Jones. He hadn't lied about his name?

"Show me your ID."

He shook his head at the imposition but did as she asked.

Sure enough, unless he'd spent a fortune on a fake, that was his real name. He stood six-two, weighed 220 and was even an organ donor.

"Now that you know I'm official, ready to meet my folks?"

She lurched when the baby gave an extra-hard shove to her appendix.

"Whoa…" Rowdy stared at her enormous belly. "Was that our little guy?"

She had a spiteful retort on the tip of her tongue about the baby technically no longer belonging to either of them, but Tiffany instead nodded.

"Mind if I…you know…" He hovered his hand above her bump.

"Knock yourself out."

When he touched her, all sense of logic short-circuited.

His fingers were big and warm and reminded her of that night when they'd both been very naughty, yet that poor behavior had felt so very good. She hadn't been with another man since.

The sad truth was that she hadn't wanted to.

This guy—the one she'd been reunited with for all of fifteen minutes—was already making her head swim with all manner of delicious possibilities for a brighter, better life.

But she didn't have just herself to consider. Even if she did, she had to remember men were the enemy—*on all fronts*. Her dad had been a ticking time bomb for a decade before exploding her and her mother's lives. Then there was her ex, Crawford. Just when she'd needed him most, he'd emotionally shredded her heart. He hadn't even had the cojones to tell her in person that he wanted a divorce. He'd had some random court-appointed suit show up at their Dallas home to serve papers. She'd tried calling him, certain there had been a mistake, but his secretary had told her Crawford was no longer accepting her calls and that the house, the furnishings, her jewelry and a sizable chunk of cash were hers free and clear.

The only stipulation?

Crawford William Ridgemont IV wanted his precious, unsoiled family name back.

Devastated didn't begin to describe how she'd felt. She'd given him what he wanted, then proceeded to sell the house and everything in it to help pay Big Daddy's legal fees.

The baby kicked again—jolting her from the past and right back into her confusing present.

"Damn..." Rowdy whistled. "He's a tough little guy. We'll need to start thinking of names. My mom's already got a half dozen, but what would you think about John Wayne—of course, as a tribute to the legend."

"John Wayne Jones? Really?" Tiffany pushed her

wheeled desk chair back so abruptly that Rowdy, who still had his hand pressed to her belly, lost his balance and fell onto his knees.

"Hell, woman." He rubbed his lower back. "What's your problem? A little advance notice of your move might've been nice."

"So would returning my call."

He groaned. "Are we back to that? I already told you about my phone and the well."

"Look," she said as she examined her sadly painted pink nails. "There's much more going on here than you could possibly understand. It's complicated." All her life, she'd had a private manicurist, and she still hadn't mastered the art of doing it herself. But she was trying—just like she was giving all she had to this real estate job. All she'd need was one good commission to build her savings and ensure Gigi and Pearl would be comfortable and warm for at least a few months if that was how long it took for her to make her next sale. "All my life, I've depended on men, and they've always, *always* let me down. Now the only person I trust with my well-being is *me*." She hugged her belly. "Don't think for one hot second I wouldn't love being a stay-at-home mom, but I've been down that road and discovered the hard way that it's a dead end."

"So you don't want to get married?" Was it her imagination, or did he look relieved?

"Excuse me?"

"I'm cool with you being a single mom. I mean, I'll always be there for you whenever I'm in the States and I plan to support my kid whether we marry or not, but it might be best if we don't tempt fate by— How do I

put this in a delicate manner?" There he went again
with his maddeningly sexy grin. "Let's just say it probably wouldn't be in either of our best interests to go at
it quite to that degree again."

"Get out." She pointed toward her closed office door.

"Aw, now, don't go getting your pretty pink panties
in a wad—I wasn't complaining. I just—"

She stood. "I don't care what you meant. And for the
record, Mr. Jones, my panties are black—like a black
widow spider. After she mates, she *kills*." Tiffany had
once heard the line in a movie and thought it made for
a great dramatic effect. She tried crossing her arms to
further emphasize she meant business, but of course,
they landed too high on the baby to be comfortable or
sufficiently menacing. Still, no way was she giving in
now. *"Get out."*

"Miss Tiffany, you are one helluva special snow-
flake." After a good long chuckle, he pushed himself
to his feet, retrieved his hat, then followed her orders.
"Want your door open or closed?"

"Closed."

"I'll be in touch."

Only after she was once again alone did Tiffany col-
lapse back into her desk chair. During previous catastro-
phes, she might have indulged in a nice long cry, then
soaked in a bubble bath with plenty of champagne and
imported chocolates.

Now? Her only option was to pull out the big guns.

With an extra-hard tug, her bottom desk drawer
popped open to reveal one of her favorite wedding
gifts—a Baccarat crystal candy dish from Crawford's
Aunt Cookie. Since they'd been married two years be-

fore their divorce, Tiffany got to keep all the gifts. She'd sold the vast majority but kept a cherished few. After all, now that she'd reached rock bottom, she needed to remember what awaited her back at the top.

Smiling, she reached into the bowl for one—okay, make that four—fun-sized Snickers.

Rowdy might have temporarily interrupted her day, but she refused to let him permanently bring her down. She had commissions to earn, a mother and grand-mother to support, and a healthy baby to raise for the Parkers. Which was why she next ate a snack-sized bag of minicarrots, followed by apple juice and ched-dar cheese cubes.

All of which should have filled her but didn't.

What was she really craving?

One of those cinnamon rolls Rowdy said his mom made.

Covering suddenly flushed cheeks, Tiffany rested her forehead against the cool laminate top of her desk. Given the fact that according to WebMD, the average cost of childbirth in America was $9,600—an uncom-plicated C-section was a whopping $15,800—she had no option other than to give her son up for adoption so his new parents could pay. Pearl offered to mortgage her home to keep her great-grandson in the family, but Tiffany could no more let her do that than she could afford health insurance—she knew she'd owe a hefty penalty come tax time for not finding coverage, but she'd worry about that next April.

What Rowdy proposed sounded crazy. Maybe if he'd presented his proposition in a more reasonable manner, she might have considered it.

All she had to do to keep her baby was marry his father, and voilà—her every financial problem would vanish. Only it wouldn't be quite that easy. Rowdy wasn't going to make her his bride for nothing, and not to be a drama queen, but she'd already learned the price for marriage was her soul.

Chapter 3

"Uh-oh…"

"That about sums up my morning." Rowdy shut the back door on nasty blowing snow, wishing he were back on a beach—or, shoot, even a desert would be preferable to this.

"I take it she didn't accept your proposal? Told you so. You should've taken a ring." Patsy Jones lounged in the kitchen's usually sun-flooded window seat, wearing the Hello Kitty grown-up footy pj's his dad had bought her last Christmas. Maybe it was best he hadn't brought Tiffany today?

"Best as I could tell, her refusal had nothing to do with a ring." He hung his hat and coat on the rack beside the door, then went straight to the oven, only to find it empty. "Thought you were making cinnamon rolls?"

"I was, but in the book I'm reading, Jack just got chased by a bear and Marcy has his gun."

Shaking his head, Rowdy settled for heating up a can of SpaghettiOs, then asked, "Where are Dad and Carl?"

"They called a while ago. Found a momma determined to have her calf in this storm. They're staying out there to make sure she's okay."

"Cool." Only it wasn't. He was used to having every minute of his days filled with action, and out here, seemed like everyone had something to do but him. He'd planned on having the mother of his child here to at least hash out plans.

He was running out of time. He needed to get back on base, and their baby wasn't going to wait for Tiffany to make a decision. "I'll be in my room."

"Why? Don't tell me you're giving up?"

He sighed. "No way, but there's not a whole lot else I can do today. Since my ambush didn't work, I need to come up with a better plan of attack."

"How about if you don't treat this like one of your military missions but like a man asking a woman to marry him for the sake of their child? Did you tell Tiffany how sweet you can be if you set your mind to it?"

"I told her I was good-looking."

"Good grief, Rowdy. No wonder she's confused."

"More like pissed. From what I can gather, this isn't her first rodeo, and she's been burned before."

His mom paled. "You mean she already has a child?"

"No. I meant her previous relationships went sour, so now she's one of those man-hater types."

Frowning, she noted, "I'm not sure what that means."

"You know—like the last guy she was with was an ass, so now she hates all men."

"That can't be true." She winced at his foul language, then rested her book on the nearest pillow. The kitchen was yellow, and by yellow, Rowdy meant every last thing save for the oak kitchen table and white marble counters was the color of a damned lemon. Her pillowed window seat was no exception. "Did you tell her you're not like that and wouldn't hurt her?"

"Sure, but by not contacting her until this late in the game, I pretty much already have hurt her. If only I'd have been here from day one of her pregnancy, you know?"

"That's a given. But it's not like you were off with another woman. Did you explain how your phone fell down a well?"

He snorted. "To Tiffany that was the equivalent of telling her my dog ate my homework. She's not buying it."

"Want me to talk to her? Vouch for you?" *Yes*. Initially, that had been exactly what he wanted. But now he wasn't sure bringing his mom into this mess would help.

"Thanks, but no." He arched his head back, slicing his fingers through his buzzed hair. "The last thing I want is for you to interfere."

She waved off his concern and ducked her head back behind her book.

In his room, Rowdy used the remote to click on the TV and flip through channels, but then he realized the TV no longer had a satellite connection—just an ancient VCR and a stack of his mom's workout and chick-flick tapes.

His desk had been replaced by a treadmill, and against the wall where his bed used to be now sat a sewing/craft station and a brass daybed with a freakin' yellow floral spread. His formerly blue walls had been painted yellow and his bikini pinups no doubt burned.

Outside, the storm raged on.

He felt restless and in a perfect world would have saddled his paint, Lucky, to go help his dad and brother. But the odds of finding them in this whiteout were slim to none, which landed him stuck in his yellow cage.

Needing a male perspective, he called Logan. The team was off for another week. Knowing his friend, he was either sleeping, playing PS4 or deep into strip beach bingo with some hottie he'd picked up at Tipsea's, the local SEAL hangout.

"Dude." Logan answered after the third ring. "I was just on a Yuengling and chip run for a 'Call of Duty' marathon—saw a pregnant chick at Food Lion and thought of you. How's it going?"

"Tiff's last words to me were *Get out*." What Rowdy wouldn't give for just one of their fave local beers.

"Damn. You've always got game. If you're not getting action with your own baby momma, there's no hope for the rest of us schmucks."

"Ha ha." Rowdy walked to the room's picture window and pressed his forehead to the cool glass. "What should I do?"

"All women are suckers for presents. I say buy her a bunch of flowers and pickles and ice cream—whatever pregnant chicks like."

"Have you seen the flower assortment up here? This

is North Dakota we're talking about. There might be a couple wilted red truck-stop roses, but that's about it."

"You're making excuses, man. I'm telling you, buy her something nice. Works every time."

Rowdy grimaced.

He'd have gotten better advice from his horse.

Should he have called Duck? Nah. Rowdy didn't need another lecture on the virtues of being a family man. He was a soldier. It was the only thing he knew how to do.

After a few minutes' more small talk with Logan, he hung up to pace.

In a roundabout way, maybe Logan's idea wasn't so bad. Rowdy just needed to take that gifting to the next level.

How many times had Tiffany mentioned that she'd intended to show him houses? He could stay in the navy for only so long and, after retirement, had always planned on returning home. He had money stashed away. What if he went ahead and bought a retirement cabin now? Not only would Tiffany get the commission, but he'd have all that house-hunting time with her to foster goodwill.

Heck, she and his son could even stay in the place when he was deployed. His mom would be close enough to check on her—as would her own mother and grandmother.

From where he was standing, the idea looked like a win-win.

So much so that he headed back downstairs for his hat, coat, boots and keys.

After a little legwork netted him Tiffany's grandmother's address, he announced his new plan to his mom. She gave him grief about driving in the storm, but he was a SEAL.

No way would he be stopped by a little snow…

"Ohmygosh!" Gigi stepped back from the front door to allow space for a snow-covered man to stumble inside Pearl's foyer. "You must be freezing. Get in here. I'm not accustomed to welcoming strange men into my home, but in this case, it's the only charitable thing to do." Once he was inside, she shut the door on a growling north wind and blowing snow. *"Tiffany! Mother!"*

"I'm right here," Tiffany said from behind her mom. "There's no need to shout." Especially since this man was no stranger, but Rowdy.

"You stupid man." Tiffany took his hat and coat, hanging them on the brass rack at the base of the stairs. Both of his personal items were snow crusted. "Why are you out in this storm? More importantly, what are you doing here?"

Mr. Bojangles yapped at Rowdy's boots.

"I—I got a g-great idea." His teeth chattered so bad he could hardly speak. Ice crystals clung to his stubble and his cheeks had turned an alarming red.

"You know him?" Gigi asked.

"Yes." Tiffany would have loved telling a little white lie, but apparently Rowdy's determination outweighed her imagination.

"You never told me you had a suitor." Gigi beamed as if she'd been handed the keys to the Dallas Galleria Neiman Marcus. "How very nice to meet you. I'm

Mrs. Gregoria Hastings-Lawson, but my friends call me Gigi."

"Mom, could you please find some towels."

"Oh, of course." She scampered off.

The dog licked from the rapidly forming snow puddle on the entry hall floor.

With her buttinsky mother temporarily out of the way, Tiffany snapped, "For heaven's sake, Rowdy, sit down and take off your wet boots—then let's get you in front of the fire."

He shivered too hard to be of much use, so she pushed him onto a small wood bench, then struggled to remove his icy cowboy boots for him.

"You do know you're crazy?" she scolded. "I had a tough time getting home after we talked, and that was pushing three hours ago. We're supposed to get twenty inches by morning."

"Swell…" His grin raised all manner of havoc in her tummy. For a woman who'd sworn off men, this was not a welcome development. "If we're snowed in together, we'll have plenty of time to come up with a game plan for keeping our baby."

"You're my future grandson's father?" Poor Gigi was past due for her Botox. How did Tiffany know? Because her mother's eyebrows rose an inch! "Why didn't you say so? But after you answer that, how about telling me where you've been. And then get this fool idea out of my daughter's head about giving my grandson up for adoption. A child doesn't need money to be loved. Tiffany's daddy grew up right here in Maple Springs and look how well he turned out—well, aside from his temporary setback. But—"

"Mom, please stay out of this."

"I will not."

"What's all the commotion?" Pearl wandered into the fray. She wore a quilted pink housecoat, slippers and a pink shower cap over her rollers, and her face was white with face cream. "*Ooooh*, how nice. Last thing I expected was to find a hottie in the house."

Tiffany closed her eyes, praying when she opened them, she'd find herself awaking from a bad dream. No such luck.

As if knowing he'd just made significant forward momentum in his mission, Rowdy delivered his stupid-handsome grin to all of the ladies, then held out his hand to her grandmother. "You must be Miss Pearl? My momma said she's never tasted a finer pumpkin pie than the one you made for the garden club's fall bake sale."

"Aren't you the charmer?" Pearl held his hand way longer than Tiffany deemed necessary. "If you don't mind my asking, who is your mother?"

"Patsy Jones. I'm her youngest, Rowdy. You've probably met my big brother, Carl? He helps my dad with our ranch and is married to a real sweetheart—Justine. She's a part-time teller down at First Trust Bank."

"Goodness gracious, what a small world. I've had my savings and checking accounts there for going on forty years. Now, since I'm older than dirt but not dumb as a box of rocks, what is this I heard about you being the father of my great-grandson. Is this true?"

"Yes, ma'am." He had the audacity to meet Tiffany's stare. "But I swear on my own grandmother's grave, I only recently heard of your beautiful granddaughter even being pregnant. I'm in the navy and have been overseas. But as soon as I got the news, I caught a flight, and here I am. Just this morning, I proposed to your granddaughter—told her if she wanted, I'd make an honest woman of her, but she flat turned me down."

Oh—he played dirty.

Pearl and Gigi both stood mooning with their hands pressed to their chests.

"I can't tell you what a relief that will be." Gigi freed one hand from her bosom to fan her flushed cheeks. "I don't consider myself old-fashioned, but nothing would make me happier than to see Tiffany married before the baby comes. Of course, she's already been married once before, but we don't speak of that."

"Mom!" Tiffany gave her a glare before turning back to their uninvited, unwelcome guest. "Rowdy, I'm not sure why you're here, but pretty sure it's time for you to go."

"Nonsense." Pearl turned for the stairs. "Give me a sec to gussy up, and then I'll make everyone a nice late lunch. Or would that be an early supper? Either way, we'll have plenty to discuss, what with a wedding and baby shower to plan."

"There's not going to be either, Grandma. We've already been over this a dozen times."

"Sounds good, Miss Pearl. My ride got stuck a ways back, and I worked up a powerful hunger walking through the snow."

"Oh, dear," Gigi said. "Sounds like you'll have to stay on for dinner and maybe even breakfast, too."

"But I do expect him to take the downstairs guest-room," Pearl noted. "Just because the rooster got into the henhouse once, doesn't mean it needs to happen again until I see a ring on our Tiffany's finger."

"Yes, ma'am." Rowdy nodded. "I couldn't agree more." As if just now noticing Mr. Bojangles, he knelt to scoop up the tiny dog. Had her traitorous mutt been a cat, he'd have purred from the scratching beneath his fussy collar. "Aren't you a silly little thing? You're smaller than our baby's going to be."

"Correction—the Parkers' baby." Before her mind's eye filled with visions of handsome Rowdy cradling their son in his big, strapping arms, Tiffany snatched her dog, who growled during the transaction. "I already told you, we can't keep this baby."

"I told you we're going to reach a mutually amenable arrangement."

"Well, that's settled." Gigi handed Tiffany the towels. "Darling, how about you help your fiancé dry off and get comfy in front of the fire—then I'll get his room ready. Maybe after that, we can all play canasta? Rowdy, sugar, what do you think?"

"Sounds like a fine plan," Pearl said. "Only thing I love more than cards is a wedding."

The second her mother and grandmother left the entry, Tiffany landed a swift kick to Rowdy's left shin.

"Ouch," he complained. "What was that for?"

From his safe perch in the crook of her arm, Mr. Bojangles barked at the commotion.

"What do you think? Those two women mean the world to me, and because of your big fat mouth—" she kicked his right shin, too "—now they both have expectations that there's no way on God's green earth we'll ever be able to fulfill."

"Hate to burst your bubble, but at the moment, God's earth is white as driven snow."

She pitched the towels at him. "Dry yourself. I need to sit down."

"Is everything okay? With the baby, I mean?"

"Our son is fine. As for my rising blood pressure? That's a whole nother story."

"Knock, knock." Quarter past ten that night, after an endless day of trying to make Tiffany remember why she'd been hot enough for him to have even made a baby, Rowdy cracked open her bedroom door and poked his head through. "You decent?"

"No!" Her whispered word was more like a hiss.

Mr. Bojangles woke to go into yapping attack mode at the foot of her bed.

Rowdy entered and shut the door behind him.

"Go away!" She sat up in a big white wrought iron bed, pulling a comfy-looking stack of quilts up to her neck. "I want Mom and Grammy Pearl to at least pretend I'm a virgin."

He cracked a smile, then grabbed the dog. "Pretty sure that cat's *way* out of the bag. The night we met— that trick you did with my... *Damn.* Woman, you've got skills."

"Stop." She covered her blazing cheeks with her hands. "Why are you here? And I'm not just talking about being in my bedroom."

"Why do you think?" Cradling the dog just as sweetly as a baby, he perched on the empty side of the double bed. "I'm here to change your mind about that adoption. Hell, if you don't want your own son, I'll raise him myself. This morning, I gave you plenty of acceptable scenarios, and now you need to choose."

When tears welled in her eyes, she looked away. The sight of him with the dog was all too easy to get tangled up with other images in her mind. Her yappy, spoiled mutt wasn't the same as a real baby. Mr. Bojangles didn't need health insurance or diapers. For her family, times were so hard that Pearl had to barter eggs for a neighbor's bacon. There was no way Tiffany could ever afford to keep her child.

"Look." He softened his tone. "I get that when I didn't call you back, you assumed I was some derelict deadbeat, and I'm sorry. But I'm here now, and if you want me to break the news to that couple you made the adoption arrangement with, I'll do it. For the sake of the baby, if you want to get hitched tomorrow, I'm on board. Whatever decision you make is fine as long as I'm part of the equation."

"You don't understand." She took a roll of toilet paper from her bedside table, then tore off a piece to blow her nose. "The night you and I hooked up, I was out of my mind with grief and trying to mask the pain. My dad had been sent to prison and my husband divorced me right down to the point that he bought back his name. I went from a life of pampered luxury to blowing my nose with toilet paper." Borderline hysterical while still trying to whisper, she waved the roll around. "It's not even a good brand, but generic. Every dime to my name went to paying off Daddy's lawyers and now I've gone from my biggest worry being what color to paint my nails or how many calories were in my morning latte to being responsible for an entire household. I *hate* my ex.

And I'm not especially fond of my dad, so forgive me if I don't buy your whole marriage scenario. We slept together—one night. So how in the world do you think I'm now ready to marry you?"

"Technically, we were together about six times that one night. And I'm not suggesting this is anything other than a solution to keep our baby. Marriage would be a means to a mutually beneficial end. That's all."

She pitched a lacy pillow at him, which he easily dodged.

Now her own dog growled at her!

"Sorry. Sounds like you've been through a rough patch, but—"

"*Rough* patch?" She was back to whisper-screeching. "I went through hell. I became that woman in Junior League and in my sorority's alumni chapter who everyone whispers about being one martini shy of having a nervous breakdown. The men I trusted the most yanked my world out from under me, so forgive me if I'm not feeling warm and fuzzy about a total stranger's vow to make me a live-in nanny. I don't know you from Adam. You could be an ax murderer or…or…shoplifter."

"Yeah." He nodded with a faint smile. "If I turned out to be one of those creepy guys who stash candy bars and gum in their pants that would be seriously bad news."

"You know what I mean."

"I do." He inched close enough to cup his hand over their baby. Even through layers of quilts, she felt a connection to him—to their son. Her every muscle tensed to resist the havoc his simple touch had created. "But here's the deal. I'm actually a really great guy, and if you'd give me a chance, I'd—"

"Tiff?" Gigi knocked, then opened the door. "Rowdy. I didn't expect to find you in my daughter's boudoir."

"Sorry, ma'am. Your daughter and I needed to talk—in private."

"About the wedding? Let's have a holiday theme. It'll be extra special, don't you think?"

"Sure," he said as if more determined than ever to see this crazy thing through.

"In that case…" She treated them to a huge wink. "I'll leave you two lovebirds alone. I need to start planning."

"Thank you." Rowdy smiled.

She smiled back and was gone.

Tiffany, however, was not smiling. If anything, her mood had turned even darker than it had been before.

"Now that I have your mother's blessing," he said, "will you at least meet my family before condemning me to the land of evil shoplifters?"

"Joke all you want." For an instant, she laughed. "But I'm serious. At any time you choose, you can walk away. I don't have that luxury. I also don't have the money to pay for our baby's birth, let alone diapers and college."

"Are you planning to have the baby at Regional Hospital here in town?"

"Yes." It was small but had a great reputation.

"If we're married, my health insurance will cover you."

"What then? I don't mean to sound bitchy, but what about everything else our baby boy is going to need—including time to care for him and love him and teach him to be a man? Let's say you are in the navy, and we marry. What happens if I hate Virginia? Or you?"

"A distinct possibility," he teased, patting her belly.

"This seems like a game to you—a challenge to win your son—but if you'd for one second be serious and think about the ramifications involved, I think you'd agree adoption is best for us both."

"Never. I was raised to accept my responsibilities. I was man enough to help create this baby, and I'll be man enough to raise him."

"But *why*? You've admitted how much your career means. Having a wife and child will only get in your way. Don't you get it? This adoption gives you an honorable out. Our baby will no longer be merely a responsibility but a blessing. The Parkers are wonderful, deserving people who will be better parents than you and I ever could."

"Look, you admitted you've had a rough year. Well, you're not the only one. What I'm about to share with you, even my parents and brother don't know..."

Chapter 4

Tiffany leaned closer. Did it make her an even more horrible person that one of the simple things she most missed about her former life was gossip? "Well? What could be so horrible?"

"Lord… Where do I even start?" He swallowed hard, rubbing her sleeping, traitorous dog behind his ears. When tears shone in Rowdy's green eyes, guilt had her offering the toilet paper roll. Whatever he was about to share, it was serious.

"Most people say start at the beginning, but I have a short attention span, so jump right in with the juicy parts."

He grinned.

She nearly swooned. *Baby, your daddy's a looker…*

"Anyone ever told you you're a little kooky?"

"All the time." She settled a pillow behind her back. "Now spill."

"Okay, but don't think badly of me. Because seriously, no one hates me more than me."

That didn't sound good, but who was she to cast stones? "Considering I got knocked up from a one-night stand, this is a judgment-free zone."

After a deep inhale, then slow exhale, words tumbled too fast, as if he'd been holding them in for far too long. "The night we met? Part of the reason I was so damned drunk was another woman. Back in Virginia, Brandi and I dated on and off—nothing serious. Then she tells me she's pregnant and the baby's mine."

Now Tiffany sucked in a deep breath. "Where's the infant and his or her momma now?"

"That's just it…" He rubbed the back of his neck. "We hardly had a great love story. It was all about sharing a few Friday-night drinks, then releasing the week's tensions. But hell, when she told me she was carrying my baby, I was prepared to do right by her and my kid. I bought her a ring, got down on one knee—the whole nine yards."

She leaned in closer. "Why aren't you married to her now?"

"Damn, woman, if you'd quit interrupting, I'd tell you."

"Sorry." To stop herself from blurting about a dozen more pertinent questions, Tiffany drew her lower lip into her mouth and bit.

"So anyway, I wasn't exactly proud of how this whole thing was going down, but we got married, and then I got shipped out. Making a long story real short, by the time I got back, she'd had the baby—a boy. I had a son. I'd had a couple hundred sleepless nights to ponder what it was going to be like when I got home—you know, taking on the role of dad and husband to this infant and woman I hardly knew."

Where in the world was this going?

"Back on base, when I stepped off our C-130 transport, she waited for me on the tarmac with all of the other wives. When I caught my first sight of her with a baby stroller—not gonna lie—I could've downed an entire bottle of Pepto. Still, she was my wife, this was my son, and I was determined to be a great dad and partner. All around us, my SEAL buddies were making out with their wives or hugging their kids, so I got into it. Or at least tried. I kissed her cheek, then reached into the stroller for my son. Only when I picked him up for our first hug, I got a helluva shock—there was no way this kid could be mine."

"*What?* How could you tell?" Tiffany could deny it all she wanted, but when it came to juicy gossip, she was every bit as bad as her mother. This story was getting *good*.

"Let's just say the little guy was cute as a button but looked more like Bruce Lee than me. As far as I knew, we didn't have any Asians on the family tree. She admitted to having slept with another guy around the same time as me and that she was already back together with him. She pulled a packet of divorce papers from a pouch on the back of the stroller. Told me that once I signed them, our marriage would be officially over, then wished me a nice life. After all those nights

I'd spent worrying about how I was going to perform as a father, just like that, the issue was off the table."

"Whoa…" Out of habit, Tiffany rubbed her baby bump. "You weren't kidding. That was nuts. But how does what Brandi did make you feel bad about yourself?"

"Because I was an idiot for landing myself in that situation. I'd always worn protection with her, but accidents happen. Now here I am again, facing the same issue with you. But the funny thing is, after another long-ass tour filled with way too much time for thinking, now maybe I am ready to be a dad."

"Do you know how crazy that sounds? After what that woman put you through, I would have figured you felt like she'd given you a get-out-of-jail-free card. I'm now offering you another one."

"But I want my son."

Tiffany shook her head. "You only think you want to be a dad. Trust me, I have bouts of suffering from baby fever, too. When those adorable diaper and baby-food ads pop up on TV, the chubby-cheeked close-ups get me teary eyed every time. But those aren't the realities of raising a child. To do right by him, to put the same time, attention and love into your son as you do being a SEAL, you might have to give up your career and move back to this dead-end town."

"Funny you mentioned that…" He set the dog between them, then cupped his hand over her belly. His palm created a warmth like a heating pad. When his barest touch felt this good, what if he spooned her? Warmed her entire aching back?

No, no, no. She might be able to squelch this impractical line of thought, but she didn't remove his hand. Selfishly, the much-needed comfort felt too good.

"I've always liked this town. I've seen a lot of the world—and granted, Paris and the Mediterranean have their perks. But honestly, there's an awful lot of ugliness out there, too. Here I'd have nothing but blue sky and the faces of everyone I love."

"And snow. You forgot about the multiple *feet* of snow."

He laughed.

"And what if this baby turns out to be not yours? Remember your not-so-nice implication that I'd made a mistake? You said as much back at my office."

"Sorry. The last thing I meant to imply was that you'd been sleeping around. I was there the night this little guy was conceived." He now added an infuriatingly distracting rub to her tummy. "I clearly remember being so hot for you that I was too out of my freakin' mind to make sure the condom was—well… How do I put this? Positioned correctly?"

Hot didn't begin to describe their chemistry.

Volcanic.

Seismic.

Cataclysmic. All sorts of -*ic* words. And now that there was a baby on the way, *apocalyptic* also applied. Before she found out she was pregnant, life had still been a disaster but at least manageable. Now? Her sheer size made most tasks three times tougher than usual. As for the pang in her heart each time the baby kicked? That was the worst. Of course she wanted to keep their baby—more than anything. But logic dictated that wasn't going to happen.

"Since you're already knocked up, why not at least try seeing if we still share a connection?" He leaned closer, all the while stroking her tummy with his thumb.

Had there ever been a more idiotic question? They didn't share just a *connection* but the kind of explosive spark she'd never even experienced with her former husband—which was probably why they were now divorced. Rowdy's warm breath tickled her upper lip, goading her into all manner of naughty thoughts.

"We could pick up right where we left off…"

He shifted the dog lower on the bed, then inched still closer until the empty space between them couldn't have been thicker than the flyer she'd found on her car window the night after having made the poor choice of being with him.

Why wasn't her dog defending her?

And speaking of poor choices…

The memory of seeing her positive pregnancy test served as a much-needed bucket of cold water to her flaming cheeks. Tiffany backed away. "You should probably go downstairs. If Grammy catches you up here, there's gonna be hell to pay."

He leaned forward, nuzzling her neck. "I never did mind dancing with the devil. Besides, I could tell straightaway your grandmother and momma like me just fine."

"I wouldn't take it too personally." Tiffany crossed her arms. "They'd love the trashman if he'd make an honest woman of me. They're both old-school and believe a woman has no business being pregnant without a wedding ring."

"So? Let's get one. First thing in the morning.

Then, come afternoon, you can get to work finding us a house."

"Stop. Are you even listening to yourself? Rowdy, you're free. The Parkers are taking our baby and giving him a better life than we ever possibly could. He'll have the best of everything. Private school. Travel. Art lessons and dressage and speaking five foreign languages. Don't you want that for him? Don't you want him to have more than two parents who—up until this morning—didn't even know each other's last names?"

"While all of that fancy stuff sounds dandy, it doesn't hold a candle to true family ties. I'll be a great dad. I've already been practicing for damn near a year."

"Yay for you. But I can't be a mom—not yet. Maybe not ever. I already have one failed marriage, a father in prison, a mother teetering on the edge of a nervous breakdown and a grandmother who refuses to see the bad in anyone, when I can't remember the last time I had a man tell me the truth—present company excluded. I think. *Hope*." She shook her head. "It doesn't matter. No matter what you say about anything, I'm not changing my mind about the adoption."

"Sorry, angel, but that decision's not entirely up to you. I have rights, too, you know?" He cupped his hand possessively over the baby. "This decision isn't just about you. We went over this at your office."

She sighed. "Please, just go."

He stared at her for the longest time.

The dim lamplight showed a weariness in him that she hadn't before seen. Shadows beneath his eyes and a sad downward turn to his lips. He was heartbreakingly handsome. Long lashes and those grassy-green eyes that called to mind sunny days spent downing Long Island ice teas on the sidelines of polo fields. What would a man like Rowdy have been like in her former world? Would she have given him the time of day?

She was so caught up in his stare that she forgot to breathe. When her body forced her to remember, her gulp went down too fast and left her coughing.

He was instantly by her side. "You okay?"

Still unable to speak, she nodded.

"We'll continue this discussion in the morning. Only you need to be ready to make concessions." Without waiting for her reply, he turned for the door.

No. He couldn't just waltz in here and dictate what she could and couldn't do. But she was tired of talking in circles, so she kept her mouth closed. Unfortunately, there was a lone question hammering at her like a woodpecker against a rickety wood shed. "Rowdy?"

"Yeah?" He didn't bother facing her.

"What did your parents say about your first marriage?"

"Not a damned thing. They don't know." With that shocker, he exited her room and shut the door.

More confused than ever, she scooped up the dog to settle him on his pillow beside her, then covered him with his own leopard-print fuzzy blanket. She turned out her bedside lamp, bunched a pillow between her legs and one behind her back and three more behind her head but still couldn't get comfortable—not the way she'd been with Rowdy alongside her for support.

Why hadn't he told his folks about his first baby scare? Embarrassment? Pride? But that morning, he'd offered right away to drive her over to meet his mom.

Why? What about their situation made such a huge difference?

The old her—the Tiffany who'd believed in happy endings—might have wondered if Rowdy had been looking for more from their union than she had, which was basically one night free from the nightmare that had become her life.

Running her hands over her belly, she closed her eyes and tried sleeping, but peace refused to come. Her lower back ached, and she was hungry and had to pee.

After a trek to the restroom, she carefully made her way down the back stairs to the kitchen. A mug of hot cocoa and a half-dozen of her grandmother's oatmeal cookies would be delicious. After that, she'd pop the rice bag she used as a heating pad into the microwave and then try going back to bed.

At the base of the stairs, she traipsed down the hall and into the kitchen, only to come to an abrupt stop.

Rowdy's entirely too-fine muscular legs and derriere clad in red-striped boxers were the only parts of him visible behind the open fridge door.

She'd just turned to tiptoe her way back up the stairs when the fridge door slammed.

"Jeez, woman!"

She spun around as fast as a seriously preggers woman could to find Rowdy clutching his chest.

"You scared the hell out of me."

"Sorry. I assumed you'd be sleeping."

"I should be, but you've got me so wound up on about eighty different topics that I'm having to stress-eat."

"You're wound up? How do you think I feel? I'm

starving." She nudged him aside to make her way to the fridge.

"For the sake of both of our growling stomachs, let's table all topics involving the baby and focus on food. Deal?"

He held out his hand for her to shake.

She should have known better than to touch him again.

The instant she pressed her palm to his, a warm tingle didn't just take hold but threw her slightly off balance, as if she were standing on the bow of a yacht when it crashed down from a wave. He was without a doubt bad for her—in the most maddeningly wonderful way. All the more reason to steer clear of him.

After breaking their brief hold, she asked, "Want me to make you a sandwich?"

"Sit." He clamped his hands over her shoulders, aiming her toward the round oak table and nearest ladder-back chair. "Your grandmother's dinner was so good that I don't see the point in messing with perfection, do you? Leftovers sound awesome."

Trying not to get caught staring at his ridiculously toned body, she nodded.

Outside, wind howled.

Gusts made the old house shiver.

But inside, Pearl kept the propane heat on a tropical high. Refilling the tank wasn't cheap, which reminded Tiffany just how much she needed to make a house-sale commission.

"Tell me about your husband." He cradled four Tupperware bowls in his arms, then dropped them all onto the gold-speckled laminate counter. His biceps were big, but not bodybuilder beefy.

Her cheeks flamed from the memory of wrapping her fingers around them while he'd—

"Sorry. I see you're turning red. Was that too intimate of a question for our first late-night snack?"

She inwardly groaned. *Would it be too much to ask for you to put on some clothes?*

"Okay… Since that subject's apparently off-limits, I'll—"

"No," she said, fanning her flushed face with a coupon circular Pearl must have left on the table. "It's not like that. I'm having a hot flash." *Caused by you!* "Crawford and I were the ultimate cliché. We met at the University of Texas. His fraternity was always paired with my sorority. Our parents ran in the same social circles. We both had the same ambitions. He wanted to conquer the business world. I wanted to rule the Junior League and raise gorgeous babies. Looking back on it, I guess the whole thing was a big, shallow mistake. He's already remarried and aside from the embarrassment of the whole thing, I'm not all that heartbroken."

"You mentioned earlier that he broke things off because of your father's conviction?"

"Yep. I should have at least cheated or something, you know? At least given him a true reason for the split."

"If you don't mind another question, what's your dad locked up for?"

"Insider trading."

He nodded. "Ever planning on going back to Texas?" Now that the lids were off all of the containers, he opened three cabinets before finding the one holding her grandmother's white china plates.

"Honestly?" A strangled laugh escaped her. "Sometimes when I can't sleep, I have visions of gliding back into town behind the wheel of a brand-new Jaguar convertible. My hair and nails and outfit will be flawless and I won't rely on a man for my well-being, since I'll run my own real estate empire."

"Nice." He spooned heaping portions of mashed potatoes, meat loaf and peas onto both plates.

"For the record—what this Crawford character did was pretty shitty. Sounds like a total douche bag. I mean, hell, he married you—not your dad."

"No kidding, right?" Her respect for Rowdy rose by a considerable margin. He could just be blowing happy smoke up her skirt, but his words seemed as genuine as his sympathetic smile. A problem, since the last thing she wanted was to be reminded of why she'd spent the night with him in the first place.

He popped one plate into the microwave, then joined her at the table with bowls of ambrosia and three-bean salad. He handed her a spoon. "Dig in."

"Thanks." She did. Never had she been more grateful for her grandmother's overabundance of side dishes at any given meal. "Mmm…" she said after swallowing her first bite of the sweet fruit salad. "When I was a kid, we used to always have this for special occasions."

"Should I take it as a compliment that Pearl made it for me on an ordinary Monday night?" His slow and easy grin was potent enough to steal her next breath.

They ate in companionable silence until both small bowls were empty. She was caught off guard by how much she enjoyed the simple pleasure of sharing a meal with him. Why was it that the harder she fought to resist him, the more he drew her in without the least bit of effort?

The microwave beeped.

She offered to get the one plate and put the other in, but he insisted on serving her, right down to delivering a napkin and fork.

"Thank you." She waited until they both had their meals to start in on hers.

"Don't wait on my account," he said. "Need anything else? Salt or pepper? Ketchup?"

"No, thank you. This is perfect."

The baby gave her an extra-hard kick. Surprise had her grasping her belly.

"Everything okay?" He eyed where she held her hands. "You're not having contractions, are you?"

"No. He just practiced his favorite soccer move. Nothing I can't handle."

Not bothering to ask permission, Rowdy knelt alongside her chair, framing their son with his big hands, then leaning forward to rest his cheek to her womb.

Their son.

Her heart twisted from the rush of affection she felt for the man and unborn child—neither of whom would ever belong to her.

Chapter 5

"You're up awfully early."

"Yes, ma'am." Rowdy had hoped to sneak out before the three women of the house were awake, but Tiffany's grandmother was an early riser. "I figured since the storm passed, I should get a head start on digging out my truck."

Sun shone on the sea of white visible beyond red gingham curtains. The sky was a deep, clear blue. According to his phone, the temperature would be in the forties by noon, so thankfully, the snow would melt as fast as it had fallen.

"Wise idea. But you're not going anywhere without a nice rib-sticking breakfast."

"Thanks." He didn't dare tell her he was still full from all the food he and Tiffany had put away the previous night. Man, oh man, could that girl eat. If her appetite was any indication, their son would be a bruiser. "Anything I can help with?"

"Since you asked, I'd be much obliged if you'd gather the eggs and make sure the chickens have feed and their water didn't freeze. The coop is just around back. You might also check their heat lamp once you're out there."

"Will do." He was glad for the busywork. It might at least give him a fighting chance of forgetting the feel of his son moving just beneath his hands.

If things were different between him and Tiffany, she might have welcomed him, placing her hands atop his to press him closer, instead of stiffening at his every touch. As it was, he'd guessed he was crossing a personal-space boundary but didn't much care. He'd already missed the first seven months of his son's life and he'd be damned if he'd miss one day more.

In the front hall, he slipped his feet into his boots, then shrugged on his coat and added his cowboy hat and gloves.

He trudged through two feet of wet snow before reaching the chickens. Their coop was a fussy yellow shed that he figured his mother would very much like, given her affinity for the color. A flower box hung askew beneath a paned window and the wooden shingled roof had turned green with moss.

Near the latch-hooked door, he spotted a lidded feed bin and opened it to get a scoop. The grains smelled good. Familiar and sweet. While for the most part, there wasn't much about his life as a SEAL that he didn't enjoy, he had to admit to missing quite a bit about growing up on his family's ranch.

He ducked his six-foot-two-inch frame through the coop's low door to find the Araucana ladies not happy about his intrusion. Cozy in their straw-filled roosting shelves, they squawked and squabbled. A rooster strutted close enough to land a peck to Rowdy's shin.

"Hey," he protested, closing the door on the chill. Judging by the muggy heat and glow, the heat lamp was working just fine. "Don't peck the legs that are attached to the hands feeding you."

He shook grain into a shallow food tray, checked that the water hadn't frozen, then gathered ten blue eggs, which he held in his sweater's upturned hem. How amazing would it be to perform these chores with his son? To teach him about different breeds. He might enjoy Easter Eggers—they laid huge eggs that ranged from rose and blue to green and brown. Rowdy's boy could raise his own chicks for a 4-H project.

Rowdy wanted his son with a visceral pull on his heart.

After what he'd been through with his first stab at parenthood, he now actually felt ready. Excited. How could he get Tiffany to feel the same?

The rooster delivered another peck to his shin.

"Thanks, buddy. You're making me feel about as welcome as Tiffany."

Rowdy left the coop to deliver the eggs to Pearl.

"You are a sweetheart," she said with a big smile. "I can't tell you what a treat it is to have a big, strapping man around the house. I have my suitors, but they mostly come by for pie and sugar." She winked. "If you know what I mean."

It took him a sec, but Rowdy eventually caught on.

"Breaks my heart to think I'm in competition for your affections, Miss Pearl."

Her cheeks reddened. "You are a silver-tongued devil. I see why Tiffany lost her senses around you. Take off your coat and let me whip some of these eggs into an omelet and pancakes."

"That sounds delicious, but how about I shovel the front and back walks while you cook. That's more of an even exchange."

"Deal. There's a snow shovel in the barn."

Rowdy found the shovel and made quick work of clearing the narrow path leading to the chicken coop. Around front, the wide brick walkway that led to the street took considerably longer, but that was okay. He wouldn't want Tiffany or her mom or grandmother risking a fall.

He'd known most of the Lawson women less than twenty-four hours yet already felt protective toward them. If he'd had his way, he and Tiffany would have already been hitched. Just because he needed her back in Virginia to watch after the baby didn't mean they couldn't also be friends.

Tiffany woke to too-bright sun streaming through her bedroom's tall, paned windows and the unnatural sound of metal scraping against rock. She winced before trying and failing to roll over and hide her ears beneath a pillow.

Mr. Bojangles peeked his head out from under his blanket.

She gave him a rub. "I know it's cold, but we need to

find your booties and go outside. Want to change your sweater now or later?"

He ducked back under his cover.

She laughed. "We go through this every morning, sweetheart, but you know you will eventually have to leave this bed."

After three failed attempts to stand left Tiffany feeling like an upside-down roly-poly, she finally made it onto her feet but had to balance herself by grasping the back of the chaise.

"Baby, you are giving me quite a workout and it's not even eight." She gave her belly an affectionate rub before waddling to the window to draw back the lacy curtain.

Rowdy, in all his sheer male beauty, shoveled the front walk. The obnoxious clanging she'd heard had been the twang of his shovel hitting the brick pavers.

Tiffany groaned.

Part of her had been hoping his reentry into her life had been a dream.

He caught sight of her. Smiled and waved.

She dropped the curtain as if it had caught fire.

The other part of her? Oh—that part unfortunately felt like a giddy schoolgirl facing her first crush. His merest brush against her made her entire body hum. When he touched the baby bump they'd created, she lost the ability to think or even breathe. The man made her crave not pickles and ice cream but kisses and hugs and settling into a home with a family of her own. But the thing she had to remember was that she'd already had all of the above and it had vanished like a morning fog. Just like a sad country song, she'd lost her man, her house and her dignity.

At least she still had her dog.

Sort of.

Mr. Bojangles had taken a particular liking to Pearl—in no doubt due to her many handouts. If even her dog preferred other company to hers, what did that say for her mothering potential? As much as she adored the idea of becoming a mom to her son, the realities proved time and again that it was never meant to be.

She forced a deep breath, brushed hot tears from her cheeks with the back of her hand, then scooped Mr. Bojangles from the bed. Whether he liked it or not, they both had to face the day. Which unfortunately also meant facing Rowdy.

"Please tell me that dog doesn't have his own red snow boots?" Rowdy leaned on the shovel's handle.

"Good morning to you, too." Tiffany set her pampered pup on the section of the walk he'd already shoveled. "Thank you for tackling this job. Usually I'm stuck doing it."

"But you're pregnant."

"Exactly. A few weeks back when we had that dusting, I figured it wouldn't be a big deal, but turns out it was. I was exhausted."

"One more reason to marry me for the sake of the baby. North Dakota isn't exactly known for balmy winters, yet my part of Virginia typically doesn't have it too bad."

She rolled her eyes before clutching the two halves of her inadequate wool coat as close as they'd go—not nearly all the way around her bulging tummy. He'd have to get her a new one. Maybe online? He couldn't let the mother of his child be cold.

"Look." Her sharp exhale clouded in the frosty air. "I appreciate you charging in here to act like my hero, but I'm perfectly capable of handling this situation on my own. There's not going to be a wedding, and right after ringing in the New Year—" she patted her belly "—our baby will be blissfully happy in his new home and you and I can get back to our separate lives as if none of this ever happened. Agreed?" She held out her hand for him to shake.

"Did you not hear a word I said last night? I'm not giving up on my son. Aren't you at least willing to try? Once you sign those papers, there's no going back. Can you honestly tell me you're that ready to give up a child that could be the best thing to ever happen to either of our lives?"

The dog left a yellow stain on the newly fallen snow.

Rowdy couldn't help but see it as a sign.

He cleared his throat. "Could you at least give me the courtesy of a reply?"

"It's cold. I need to get Mr. Bojangles inside." She scooped up her dog and left.

Rowdy took that as his cue to do the same.

He finished clearing the walk, returned the shovel to the barn, then trudged his way back to his truck. Since his words were clearly useless, he took his frustration with Tiffany out on the melting snow. Enough horsepower had gotten him out of a helluva lot of jams, and this time was no exception. The melting drift was no match for his dad's one-ton truck. As for this mess with Tiffany and his baby, looked like he'd need to re-think his strategy.

His specialty was brute force.

This situation called for a bit more finesse.

Meaning it was time to call in the big guns—his mother.

"Might've been nice for you to let me know you were alive."

Rowdy entered his family home through the back door.

Patsy sat at the kitchen table. Judging by the array of paperwork spread around her, she was paying bills. Never the best time for a heart-to-heart.

"Sorry." He took off his boots before stepping onto her prized maple floor.

A welcoming fire crackled in the hearth, and sun-shine added to the yellow room's already-cheery feel. So why did he still feel defeated?

"You'd better thank your lucky stars Pearl Lawson had the decency to let me know you were staying with her during the storm. I'd have called out the National Guard looking for you."

"Not to discount their great work, but I'm a SEAL. Think I could have survived a night in my truck." He rummaged in the fridge for sandwich fixings.

"Don't sass me. I'm already in a foul enough mood over your father's Visa bill. That man charged five hundred dollars' worth of fishing lures. How is that even possible? With the baby coming, we're going to need every spare dime to set up a nursery for when the baby stays here. I was thinking pale blue walls with an adorable cow-jumping-over-the-moon theme. What do you think?"

After opening the mayo, he sighed. "What I think is that unless you help me devise a plan to get Tiffany to change her mind about giving your grandson up for adoption, we could be in for one helluva fight."

"Oh, honey…" She put down the Visa bill and removed her reading glasses. "What are you going to do?"

"I told her that for the sake of the baby, we should get married. Her mom and grandma seemed on board with the plan. Tiffany's the problem. She's got some fool notion that she's not fit to be a mom, but she babies her rat-sized dog like he's heir to the Lawson throne. Oh—and I guess money's a factor, but when I pointed out that I've got more than enough saved to provide a comfortable life for her and our baby, her pride kicks in and she starts spouting off about how she can do everything herself."

"Sweetheart, of course every woman is capable of supporting herself, but have you stopped to think about what that poor girl has been through? With her father in prison and her husband having left her, it's no wonder she's wary about jumping into another relationship."

He'd added mayo, shaved ham, lettuce and pickles to the bread and now slapped a second piece of bread atop his creation.

"Didn't Pearl cook you a big country breakfast?"

"She offered, but Tiffany got me so riled I left before eating."

The back door opened, ushering in not only Rowdy's dad, James, but his big brother, Carl.

"Look what the cat dragged in," James said. "We

sure could have used your help around here last night. That storm had cattle scattered all over hell and creation."

"Cut him some slack." Carl removed his long duster to hang it on the wall-mounted rack. He slapped his brown leather cowboy hat on the peg beside it. "Poor guy's had lady trouble. Justine said her friend Darcy, from Sunday school, told her that she knows a friend who plays bridge with the couple all set to adopt Tiffany's baby. They've been trying for years and couldn't be more pleased that they're getting a son."

"That's gotta be a special hell—" James sat on the entry bench to tug off his worn work boots "—to want a child and not be able to have one."

"No kidding, right? Lucky for us Jones men that we're nice and fertile."

James and Carl shared a laugh.

Rowdy didn't see a damned thing about his situation that was funny.

"Those people are *not* getting my son." Rowdy had held his sandwich to his mouth but now slapped it to the counter.

"Hon," Patsy said, "I've told you a million times to use a plate when you eat. You know I can't stand crumbs."

"Would you all listen to yourselves? This is my flesh and blood we're talking about. Yours, too. I'm all set to marry this woman, but she acts like my opinions don't even count. But I have rights. She can't just sign away my kid at her whim, can she?"

"I think the bigger question—" Carl helped himself to Rowdy's sandwich "—is what you are going to do with a kid. Have you set aside your own bull-headed pride long enough to consider the fact that Tiffany might be doing you a favor? I'm not saying this is by any means an easy decision, but it just might be the right one. This couple she's talking to seem like good people. They'll make equally good parents to some lucky kid—maybe even yours. Realistically, what do you have to offer?" He paused his rant to take another bite of Rowdy's sandwich. "A ratty apartment you share with four other guys. But that doesn't even matter when you're gone three hundred days out of the year. When you are home, you're on call or training. You're a full-fledged adrenaline junkie. How are you going to choose between sitting in the stands at your kid's fiftieth losing Little League game versus planting explosives beneath some bad guy's ship? You think you're obligated to marry this woman, but take a good hard look at the bigger picture. Make no mistake, I love Justine and the girls, but I'd be lying if I said there are times I don't envy your path. But let's say you do convince Tiffany to marry your sorry ass? What then? What kind of life is that going to make for your son? Let alone his mom. What's she supposed to do with her days? Just sit around pining for you?"

"Your brother raises valid points," his dad said.

"Whose side are y'all on?" Rowdy hardened his jaw. "This is *my son* you're so casually talking about. All of our flesh and blood. Sure, I'll be first to admit changes will have to be made to my current way of life, but plenty of guys I serve with have kids and they all seem to do just fine."

"They're the exception," Patsy said. "Have you seen

the statistics on SEAL divorce rates? And those marriages started out with love. What you're proposing is more of a business arrangement."

"Stop." Rowdy pressed the heels of his hands against his closed eyes. With everything in him, he wanted to tell his family about what he'd been through with Brandi, but what would that do other than reinforce the fact that they were probably right—especially his mom with her divorce-rate statistics. He was a walking example of how easily a lonely woman found *entertainment*.

"Honey..." His mom left the table to give him a sideways hug. "No matter what you decide, we're all on Team Rowdy. If you're determined to see this through with Tiffany—make her your wife—just tell us how to help."

"That's just it," he said. "At this point, I'm not sure what to do. I proposed. She turned me down."

"Well, hell, son." Now his dad gave him a pat on his back. "You've got to woo her. And I'm talking a much deeper level than flowers and drugstore chocolates. You'll have to go all in. Really prove to this woman that you're husband and father material."

"How am I supposed to do that? I don't even have my own house."

Carl snorted. "Thought the navy was supposed to give him smarts. Tiffany's a Realtor, right? Kill two birds with one mortgage-sized stone. Have her show you every damned house in the county, then during all that time together, you can wow her with your charm."

"Duh. That was already my plan," Rowdy said with a put-upon sigh.

"For the record—" Patsy had left his side to take

a pencil and notepad from the junk drawer, then get comfy on the window seat "—I think you're all wrong. Oh—I'm all for Rowdy showing Tiffany what a great catch he is, but in a roundabout way. Since you've already tried the direct approach and bombed, looks like you'll need to be sneakier. Now, I'm not usually in favor of playing games, but from what you've told me, this poor girl has been hurt to the point that she no longer takes a man's word at face value. What I want you to do is not *tell* her she's going to marry you but make her *ache* to marry you."

Rowdy frowned. "Mom, you might as well be speaking Martian. What does any of that mean?"

"Have a seat." She patted the cushion beside her. "I'll teach you everything I know…"

Chapter 6

"Grammy, what is this?" Two days after her last run-in with Rowdy, Tiffany had just come home after an endless day at the office to find a disturbing letter from the First Trust Bank lying on the desk she shared with her mom and grandmother.

Pearl snatched it from her hand. "Didn't your mother teach you it's not polite to snoop?"

"Please tell me this is a mistake?" The letter was a notice that Pearl was two months in arrears on paying her mortgage—a mortgage Tiffany hadn't even known existed. "I thought Daddy paid off your house a long time ago?"

"He did, but then he needed cash for legal fees, and Tommy Peterson down at the bank was nice enough to help me fill out a few forms, and voilà—your father's legal fees were paid, so you and your mom didn't have to worry about them."

"But, Grammy, you now have to pay this bill every month. If you don't, that *nice* Tommy Peterson will take your house. You're already two payments behind. That's over a thousand dollars with late fees."

Her grandmother paled.

Which made Tiffany feel horrible for scolding one of the people she held most dear in the world. But she had enough on her plate with just paying utilities, car insurance, gasoline and grocery bills. How in the world would she ever manage an extra five hundred per month? Thank goodness the Parkers were covering her obstetrician fees and prenatal vitamins.

"I'm sorry," Pearl said. "I figured we'd find the money somewhere."

Tiffany groaned, leaning forward in the desk chair. "We will, Grammy. Don't worry about it, okay? I'll figure something out."

"Of course you will. You've always been such a clever girl." Pearl kissed the crown of her head, then shuffled off toward the kitchen. "I'm making pork chops for dinner. Why don't you invite your handsome fiancé over for a nice hot meal?"

"Grammy, I already told you, Rowdy and I aren't getting married."

Pearl gave her a backhanded wave. "Sure you are, honey. You're carrying his baby. Maple Springs is a small town. If you don't marry him, tongues are going to wag."

"Grammy, no one cares about single women having babies anymore. Besides, Susie and Jeb Parker are adopting the baby, remember?"

Why had she wasted her breath on the speech?

Pearl had already left the room, leaving Tiffany alone with too many worries and fears for one heart to bear.

"Wait—please don't tell me you're Mr. *Gosee*?" Tiffany groaned before leaning back in her desk chair at Hearth and Home Realty. It had been a blessed whole week since she'd seen Rowdy. Halloween had come and gone, and she'd thought he'd returned to his submarine or ship or wherever it was navy SEALs spent their time.

"Right. Get it? As in I need to *go see* a few houses?" Rowdy flashed her that lopsided, toothy grin that got her all hot and bothered and wishing for a pitcher of margaritas and a dark dance floor on which she'd spend a few hours kissing him. All of which was stupid, considering as soon as their baby was born, odds were she'd never see him again. "I emailed all my needs. Do you have any properties lined up?"

"I did for your alter ego. But none for you."

"Aw, come on. My money spends just as good as his, and from what you've told me, you could use the commission."

"Of course I could, but do you have any idea how much trouble I'm in with Gigi and Pearl? I told them I have no intention of marrying you, and neither has spoken to me since. Even Mr. Bojangles is giving me the cold shoulder. He slept with Grammy last night."

"Can you blame him? Not only is she a great cook, but I like her sunny disposition. You're about as welcoming as barbed wire."

"I hate you."

"No, you don't."

"Oh—I really do." As if excited just hearing his daddy's voice, her traitor baby kicked. "I have a plan. A good plan. You can't just come in here—"

"Whoa. Stop right there. I'm not here to discuss my son or our pending nuptials or anything other than buying a house. If you're not interested in making my home-ownership dreams a reality, then I'll ask your boss if he'd be willing to show me a few places." He stood.

"Sit down. If you promise to keep talk strictly on houses, I did find a few I think *Mr. Gosee* will like. But I'm warning you, if I get one hint that this is a trick and all you're really after is another shot at changing my mind about the adoption, I'll dump you right in the middle of the road—any road."

"Fair enough." He offered her his hand to shake.

After eyeing his outstretched hand with a narrow-eyed glare, she turned her attention to her computer, printing fact sheets for three small ranches. "Per *Mr. Gosee's* request, these are all horse properties. One has a full barn—the others have rustic lean-tos that could, of course, be improved." She handed him the papers, then retrieved her purse and three mini Snickers bars from her bottom drawer. Since tequila was off the table as a stress reliever, chocolate would have to do.

Keys jingling, she squeezed into her coat, then led the way from her office, all too conscious of his presence. He made her feel hot and tingly and hyperaware. The last place she wanted him was behind her, but if he'd been in front, then she'd have been tortured by the view of his backside hugged by faded Wranglers.

"Would you rather I drive?" he asked when she struggled to fit behind the wheel.

"I can manage."

"I don't doubt you can, but what would it hurt for you to kick back and let me serve as your chauffeur?"

His offer was tempting…

It was only ten thirty, yet her lower back throbbed. Don't get her started on how her swollen feet had turned numb from being squeezed into heels.

"You forget, I grew up around here and know all the best shortcuts."

"Okay." She handed over her keys and they made the seating transition. "But no funny business. We're strictly house-hunting. That's all."

"You have my solemn vow."

She snorted. "Seems like you gave me that the night I got pregnant. Let's see… How did that go?" She lowered her voice to mock him. "'Baby, I give you my solemn vow as a bull rider that you'll never have another ride anywhere near as fine as this.'" She tried folding her arms, but her sleeves were mortifyingly too tight to allow for the simple movement, so she settled for glaring out the passenger-side window. "Have you ever even ridden a bull?"

"That hurts." He clutched his chest before backing out of her assigned space in the lot behind the office. "I'll have you know I was almost state champion back in— Well, let me think about it. It was three years before I graduated high school, so that would've been—"

"Never mind." She glared harder.

"Turnabout's fair play. You told me you were a rodeo queen. Is that true?"

"Absolutely. I've won several titles."

"Name one."

"Name one of yours."

"I asked you first."

"So you weren't a rodeo queen?"

"So you weren't a bull-riding champion?"

At a stop sign, he slanted a breathtaking grin in her direction and she lost it. She laughed and he laughed and then pregnancy hormones had her crying from the absurdity of their situation.

"Truth—" she dabbed the corners of her eyes with a tissue she'd taken from her purse "—I was fourth runner-up in the Miss Rodeo Fort Worth competition when I was sixteen. But a horrible girl named Windy—spelled with an *i*—*accidentally* spilled nachos down the front of my custom-made white satin pantsuit. If it hadn't been for her, I have no doubt I would have worn the crown."

"Hell, yeah, you would have." At a four-way stop, he fixed her with a look so intense, so downright mesmerizing, her heart skipped a beat. "You're gorgeous."

"You're sweet." Pulse on a treacherous gallop, she looked at her hands clasped atop their baby. How long had it been since a man told her she was pretty? A while. Not since she and Rowdy had first been together. "She was a far better barrel racer. Even without the sabotage, she probably would have won."

"Don't sell yourself short. A lot of women might have fallen apart after what you've been through, but adversity seems to have made you stronger."

His kind words were hot chocolate. A crackling fire. A foot massage followed by—

From behind them a FedEx driver honked.

"Sorry," he said along with a backward courtesy wave. "To him—not to you."

They rode the rest of the way to the first house in silence, but something about his compliment warmed her on a fundamental level. She had fought for so long— for *everything*. Not just for money to pay bills, but to keep her mother and grandmother comfortable. To eat healthy and care for the miracle growing inside her that she would all too soon gift to a more deserving mother.

Truth be told, she didn't used to be a nice person. Maybe she hadn't loved Crawford the way she should have? Maybe if she'd been more focused on his needs instead of planning what to wear to her next charity event, he might have stood by her side when her dad's business had taken such an ugly fall?

"This it?" His question provided a welcome respite from her dark thoughts.

Since she could no longer afford her smartphone, she eyed her county map. "Looks like it. The home is vacant, so pull right into the drive."

Though the main roads were clear, patches of slushy snow made the trek down the dirt drive less than ideal.

"I apologize for this. The owner's out of state. I should have thought to have it plowed."

"No worries. I'll park in a dry patch so you don't ruin those fancy shoes."

"Thanks." He noticed? Rowdy was full of all kinds of surprises this morning.

The two-story classic American bungalow featured a

wide front porch supported by sturdy square columns. But the place was in need of a thorough cleaning, as brown leaves and a thick coating of dust covered the wood-plank porch floor.

Tiffany fumbled with the lockbox but eventually led them into the dark home. "It's a total fixer-upper, but with a price of fifty thousand, you'd have plenty of room in your budget to renovate. There are four bedrooms. One full bathroom to share upstairs and a powder room on the ground floor for guests."

The carpet was gold '70s shag and birds could be heard chattering in the chimney. Heavy gold velvet drapes were drawn and mildew was the prevailing scent in the air. Water stains marred the sagging ceiling.

"There's probably hardwood under the carpet. Want me to tug back a corner so you can take a look?"

"Thanks for the offer, but I'm getting serious haunted vibes from this place. Let's check out the next place on our list."

"Are you sure? We haven't even seen the kitchen. Plus, there are ten acres of good grazing land for your horse."

"Thanks, but no thanks. I mean, come on. At any price, could you see yourself living here?"

"Rowdy…" she warned. "You promised your sudden drive to become a homeowner had nothing to do with me."

"It doesn't. It was a rhetorical question."

"Oh—well, in that case, no. This place gives me the creeps."

Tiffany locked up the house and had never been more relieved to be back in a car—any car. Not because she'd been that afraid of the spooky old house but because her feet seriously hurt. What had she been thinking? Heels and her seventh month of pregnancy had been an awful idea.

Upon reaching the end of the drive, Rowdy took a left. "The info sheet says this next house has a hot tub. I'm excited to see that."

She leaned her head back and closed her eyes. "Hate to be a party pooper, but don't hold your breath. I can't count the number of listings I get all jacked up to see, then they wind up being an agent's work of fiction. Like this one time, I saw that a listing featured an atrium. My client had been transferred here from Jacksonville, Florida, and missed her sunshine. Well, that was before I learned to preview properties, and boy, did we get a surprise. That sun-flooded atrium we envisioned to be glass walled with palm trees and parrots? Turned out to be a hallway that had a leaky ceiling. The owner's solution had been to bust the roof all the way out, staple tarps to the edges, and sledgehammer holes in the walls of other rooms that they then used for a new hall. It was bizarre."

Rowdy whistled. "Gotta give 'em points for creativity."

He punched the new address into his phone, then set the route. "What did you do before selling homes?"

"I'm kind of embarrassed to say, but nothing."

"You had to do something."

She shrugged. "I lunched. Shopped. Did charity work."

"See? Charity's a good thing."

"I suppose."

"Why do you sound so down? As my Realtor, aren't you supposed to be chatting me up?"

"Sorry." She forced a smile. "Something occurred to me, and I haven't been able to get the thought from my mind."

"Lay it on me." He turned onto Ponderosa Court.

"Remember what you said earlier? About adversity having made me stronger?"

"Sure. What about it?"

"When Brandi did what she did—you know, sleeping around on you—did you feel guilty?"

"No way. Why should I feel bad because of what she did? But what does any of what I went through have to do with you?"

"Nothing." She shook her head, aiming the heater vent down from her flushed face. "At least not directly. But part of me wonders if I had been a better wife, maybe Crawford would have stood by my side through Daddy's troubles."

"Back up the truck." He cast her a sideways glance. "You don't really believe that, do you? That somehow you're to blame for your idiot husband leaving you when you needed him most? That's BS. I'm assuming you two went with the traditional vows, meaning he was aware of the whole for-better-or-worse scenario? Plus, he was hitched to you—not your father."

"You make it sound so black-and-white."

"It is. A man doesn't leave a woman when she's down—at least not me. I wasn't raised that way."

"Remember when you wanted me to meet your mom?"

"Sure. Want to come for dinner some night? Or we

could just stick with the original offer of cinnamon rolls."

"That sounds nice, but…" Suddenly emotional for no reason, Tiffany wanted to say yes but shook her head. Getting close to Rowdy's family would only make her decision more painful for all involved. Before now, she hadn't considered the fact that it wasn't just Rowdy whose life would be impacted by her giving up the baby. Though his big brother had already given his parents two granddaughters, did they want more? Obviously, they must be proud of their hotshot SEAL son, but did they want more for him? A daughter-in-law and more grandchildren and for him to settle down closer to their family home? "Definitely no."

"Why not? Mom and Dad are great. You'd like them."

"I'm sure I would." Which was the problem. The bigger her baby grew, the closer she came to her heart officially breaking when it was time to hand him over to the Parkers. She couldn't then turn around and do that to Rowdy's family, too.

"Then why not come for dinner?"

"Rowdy…" She sighed.

He held up his hands. "Invitation rescinded."

"Thanks." It crushed her that he gave up so easily, but then, why had she expected anything different when she'd asked to keep their dealings on a professional level?

They arrived at the next house.

This one was an A-frame overlooking a four-acre lake. Though the home had been painted an unfortunate shade of electric blue, the landscaping was lovely.

Rolling hills dotted with patches of forest and snow-covered pasture.

"Hope this comes with a riding mower." Out of the car, Rowdy held his hand to his forehead, shading his eyes from the sun.

"Why would you need to mow anything? Can't your horse eat the grass?"

"See those fences?" He pointed to newish-looking split-rail fences rimming the property. "Since it says on the info sheet that this has thirty-six acres, it stands to reason that the area not fenced is what they consider a lawn. I'm a fairly good judge of distance, and I'm going to say that's about three football fields' worth of lawn my wife is going to want me to mow every Saturday afternoon when I'd rather be watching college football."

"But you're not married." Her chest squeezed uncomfortably at the thought of him one day living here—or anywhere—with another woman. What was the significance of the fact that she didn't want him but she sure didn't want him canoodling with anyone else?

"For now, I'm single. But I'm a great catch. Out on the open market, I won't last long."

She rolled her eyes.

He winked.

Butterflies fluttered in her tummy.

"Buying a house is a big commitment," Rowdy said. "Eventually, when I retire from the navy, I'll end up back here, helping my dad and brother. Whoever I marry will have to get along with my mom and Justine. I assume they'll go shopping and garden and bake together. Plus, they do charity work."

On the meandering path to the home's front door,

Tiffany asked, "What sorts of charities? In Dallas I volunteered for the local animal shelter."

"Nice. I think Mom works at the hospital—showing visitors to patient rooms, delivering flowers, that kind of stuff. Justine reads books to old folks at Pine Manor. It's a retirement center."

"They sound like sweethearts."

"They are."

For some unfathomable reason, her hands shook while trying to work the combination on the lockbox. What would Rowdy's mom and sister-in-law think about her giving her son up for adoption? As mothers, would they look down on her? Or understand?

Most days, Tiffany didn't even understand.

But she felt backed into a corner.

Not only did she not feel emotionally strong enough to be a good mother, but the whole financial strain seemed insurmountable. She truly had no other option.

What about Rowdy? her conscience nudged. *How many times has he proposed?*

Funny, but accepting his offer of marriage struck her as a cop-out. The coward's solution to her problems. He hadn't gotten her into this money mess. How would it then be fair to expect his help? They were virtual strangers. Aside from their lone hot night, they had nothing in common. Sure, the baby was half his responsibility, but the last thing she wanted was for him to feel trapped like he had with Brandi.

Most important, Tiffany deserved more than what would essentially be a marriage of convenience. *If* she ever married again, it would be forever. Rowdy was sweet, but not exactly a forever kind of guy.

"Need help?"

She looked up to find him kneeling alongside her.

His face was close enough to hers that with minimum effort, she could have leaned forward to press her lips to his. She could have. And it was an undeniable fact that kissing him would feel beyond amazing. *Sublime*. But what would that solve? There was no denying their physical chemistry. But that had nothing to do with the kind of love it took to sustain a forever kind of marriage.

"Tiff?" He cleared his throat. "You okay?"

Free hand to her throat, she hastily nodded.

"You look pale. Need a break?"

"No. I'm good. Great." The lockbox popped and the house keys dropped into her open palm. "Okay, we're in."

She opened the door to enter a space that more closely resembled a taxidermy shop than living room.

"Hmm…" Rowdy arched his head back, taking it all in. The area featured an at-least-twenty-five-foot vaulted ceiling. Every inch of available wall space was covered in heads—deer, antelope, elk, bighorn sheep. An eight-foot grizzly stood in a corner. The air felt oppressive from the creatures' ghosts. "I guess this beats my roommate's centerfold pics."

"Look beyond the current decor. Remember, all of this will be going along with the owners."

"And their plaid furniture? Never been a fan of plaid."

"What if your wife loves it?"

"She won't."

"How do you know?"

"It's a deal breaker. If we get to the stage in our relationship where I'm thinking of popping the question, then I'll first ask about her relationship with plaid."

Tiffany rolled her eyes. "If you'll follow me upstairs, we'll look at the bedrooms."

"I've seen enough. We can move on."

"But don't you at least want to see the kitchen? And what about the hot tub?" She pointed toward the sliding glass windows leading to the deck.

"I'm good. I'll know the right place when I see it, and sorry, but this isn't it."

Tiffany sighed.

In her perfect dream scenario, *Mr. Gosee* would have fallen for the very first house they'd toured. The more she was forced to be with Rowdy, the more curious she grew about the type of woman he would one day be with. Beyond a physical type, what personality traits would he find irresistible? A sense of humor? Intellect? Was he looking for a great conversationalist or lover?

She shouldn't care but oddly did.

Her cheeks heated at the realization that she already knew what qualities he appreciated in the bedroom. The sex between them had been—

"Tiff, holy crap." He pointed at her feet. "Why didn't you tell me you need a break?"

"Huh?" She'd been so deep in thought about her baby's father that she'd forgotten her own rule about their house-seeking mission being strictly platonic. "What do you mean? We still have another house to see."

"You're not going anywhere but home. You have to get off of those footballs you call feet."

She glanced down to find that her feet and ankles had swollen to the point that the skin beneath her nude pantyhose had reddened. She hadn't felt any pain, because they'd gone past that point to numb.

Fear slithered through her in disorientating waves. "I've read about this in books. Do you think something's wrong with the baby?"

"There's only one way to find out. We're taking you to the ER." Before she could even think about launching a protest, he scooped her into his arms.

Chapter 7

*O*ur baby.

While the doctor examined Tiffany, Rowdy paced in the ER's crowded waiting area. A TV blared some god-awful kid show and an assortment of moans, coughs and general conversations interfered with the signal usually telling his brain to chill during emergencies.

But that was when bad guys shot at him.

This was a whole nother ball game.

He'd gladly take a bullet over the emotional strain of wondering what was going on behind closed exam room doors. He'd been seated in the hard plastic chair for two freakin' hours. What could be taking so long? Should he call Tiffany's mom and grandmother? Should he call his parents? What was the protocol on this situ-

ation? He needed a manual. At the very least, an officer barking orders.

But if he was on the verge of becoming a father, what
did that say about his parenting skills? When it came to
any family emergency, his mom and dad always seemed
to know exactly what to do. What was wrong with him
that he didn't?

And what was happening with the hospital bill? As
the baby's father, shouldn't someone have asked him
about insurance? He assumed his military coverage
would automatically include his unborn child, but that
was another issue he'd need to look into.

A pinched voice said over an intercom, "Mr. Jones,
please come to the service desk."

Rowdy stood, but then so did an elderly man dressed
in overalls and a red shirt. His green ball cap read Mc-
Ginty's Tack and Feed.

They reached the desk at about the same time.

In deference to the man's age, Rowdy gestured for
him to approach the clerk first. He wanted to think the
kindness was because his folks raised him right, but
the God's honest truth was that he wasn't sure he was
ready to handle bad news should something be wrong
with Tiffany or their baby.

Turned out the older gentleman had been the Mr.
Jones in question, so Rowdy started to sit back down,
but his seat had been taken by a teen boy with a nose
ring and green hair. If that were his kid, he'd shave him
bald and yank the ring out with pliers.

But then, hell. What kind of parent didn't allow their
child to experiment with his or her personal sense of
style? The summer between his junior and senior years

of high school, he'd gone through his own brief Goth stage. His folks hadn't much liked it, but they hadn't stopped him.

Could Tiffany be right? Could neither one of them be ready to be parents to this baby who was barreling their way?

He paced in front of the snack machines for a good thirty minutes before hearing his name again called over the intercom. This time an orderly greeted him and led him to the curtained-off room where Tiffany and her enormous belly sat up on a too-narrow bed. Her complexion had turned sallow, her formerly tidy bun had fallen and she'd sucked her lower lip into her mouth as if trying with all her might not to cry.

"Babe, what's wrong?" he asked at her side, forgetting his mother's order not to show how much he actually cared.

"I have edema and my blood pressure's too high. The doctor put me on bed rest for the week. But I have showings scheduled for three clients. I can't just lounge in bed. Mom and Grammy need the money from those potential sales."

"Slow down..." He took her hand, giving her a gentle squeeze. "Right now all that matters is keeping you and the baby healthy. Everything else can wait."

She shook her head. "If I don't get those commissions, who knows what could happen? Grammy could lose her house. She didn't want anyone to know, but I found out by accident that she mortgaged it to pay off Dad's legal fees." Her heart rate skyrocketed on the monitor, as did the baby's.

"Relax..." Rowdy coached. "Take a few deep breaths.

It takes a long time for a bank to officially foreclose. One of my idiot roommates, Connor, bought a great condo he was going to fix up on weekends and sell for a nice profit, but then we got deployed. He thought he'd set up auto-payments but never went to the bank to sign the forms. Long story short—he didn't make his payment for six months, but once he got back, he got it all sorted out and he eventually made a killing. If it makes you feel better, I'll go show the houses on your behalf."

"If only that would be legal. But if it were, you'd do that?" She met his gaze and the intensity of their connection caused his pulse to race as fast as hers. Didn't she know by now that he'd do anything for her and their unborn child? But why? He barely knew her yet couldn't shake the sensation that he'd always known her. That he couldn't imagine life without her. Not a good thing considering maybe she'd been right about the adoption all along.

"Sure." He strove for a light tone. Like she hadn't turned his entire world upside down and inside out and every damned way in between.

She sharply exhaled. "That would've been great. Thanks for the offer."

"No problem."

A man and woman suddenly rushed into the room. "Thank goodness you're okay."

Rowdy glanced over his shoulder to find the sort of power couple he'd seen only on TV. The man with slicked-back blond hair wore a navy suit, pin-striped shirt and red power tie. The set of his mouth was pinched with worry. The woman with him had sleek dark hair. A red dress with black stockings and heels.

More gold around her neck, wrists and fingers than Fort Knox. Yet her bloodshot eyes looked as if she'd been crying. She clenched a tissue in her hand.

Let me guess—Jeb and Susie Parker? His son's adoptive parents.

No wonder no emergency room staff had asked him about payment. When Tiffany called in the cavalry, they'd probably made all the necessary arrangements for the bill to be paid.

Rowdy wanted to hate them but felt an odd compassion for this couple who for all outward appearances seemed to have everything yet lacked the ability to conceive their own child.

"Tiffany…" The woman dabbed the corners of her eyes with a tissue. "We got your call and I swear I haven't breathed since. But the doctor said you and the baby will be all right? You just need rest?"

Tiffany nodded. Her gaze darted from him to the couple. "Susie, Jeb—this is Rowdy. He's the baby's biological father."

"Oh." Susie looked from Tiffany to Rowdy, then raised her trembling hands to her mouth. "Oh, God…" She shook her head, then turned to her husband, hiding her face against his pricey suit's lapel. Suddenly, they were no longer powerful and all the money in the world meant nothing compared to the gift of a newborn son they believed they were receiving.

"Shh…" Jeb said to his wife. "Don't jump to conclusions." He held out his hand to Rowdy, forcing a tight smile. "Nice to meet you. We, ah, can't thank you enough for your remarkable sacrifice."

About that…

"Yeah. Sure." Rowdy shook the guy's hand but then felt so overcome by raw emotion that he cleared his throat, then said, "I'll leave you all alone. Tiff, I'm guessing you'll want the Parkers to drive you home?"

Her eyes also shone with tears. She opened her mouth to speak but then clamped her lips shut and merely nodded.

Rowdy's heart felt near exploding from pain and confusion, so he left.

He should have stayed.

He should have told this couple here and now that there was no way in hell they'd ever be raising *his* son. But how could he claim any of that when he'd never been more confused?

After driving aimlessly for thirty minutes in Tiffany's SUV, knowing he'd have to at least see her again to return her vehicle, he wound up back at his family's ranch.

The day had turned into the perfect Indian-summer afternoon. After the early snow, what few leaves remained on the oaks and maples surrounding the house and barn were putting on a colorful show.

While parking Tiffany's SUV—his truck was back at her office—Rowdy spotted his brother teaching a gelding, Dandy, manners in the round pen, so he sauntered that way, appreciating the scents of loamy soil and hay.

"You look like hell," Carl said. He gave the black gelding a rub, then led him out the gate to play. The last time Rowdy had been in, the gelding had been a little guy. Now he was almost ready for saddling. He missed a lot being gone from the ranch. But he loved serving his country.

He loved being a SEAL.

His job wasn't merely a paycheck but his calling.

Rowdy said, "Feel like it, too."

"What's up?"

Where did he start? Why hadn't he told the Parkers that his son would never be theirs? "You're a dad—a great one."

"Yeah. What about it?" Carl aimed for the barn.

Rowdy climbed over the fence to meet him inside. It took his eyes time to adjust to the shadows. He'd always felt at peace in the quiet barn. In a way, it was his church—slanted sunbeams filled with dust motes his dad used to tell him were angels, watching over him and keeping him safe. The rich aroma of leather tack that had been in the family for generations, lovingly cared for and oiled, made him feel a profoundly deep connection to not only his family but the land.

Carl said, "Prying words out of you is about as easy as it's been getting Dandy prepped for saddling." He took a pair of well-worn leather gloves from a shelf and handed them to him. "If you can't tell me what's wrong, at least make yourself useful. The stalls all need cleaning. Ingrid has an ear infection, so I had to run her to the pediatrician this morning instead of doing my usual chores."

"Where's Dad?"

"South pasture. He found a calf with scours, so he's bringing him in for treatment."

Rowdy nodded.

Carl handed him a pitchfork, then took a wheelbarrow down to the last stall. This time of year, they brought most of the horses in for the night. Though cattle were the ranch's biggest source of income, they also raised and trained horses. Carl and his father had earned the reputation of being a couple of the best trainers around.

What was Rowdy good at? Sniffing trouble.

His nickname with his buddies was Voodoo because he had an uncanny knack for exposing the earth's human scum. This ability came in real handy while on active duty in Iraq or Afghanistan, but it wouldn't do beans for him in North Dakota.

One more reason to reconsider becoming a father?

His chest ached from the decision rocketing toward him faster than enemy fire. By his calculations, Tiffany had about six weeks until she delivered their son. In that time, he'd have to make what now struck him as an impossible choice.

Together, Rowdy and Carl cleaned three stalls without saying a word.

But then Rowdy's dam of silence broke. "I was out with Tiffany this afternoon, looking at houses like y'all told me to, when I noticed her feet looked like a pair of footballs."

"It happens. With both pregnancies, Justine had to spend a lot of time off her feet. She teased that was nature's way of telling me to spoil her rotten." He smiled. "Damn, I love that woman."

In the moment, Rowdy envied his big brother and his friend Duck. Both of them seemed to have life figured out.

"Did you take her to her doctor?"

"Her feet were so big I ran her straight to the ER. Long story short, you're right. The doc told her to stay off her feet for the next few days. Oh—and she needs to stop cramming her toes into silly high heels."

"Sounds like a solid plan. So what's the problem?"

Rowdy shoveled faster. "While we were at the hospital, this frantic couple stormed into Tiff's room. Turns out they're the adoptive parents she selected."

Carl whistled. "Bet that was an ugly scene. How'd they take the news that your son is no longer on the market?"

"That's just it." Rowdy froze, resting his hands atop the pitchfork. "I couldn't tell them. The woman— Susie—was crying with worry over the baby. Her husband, Jeb, was a real professional type. Suit. Tie. The whole nine yards. But even he had tears in his eyes. And I stood there looking at them, thinking they already love my son. They have loved him longer than I've even known he existed. They probably have a nursery already in place and, hell, a preschool application at some fancy-ass academy where rich folks send their kids to get trained to be even richer. But what do I have to offer? Like Mom pointed out, the vast majority of the year, I'm not even in the country. Can you imagine being away from Isobel and Ingrid for that long?"

"Honestly? No."

"See? So what if I was wrong to head up here, demanding Tiffany and I force a marriage when neither one of us are anywhere near ready to settle down? We don't know the first thing about raising a baby. Hell, what do I know about changing diapers or making formula? I like to think someday I'd make a good dad, but how do I know now is that time?"

"You know when you know."

"What's that mean?"

"Just what I said. Look, when Justine first told me she was pregnant with Izzy—not gonna lie, I was scared shitless. But that's why the good Lord saw fit to give us nine months to get used to the idea. So that by the time the baby enters the world, you've got yourself good and psyched up. Then, once you see him or her..." his eyes welled and he tapped the center of his chest "... it's magic. Indescribable. You just know that suddenly the most important person in your world is this tiny, squalling, red-faced creature who holds your heart in her tiny hands. Or, in your case, his hands." He sighed. "I'm not passing judgment. If you don't feel like now is the time for you to be a dad, I can't say I understand, but I'm not going to love you any less. I'm sure as hell not going to judge—neither are Mom and Dad. Only you can decide if you're ready to be a father. And if Tiffany maintains that she can't handle custody, then it might come down to you having to raise this baby boy on your own. Not sure how you'd do that while deployed, but we're a family and we'd figure it out."

Rowdy wished his big brother's sage words made him feel better, but if anything, he'd only grown more confused.

Chapter 8

"How exciting," Pearl said not thirty seconds after Tiffany and the Parkers entered the house. "It's rare to have company around here, and you all make for three in the same week. How do you know our Tiffany?"

"Grammy, these are the baby's adoptive parents." Tiffany made formal introductions. "I had a problem with swollen feet this afternoon, so Rowdy took me to the ER. Jeb and Susie were kind enough to give me a ride home. I guess Rowdy will stop by later with my car."

"Gracious." Hand to her chest, Pearl made a clucking sound. "Hope it's nothing serious?"

Mr. Bojangles danced at Susie's and Jeb's feet. He wasn't wearing the black sweater she'd put on him that morning. Was he cold?

Gigi wandered in, fluffing her hair. "Why didn't any-one tell me we have guests? I would have done some-thing with myself." Of course, Gigi looked flawless in full makeup, curled hair and a flowing, bejeweled caf-tan far more suited to Dubai than North Dakota.

"Hush." Pearl landed a light swat to her daughter-in-law's shoulder. "Tiffany's sick, and these are the people who will be taking her baby."

"But I thought she was marrying Rowdy and keep-ing the baby? I've been on the phone with florists and caterers most of the afternoon."

Poor Susie paled.

Jeb wrapped his arm around her shoulders as sup-port.

For some unfathomable reason, Tiffany wished for Rowdy to give her the same comforting treatment, but that train had long left the station. Judging by the dark look he'd sported while meeting their son's adoptive parents, he'd been as shocked to see them as they had been upon meeting him.

Susie's eyes teared, but she managed to say, "We were under the impression the baby's father was no longer in the picture?"

"He wasn't. He's not," Tiffany assured them. The drive over, Susie had been on the phone with a private nursing company. Despite Tiffany's protests, she'd been determined to provide round-the-clock care.

"That's not what he told us," Pearl stated. "That man declared his intentions, so I'm real sorry," she said to Susie and Jeb, "but Tiffany and Rowdy will be keep-ing their baby."

"Don't listen to them." For the baby, Tiffany needed

to get this issue behind her and sit down. Her feet were already once again starting to swell. "Susie, Jeb, I know the baby's father showing up has put a slight kink in our plans, but I wholeheartedly believe he'll come around. Please, for now, I can't thank you enough for charging to my rescue, but I need rest."

"What about the private nurses?" Jeb asked.

Pearl raised her chin. "I might be old, but I'm plenty capable of caring for my own grandchild."

As if sensing the tension, Mr. Bojangles barked.

"Grammy—" Tiffany awkwardly knelt to pick up her anxious dog "—the doctor told me I need to be on bed rest for the week. I can't burden you with that."

"Nonsense. I—"

A brief knock sounded on the still-ajar front door. Then Rowdy stepped into the fray. "If anyone's going to care for Tiffany and our baby, it'll be me."

Once again Tiffany nearly swooned.

She scolded her stupid, romantic heart. The only service Rowdy currently performed was acting as one more person wanting something from her that she wasn't equipped to give.

"So that's it?" Jeb asked. "Man-to-man, you're not willing to sign away your parental rights?"

"Honestly?" Rowdy's whisker-stubbled jaw hardened and he shoved his hands in his jeans pockets. "I'm not sure. I'd be lying if I said I wasn't leaning in that direction, but my military career isn't exactly family friendly, so that's got me wondering if maybe an adoption would be best?"

Susie took a tissue from her purse and blotted her watery eyes. Tiffany's heart ached for the poor woman.

She'd been trying to get pregnant for nearly a decade. Wanting a baby consumed her. To now snatch back this most precious gift would be beyond cruel.

"We'll need a definitive answer," Jeb said. "My wife is a strong woman, but—"

"I can speak for myself," Susie said. "Rowdy, Tiffany explained how you only just recently found out you were going to be a father, so I'm sure you're still adjusting to the news. Please know that if you were to decide to go through with the adoption, we'd be forever in your debt. Your son would never want for love or anything else."

"I appreciate that," Rowdy said, "but you've got to understand that this decision is going to take a minute."

"Of course." She bowed her head.

"If I did decide to sign over my parental rights, would I at least be involved in my child's life? Or are we talking about a closed adoption?"

"Closed," Jeb said. "Sorry, but I think it's best for the child to believe we're his parents in every sense of the word. Someday down the line—maybe when he's in college, we could tell him the truth, but—"

"I get it." Rowdy held up his hands to stop Jeb's speech.

"What about the wedding?" Gigi asked.

"Mom, please, stay out of this. And for the last time, there's not going to be a…" Suddenly light-headed, Tiffany grasped the newel post for support.

"This party's over," Rowdy said, already by her side, scooping her into his arms. "Jeb, Susie, we'll let you know when we have an answer. Until then, please respect the fact that this isn't an easy choice for any of us. We'll let you know what we've decided as soon as we know."

He carried her up the stairs, tenderly deposited her on the bed, then took the dog from her to set him atop her towering belly, where he served as king of the mountain.

She didn't have the energy to move him.

It was only a little past five, but the afternoon had been beyond exhausting.

To the dog, Rowdy said, "Watch over your mom and my son, okay? I'll be right back."

"Where are you going?" Tiffany asked.

"To finish a conversation." He removed her heels, then pitched them across the room. He took her favorite fuzzy blanket from the foot of the bed, lifted Mr. Bojangles long enough to cover her, then set the dog back on her belly while adjusting her pillows. "Comfortable?"

She nodded.

"I'll be back with food and something to drink. Don't you dare move a muscle. Are we clear?"

"Yes, sir." She made a sassy salute.

Her SEAL growled before storming out her bedroom door, closing it behind him.

She closed her eyes and tried sleeping, but that was kind of tough considering the raised voices floating up the stairs. Not to mention the fact that she'd just thought of Rowdy in terms of being *hers*, when nothing could be further from the truth.

Rowdy descended the stairs to find himself immersed in the sort of verbal ugliness he hadn't seen since his last visit to Mogadishu.

Jeb fought with Pearl.

Susie warred with Gigi.

What all of them had forgotten was that upstairs, the woman carrying the unborn child they bickered over was in less-than-ideal health. Tiffany needed care and support—not infighting over custody of a child who would rightfully be his.

Sick of the noise, he put his fingers in his mouth for an ear-piercing whistle. When all four of them stopped yammering to stare, he said, "Susie and Jeb, I appreciate your help." He fished one of his family ranch business cards from his wallet to hand to Jeb. "Whatever the medical costs turn out to be, please forward them to me at this address."

"This isn't about money," Susie said. "We want your baby."

"I get that. Your message has come through loud and clear. But right now my sole focus is Tiffany. She needs peace and quiet. Which means you two need to leave."

"I thought you said you just needed time. D-does this mean you've already made a decision?" Tears streamed down Susie's cheeks.

"I honestly don't know. At the moment, all I do know is that like I already told you, the best I can offer is to give you a decision closer to when the baby's due. Until then, I'd appreciate not seeing either of you again."

"We do have rights," Jeb noted. "The adoption will be legal just as soon as Tiffany signs a contract."

"Yeah…" He opened the front door and gestured the way out. "Well, that was before I was in the picture. Now that I'm back in, you can take your contract and shove it up your—"

"I think they get the message," Pearl said with a

calming hand to his back. "Susie and Jeb, I'm sure Tiffany will call should her condition change."

"You'll be hearing from my lawyer," Jeb said before ushering a sobbing Susie out the door.

Once they'd left, Rowdy leaned hard against the nearest wall, closing his eyes for a moment to drag in an extra-deep breath.

"I had no idea you were such a powerful orator," Gigi said. "Perhaps at the wedding, you and Tiffany should write your own vows?"

If a guy like Jeb had said that, Rowdy probably would have decked him for the ridiculous comment, but Tiffany's mother looked so sincere all he could do was laugh. "If it comes to that, we'll see. But for now, could one of you please help me make Tiff a cup of herbal tea?"

"It would be my most sincere pleasure," Pearl said. "I have fresh-baked oatmeal cookies, too. I always add a smidge more vanilla than the recipe calls for. Makes them extra tasty."

"I can't wait to find out." Rowdy followed both women to the kitchen, where Gigi chattered about the holiday-themed wedding that was never going to happen. Meanwhile, Pearl prepared a tray loaded with three small baskets of cookies, muffins and grapes. Once the teakettle whistled on the gas stove, she poured steaming water over the tea bag she'd already placed in a dainty floral cup.

"Here you go," she said once she'd finished. "Need help delivering it to our patient?"

"No, thank you. You've done enough by putting all this together."

His simple praise left the kindly old woman beaming.

Gigi sported a huge smile, too. "Mother Lawson, it sure is nice having a man around the house, isn't it?"

"Yes, ma'am, it sure is. I'm excited for the wedding. I might tackle the cake all on my own."

"You do make beautiful cakes." Gigi snatched a cookie from her daughter's tray.

Rowdy didn't have the heart to tell them the wedding was a figment of their imaginations, so he retreated up the rambling farmhouse's back stairs.

It was tricky cradling the tray in the crook of one arm while turning the crystal doorknob to Tiffany's room, but once he was in, the sight awaiting him took his breath away.

Tiffany and her sorry excuse for a guard dog had fallen asleep. Both lightly snored, and both were bathed in the setting sun's golden glow.

She was a beauty.

He recalled the night they'd met like it had happened eight minutes earlier as opposed to eight months.

How had all of this gotten so messy?

When he'd learned of her pregnancy, he'd planned for a simple extraction mission. Pick up the woman carrying his baby, bring her back to Virginia, set her up in a house. Problem solved, right? But somewhere along the way, she'd gotten under his skin. He found himself wanting to do little things for her. Hefting her into his arms more because he craved holding her rather than because she wasn't able to walk.

Swiping his hands through his hair, he tried looking at this cluster bomb of a situation with a clinical view.

But a pang in his chest stopped all signals from going to his brain. Where his logic used to live now resided an unfamiliar craving for a more elusive something he couldn't wholly identify, let alone find.

His every current problem stemmed from this woman.

Her blond hair streamed across the pillow, catching glints from the sun as if she were his own personal siren. In that moment, he didn't want to be with her for the sake of the baby, but because he wanted to kiss her.

For a guy whose tightest relationship was with the US Navy? Craving a woman was a very bad thing.

Chapter 9

It was just her luck that when Tiffany woke from her dream of yachting on the Amalfi Coast, being ravished by a dark, brooding sort who looked suspiciously like Rowdy, she'd find herself being assaulted by Mr. Bojangles's overexcited tongue.

"Sorry," Rowdy said. "I tried getting him off of you, but it was tough while trying not to spill your tea."

"I understand." After setting her dog on the pillow beside her, she struggled to push herself up in the bed. "Thank you. You didn't have to go to so much trouble."

He shrugged. "Pearl did all of the work. I just carried it upstairs." After placing her still-steaming tea on the nightstand, he asked, "Cookie or muffin?"

"Both." She frowned. "I'm horrible. Once this baby

pops out, the carb police are going to lock me in solitary confinement for a year with nothing but celery."

"Knock it off. You're beautiful." After delivering her baked goods, he sat on the ultrafeminine chaise where Gigi usually lounged. At first he looked uncertain about what to do with his long legs, but then he figured it out and leisurely stretched as if he'd taken lessons on being a royal from her spoiled-rotten dog.

He cast her an indecipherable grin.

"What's that about?"

"What?"

"That grin. You look suspicious."

He crossed his legs. "You're way off base."

"Okay, then, what's up?"

"I'm not touching that with a ten-foot pole—especially when you're currently giving me a rather lengthy one." He winked.

It took her a sec, but then she flung a pillow at him. "You're horrible! How can you think of sex when I'm huge?"

"Because you're still the hottest woman I've ever seen, and when I walked in the room, your expression reminded me of the morning I woke up beside you— not to mention the crazy shit we did the night before."

Her cheeks flamed. Not that she protested him finding her ginormous body desirable, but she had to add, "In light of what we just went through with Susie and Jeb and my football-sized feet, how is any of that relevant?"

"How is it not?" He sat up, swinging his legs around to plant his feet flat on the floor and elbows on his knees. "Think about it. If it wasn't for that night, the two of us might never have spoken again. That has to mean something, don't you think?"

"Like in a touchy-feely universal kind of way?"

"Exactly. What if we're soul mates? And our son is the thread binding us together?"

"Soul mates?" She struggled not to laugh. "My future soul mate is waiting for me back in Texas. He will own a twenty-room Dallas mansion, a log cabin in Aspen and a French château we don't visit as often as we'd like, because it's so fabulous that it's always being rented for movies."

He rolled his eyes. "I refuse to believe you're that narrow-minded when it comes to finding a good man."

She didn't used to be. Back when Crawford asked her to marry him, she'd still believed in happy endings. "Right about the time Big Daddy landed himself in jail and Crawford served divorce papers, I gave up on love. It's an antiquated emotion best saved for sappy greeting cards. I'll be the first to admit, the night you and I shared was incredible—hands down, best sex I've ever had. But what did that get me? A bun in the oven and some navy SEAL cowboy who won't stick around any longer than the horse-riding version. If I told you this second I want to keep our baby and ride off into the sunset with you, what would you say?"

"Depends. Would this marriage have benefits?"

"No." She frowned. "Give me your real answer. Not the first one that pops into your dirty mind. Or your heroic, save-the-world SEAL mind. Take both of those what-you-think-you-should-do urges out of the equation to give this topic rational thought. What happens when our little Johnny has a bad flu or lands the lead role in his school play or is—"

"Since this is my son we're talking about, he'll be a quarterback like his old man."

Now she was rolling her eyes. "You didn't let me get to the heart of the matter. Let's say I did believe in love and marriage. With you gone the vast majority of the time, what good does a piece of paper do me when I need a hand to hold when Johnny's got the ball, there's five seconds left on the clock and his team is down by two points? If he makes the game-winning touchdown, who do we party with? If he doesn't and his whole team blames him for the loss, who do I console him with? Oh, sure, you're more than willing to step up and do the supposed right thing by marrying me—giving our baby your name and a roof over his head—but have you ever stopped to think about what that even means? I've been brutally honest with you about the fact that I'm not sure I have what it takes to be a parent—let alone a single parent. If I married you, wouldn't I essentially be signing up for just that?"

Rowdy didn't have an answer for her, so he mumbled an awkward goodbye, kissed her cheek, then fed her some BS line about needing to meet his brother to get his truck from her office lot.

The second he'd slipped from the house without being caught by Gigi or Pearl, he did call his brother for a ride, but he started walking in the hopes of clearing his mind.

He didn't want to admit it, but Tiffany's speech made a lot of sense. With him constantly deployed, she would be a single parent. But hell, he knew lots of guys who were married and had kids and they seemed happy enough. Grady and Jessie. Wiley and Macy. But Grady had chosen to leave the navy and Wiley had been forced out by an injury.

Rowdy didn't just love his job as a SEAL but needed it.

The rush.

It was the closest thing to being Rambo that America had to offer. The United States government gifted him the latest weaponry and cutting-edge gadgets. He worked with a band of brothers who would literally give their lives for him in a crisis. Hazard pay was pretty damned sweet, too. What else did Tiffany think made him able to afford the cozy house he planned to buy?

The thought of going without all of the above—quitting cold turkey—made him nauseous. What would he do with himself all day? How would he handle what most people considered a normal life when to him, *normal* meant disarming a terrorist nuke with ten seconds to spare?

He'd stormed his way past the neighborhood and now walked alongside the highway leading out of town. Tall weeds made the hike a struggle, but he was used to a lot worse.

A truck towing a horse trailer whizzed by. The resulting breeze was damned cold, so he jammed his frozen fingers in his jeans pockets.

His most pressing hardship wasn't the rapidly falling temperature but the turmoil in his mind. In figuring out how to keep his son while still hanging on to the career he held dear. And what happened with Tiffany? Beyond their chemistry between the sheets, what would make a marriage between them work? And he was talking a real marriage—like what his folks shared. Carl and Justine. But in order to get that kind of lasting relationship, what was he prepared to give? What, beyond his paycheck, was he willing to leave on their familial table?

A couple miles farther, he winced as Carl approached and the old farm truck's lights blinded him. "Little brother, you are one crazy SOB."

"Tell me about it." Rowdy held his hands in front of blasting heater vents.

"What'd your gal do this time that got you all wound up?"

How did he answer without making himself look like an ass? Hell, maybe he was an ass? "We were right in the middle of what's starting to be our usual debate when she tells me she's never wanted to be a single mother. No shit, right? I wouldn't especially want to be a single father. But if that's the case, then why shouldn't I be on board for giving our baby to this Jeb and Susie couple who seem a helluva lot better equipped to handle raising a child than either me or Tiffany."

Carl gunned the vehicle toward town. "I don't get this. When I picked you up from the airport, you were all about keeping your son. Now you're filled with doubts?"

"I can't help it. Tiffany does raise valid points. Plus, how do I stay in the navy while having a kid?"

"Did you honestly just ask such an asinine question? I'm not saying it would be easy, but thousands of active military and veterans manage just fine. So if that's your biggest parenting hurdle? I'm not buying it. Did you ever think it's time to man up and claim your son?"

"Well, yeah. That's why I'm here. But what if Tiffany's right? And our son would be better off being raised by another couple? They've got time and money."

"If you ask me, you're both being selfish."

"Selfish? What the hell? If anything, we're being *selfless*."

"Whatever. I'm sick of hearing about it. If you were man enough to get Tiffany pregnant, then you should be man enough to put your son's needs ahead of your own."

They'd almost reached Tiffany's office.

Despite Thanksgiving being two weeks away, downtown merchants had already swapped Halloween decorations for Christmas. The rush toward the holidays made Rowdy all the more incensed. Why the hell was everything in his life set on fast-forward?

What was wrong with him that he equated the birth of his newborn son with a sort of death? If he wanted to be a dad, his days as a SEAL seemed destined to die. As for the fact that Rowdy struggled to decide which life path he most wanted, did that make Carl right? Was he selfish?

He and his brother had always had their minor squabbles, but this felt different.

Carl pulled his truck behind Rowdy's.

Without a word, Rowdy climbed out and slammed his door.

Carl shouted out the now-open passenger-side window, "Call Mom if you're going to be late. She worries!"

Having delivered his cargo and message, Carl gunned from the lot, leaving Rowdy eating his exhaust.

He should've at the very least flipped Carl a bird, but honestly? He was too drained to care. Count on his big brother to twist the guilt knife a little deeper as to his mother's worry.

One more nail in the coffin of his career?

He climbed into his vehicle and turned the engine. The starter clicked a few times before catching. Great. On top of everything else, he now had more truck problems?

Since his ride seemed to be running fine, Rowdy aimed for the ranch but changed his mind in favor of checking on Tiffany again.

After a quick call to his mother, he ended up at Pearl's.

Gigi opened the door. "Get in here, handsome. We wondered where you'd run off to."

"I had to get my truck." He hitched his thumb toward the street where he'd parked.

"Actually…" She grabbed his forearm, tugging him inside. The air smelled rich. Chicken and dumplings? His stomach growled. "I'm glad for this moment alone."

His formerly excited stomach fell. What was she up to?

"I've had to keep this under wraps, because Tiffany gets all bent out of shape when I use the color printer for nonessentials, but I think nothing could be more important than uniting the both of you with your child."

Beyond uncomfortable with the conversation, Rowdy cleared his throat. "Thanks. Can we talk later? Right now I've gotta check on Tiff."

"Leave her bedroom door open!" Pearl shouted from

the kitchen. "No funny business until after the wedding!"

"Yes, ma'am." To hasten his exit, Rowdy took the stairs two at a time.

He entered Tiffany's domain to find her brushing Mr. Bojangles while softly humming.

He cleared his throat. "Hey."

"You're back."

He shrugged. "My brother, Carl, said a few things I wanted to run past you."

"Shoot." Her silly little dog looked ready to purr from pleasure. She set down his brush to grab a pint-size sweater from a basket on her nightstand, then fit it over the dog's head.

Moments earlier he'd known just what to say, but now he couldn't find the right words. Carl's accusation cut Rowdy deep. He couldn't be that direct with a pregnant woman who was already under too much stress.

"Well?" She'd finished dressing the dog and now held him to her cheek for a cuddle.

"You know how you keep telling me part of the reason you want to give our baby up for adoption is that you won't make a good mom?"

She bowed her head. "It's the truth."

"I call BS. You don't think what you do for your pet is mothering?"

"It's hardly the same and you know it." She set the pooch alongside her on the bed. "If I need to run an errand, I can take him with me or leave him with my mom or…"

"Exactly. You could also do the same with our son." He sat on the chaise, facing her. "Look, you've actually made surprisingly valid points with this whole adoption thing. So many that I'm seriously thinking about agreeing with your position. But then I get this gnawing ache…" He patted his chest. "I can't even conceive of my son—our son—being in this world without us. And then Carl said something…" Rowdy hadn't planned to repeat his brother's hurtful sentiments, but maybe she needed to hear them? Maybe she needed the same verbal punch? "He accused us of being selfish."

"What?" She sucked in her next breath fast enough to cough.

Mr. Bojangles barked.

"Are you kidding?" Her eyes shined with tears.

"Afraid not."

"The whole reason adoption is even on the table is because I realize maybe I'm not the best woman for the job. Isn't that being selfless?"

"Exactly." Rowdy finally exhaled. "That's what I said. I was pissed. Where does he come off getting in our business like that?" Too antsy to sit, he made the short trek to her dresser for a cookie, then took the tray to her. "Eat. You need to keep up your strength."

"Yes, sir." She took a cookie and muffin. "But as soon as this baby pops out, carbs are out of my picture."

"Whatever. But here's another thing. You know I'm considering adoption as a viable option?"

She nodded.

"I want you to do the same in regard to keeping our son."

"Rowdy, we—"

"Trust me, I am one hundred percent on board with every shred of your rationale. No one's life stands to be changed more than mine by adding a wife and baby. But what if that change was positive? For both of us. We've given the whole adoption thing a good look, but it's only been a couple weeks since I've been back in your picture. What would it hurt for you to give my way a chance? Especially since for now, it would only be in your head."

A week later, Tiffany still couldn't stop thinking about Rowdy's haunted expression.

She sat across from him in her obstetrician's crowded waiting room. He made faces at a six-month-old in a carrier at his feet.

The little girl giggled every time he raised his eyebrows and stuck out his tongue.

That pang in his chest he'd talked about? She felt it now.

Would he be this playful with their son?

Her imagination went straight to a cozy shared breakfast with her making pancakes and him feeding the baby oatmeal. He'd make adorable vrooming truck noises for their son and little Johnny would giggle and kick in his high chair, squealing with delight. She'd deliver Rowdy's pancakes, and he'd wrap his arm around her waist, reeling her in for a thank-you kiss.

She closed her eyes and knew much too well the feel of his lips crushing hers in every variation. Dizzying pressure to a butterfly-soft whisper. His kisses made her lose her mind, and she'd all too willingly signed up for the trip. His lightest touch—

"Miss Lawson? The doctor's ready for you."

Jolted from her daydream, Tiffany touched her heated cheeks, then the baby.

"Want me to go with?" Rowdy asked.

"No." *Yes!* How adorable would it be watching him see their son and hear his heartbeat for the first time?

"What if I want to?"

"Suit yourself."

He waved goodbye to his adorable friend.

She waved back.

A knot lurked at the back of Tiffany's throat.

If they were to marry and set up a home and Rowdy left to go off to war, how hard would it be watching their son wave goodbye? She blinked back tears.

"You okay?" Rowdy asked. He'd placed his big hand in the small of her back. The simple gesture made her huge pregnant body feel small and protected.

"I'm good," she said, even though she clearly needed time away from the stupid-handsome man to clear her head and return her last shred of sanity.

It didn't escape her notice when he politely turned away during her weigh-in. He also knelt to help her slip off the ugly loafers she'd been reduced to wearing since they were the only shoes in her closet that fit.

In the exam room, after the nurse took her blood pressure and delivered the reading, he asked, "Is that normal?"

"Yep. Our momma is doing great." She handed Tiffany a floral hospital-style gown and heated blanket. "You know the drill. It shouldn't be too long until the doctor's in."

"Great. Thanks."

Tiffany glanced at the gown, then to Rowdy. "Mind stepping out?"

"It's not like I haven't seen it before," he said with a grin. "Just kidding. But in case you need help, I'll be right outside."

"Thanks." She changed as quickly as she could, given her condition. Her hot-pink socks that had seemed like a good match for the Baby On Board sweater, which had been the only clean one that still fit, now looked silly with her pale green gown.

She was attempting to heft herself back onto the exam table when Rowdy knocked, then poked his head back in the room. "All clear?"

"Sort of." She hugged the still-warm blanket, hating herself for wishing it were him. "Don't look at my butt."

"Wouldn't dream of it—though, for the record, it's an awfully cute butt."

"Rowdy!" she scolded in a loud whisper. "You can't say things like that."

"Why not?"

She didn't have an answer.

Luckily, the doctor knocked, then entered. "The nurse said your blood pressure is good. How are those poor feet?"

"Better. So can I go back to work?"

"Sure. But try keeping it to only a few hours a day. You're a Realtor, right?"

"Yes."

"We have a new physician joining our clinic. She's temporarily staying with family, but would you be able to show her something on Thursday?"

"I'd love to. Thank you. I'll get you a card when

we're done so you can give your friend my contact information."

"Perfect." To Rowdy, the doctor said, "I haven't seen you around here before."

"I'm the baby's father."

"This is an interesting development." She helped Tiffany lie back on the exam table. "It's always more fun for Mommy when the daddy's around. Tiffany, I have to ask, have you changed your mind about the adoption?"

"I'm not sure," Tiffany admitted.

The doctor strategically placed blankets so as to reveal only the baby bump.

The nurse stepped in and quickly shut the door.

Usually, the exam room felt plenty big. The pale lilac walls were soothing, as were the dim lights and collection of four-leaf-clover photographs artfully grouped on the far wall.

Rowdy's presence overwhelmed her not only physically but emotionally. For some unfathomable reason, what she could describe only as giddiness rose from deep within her soul when the doctor rubbed ultrasound gel on her tummy, then waved the magic wand for Rowdy to get his first glimpse and listen of their son.

How would he react? Would he be excited? Nervous? A little scared?

"There he is…" the doctor said. The gallop of her baby's little heart never failed to give Tiffany a thrill. Knowing she had to give him away, she'd purposely tried to disconnect, but with each visit, that task grew harder. "Well, Rowdy? What do you think?"

Thanks, Doc, for asking what my heart needs to know…

Chapter 10

Rowdy tried not to crowd Tiffany's personal space, but when the doctor waved the ultrasound wand across her tummy and he not only saw his son but heard his heartbeat, Rowdy was a goner.

Tears stinging his eyes, he leaned closer.

The doctor had asked him a direct question, but he'd be damned if he could remember what she'd said.

"Speechless is always a fun response," she said with a laugh.

"I'm sorry, what?" Rowdy asked. "I'm kind of..." He wasn't sure what he was feeling. Mostly overwhelming happiness and then sadness for the uncertainty still in the air.

He looked to Tiffany. Her blue eyes shone with unshed tears and she'd drawn her lower lip into her mouth for a sexy nibble. God, she was a beauty.

"I'm not entirely sure if I'm seeing our kid's elbow or a hockey stick, but regardless, Tiff, you made a good-looking baby." He skimmed his hand atop the crown of her head. "Seriously, he's..." He could hardly speak past the well of emotions threatening to overflow. "He's great."

"Thanks." Tiffany beamed.

The nurse handed them each a tissue when neither did a good job of holding back silent tears.

"You two stop, or you're going to get me going," the doctor said. "Your baby's heart rate is strong and right where we need it to be. Everything else looks good. Rowdy, if I could get you to step out of the room, I need to take my exam down below."

It took him a sec to catch on. But then he bent forward to kiss Tiffany's forehead before leaving the room, secretly glad for the chance to regain his composure.

He raked his hands through his hair.

This was a game changer.

After actually getting a look at his son, he couldn't even think of handing him over after his birth. But was he ready for a lifelong commitment?

He paced the hall, wishing for an easy answer, but there was none.

His stomach lurched when the door opened and the doctor and nurse stepped out.

The nurse said, "Tiffany's good to go as soon as she's dressed."

"Cool. Thanks." Rowdy struggled to find his next breath. Maybe he shouldn't have tagged along? Maybe he'd OD'd on the recommended dose of touchy-feely emotions for one day?

"Nice meeting you," the doctor said. "Hopefully, you plan on staying in town?" Her tone implied what her words hadn't directly asked. Was he going to play an active role in his son's life?

Yes.

I mean, probably.

What am I thinking? Absolutely.

But how? How did he dive right into a second marriage with a woman he hardly knew? How did he know he'd even like being a dad? But who was he to assume he had a choice? If he'd been man enough to share in making the child, then he had the moral obligation to raise him.

"Yeah," he mumbled. "It was good meeting you, too."

With the doctor and nurse gone, Rowdy was back on his own and brushing his sweating palms against the thighs of his jeans. His pulse galloped as fast as his son's and his mouth had gone dry.

He was a navy SEAL—supposedly one of the toughest men on the planet. So why did this issue have him feeling weak in the knees? His father and brother were much better equipped to handle this situation. But why? Especially when Rowdy had been trained to tackle any possible contingency with zero complaints. When he was assigned a mission, he'd never been the kind of guy to hem and haw. He was a soldier. He made a decision and saw it through. Period.

"Ready?"

"Yeah." He glanced up to find Tiffany leaving the exam room. Her long blond hair was tousled and her giant pink sweater hung crooked. Despite all of that, he'd never seen her look more beautiful. She was the mother of his child.

The freaking mother of his child.

She carried his precious son inside her body.

He took a moment to let that sink in. Was there any deeper intimacy a man and woman could share?

"Can you believe that just happened?" she asked.

"I know, right? Seeing our baby was—*wow*."

"I try not to look. It's too hard, knowing I have to get off at the end of the ride."

"But you don't. We don't." They'd reached the end of the corridor and stood in a quiet corner leading to the patient checkout. "How can you tell me what happened in there didn't matter?"

"Of course it *mattered*, but to what end? Just because it's a modern-day miracle being able to see our unborn child doesn't change anything. It doesn't pay off Grammy's new mortgage or medical bills or—"

"Shh." He pressed the tip of his index finger over her lips.

She opened her mouth and nipped him. "Don't shush me. Especially when you know I'm right."

"What if you sell this new doctor a big, fancy house?"

"Realistically, what are the odds of her buying from me?" She tugged the front of her sweater. "*Webster's* has a picture of me under their definition of *hot mess*."

"Your defeatist attitude is getting old. I understand you're going through a rough patch, but you seriously need to work on your mental toughness."

"You need to stick your mental toughness where the sun doesn't—"

"Excuse me?" From behind them, a woman cleared

her throat. She pushed a stroller carrying twin infant girls.

Rowdy opened the door for her, then propelled Tiffany in the same direction. This constant bickering had to stop. It wasn't good for her or their baby.

When it was their turn at the checkout counter, the clerk asked, "Ms. Lawson, the doctor wants to see you again next week. What's a good day for you?"

Tiffany scheduled her appointment.

"What's going on with her bill?" Rowdy asked.

"It's been paid in full. We offer complete delivery packages." The number she read produced instant indigestion that made him feel as if his son were a box on a shelf. Right here and now, he'd send the message that his child was no longer for sale.

"I need to call my bank out east and transfer funds, but is there any way to refund that previous payment and allow me to pay instead?"

"Rowdy, what are you doing?" Tiffany sported a Texas-sized scowl.

"I suppose we could," the clerk said. "But it's highly unusual. Let me check with my supervisor."

"Thanks," Tiffany said, "but there's no need for that. He's just messing around."

"No, Tiff, I'm not. I'm damned sick and tired of—"

"Sir…" The clerk raised her eyebrows, then nodded toward the waiting room's staring audience—many of whom were a G-rated crowd.

"Right. Sorry. I'll come back another time."

"What was that about?" Tiffany asked after reaching the privacy of his truck.

Much to her ever-increasing displeasure, Rowdy not

only opened her door but scooped her up to set her on the tall vehicle's seat. She was still tingling from his touch when, once he sat behind the wheel, he further complicated matters by reaching over her to fasten her seat belt, in the process brushing his arms against her baby bump and breasts.

Nipples standing at attention, she crossed her arms. The man made her all kinds of crazy.

When he turned the key in the ignition, it made a few clicking noises, which seemed to get him all riled up. Fortunately, on his next try, the engine turned over.

He drove them out of the clinic's crowded lot and through the few blocks leading to her grandmother's house, only to then turn onto the highway leading out of town.

"First," she said, "where are you taking me? And second, explain that stunt back at the obstetrician's."

"Where I'm taking you is a surprise that will hopefully, for once, shut you the hell up. And my *stunt* was the first step in reclaiming our lives. Jeb and Susie Parker might have put a down payment on our son, but effective today, he's off the market."

"I'm so sick of this." Pressing the heels of her hands to her throbbing forehead, she said, "One sonogram doesn't change a thing. Jeb and Susie have merely paid my medical bills because I couldn't. As for you implying I'm somehow profiting on the birth of our child?" She couldn't even look at his stupid face. And yes, she was purposely leaving out her usual *handsome* assessment, because after his latest streak of bad behavior, she no longer found him the least bit desirable.

Liar!

"I never said that, and you know it. Look at me."

"No."

"Tiff…" With far too tender a touch for her to keep a nice tight hold to her rage, he placed his hand under her chin, urging her to at least glance his way. "You put words in my mouth I would never say. I know the adoption is your way of doing what you wholeheartedly believe is best for our child. I know all these months without me, you have to have been worried out of your mind. But now I'm here. And I'm going to help. And you know what?"

She shook her head, swatting away his warm, gentle, stupid touch.

"For the rest of the day, you and I are going to stop fighting and work on becoming friends."

"Impossible."

"Try."

"I need to get home. Mr. Bojangles has started wriggling out of his sweaters and by this afternoon we're supposed to get more snow. I don't want him catching a chill." To calm the mental chaos the man never failed to produce, she nibbled her pinkie.

He shocked her by taking her hand, then slowly, with what to her chaotic pulse felt downright erotic, eased his fingers between hers. The heat, the electric awareness, the instant need, robbed her of all rational thought. When he further muddled her mind by raising her hand to his lips—those lips she knew all too well?

She closed her eyes and gulped.

I am Tiffany Lawson, she reminded herself.

I am a society darling.

I am strong and smart and talented and capable of

caring for myself and everyone I love. I am fully in control of everything I do and say.

I don't want this man to hold me or kiss me or...

The second his lips touched the sensitive skin on the back of her hand, freeze-framed images of their wild night hit like a sensual firestorm.

For an instant, she squeezed her eyes shut.

Like my tongue here? Lower?

Turn around. I need to kiss you.

What if I brushed my lips across—

"Tiff?" he asked with a concerned glance her way. "You feeling all right? You look hot and splotchy."

"I'm fine." She snatched her hand free. "You focus on driving, and I'll worry about me."

"Yes, ma'am." His cocky sideways grin wrought all manner of havoc. She couldn't remember the last time she'd felt good old-fashioned desire, but an unforgettable humming between her legs reminded her of Rowdy's bedroom potential. "Why don't you take a nap? Bismarck's a fair piece down the road, and—"

"Why are we going there? I have to get ready for when my new client calls."

"That's exactly what we're going to do. Relax. Promise, you'll enjoy every second of the rest of our day..."

No truer words had ever been spoken.

An hour later, Rowdy had delivered her to a mall nail salon, where she was indulging in a decadent foot massage to be followed by a pedicure and manicure.

He sat patiently in the waiting area, flipping through fashion magazines as if he were actually interested. Every so often, he looked her way. When their gazes met, her body turned all hot and bothered. Thank goodness he was across the room, because she wouldn't know what to say. Had any man ever done something so thoughtful? No.

In Rowdy some lucky lady would land a real keeper. Too bad that woman wouldn't be her.

Why not? her buttinsky conscience nudged.

How many times had he asked to marry her? Offered to take care of her and their son? Marrying him would be easy.

Until it wasn't.

Until she went and did something reckless with her wounded heart by falling for him harder than she feared she already had. If she allowed feelings for him to ever pass this current superficial-physical-attraction stage? She'd be a goner. Her father and ex had taught her all too well what happened when men she loved abandoned her.

She wouldn't put herself through that kind of pain again.

The woman doing her pedicure raised her feet from the bubbling footbath to wrap them both in hot towels.

The sensation was beyond bliss and deep into a realm of unicorns and rainbows and lots and lots of still-warm-from-the-oven cookies.

Tiffany glanced up to find Rowdy staring.

His green eyes punched through her every excuse to stay away. And then he blew such a faint kiss that she couldn't be sure she hadn't imagined it.

Not only did her pulse surge, but the baby kicked.

Protecting her wary heart, she dropped her gaze, only to raise it back up. To find his stupid, sexy grin and lose herself all over again.

For the rest of their time at the nail salon, she didn't

look at him. She couldn't. The results were far too dangerous. The fact that he'd returned her to her natural salon habitat clearly had her punch-drunk on nail-polish fumes!

She'd opted for a fast-drying shellac finish, so as soon as Rowdy paid for her services, they reentered the bustling mall, which was already decked out for Christmas.

Santa reigned over the North Pole, aka former food court. Along with soaring mall-sponsored trees festooned in silver, powder-blue and white glittering ornaments stood hundreds of smaller trees that had been decorated in themes by different organizations. They all helped raise money for charity when mallgoers paid a dollar to vote for their favorites.

She put a dollar in the collection pot for the Barbie-themed tree.

Rowdy opted for a beach-themed tree that had sand and shells bunched around the base in lieu of a traditional skirt.

"It's Beginning to Look a Lot Like Christmas" played over the sound system.

Everywhere she looked, frazzled parents chased hyper kids.

Would that be her and Rowdy one day? Those moms and dads didn't look especially happy. They looked exhausted.

"Feel better?" he asked.

"Much. Thank you." Assuming he'd meant in regard to her nails, she avoided the deeper subject of the adoption that always lurked just beneath the glassy surface of their conversational waters. If she—they—did go through with giving their baby to Susie and Jeb, would she regret it? Would every holiday for the rest of her life be spent wondering *what if*?

He shrugged. "No biggie."

"To me it was." She forced a smile. Professionally manicured nails were a luxury she hadn't been able to afford for quite some time, and she refused to spend a moment more on worry. "Ready to head home?"

"Not a chance, princess. Your party's only just begun. While you were getting your nails and toes pretty, the ladies around me helped me out with the location of a maternity store. We're going to find you a few fancy Realtor dresses, a new coat—and shoes. Sensible, but still nice enough to make you feel like the ice queen I first met all those months ago."

He'd delivered his assessment in a playful tone, but she had to ask, "Is that how you saw me? As a cold-hearted bitch?"

"There you go again." He bumped her shoulder with his upper arm. "Putting words in my mouth. You were dressed all in white, right down to those sky-high heels. In that run-down old bar, you looked like an angel. Unobtainable. Ethereal. So far out of my reach that I shouldn't have wasted my breath even talking to you. But I did, and we did and…"

She remembered the play-by-play of what happened next, and damn if her body wasn't craving a repeat performance.

In the center of the crowded mall, they'd stopped.

Turned to each other.

Was he going to kiss her? Here? In front of God, hundreds of families and Santa?

Please... her body yearned.

Don't even think about it, her carefully structured defenses railed.

She licked suddenly parched lips. Had he always been so tall? Had his chest always been so broad? Had he always smelled of sun-warmed leather?

He leaned closer.

She leaned closer.

He tilted his head.

She tilted hers.

He inched closer and closer until his warm breath tickled her lips and her heart thundered like a runaway herd of reindeer. She wanted his kiss more than anything, but badly enough to risk lowering the gate on her heart?

"Shoes," she blurted.

"What about them?"

"If you're sure—I mean, if you were serious about gifting me with a new work outfit—we should start with shoes." *Because if I stand here looking at your stupid-handsome, whisker-stubbled face for one second longer, I'll break. And then I'll be kissing you. And that wouldn't be good for either of us!*

"Right. Shoes. Lead the way..." He looked as dazed as she felt. *Had* he been on the verge of kissing her? Before her first marriage and divorce and this mess with Big Daddy, she used to know when a man desired her. Attraction had been second nature. As simple as knowing when she needed a cool sip of champagne. Now? For all she knew, Rowdy might have been pondering whether to have a cheeseburger or spaghetti for dinner.

A long waddle from their current location landed

them in comfy leather seats with an eager salesman grabbing three pairs of shoes in various sizes. Fortunately, when it came to finding gorgeous shoes, her instincts were still sharp, and she'd found low-heeled black leather boots, somewhat-sensible black leather pumps and black flats.

"I like the boots," Rowdy said, "but how are those other two going to work in the snow?"

She waved off his concern. "Snow is no big deal. I just need to watch the heel height."

"If you say so…"

The salesman returned, and if it weren't already bad enough that her normally perfect size-six feet had exploded into size nine, her calves and ankles had grown so huge that the boots wouldn't zip.

"Try again," she asked the college-aged kid. "Maybe the zipper's stuck?"

"Nah. They're too tight. My manager will kill me if I break it."

She cringed with embarrassment.

The salesman moved on to the heels. "You'll probably want to trade your socks for these." He wagged a pair of those crumpled panty-hose feet that looked like dead hamsters. The old Tiffany would have brought her own knee-high stockings. But then, in her defense, she hadn't exactly known their destination.

In regard to fit, her feet told the same sad story with a different shoe.

The baby wasn't due until January. At her body's current rate of expansion, how was she supposed to remain presentable till then?

Rowdy said, "I think you'd look cute in those red

sparkly ones." He pointed to a corner shelf filled with jewel-toned shoe heaven. Most were stilettos, but there were a few flats. The red ones in question? Darling, but a bit over the top for your average Tuesday in Maple Springs.

"I don't know…" Tiffany grumbled. "They probably won't even fit. And they're way too dressy for work."

"Bring them in a size ten," Rowdy said.

"A ten?" Tiffany's eyes stung. "I wear a six."

"Correction." He patted her huge baby bump. "You used to wear a six. But for now, let's just try a ten, okay? Besides, it's not like anyone except me will even know the size."

"I guess you have a point. But still, they'd be way too fancy for work."

"Since when is Tiffany Lawson, rodeo queen, afraid of being fancy?"

"You have another point…" She couldn't help but smile.

The salesman returned.

She nibbled her pinkie while waiting for him to take the sparkling creations from a white satin drawstring case. The new-shoe smell served as the best possible aphrodisiac.

"Let me…" Rowdy left his chair, holding out his hand for the shoe.

"Of course." The salesman handed it over.

Grinning, Rowdy said, "This moment has Prince Charming written all over it, don't you think?" Kneeling, he'd clasped her foot, but not in a clinical trying-on-shoes way. More like a territorial stroking-her-sole-with-his-thumb kind of way, making her dangerously close to having a drag-him-into-the-nearest-janitor's-closet-for-a-make-out-session impulse. He finally slid on the left shoe and it must have been an early Christmas miracle, because it fit. "How's that feel?"

"Good." *Ridiculously good.* But she wasn't just talking about the shoe's cozy fit. She had to hand it to him, the man was skilled with his hands. "Put on the other."

He did.

Had it been possible for feet to sing, hers would have.

The power of her mani-pedi and new shoes was an intoxicating thing. In that moment, she remembered what it was like to have fun. She remembered how to laugh. Most important, remembered how good it felt to share her laughter with Rowdy.

"Well?" he prompted. "The whole time I've known you, you've never been this quiet."

"I love them." She leaned forward, wrapping her arms around his neck for a hug. *I love you*, her heart sang. But she didn't. Not really. She was clearly still high from nail-polish fumes. Toss in new-shoe leather and that special something that was all Rowdy and she was lost. Rendered incapable of snark. Head bowed, she said, "Seriously, I know this must sound silly, but something about new shoes makes everything better. It wouldn't surprise me if we left the mall to find the sun shining and birds chirping in a balmy eighty degrees."

He laughed. "If that's true, I think the state would issue a new tax to keep your new-shoe fund afloat. Hell, you might single-handedly transform North Dakota into the next Florida." His words might be teasing, but the sultry heat stemming from his secure hold couldn't be more real.

She backed away before her body grew any more at home in his arms.

The salesman returned. "How did they work?"

"Like a charm," Rowdy said. "Let's take two more pairs. Black and that funky green."

"Rowdy, no. That's too much."

"Welcome to life with me, darlin'. My wicked plan is to spoil you rotten."

As much as Tiffany liked the sound of that, she couldn't let down her guard. She couldn't trust that Rowdy's charm didn't come with a price far higher than shoes. It was no secret he didn't want to go through with the adoption. She had to make him understand that neither did she—not really. Not in the deep-down, quiet moments of her heart. But she was backed into a corner and nothing about her once carefully structured adoption plan now felt right. The only thing currently making sense was profusely thanking Rowdy, then accepting his proffered hand.

With the shoes purchased and bagged, strolling through the bustling mall with her naked palm pressed to his made it easy to envision him always being in her life. She could far too easily picture them this time next year, when they'd try holding hands but it would be too awkward while pushing a stroller and gathering up their dozens of Christmas packages. She'd have a thriving real estate business and he'd— That's where the dream died.

What would Rowdy do for work if he gave up his job as a SEAL? Would he join his father and brother on their family ranch? Would he use the money he'd saved to start his own cattle ranch?

Bing Crosby crooned "Silent Night" over the mall's sound system. The song, the nagging questions, sobered her mood.

If Rowdy did take an early retirement from the navy, how long would it be until dissatisfaction with his new line of work turned to resentment for her and their son? After that, it would be only a hop, skip and jump to their inevitable divorce.

Tiffany had to face facts. No matter how delectable this very moment might be, once she surrendered her heart, all roads eventually led to her emotional ruin.

"Why so glum?" he asked. "Don't tell me your new-shoe glow already wore off?"

She forced a smile. "Not at all. I was actually thinking about how nice this is. Being with you. Taking in all the decorations." Hormonal tears wet her cheeks.

"Hey…" He dropped her hand so he could dry them with his thumbs. The shoe bag dangling from his wrist bumped the baby, causing them both to grin. "If we're having such a nice time, what's with the waterworks?"

I'm afraid you're going to leave me.

Even worse, she was terrified it wasn't her he wanted but their baby. Like some girls wanted to get married only for their fancy wedding, maybe holiday cheer had him enamored with the Norman Rockwell ideal of having a family?

"Tiff?"

"I'm good." She sniffed. "Let's get something to eat. My treat—meaning, corn dogs."

He laughed. "No offense, but there's a surprisingly

good steak place just past the next fountain. Then we need to find new duds to go with your shoes."

"You've already done too much."

"Baby…" There they were, once again standing face-to-face in the throng. Her heart beat at an alarming rate. Only this time, her galloping pulse had little to do with their son and everything to do with the baby's father. She instinctively leaned closer, raising her chin.

Are you ever going to kiss me?

Chapter 11

*D*amn.

Through what had felt like an endless meal, Rowdy struggled to focus on his steak rather than Tiffany's mouth. Her perfect mouth, with full, kissable lips...

Candlelight wasn't helping his frustration.

Neither was the dark paneling or wandering classical guitarist.

All of it set a mood that was essentially a lie.

A glance in Tiffany's direction showed her to be oblivious to the restaurant's romantic vibe. She happily munched her steak, chatting about whether slacks or a dress would look best with her shoes.

"I'm thinking slacks. A nice flat is always a cute pairing, don't you think?"

"Huh?"

"Haven't you heard a word I've said?"

"Sure." He'd heard lots of words. He just didn't much care about any of them. "Are you going to eat your bread?"

"No. Go for it."

He did. And when she changed the topic to the option of blouses or sweaters, he'd had just about all any reasonable man could take of discussing fashion.

"You ever think about it?" he blurted.

"What?"

"The night we…" he pointed toward the baby "… you know."

"Oh…" Her cheeks reddened. "Well, sure, but I try not to. It was a mistake. All of it. I never should have gone to that bar, and I sure shouldn't have gotten that motel room with you."

"Why not? Are you saying it wasn't a good time?"

She refused to meet his gaze.

"I'll take your silence as an admission that you enjoyed it as much as I did but you're too stubborn to admit it."

She shook an obscene amount of steak sauce onto her meat.

"In fact, if we were to end up back in a motel room, alone, with nothing better to do than take advantage of each other, I'll bet you'd do it all over again."

"Never."

"Wanna bet?"

"No—but only because I don't have the cash to blow on something so frivolous."

"Then you're admitting you'd lose?"

"Not at all. I'm just saying it's a dumb bet."

He eased back in his chair and smiled. "You'd be all over me, and you know it."

She sighed. "If you're done, can we please get back to shopping? The mall's probably closing at nine and it's already seven."

"Yes, ma'am." He signaled the waiter for the check, then took the last few bites of his meat.

Ten minutes later, they were back to fighting holiday shoppers. "Jingle Bells" blared over the sound system and no fewer than six kids were pitching screaming fits over wanting to see Santa.

He found a map of the mall's layout and located the only maternity store.

When they finally made their way there, the long walk was worth it, judging by the size of Tiffany's smile.

"Just look at all of this. I found my other maternity stuff at thrift stores, but the sizes were always off. How exciting is it to get to try on something new?"

"Sorry," he said while she sorted through a rack of holiday-themed sequined sweaters.

"About what? You're beyond sweet for bringing me here. Really, I can't thank you enough."

"I wish I had been here with you from the start— sharing everything. Your first doctor visits and buying maternity clothes and baby gear. Painting his nursery and assembling his crib."

"But why would you have done all of that when he's not even ours?"

"He'll always be ours, which is another reason why this whole adoption thing is unnerving. I can't wrap my head around how it would feel this time next year without him."

"What about me?" She covered her mouth. "I didn't mean to say that out loud."

"It's a legitimate question. And for the record—yes, I would miss you. You're argumentative, sassy, some-times don't make any sense and infuriatingly stubborn. Despite all of that, Tiffany Lawson, you're growing on me."

"Aw, thanks." She elbowed him. "You had me at new shoes."

From where she summoned the energy to try on so many clothes, Rowdy would never know, but by the time they left the store, she'd found a coat and two outfits to match each pair of shoes. Most of it had been on sale, even though he'd told her he didn't care about the price. In his experience, a lot of women would have taken him for all they could. He liked her even more for the fact that she didn't try to take advantage of him.

"Hope you remember where we came in?" she said as they paused to get their bearings alongside a giant candy cane.

"We need to take a left by Santa's workshop."

"That's right. I remember thinking how much I'd like a candy cane."

"Want me to get you one?"

"Would you?"

He handed an "elf" a five-dollar bill for a handful. "Think this will be enough?"

"You're amazing. How can I ever thank you?"

I can think of a few ways.

"I mean, back when I had all the money in the world,

I took shopping for granted. Now I realize what a big deal it is to look and feel my best, and…" Her eyes shone with tears. "Thank you."

"You're welcome." He tried wrapping her in a hug, but it was tough with not only the baby but shopping bags between them. "You're going to sell this new doctor a big house, and the commission will keep you afloat for months."

"From your lips to God's ears."

They continued the hike to the car only to round the last corner and freeze.

"Is that what I think it is?" Rowdy asked.

"I knew snow was in the forecast, but the weatherman said nothing about a *snowpocalypse*."

Apparently, the entire time they'd been in the mall, Mother Nature had dumped white stuff. They'd already gotten a good two feet, and more thick flakes fell by the minute.

"Wait here." He parked Tiffany on a bench in the heated vestibule, then set the packages beside her. "I'm going to get the truck. Don't leave this spot until you see me pull up outside, okay?"

She nodded.

Not wanting to haul his coat around the mall, he'd left it in the truck. Now Rowdy sorely missed it. Frigid air mixed with high winds meant his teeth were chattering only halfway to his destination. Holy hell, it was cold. He'd need to get the truck nice and toasty before bringing Tiffany outside.

Plows worked the lot, but with so many cars it was a losing battle. They'd piled snow behind the smaller vehicles and now dozens were stuck.

He reached his pickup and climbed behind the wheel to ram the key into the ignition, but instead of a satisfying roar, all he got was clicking.

Great. His wonky starter was now officially busted.

Over an hour from home.

In the middle of a blizzard.

He slammed the heel of his hand against the dash, then slipped on his coat before trudging back to the mall to deliver the news.

But when he reached the vestibule? The exact bench from where he'd specifically told her not to move? She'd moved.

Tiffany and all of her shopping bags were gone.

The line for the bathroom was insane.

At least fifteen women and little girls deep.

The handles from her heavy bags were digging lines into her palms and her feet had started to swell.

By the time she finished, washed her hands, then started the long walk back to where Rowdy had left her, each step felt like a hundred.

Never had she been happier to see his scowling face approach. "Where the hell did you go? I told you not to move."

"You can't tell a pregnant lady's bladder not to move. I had to go—bad." Relief shimmered through her when he took the bags.

"Okay, well, you scared the hell out of me. I thought you'd been abducted."

"Right. Because so many stalkers have the hots for giant pregnant women." She waddled to a seating area and collapsed into an armchair.

"What's wrong? You look pale."

"I'm exhausted but otherwise all right. Did you get the truck?" She couldn't wait to get home, have a nice long soak in Pearl's roomy claw-foot tub, then cuddle with Mr. Bojangles.

"About that…"

"You couldn't find it? Were you in the wrong lot?"

"Not exactly."

"Hurry up and tell me before I have to pee again."

He gave her the CliffsNotes version.

"Let me get this straight. Even though you knew the starter was going out, you thought it was a great idea to take your truck on a road trip?" She took her phone from the small purse she wore slung across her chest. "I could call Jeb and Susie. He has a four-wheel drive. I'm sure they'd be happy to help."

"I have no doubt they would, but I've got everything handled. There's a Holiday Inn across the street. I already made a reservation and called a towing company, but because of the snow, they're pretty backed up."

"Did you get two rooms? Because I'm not sleeping with you."

"Yes, as a matter of fact, you are. They only had one room available, and it has a king-size bed."

"Rowdy Jones, if this is all some elaborate ruse to—"

"Trust me, if I wanted in your pants that bad, I'd already be there." He winked.

"Pig."

"Oink, oink." He held out his hand to help her from the chair. "Come on. The hotel runs a mall shuttle every thirty minutes. I don't want to miss it."

She tried getting up from the deep chair without his assistance, but her efforts proved to be an epic fail.

He abandoned her shopping bags to plant his hands under her arms, hefting her up and out. "Damn, our son's getting big."

"Thanks. Tell me something I don't know."

They bickered back to the vestibule. While he helped her into her new red coat. During the short ride to the hotel. While waiting in line to get registered. Again in the elevator and all the way down the long corridor leading to their room.

"Here we are…" He opened the door with a flourish. "Home, sweet home."

Even from the shadowy light rising from the brightly lit parking lot, she saw the room was a step up from the last one they'd shared.

He reached around her to flip on an overhead light switch for the hall leading from the bathroom to the bed and sitting area.

She veered to her left, allowing him to pass on her right, praying he wouldn't brush against her—not because it didn't feel good. But because it always managed to feel so right.

Her attraction for him felt wrong on a zillion different levels. It distracted her from what was most important—caring for her mother and grandmother. Keeping them safe. If her grandmother lost her home…

The mere thought was enough to cue hormonal tears.

She ducked into the restroom and closed the door.

"Tiff?" Rowdy's voice was muffled. "Everything okay?"

"Fine." Only it wasn't. Because she was trapped in a warm and cozy hotel room with a man who made her lose all rational thought. What she needed was to redirect her attention on to anything other than him. So she filled the tub with steaming water, squirting in the peach-scented body wash the hotel had provided.

Once she'd stripped and then sunk up to her neck in delicious-smelling bubbles, for an instant, the hot water made her wholly content. Then she realized her baby bump rose from the suds like an island. And then her mind skipped to the stupid-handsome man who'd helped make her baby.

"Tiff?"

"Yes?" Her cheeks blazed hotter than the water.

What had she been thinking? How was getting naked supposed to make her think of anything other than Rowdy?

"I called your grandmother to let her know you wouldn't be home until tomorrow."

"Thanks." She'd called on their way to the mall to let the two women in her life know she'd be late, but never had she intended to be gone overnight.

"I know it's only been a few hours since we ate, but I'm hungry and thought you might be, too? I ordered a pizza. Hope sausage and mushroom is all right?"

"Sure." Every inch of her glowed. The mere sound of his voice made her crave more of him.

Eyes closed, she gulped.

"Tiff?" His voice sounded clearer. Almost as if he were alongside her in the room.

Wait—he wouldn't dare. Would he?

Eyes wide open, she found him near the sink, holding his hands over his gaze.

"Go away!" she shrieked, covering her embarrassingly huge breasts with her hands.

"I wanna see the baby."

"Are you crazy?"

"Just one peek."

"No."

"Please?"

"Absolutely not."

"Just one little peek, and I promise to leave you alone."

"Rowdy…"

"Come on. No funny business. I just want to see my son."

"All you can see is my giant stomach. It's not all that attractive."

"Bull. I'll bet your body is even more beautiful now than it used to be." He'd come perilously close and now crouched a mere foot from the tub. His voice was smooth and decadent. Warm caramel. She pressed her legs closer in what she feared to be a futile effort to stop the needy hum. "Let me see, Tiff…"

"Okay, but…" *Please, don't hurt me by telling me how fat I've gotten or how my stretch marks turn you off or—*

He sharply exhaled. "Damn, you're sexy. Already a MILF."

"I'm not." *But I appreciate your fib.*

He'd repositioned onto his knees and pressed his big hand atop the baby. His every fingerprint strummed her with awareness. Pleasure. Cravings for more of anything he had to offer.

He kept his hand on the baby, but his fingers drifted higher. Her nipples puckered beneath her palms.

"I want to kiss you."

Their gazes locked.

I want that, too.

"And then I want to carry you to the bed and figure out a position that allows me to bury myself inside you."

She licked suddenly parched lips.

"I promised Pearl we'd behave, but..." he played dirty by flashing his stupid-handsome grin "...you know what they say about promises."

They were made to be broken.

What would it hurt to be with him one more time? What was the worst that could happen? It wasn't as if she could get any more pregnant.

"Talk to me, Tiff. What are you thinking?" He slid his hand lower, to the V between her legs. Without saying a word, she answered his question by opening for him.

The instant he touched her, she lost all ability to think or speak. And when he leaned in to hover his lips above hers, she refused to care about anything other than finally getting his kiss.

At least until a knock sounded on the room's outer door.

A man called, "Pizza delivery!"

"Shit." He looked to the door, then her. "Don't budge. I'll be right back."

With him gone, her sanity returned along with her ability to breathe.

He'd closed the bathroom door, so she gripped the tub's safety bar to pull herself up, then as quickly as possible toweled herself dry. She was just attempting to draw up her panties when Rowdy rejoined her.

"I was afraid of this." He stepped disturbingly close

and smelled of the strongest aphrodisiac on the planet—pizza. "As usual, you refuse to follow directions." He settled his big hands low on her hips and then drew her as close as the baby allowed.

With only her towel between them, her pulse went haywire. "Rowdy..." She licked her lips. "Maybe this isn't such a good idea? Being around you like this... I—I can't think."

"For once, what would it hurt for you to stop analyzing and simply *feel*?" His warm breath fanned her upper lip.

She ached from the effort of denying her attraction. She didn't just want to kiss him—she wanted to lose herself to him. She wanted to forget everything but how right they felt together—at least physically.

Everything else could sort itself out later.

Here, now, she pressed her palms to his chest, fisting his shirt when he inched still closer.

Anticipation for his kiss balled in her chest.

Kiss me, her soul cried.

And then he did.

He slanted his lips atop hers, and in that instant, she'd found home. A butterfly-soft brush morphed into a fevered, desperate give-and-take as she helped Rowdy strip and then he made good on his earlier statement to carry her to bed.

They bumped and fumbled and kissed, only to find it wasn't all that easy for him to enter her in a conventional way. Finally, necessity provided a solution when he helped her straddle him, then settled in for a nice long ride.

With his hands on her hips, he plunged deeper.

She closed her eyes and tipped her head back, abandoning herself to the heady sensations that only he'd ever been able to give.

How heavenly would it be to wake to this kind of pleasure every morning and fall asleep the same way each night? Truly giving herself to him would be way too easy. It was his leaving that would be impossibly hard.

Just like every other man she'd loved, he would eventually leave…

Her climax struck with such exquisite beauty that tears stung her closed eyes.

He stiffened, tightening his hold before releasing a rugged sigh. "Damn. What you do to me is criminal."

"I'm sorry?" she said with a half laugh. "If it helps, you do the same to me."

He sat up a little, and she leaned down a little, touching her forehead to his.

"You do know I won the bet."

"What bet?"

"Remember the wager we made back at the mall? About how if we ever ended up back in a motel room, that we'd…" He winked.

"Hush. It was stupid. And I never agreed."

"Doesn't matter. I still won."

"Whatever."

He spiraled a few locks of her hair around his pinkie. "Does this mean you changed your mind?" he asked.

"About what?"

"Marrying me. You know it's the right thing for the baby. Plus, we'd get to have great sex."

It's the right thing.

We'd get to have great sex.

Nowhere in his speech did he mention having fallen deeply, madly in love. Not that it would have mattered. She'd been told she was loved by lots of guys. It wasn't the words that mattered but actions.

"Tiff? Marry me?"

Swallowing hard, she shook her head. "Could you please help me to the restroom? I think I'm going to be sick."

Chapter 12

Rowdy was no saint.

He'd seen plenty of freaky things in his thirty-odd years. But having a woman puke her guts out right after they'd made love? That ranked right up there with slogging a fully-loaded raft across a lake bed that turned out to be more mud than lake.

"Babe, what can I get you?" he asked from his seat on the edge of the tub.

"Do something with my hair. I'm hot."

It was on the tip of his tongue to ask what specifically she wanted done, but self-preservation told him this was one of those times when he'd be better off figuring it out for himself.

When she sat back on her knees in front of the commode, he readjusted the blanket around her slim shoulders, then finger-combed her long hair back, weaving it into a braid. His friend Grady had a little girl who'd taught him the skill.

"Thank you," she said. "I'm sorry."

"You're welcome and you've got nothing to apologize for." He stood and wet a washcloth with cold water. Stroking her forehead and cheeks, he said, "Think it was something you ate?"

"Probably. I gobbled twice my weight in butter."

"Then I guess I'm lucky you didn't melt?"

Her slit-eyed gaze only encouraged him. "Get it? The two of us together were so hot that—"

"I get it." Silent tears shimmered on her cheeks.

"Hey…" Sobering, he set down the washcloth to sit beside her, drawing her into his arms. "If you're hurting that bad, need me to call for help?"

She shook her head. "I don't know why I'm crying. It's stupid. Hormones have turned me into a lunatic."

"If it helps—" he kissed her left temple "—when my brother's wife was pregnant, she nearly ran him out of the house. She was always hopping mad about something. He's got a thing for beef jerky, but if he so much as had it in the same room as her, he'd have hell to pay."

Tiffany laughed. "Smells are bad. They're all magnified. Like I'm a great big basset hound."

"You are cuddly." He gave her an extra-firm squeeze. "But I don't see any drool."

She gave his forearm a light swat. "Don't make me laugh."

"Yes, ma'am." He kissed the crown of her head. "Want me to run you another bath?"

"Yes, please. And when I'm feeling better, I promise to do something nice for you."

Like marrying me? Keeping our son?

What would it take for her to see both items needed to be on her agenda? Or was he jumping the gun? Had being with her again in the biblical sense made him think they'd created a bond that wasn't really there? Oh—make no mistake, he wanted it to be. But it wasn't the kind of thing a man could force.

He'd already been with one woman who hadn't been all that into him. Was he really up for reliving that scenario?

"Rowdy?"

"You're a royal pain in my ass," he said into his cell before wiping sweat from his brow with his flannel shirtsleeve. It had been four days since they'd talked. In that time, Tiffany had avoided his calls, dodged repeated visits to her family home and even driven the other way when she'd seen him walking down the street toward her office. "What's up with the evasion tactics?"

"I don't know what you mean."

"The hell you don't." He leaned on the end of his pitchfork. He'd once again landed the crap job of mucking out the barn stalls. It had only served as a reminder that if he stayed here in town, this was what he had to look forward to for the next fifty years. "Why did you even call?"

"I have news."

"Oh?" Had Jeb and Susie backed out of the adoption? If that was her news, part of him would be elated to keep his son. Another part of him? Well, that guy was still scared shitless by the prospect of becoming a father.

"Remember that new doctor who was coming to town? And how she needed a new house?"

"Did you sell her one?" The words spilled out of him in a rush.

"I think so. We have one more to see tomorrow, but she loved the one we saw today. It was amazing—a modern log cabin with great big windows and a river-stone foundation. First class all the way. It looked like a five-star ski lodge."

"Nice." *So why are you calling?*

"It really was. She has three kids. Her husband's a doctor, too."

And? Get to the point.

"Thanks again for the new shoes, coat and clothes. If I do end up with the sale, I'll have your generosity to thank."

"Any man in my position would have done the same." Or more. He'd barreled into town intent on making an honest woman of her and giving his son a proper last name. Now more times than not, he felt all messed up inside. Like the yard after a nasty storm. Filled with fallen twigs and debris. Cluttered and chaotic.

"Maybe. But you did. So, thanks."

After an uncomfortably long pause, he forced his lungs full of the chilly barn air. "Is that why you called? About the clothes?"

She blurted, "Remember how your brother called us selfish?"

"Yeah." Mad all over again, he tightened his grip on the fork's handle.

"Well, I was in the middle of a house tour, making polite small talk, when we entered this awesome home theater. It was seriously pimped out. Built-in leather recliners, curtains over the screen—even a popcorn machine and movie-butter dispenser."

"Sweet."

"She started talking about how much her kids would love the room, and then she got all misty-eyed, telling me how much she missed them. I asked how she did it—worked such a demanding job while raising three kids. She said her kids were her reason for living. And that sometimes it was hard juggling family and work responsibilities but that she and her husband wouldn't have it any other way. The rest of the afternoon, her words stayed with me. And I thought about how I have been avoiding you—not because I didn't want to talk to you and kiss you and do lots of other things we have no business doing, but because the God's honest truth is that I'm scared maybe your brother's right. Maybe we are selfish? Maybe if we really put our son's needs ahead of our own, nothing else would matter but him?"

Lips pressed tight, Rowdy tugged the brim of his battered leather cowboy hat.

"Aren't you going to say anything?"

"I like that you've at least been thinking about me."

"Rowdy, I'm serious. When my client went on and on about how her kids matter more than anything, I felt a pang in my chest that's still there. What if we sign those adoption papers but regret it? How would we cope with the guilt and loss?"

"Wish I had an answer for you." He really did.

His call waiting beeped. A glance at the screen

showed a number he didn't want to see. His commanding officer's.

"Babe," he said, "I'm sorry, but can I call you back? My boss is calling."

"Sure. But don't forget."

He answered his CO's call.

Then he had his brother drive him to Bismarck Municipal Airport.

And parachuted into Africa two days later.

Tiffany pouted when Rowdy hadn't called back within thirty minutes. She got a little teary when it was time to feed Mr. Bojangles his supper and Rowdy called, but before they'd said more than hello, the service dropped.

When a week passed, she was pissed but assumed turnabout was fair play. He must be playing a tit-for-tat head game. She'd avoided him, so now it was her turn to feel the burn.

But when two weeks passed, she made her first big house sale, Thanksgiving came and went, and she still hadn't heard from him, worry took hold. Had he fallen ill? Been in a wreck? Should she ask Pearl for his mother's number?

"Fretting never solved any problem," Pearl said as she took a fresh batch of oatmeal cookies from the oven. They reminded Tiffany of the time Rowdy had brought her cookies in bed. And how he was always doing nice things for her but she was always so snippy. "Neither did pretending you don't give two figs about a man when you clearly do."

"What man?" Tiffany asked from the table, where

she sat peeling potatoes. The last thing she needed was for Pearl to get wind of the fact that as much as she'd struggled not to fall for Rowdy, she'd been stupid enough to do that very thing.

There was so much she wanted to say to him, but he was gone. Had her constant complaining driven him away?

"If you worry any louder, you'll wake your lazy, spoiled-rotten mutt."

"Who said I'm worrying?" As for her dog, he slept on his zebra-striped pillow in front of the heater vent, oblivious to anything other than his own comfort.

"We've both noticed," Gigi said upon entering the room. "You haven't been yourself since Rowdy's been gone. But he'll be back soon, you know."

"What do you mean?" She hugged her baby. "Do you know where he is?"

"Of course. Don't you?"

"Mom, are you kidding me?" Tiffany tossed the peeler into the metal bowl.

"I just assumed you knew." Gigi joined her at the table. "You get so prickly every time I bring up the wedding that I didn't want to further upset you by bringing up the fact that Rowdy got emergency orders to ship out. His mom told me she doesn't even know where he went or when he'll be back. She hates how secretive he has to be, but I guess that's part of his job."

He left without telling me?

Right at this very moment, he could be in some god-forsaken country alone in a ditch or hurt or…

She refused to even think the last part. If he were

to die without seeing his son—their son— Her breath caught at the back her throat.

Pushing her chair back from the table, Tiffany made a mad dash for the bathroom to be sick.

Two weeks before Christmas, Rowdy stood in line with at least four dozen fellow SEALs, awaiting his turn to place his trident on top of Duck's casket.

The chain of events that had led him to this place and time still didn't seem real. He couldn't wrap his head around the fact that one minute Duck had been asking him for a stick of Juicy Fruit, and the next they'd heard the pop of enemy fire and taken cover.

By the time Rowdy realized Duck was no longer beside him, it was too late. His body armor had done no good against a shitstorm of bullets.

Their team's plans had been precise.

They'd each played an assigned role and there shouldn't have been a problem. But there was.

Faulty intel led their team into a trap. It was a damned miracle more of them hadn't died.

In the belly of the Chinook chopper, Rowdy and Logan had held Duck's hand till the end. The guy had a wife and four kids—one of them a girl, barely a month old.

He looked up to see Ginny, Duck's wife, standing stoically, bravely, as if her entire life hadn't shattered. She held the baby in the crook of one arm and the hand of their smallest son. The two oldest boys flanked her.

Her dark sunglasses hid her eyes but couldn't mask the glint of sun on silent tears.

The Norfolk, Virginia, day was ridiculously pleasant.

Birds chirped and a hint of a breeze waved count-less American flags. The air smelled of freshly mowed grass and Logan's annoying aftershave.

Rowdy missed Tiffany.

He'd lost track of how many times he'd started di-aling her number but stopped himself short. Whatever emotions simmered between them had to stop. It had taken a front-row seat to seeing one of his best friends dying to make Rowdy understand how real shit had gotten. Committing to being a father wasn't a game.

It killed Rowdy that he hadn't been able to save Duck. He'd played the scene over and over in his head. If only he'd been closer, faster, more agile.

It was finally his turn to press his pin into the top of Duck's casket. The sign of respect was a time-honored SEAL tradition, but Rowdy hardly felt worthy. Duck's family haunted him. The boys looked just like him—right down to the blue eyes, freckles, sandy-brown hair and cowlicks on the right side of their teary faces.

Rowdy pressed his palm to the casket's sun-warmed wood.

I'm sorry, man. It all happened too fast. There was nothing I could do.

The knot in his throat made it tough to breathe.

"Dude…" Logan placed his hand on Rowdy's shoul-der. "Let him go."

Rowdy nodded.

Let him go.

Logan's words were unwittingly profound. Yes. He had to let him go. Only Rowdy wasn't just talking about Duck but his son.

* * *

The next day, Rowdy was finally back in Maple Springs.

Big surprise, it was snowing. Hard.

So hard that he had to lean forward behind the wheel of his pickup to see the reflective poles marking the road's edge.

His mom's car had been in the shop for the past few days, and she'd gotten a Christmas-carol CD stuck in his truck's player. If he heard one more line about a drummer boy or figgy pudding, he'd shoot the damned thing out.

He'd been in a foul mood since getting back.

Everything felt out of whack. He hadn't been sleeping and foods no longer tasted right. He was no good to himself or anyone else. Every time he closed his eyes, he saw Ginny and those four fatherless kids.

When Rowdy finally reached Pearl's street, snow fell so fast the wipers had a hard time keeping up.

In front of the old house, he killed the engine, grabbed his overnight bag, then dashed for the house.

On the porch, he stomped snow from his boots, then rang the bell.

"Good gracious," Pearl said upon opening the door. "Why am I always finding you playing out in the snow?"

"Couldn't tell you, ma'am. Is Tiffany here?"

"Of course. She's in the office. Take off your coat and boots. I'll go get her."

Tiffany's dog barked himself silly, trying to attack Rowdy's feet. The mutt wore a hot-pink rhinestone sweater with a fur collar. The ridiculous sight gave

Rowdy his first faint smile in what felt like a damned long time.

Rowdy scooped him up.

A rub behind his ears was all it took for the little dog to quiet.

"I could slap you into the next county," Tiffany said, practically waddling down the hall in a too-tight T-shirt and sweatpants. Her baby bump was huge, but her cheeks looked hollowed. Dark circles were under her eyes. "Why didn't you call?" As if maybe wanting a hug, she stepped in close but then backed away, hugging herself. "I've literally been worried sick."

"Sorry. Honestly, I figured you'd be glad having me out of your hair."

"You're an ass."

"Probably."

"I mean it. How dare you leave the country without telling me? What's wrong with you? What kind of father leaves his child without even saying goodbye?"

"I tried calling, but my battery died."

"Likely story. Ranks right up there with you losing your phone down a well. I hate you!"

"Tiffany Anne!" Gigi floated into the entry. She wore a red-sequined muumuu and carried a string of Christmas lights. The house smelled of cinnamon and fresh-baked bread. "Is that any way to talk to your fiancé?"

"Stay out of this, Mom. Rowdy was just leaving." She snatched the dog from his arms.

"The hell I am. Have you seen how hard it's coming down?"

"I don't care where you go," Tiffany said near the stairs, "but you're not staying here."

"Rowdy." Gigi pressed her hand to his forearm. "You are welcome to stay as long as you like—just remember, no relations until after the wedding."

"Yes, ma'am."

When Gigi headed back to the living room, Rowdy chased Tiffany up the stairs. "For looking about ten months pregnant, you're fast."

"Shut up. I hate you."

"No, you don't." He hovered behind her, making sure she didn't fall.

"I seriously do. I've been sick for days. Why? Because you're too damned inconsiderate to give me a single call." At the top of the stairs, she paused to catch her breath.

Mr. Bojangles had fallen asleep in her arms.

Rowdy hefted both of them into his arms, carrying them to Tiffany's bed.

"Put me down," she said, launching a halfhearted fight. But by the time she'd really worked up a head of steam, he'd already settled her on the mattress.

"We need to talk." He took a seat on the chaise.

"The time for talking was back in November. Now I'd just as soon spit on you as look at you."

"Fair enough. I'm sorry. When I left…" He glanced at the ceiling, wishing for an eloquent way to explain the chaos in his heart. "I thought I was sure about a lot of things. I wanted to marry you and raise our baby boy, but—"

"Now you don't?" She gulped, rubbing her palms over the baby.

He leaned forward, cupping his hands over hers.

The fascination, the heat, was still there. He couldn't deny he wanted her just as bad now as he ever had. But as long as he was a SEAL, he had no right becoming a dad. He'd seen the pain of losing their father etched on the faces of Duck's boys and they haunted him. As did the thought of his baby girl never truly knowing her father. She wouldn't have anyone to take to daddy-daughter dances or to give her away at her wedding. It was tragic. Only one thing could have stopped it—if Duck had never married or had kids at all.

After forcing a breath, he said, "I think we should go ahead with the adoption."

"What?" She shook her head. Tears shone in her eyes. "After our night together and I found out you were in danger, I realized we should keep our baby boy. I don't know what I feel for you, but I do know it was awful having you gone. Let's resume your house hunt. Find you a nice little ranch where your only real danger would be falling off your horse."

"Here's the thing." A muscle ticked in his jaw. "I need the danger. The revenge. I know I must sound sick, but I'm afraid it might be the only thing keeping me alive. My friend Duck—" His voice cracked with emotion. "He died. When it happened, it didn't seem real. It was like a video game. I watched him going down—it was in slow motion, blood gushing from his side. I kept thinking, *This isn't real. It can't be real.* But it was. And he—he died. And I…"

"Hey…" Tiffany left the bed to sit beside him on the chaise, wrapping him in a sideways hug. "I'm sorry. Death hits everyone in different ways."

"I guess." He leaned forward, sliding his hands into his hair. "My only real takeaway is that if he can die, so can I. How stupid is it that before losing Duck, the fact never sank in?"

"You've never seen other soldiers pass?"

"Sure, I have. But this was different. Before, I knew them, but they weren't close friends. I didn't know they preferred yogurt and granola for breakfast and listened to Aerosmith on endless flights. I didn't know they had a wife and kids waiting for them to come home. Only Duck never will. And that *kills* me." He rubbed his chest. "Losing him hurts so bad, but I have to keep it together. For you. For our son."

"You don't have to do anything," she softly said, "except let me take care of you. I've got this." As she cupped her hand to his cheek, he couldn't stop himself from closing his eyes and leaning in to her touch.

"I'm tired," he admitted.

"Then sleep." She took his hand, tugging him onto the bed. "Everything will look better after a good long rest."

"Promise?" he asked with a sad, strangled laugh.

"Considering our current situation, all bets and promises are off. All I can tell you with one-hundred-percent accuracy is that my bed is awfully warm and cozy. Assuming Mr. Bojangles makes room, there should be plenty of space for the three of us."

Thank you, he wanted to say. But he was too tired. His confessions had taken a costly emotional toll. She consistently brought out the best in him, but what could he offer her?

Chapter 13

The next morning, Tiffany woke to bright sun streaming through her bedroom windows. As usual, her lower back throbbed, as did her feet, but the blissful warmth of being spooned against Rowdy overrode all complaints. He rested his big hand on her even bigger tummy and suddenly, for the first time since she couldn't remember when, all seemed right in her world.

But for how long?

Her growling stomach and the fact that she had to pee provided excellent reasons to ignore the nagging question.

She eased from the bed without waking Rowdy—or Mr. Bojangles, who shared Rowdy's pillow—shoved her giant feet into cozy slippers, wrapped herself in her robe, then visited the bathroom before trudging down the stairs to find food.

Heavenly smells led her to the oven-warmed kitchen, where Pearl was already busy baking.

"It's about time." Pearl clanged her wooden spoon on the edge of a pot simmering with apple pie filling. The sweet-spicy smell of cinnamon and nutmeg and brown sugar made Tiffany even hungrier. Hands on her hips, Pearl said, "I don't have many rules around here, but as an unmarried, pregnant young woman, I would appreciate you not fornicating in my—"

"Grammy, promise, all Rowdy and I did was sleep." She gave her grandmother the abridged version of what had happened with Rowdy while he'd been overseas. "He was exhausted and needed a soft place to land. That's it."

"Now that he knows how precious life is, I'm assuming this adoption business has once and for all been taken off the table?"

"That's just it…" Tiffany took an iced Santa cookie from a plate on the counter. "He's more determined than ever to go through with the adoption. He basically said he can't quit his job. Because of that, he doesn't feel justified in raising a child only to potentially leave him."

Pearl scowled. "That's the biggest bunch of hogwash I've heard in all my days. Not a single one of us are given out guarantees along with our birth certificates. In this life, you get what hand you're dealt, and you deal with it. Period. Look what happened with you and your mom. I don't say this often, but I'm proud of the way you two have managed to carry on."

"Thank you." Tiffany bowed her head. Coming from her strong, proud grandmother, who had buried her husband and seen her only son imprisoned, the praise meant a lot.

"I think you and Rowdy ought to put this whole baby business aside—at least as long as you can. Enjoy the holidays and get to know each other the way a man and woman should. You two put your cart *waaaay* before the horse with your baby. How about slowing things down? Help me decorate cookies and then help your mom with her giant fancy tree. Try acting like a couple instead of already frazzled parents."

Misty-eyed at her grandmother's practical yet much-needed advice, Tiffany nodded.

"Never thought I'd get used to all this white stuff," Gigi said. She flounced into the kitchen wearing an emerald-green caftan with ostrich feathers and jewels around the neck. She already wore full makeup—including her false eyelashes. "But look at it shining in the sun. Looks like an entire world filled with diamonds." She gave Tiffany a hug, then Pearl.

"What's got you so chipper this morning?" Pearl asked.

"It's almost Christmas, my very pregnant daughter is almost married and I have an afternoon call scheduled with Big Daddy. What more could a girl need?" She giggled.

"Indeed," Pearl said. "Although, this girl could use help with the dishes. Any volunteers?"

"I'll do it."

All three women turned to find Rowdy standing on the kitchen threshold. He wore faded Wranglers and a US Navy sweatshirt, and his short hair looked adorably mussed. Stubble lent him a bad-boy appeal. The way he cradled Mr. Bojangles made it entirely too easy for Tiffany to imagine him carrying their son. His good looks made it impossible to find her next words. His willingness to help her grandmother only compounded his charm.

"You're a good man, Rowdy Jones." Pearl wiped her hands on her white apron. "After that, you and Tiffany eat a nice hearty breakfast. Then there's plenty more to do around here to get this old house decorated and spit shined for Christmas. Oh—and if you really want to get on my good side, the chickens need checking on, and the front and back walks need shoveling again."

"Yes, ma'am."

Two hours into his chore list, the man wasn't even winded.

Meanwhile, Tiffany's lower back was on fire and her feet felt like great big Christmas hams.

Mr. Bojangles, being the ultimate diva, snoozed on a sofa pillow in a patch of living room sun.

A fire crackled in the hearth, Dean Martin crooned carols and the air smelled heavenly from her grandmother's latest batch of gingerbread men.

Gigi sat at the dining room table, polishing heirloom silver Tiffany prayed wouldn't have to be sold.

"You made this?" In front of the fresh-cut tree a neighbor had delivered and settled into its stand not an hour earlier, Rowdy held up a pink salt-dough snowman ornament. After twenty years, crooked rhinestones and heavy-handed glitter still shone.

"Yes, I did." Afraid he might be poking fun at the treasured keepsake, she snatched it from him. "What about it? Think it's lame?"

"I like it." When Gigi wasn't looking, he stole a kiss hot enough to at least temporarily make her forget how bad she was hurting. "In fact, it's the cutest damned thing I've seen in a while—aside from its creator." The look in his eyes made her knees as unsteady as her feet. As it generally did whenever she was around him, her pulse went haywire. "I love learning more about you from happier times—assuming when you made this you were happy?"

Before nodding, she wiped away silly, sentimental tears. "I was a blessed child. Mom and Daddy spoiled me rotten—not just with material things but love and attention. When they couldn't be with me, I had nannies." While she added red velvet bows to the tree, her voice took on a wistful tone. "We traveled the world. London, Paris, Switzerland, Milan."

"What was your favorite?"

"The Alps. No contest."

"Interesting." He placed another homemade ornament front and center. A small-sized paper plate with horrible green paint, an obscene amount of glitter and an adorable, crooked photo of her with no front teeth. "I had you pegged for more of a Paris gal."

She shook her head. "Don't get me wrong, I love everything about Paris, but something about those mountain views…" The longing in her voice made him want to be the next man to show her that view. Impossible, since he'd return to duty as soon as the baby was born and safely transferred to Jeb's and Susie's capable arms.

Just thinking about that moment—handing over his son—made him physically ill. But if Rowdy intended to stay in the navy, it had to be done. The last thing he wanted was for his boy or Tiffany to wear the same grief-stricken look in their eyes as Duck's wife and sons. "Does your grandma have any antacid?"

"In the hall bathroom's medicine cabinet. Are you okay?"

"Yeah," he covered. "I just ate two more servings of Pearl's biscuits and gravy than I should have."

"I know the feeling." Her grin brightened his world. It was the same one from the ornament's picture. Sure, she now had all of her teeth and wore her hair swept up instead of in pigtails, but for an instant, her happy glow was back.

How could he make it stay after the adoption, after he'd gone?

By late that afternoon, even Tiffany was shocked by the progress they'd made. Fresh fir garlands had been hung from the stair railing—courtesy of another neighbor in exchange for six dozen of her grandmother's frosted cookie masterpieces. The tree was trimmed, and more garland hung from the mantel, as did cards from Pearl's many friends. Pearl punched holes in the corners of each one and hung them by ribbons from the garland and tree.

Her mother's Christmas village had come to life on the dining room buffet, and the nativity scene played out on the entry hall table.

Rowdy sat on the floor beneath the tree, putting together a train track. His focus made her smile from her perch on the sofa, where she assembled festive bags of candy for her grandmother to gift to friends who stopped by.

For only a moment, Tiffany allowed herself the indulgence of imagining Rowdy and their son putting the train on its track together. It could be their annual thing—just the way when she was little, Big Daddy used to heft her high enough to put the angel on top of their tree.

"Hold your breath…" Rowdy flipped the on switch for the train's engine. "The *North Pole Express* will soon be chugging down the track."

Nothing happened.

Mr. Bojangles barked at the still train.

"Damn." Rowdy's little-boy expression of disappointment squeezed her heart. Her mind swirled with future possibilities for their son that would never come true. He opened the engine's bottom panel. "Got any AAA batteries?"

"I'll see…" The walk from the living room to the kitchen was a killer. Her lower back ached as if she'd spent her morning hauling hay bales as opposed to featherlight ornaments.

She returned with the batteries, then thankfully sank back onto the sofa cushions alongside her dog.

"All right." After replacing the batteries, Rowdy flipped the engine's switch. When it rhythmically chugged, he reattached it to the rest of the train. "Oh, yeah." His broad smile eased her pain. "Santa's gonna for sure visit your house. And when he does, you'll have me to thank." He winked before rising to join her and Mr. Bojangles. "This old house looks pretty damned good."

"Hey—I helped."

"Yes, you did. From the looks of your feet—too much." He eyed her swollen ankles. "You should have stopped working four hours ago."

"Probably, but then—" she lowered her voice, nodding to Pearl, who stood in the dining room, tears glistening in her eyes "—we wouldn't have the pleasure of seeing my grandmother so happy."

"But she's crying," he said.

"Trust me, those are the good kind of tears. Clearly, you haven't been around enough women to know the difference."

Their gazes caught and locked. For the longest time, she forgot to breathe. Was he on the verge of kissing her again? Did she want him to?

No.

Maybe?

Yes.

Their physical chemistry made their rocky emotional connection all the more confusing. Just because he'd given her a second fabulous night between the sheets didn't mean squat. Not really. To marry him, to keep their son and make a family, they shouldn't have had sex but made love.

"Need a glass of water?" Rowdy asked. "You've got that blotchy-and-red look again."

"Thanks." She grimaced. Just what every girl longed to hear.

"You two have made me so happy." Pearl touched tree branches as if ensuring they were real. "The only thing that would make this Christmas brighter is if your father could be with us, but he'll come home soon enough. In the meantime, we have your wedding and the baby to look forward to."

"Grandma…" Tiffany forced a breath. "You know there's not going to be a wedding. Jeb and Susie will be raising our baby. It's for the best." After her and Rowdy's hot reunion, she'd thought the two of them as a couple—the three of them as a family—might actually make sense, but with the death of his friend, it seemed as if Rowdy's mind was as set on the adoption plan as hers had once been.

Pearl waved off Tiffany's comment. "Rowdy, I hate to trouble you after you've already put in such a long day, but could you please check the chickens' heating lamp? I took them some scraps and it's cold enough out there for my son's lawyers to put their hands in their own pockets."

"Yes, ma'am. I'll get right on it." To Tiffany he asked, "Need anything before I go? A cup of that herbal tea you like? A cookie or muffin?"

She shook her head.

Once he left, the lights on the tree seemed dimmer. The pine boughs didn't smell nearly as fresh. What was wrong with her? He'd been gone literally one minute, yet she missed him. She wasn't supposed to feel anything for him. But what if she did?

She pressed her hands to their baby. "Is it wrong for me to wish Rowdy had never come home?" Because if he hadn't, she wouldn't now be panic-stricken by the thought of him leaving again.

* * *

"I was beginning to wonder when we'd next see the whites of your eyes." James sat astride his favorite paint, Charlie.

"Sorry." Rowdy rode Lucky on their way out to the southeast pasture, where a momma and her new calf needed checking. With a herd as big as theirs, it never failed that at least once during a winter storm, something would go wrong. "For the past few days, Tiffany's been complaining of her back hurting, so I've been taking care of her while doing odd jobs for her kooky mom and grandma."

"Those two are quite a pair," his dad chuckled. "Good folks, though. At the last church charity auction, Gigi brought in some fancy brand of shoes. The womenfolk damn near gave themselves aneurysms trying to outbid each other. Boy, was I relieved your mom didn't win."

Rowdy laughed, tipping the brim of his cowboy hat lower to cut the wind's icy licks at his cheeks.

For as far as he could see, the world was white.

The sky kissed the ground in an angry slash of gunmetal gray, promising more snow by morning. The very air smelled cold and forlorn. The horses exhaled deeply as they struggled through the snow.

"Your brother tells me you decided to go along with the adoption?"

"I s'pose."

"You're a grown man, so I guess it's none of my business, but for the record, this news didn't sit well."

Rowdy clamped his lips tight.

"You're breaking your momma's heart."

"What do you want me to say, Dad? I just had a close friend die while clenching my hand. Know what the last thing he said was? He asked me to tell his wife and kids how much he loved them. Carl accused me of being selfish for giving my kid up for adoption. But you know what I think is even more selfish? Willingly bringing not just one child into this world but multiples, knowing the whole while that at any given time, you could be shot down and leave not just them but their mom. To me, that's unconscionable."

"Are you honestly that dense?"

"Excuse me?"

"Do you think you and your hotshot SEAL buddies own the patent on dying? Hell, son, I've had more than a few close calls in my day. For that matter, so has your mom—namely, while giving birth to you. In the end, all any of us are guaranteed is the here and now. Which means you need to embrace life by the cojones and live every day as if it may be your last. I'm sorry your friend died, but do you think his wife or children regret having had him in their lives?"

For the rest of the ride, Rowdy remained silent.

Cold air seared his lungs.

It crept into his bones until every inch of his body ached.

By the time they'd returned to the barn, cared for the horses and headed for the house, light snow was already falling.

"Weatherman says this one's going to be a real dandy," his father said.

Rowdy merely grunted.

"Izzy and Ingrid have their school Christmas show

tonight. Hope the storm holds off till they get done singing."

"I should probably go check on Tiffany."

"Why don't you bring her? You've been around the house so little your nieces aren't going to recognize you."

"I'm sure Carl and Justine wouldn't want us ruining the girls' big night."

"Nonsense." His dad patted his back. "Get washed up, then go grab your girl. Show starts at seven, but the gym gets awfully crowded, so you shouldn't be late."

"This isn't a good idea," Tiffany said once they'd made it down Pearl's front walk, which Rowdy had just shoveled.

Snow tumbled like clumps of white cotton candy.

The neighbors' Christmas lights lent the street a magical glow.

He pretty much lifted her onto the passenger seat of his truck, and the close contact made her treacherous body hum. Even worse, the baby kicked her ribs. The pain ricocheted through her, making her back hurt all the more. But then his stupid-handsome face was within kissing range and she forgot everything except how good it had felt when the two of them had finally come together. Desperate to think of anything but being with him again, she asked, "What if your mom and sister-in-law hate me?"

"Why would you care? Once you have the baby, aside from running into them at the grocery store, odds are that you won't see them again."

"Nice…" She shivered as he climbed in beside her.

"The only reason I'm even bringing you is because my dad gave me a guilt trip."

A wall formed at the back of her throat.

Was he deliberately trying to hurt her? Losing his friend had changed him. He'd lost his playful edge.

"I know that pouty look." He started the engine. Let it idle until warm air spilled from the heater vents. "Apparently, Mom wants to meet you—not that it will make a difference in how either of us feels, right? I mean, we're both still full speed ahead with the adoption?"

Darting her gaze away from him and out the fogging window, she nodded.

"Tonight is all about getting our point across. We need to make my family understand why we've decided on this mutually beneficial arrangement."

"What are you afraid of, Rowdy? And don't give me that line about you losing your friend. I understand that was rough on you, but what else changed?"

"Excuse me?" He pulled his truck into the already snow-packed street.

"Remember when you first blew back into town like a bull charging a rodeo clown? How you demanded to have custody of your son, and how you refused to even think about adoption?"

"Sure. But clearly, I was wrong." He'd reached the stop sign at the end of the street. "Doesn't that make you happy?"

No.

The house on the corner had a giant inflatable Santa all lit up and waving in the gusty wind. The cheery sight made Tiffany sadder. Hugging her baby—their baby—she wished she knew when all of this had gone so horribly wrong. Before Rowdy came back to town, she'd been sure about the adoption, too. Now?

Nothing made sense. Especially not how much she'd grown to depend upon Rowdy for everything, from getting her tea and cookies to helping her in and out of cars. Just like every other man in her life, he'd soon be leaving. She had to not only accept that fact but make peace with it.

Besides, what she felt for Rowdy was purely physical. She didn't especially care for his stupid-handsome grin or the way his hair usually stuck out at crazy angles or how his Wranglers fit just right. She sure wasn't attracted to his goofy jokes or the way he was always accommodating and kind with her mom, grandmother and even Mr. Bojangles.

Considering all of those points, why did she care if he'd soon be leaving?

Good question.

One for which her aching heart had no answer.

Chapter 14

What are you afraid of?

Through the entire awful holiday show, which included dancing candy canes, an evil elf and a pint-size Santa stuffed with so much padding that the poor kid could hardly walk, Rowdy pondered Tiffany's question.

He tried blaming his dour mood on the gymnasium's sweltering heat. Or how the lady in the seat next to him had been far too generous with her sticky-sweet perfume. He even hated the way his mom and Justine instantly sat Tiffany between them, coddling her like she was a rare and precious jewel.

Why did he resent them treating her like she was something special?

Because she was.

Only he was too big of a coward to step up and admit

it. Damn right he was afraid. Not just of being a screwup as a dad, or dying, but of being equally as bad at this whole relationship thing he and Tiffany kept dancing around.

Stepping up?

Doing the so-called right thing by her and his child?

That would mean giving up the only way of life he knew. Sure, he could marry and still be a SEAL. Guys did it all the time. And they didn't die. But like his mom had long ago pointed out, a whole lot of them ended up divorced. Most had kids who lived full-time with their mothers. They saw them only on weekends or holidays—not nearly enough to make a real difference in their lives.

When the show finally ended and the entire family moved to the cafeteria for cake and punch and cookies, Rowdy stayed on the fringe, watching how naturally Tiffany interacted with his nieces. She wore one of the outfits he'd bought for her in Bismarck—a green sweater with the matching glitter shoes. The color made her eyes spark. He wanted her with a visceral pull. He wanted her away from all of these people to selfishly keep her to himself. But how did that desire fit in with his equally strong need to get out of Dodge?

Blaring Christmas carols combined with kids hyped up on sugar made his head scream for peace and quiet.

"She's pretty special," Justine said with a nudge to his arm. "Don't you dare think of letting her and your baby go."

"Mind your own business," he said in a gruff tone.

"Unfortunately, once I married your brother, that made you family, which makes you—and now Tiffany—very much my business. Not only is she gorgeous, but she's educated and funny and sweet. A real keeper."

He growled.

Rowdy escaped his sister-in-law to help himself to the syrupy-sweet punch. He would have gotten some for Tiffany, but his dad had already beaten him to it.

His mom caught up with him just as he filled a red Solo cup. "Don't think it hasn't escaped my notice that you're avoiding me."

"Mom…" He sighed.

"Tiffany's a lovely girl. She'll make a wonderful addition to our family."

Yeah, too bad it's not gonna happen.

"At first, when Tiffany's mother approached me about a holiday wedding, I thought we might be jumping the gun, but now I think—"

"Drop it." The instant his gruff command sprang tears to his kindhearted mother's eyes, he regretted it. He reached out to hug her, but after a look of disgust, she spun on her heels and was gone.

What are you afraid of?

Tiffany's question raised its ugly head.

Hell, maybe he was afraid of everything? Not just of dying but of truly living.

Any time he'd taken a stab at even a brief relationship, it had ended in disaster. Why should this time be different?

Because Tiffany's different. Better. She makes you better.

He felt her gravitational pull as if she were the sun and he a lowly planet. A glance up had their gazes locked. When she shyly smiled and waved, resting her free hand on their baby, his chest tightened.

Despite the hundreds of people milling about the room, he had eyes only for her. What did that mean?

He raked his fingers through his hair, forcing himself to look away first. Out of all the missions he'd been on, Tiffany Lawson was by far the most dangerous.

If he allowed himself to fall for her, he feared losing the only life he'd ever known.

"Promise you'll come Saturday to help Justine and me make cranberry bread? Bring your mom and Pearl, too."

Tiffany nodded, then stepped into Rowdy's mother's latest hug. Had there ever been a sweeter, gentler woman? No. Which begged the question, how in the world had she created such a glowering son?

"It was great finally meeting you," Justine said. "We were beginning to think you were Rowdy's imaginary friend."

Tiffany laughed.

Isobel and Ingrid, still wearing their matching icicle costumes, danced around their mom.

"Miss Tiffany?" asked Isobel, the oldest girl, who sported longer strawberry blond hair and a constellation of adorable freckles.

"Yes?" Tiffany said.

"When my mom had Ingrid inside her, she said it was because Daddy gave her too much watermelon and she swallowed a seed and it growed inside her. Did Uncle Rowdy give you too much watermelon?"

Tiffany's cheeks superheated. "Something like that."

Justine covered her inquisitive daughter's ears.

"Sorry. Seemed like the most reasonable explanation at the time."

"I understand," Tiffany said with a smile. What she didn't understand was why she hadn't met Rowdy's awesome family sooner. Was he ashamed of her? Those first days when he'd roared into town, he'd practically forced her to see his mom and try one of her homemade cinnamon rolls. But then he'd dropped the whole matter the way he had the idea of keeping their baby.

After more laughter and hugs and plenty of opportunities for Tiffany to see firsthand what amazing people had raised her baby's father, she grew all the more confused. Right now—through the baby she carried inside her—she shared a connection with these lovely people. They had to know about her plans for adoption, but there hadn't been any pressure from James or Patsy to keep their grandchild in the family.

Did they not care whether she and Rowdy kept the baby? Or did they care so much that they trusted them to make the right decision—whatever that might be?

After paying a dollar to retrieve her coat, hat and gloves from the Scouts, who'd made a fund-raiser out of their coat-check services, Rowdy led her outside.

The snow had stopped looking pretty and was now wind-driven pellets that stung when they hit her exposed cheeks.

"Get back inside," Rowdy said. "I'll go get the truck."

She usually would have argued, but in the past hour, the pain in her lower back had amped up to an alarming degree. Assuming it was from standing too long while chatting with Rowdy's family, she'd put the pain from her mind to enjoy the evening, but now the sharp stabs were growing harder to ignore.

Rowdy helped her to a bench in the school lobby, then said, "This time, please be here when I get back."

"Can't make any—" She winced.

"What's wrong?"

"Nothing." She shooed him away. "Just my back. I'm fine."

His gaze narrowed, but then he said, "If you do happen to need the facilities, leave your hat to let me know you're okay."

"Yes, sir." She'd intended to give him a sassy salute, but the latest round of pain hit sharp enough to make her gasp. She clutched her lower back.

"When did this start?"

"I don't know," she said through clenched teeth. "My back always hurts, but this—"

"Shit." He looked to her, then at the blowing snow. "To be safe, we should probably call 9-1-1, but with this storm, my gut's telling me I could probably get you to the hospital faster."

She shook her head. "I'll be fine. It's just those Braxton Hicks contractions my baby books talk about."

An hour later, while being prepped for an emergency C-section because of tests showing she'd suffered a placental abruption, Tiffany learned she couldn't have been more wrong.

She held out her hand to Rowdy. "I'm scared."

"Me, too. But everything's going to be okay." He kissed her forehead. She wanted him to kiss her lips. To claim her and their baby as his own.

Three nurses and two doctors bustled about her in

the birthing room's cramped space. The fetal monitor reminded her with each rapid-fire beep that their son was in distress. He was a month premature, yet without the surgery, odds were he wouldn't survive at all.

Rowdy held her hand until she was being wheeled away from him and toward an operating room.

Terror didn't come close to describing her turbulent emotions.

Would her baby be okay?

Would she live to meet him?

Once she held him in her arms, would she ever have the strength to let him go?

"Mr. Jones?" A nurse hovered near the waiting room's entrance.

"Yeah. That's me." Startled, Rowdy glanced up from where he'd sat in the uncomfortable chair for the past hour. "How is the baby? And Tiffany? She okay?"

"They're both fine. Your son is small, but thankfully, his lungs are fully developed and at five pounds three ounces, he's a good size for being a month premature. As for his momma, she's good, too. But will be sore and sleepy for a while."

He nodded.

"I saw on your wife's birth plan that—"

"We're not married."

"I'm sorry. I just assumed…"

"It's okay."

"Well, since you're not together, I guess it makes sense that your baby is being adopted. I notified the adoptive parents of his safe delivery, but because of the storm, it may take them a while to get here. I thought you might like a few minutes alone with him?"

"Sure. Thanks." Rowdy swallowed hard.

Everything had happened so fast after his nieces' show that he hadn't called his parents or even Gigi or Pearl. All he'd been capable of focusing on was Tiffany and his son.

At 10:00 p.m. the nursery was quiet. The overhead lights had been dimmed. Two infant girls snoozed in clear plastic bassinets. Three nurses talked quietly at their station.

"Wash your hands." The nurse who had come to get him pointed toward a counter-mounted sink. "Then please put this on." She handed him a yellow paper gown. "When you're done, have a seat in the rocker, and I'll bring your son."

Rowdy forced a few deep breaths.

He wasn't sure what he'd expected, but this overwhelming panic wasn't it. What if he dropped the kid? What if he squeezed him too hard?

Finished with the nurse's instructions, he sat in the appointed chair, and she placed the impossibly small creature in his arms. It was then Rowdy realized his biggest problem—what if he fell in love?

Staring down at this tiny sleeping miracle, Rowdy found himself gaping in awe. This was his son.

His son.

For all these weeks, he'd fretted about the adoption issue, wavering back and forth. But in this most sacred moment, the decision had already been made. No matter what, he was keeping his child.

Period.

End of story.

He wiped tears with the sleeves of his gown, then

inspected his little guy's perfect pink fingers. He was wrapped snug in his fuzzy blue blanket, so Rowdy figured there'd be plenty of time later to count his toes.

John Wayne Jones was already a looker.

And then he opened dazzling blue eyes. Rowdy knew lots of babies were born with blue eyes, but there was no denying an instant connection.

"Hey, buddy. You popped out early, but that's okay. Now that you're here, I'm never letting you go." In that instant, Rowdy knew why his brother called him selfish. But in his defense, before cradling his son in his arms, Rowdy had had no idea the lengths he'd go to fight for him. For Tiffany. For the family it only made sense for them to form.

He supposed he needed to run all of this past her, but proposing was a formality. Now that their son had entered their world, nothing else mattered besides making sure he had the best possible life.

Two hours passed before a nurse took him to the room to which Tiffany had been assigned.

"Hey, gorgeous." He presented her with a bundle of limp blue carnations he'd found for sale in the cafeteria. "How are you feeling?"

"Awful," she said with a faint smile. "How's the baby? Have you seen him?"

"He's spectacular. But with a mom and dad as good-looking as us, how could he be anything but gorgeous, right?"

"You're not getting attached, are you? The nurse told me Jeb and Susie are on their way. I can't—" Tears streamed down her cheeks. She looked away. "I don't think I can see him and still let him go."

"Babe…" He touched his fingers to her chin, urging her to look his way. "Our son's not going anywhere. Once you get your first look at him, I know you'll agree. He's the most perfect kid ever in the history of kids."

"Really?" Her voice quivered. "You think we should keep him?"

"There's nothing to think about. This is a no-brainer. The second I held him, I knew I was destined to be his dad. You're going to make a great mom. Together, we'll be the best parents any kid ever had."

"What about your career?"

"As soon as my current enlistment ends, I'll retire."

"Just like that?"

He snapped his fingers. "Just. Like. That."

Crying harder, she nodded and sniffled.

He kissed her, vowing to never again allow her lips to taste of salty tears. From here on out, he would do his best to make sure her life consisted of nothing but smiles.

"I want to see him," she said. "Hold him."

"I can make that happen." Rowdy pressed the nurse's call button.

Minutes later, the woman wheeled in their sleeping son and placed him in Tiffany's arms.

Once the nurse left them alone, Tiffany teared again, touching her pinkie finger to the tip of the infant's nose, to his chin, his suckling lips. "He is beautiful, isn't he?" Her voice held a note of awe. "I didn't dare let myself dream of a moment like this. I knew giving him up would be the hardest thing I'd ever done, but better for him, you know?"

"I get it. I thought the same. The whole adoption plan

made so much sense—it was the *only* thing that made sense. But then I saw him and…" She wasn't the only one who'd gone soft. For a guy who was supposedly a big strong SEAL, Rowdy had turned into a gentle giant.

"What are we going to tell Susie and Jeb?" she asked in a whisper. "They'll be devastated."

"Sorry, but we can't give them our child to save hurt feelings."

She sniffled but nodded.

Outside big picture windows, snow fell harder, frosting the world in white. Deep satisfaction settled over Rowdy. Though he felt physically exhausted, he was on such an emotional high that he doubted he'd ever be able to sleep.

"What should we name him?" Tiffany asked.

"Is there any doubt?"

"No…" She shook her head.

"Oh, yes. While you were still out of it, I already christened him John Wayne Jones."

"Absolutely not."

"Yes." He leaned over her bed rail, kissing her forehead.

"No."

Her cheeks.

"No."

Her nose.

"Rowdy…"

Finally, her lips.

When she sighed, then groaned, opening her mouth to the sweep of his tongue, he knew he'd gotten his way. As for whether or not the rest of their lives would go as planned, only time would tell.

Chapter 15

"We got here as soon as we— Oh." Susie froze before fully entering Tiffany's room.

The moment Tiffany had been dreading ever since she and Rowdy made their late-night decision to keep their son had arrived.

Susie paled, then clung to her husband.

Tiffany tugged the receiving blanket higher over her left breast, from which she'd been trying to get Johnny to suckle. The connection was painfully clear. If Tiffany and Rowdy had planned on going through with the adoption, she wouldn't now have been breast-feeding her son.

"I'm sorry," Tiffany said. The words felt woefully inadequate in light of the gift she'd rescinded. "I promise to pay back every dime you've spent on my medical care."

"It's not the money," Susie said. "This has never been about that. If we could just buy a baby, don't you think we would have?" Tears streamed down her cheeks, dredging a deep crevasse through Tiffany's heart. "I knew this would happen. All along, this has been my biggest fear. Why couldn't you have told us sooner? Why did you have to string us along?"

"Because she honestly didn't know." Rowdy entered the room behind them. He carried the lime Jell-O she'd craved from the cafeteria, as well as a coffee for himself. "If you need a punching bag, use me. This was one of those things we never saw coming."

"I don't believe that for a second," Susie said. Her low tone was angry enough that it might as well have been a scream. "The day you entered the picture, everything changed."

"Let's go." Jeb turned his wife toward the door. The consummate politician, he bowed his head. "Tiffany, Rowdy, we wish you well."

They were gone, but Tiffany couldn't stop shivering.

"Need me to turn up the heat?" Rowdy asked.

She shook her head. "That whole exchange left me feeling cold on the inside. Like I've made a horrible mistake in hurting Susie and Jeb so deeply."

"What about you? Me? Our son? Don't our feelings matter?"

"Of course. But I made them a promise I couldn't keep. Maybe I was wrong in ever thinking I could?"

"It doesn't matter." He slipped his arm around her shoulders. "I feel for what Jeb and Susie must be going through, but hon, this wasn't just your decision. They'll grieve for a while, but hopefully, find another child. I'm sure they don't blame you."

"You make it sound so simple. So black-and-white."

"It is."

"It's not, Rowdy. This whole situation is a thousand murky shades of gray. You and I don't know the first thing about being parents or a couple. What if we're making a mistake?"

Baby Johnny whimpered at her breast.

Her milk hadn't yet come in, and even if it had, it didn't feel as if Johnny had latched on properly to her nipple—not like her books said he was supposed to. Where was the euphoria new mothers supposedly felt when feeding?

Johnny's whimper grew into a full-blown cry.

She tried jiggling him and humming, but that only made his face turn screaming-baby red.

"Could you please take him?" She swaddled her son, then drew her hospital gown over her breast.

"Of course." Rowdy cradled the infant to his chest, but that didn't help, either.

"Should we call the nurse?" Tiffany asked.

"Yes. I'm sure she'll have a trick up her sleeve that'll make him smile."

She didn't.

Rowdy called both of their families.

By midmorning, grandmothers appeared in full force, cooing and rocking and singing, but no matter how much comfort any of them gave, Johnny remained fussy. Even in his sleep, he appeared restless.

"When your milk comes in," Pearl said two days

after his birth, "he'll calm right down. Seen it a hundred times with babies at the church nursery."

"He's got gas," Patsy said three days after his birth.

Almost four days after his birth, Justine said, "I just read an article that said he might be missing the safety of your womb."

Tiffany struggled not to frown. Even if her son did miss his former cocoon, what was she supposed to do about it?

She envied all the moms pictured in the bucolic scenes in her parenting books. They sat up in their freshly made beds with their hair and makeup perfect while holding court, everyone congratulating them on their sweet-tempered babies.

Tiffany's surgical incision wasn't healing as expected, so her obstetrician opted to keep her a fifth day and night in the hospital. The more she thought about the mounting medical bill, the more panicked she grew, which in turn seemed to make her son all the more agitated.

The fact that she couldn't even manage to feed him, let alone nurture and soothe him the way a mother should, made her feel like a failure in every facet of her life.

Then there was Rowdy.

He helped as much as he could, but aside from bottle feedings, there wasn't much to be done. He haunted the cramped room's perimeters, most often standing with arms folded, a grim set to his mouth.

Once his mother and Justine and Pearl and Gigi left for the day and Tiffany and Rowdy were alone with their son, who finally slept, she summoned the courage to ask, "Do you ever regret keeping Johnny?"

The room was too dark for her to see him clearly, but his heavy sigh was unmistakable.

"Should I take that as a yes?"

"It's more complicated than that." He left the bench seat by the window to cautiously approach the bed. Afraid of waking their son? "I'd be lying if I said I hadn't had doubts, but my issues are more long-term. I'm already worrying about how to pay for college if I quit the navy. Logically, he'll grow out of this cranky stage, right?"

"I guess?" She managed a faint laugh. "When he's crying, do you ever feel panic? Like if he doesn't stop, you'll lose what little's left of your sanity?"

"Absolutely." As if relieved to not be alone on that count, he released a rush of air. "Another thing bugging the hell out of me? Our hovering families—always giving advice. If they're all such experts, then how come none of the crap they say to do actually works?"

"Excellent point."

They both fell silent.

Aside from the faint sound of a doctor being paged over the hall intercom, all in their world was blissfully silent, making Tiffany believe maybe everything would be okay.

If only Rowdy would step closer.

Take her hand.

Hug her or kiss her or reassure her he was in this for the long haul, she might even believe he cared for her as a woman instead of just as the mother of his son.

Rowdy cleared his throat, then pointed at the general

vicinity of her chest. "I, ah, don't mean to be staring at your boobs, but…"

After a flustered moment of embarrassment over his bizarre statement, she glanced down to find twin wet spots on her gown. She'd been so consumed by a multitude of worries that she hadn't noticed the new sensation of achy fullness in her breasts or the slight tingling to her nipples.

"Think your milk finally came in?"

"Yes. What should I do? Wake Johnny to see if he's ready to eat?"

"No," Rowdy said with a firm shake of his head. "One bit of advice my brother gave is to never under any circumstance wake a sleeping baby."

"Sounds wise." Tiffany grinned. For the first time since Johnny's birth, she felt a glimmer of hope that she and Rowdy might actually survive their son's infancy—at least physically.

As for the two of them as a couple?

It was too soon to tell.

Two days before Christmas, while Rowdy sat on the chaise in Tiffany's room, watching her breast-feed their son, he realized the sight never got old. What did?

Gigi's blaring Sinatra holiday CD.

Pearl's never-ending parade of friends and cookie clientele all clamoring to see and hold the baby.

Most annoying of all? Tiffany's general vibe.

He was all the time catching her in a stare. He got the oddest sense she wanted—even expected—something from him, but what?

Finally, after their son had a turn on each breast,

Rowdy came right out and asked, "Did I do something to piss you off?"

"No. Why?" Since having the baby, she'd lost her feisty edge. He used to love their epic bickering matches. The way her cheeks flushed when she was good and mad. How many times had he craved kissing the anger right out of her? Now he couldn't get a feel for what was even appropriate when it came to touching her. She always, always held Johnny in her arms.

Poor Mr. Bojangles sulked at the foot of the bed. He'd worn the same purple sweater for three days.

"Babe," Rowdy said, "you've changed."

"Of course I have. I'm a mother. Are you faulting me for caring for our son?" She touched her free hand to her messy ponytail.

"How long has it been since you put the baby down long enough to have a shower?"

"I don't know. Why? Do I smell?"

"No. And you're totally missing my point. What are we doing? How long are we going to stay with your mom and grandmother when we should be setting up our own house?"

"Is that what you want to do?"

"I thought it was understood?" Along with the fact that they'd get married and, as soon as she was medically able, resume bedroom activities that had nothing to do with their son and everything to do with exploring every inch of Tiffany's beautifully curvy body.

"How could any of that be understood when I can't remember the last time you touched me? Let alone kissed me?"

"Is that what you want? A kiss?"

"No." A strangled half laugh escaped her like a gas bubble. "That's the last thing I want from you. What would be great? Is you running to the store before it closes. We're almost out of diapers."

"Why don't you come with me? Leave the baby with Pearl and Gigi. Might do you good to get out of the house. The Christmas lights around the square are gorgeous with all the snow." *We could pretend we were on a date. Everything between us has been backward as hell. Most couples get to know each other before having a baby. But we...*

Hell, he couldn't finish his own thought. What he and Tiffany had become was untenable. The two of them weren't working on any level. But how did he fix a relationship that had never officially formed? Let alone been broken?

Gigi and Pearl maintained a firm stance on Rowdy not spending the night with her and the baby until they were married.

If Tiffany had a quarter for every time she'd told her mother a wedding wasn't happening, she'd wipe out all family debt and still have enough for new shoes.

It was now 3:00 a.m., Johnny suckled her breast and she'd be lying if she said she didn't miss her son's father. She had flat-out lied when she'd told him she didn't want him to kiss her or hold her or assure her everything would one day be all right. More than anything, she longed for the two of them to find a cozy home of their own. She wanted to fall asleep with him at night and wake up next to him each morning.

Did she love him?

She didn't know.

All she did know was that life was better with him in it. The time he'd been gone had proven that. But lately she'd noticed he wasn't as quick with his smiles. He didn't carry his shoulders as straight, and gone was his usual confident stride.

Since they no longer talked like they used to when he'd first come to town, she could only guess at the meaning behind his funk. The only logical conclusion was that he regretted his hasty decision to keep Johnny. To stay with her.

"I love you," she whispered to her son, smoothing the tip of her pinkie across his soft cheek. "Keeping you was the best decision of my life—even if we don't end up keeping your dad."

The last thing she'd want was for Rowdy to feel trapped.

Even more than she feared him leaving her, she feared him staying for all the wrong reasons, then growing to resent her and Johnny for taking him from the life he loved.

She could handle being a navy wife.

She could handle spending a large chunk of her life raising their son on her own. What she couldn't do was know Rowdy was with her only out of a sense of obligation. Because his family expected him to do the right thing.

If there was anything she'd learned during this experience, it was that there was no singular correct path in life. Every person had to make his or her own way. His or her own decisions. If Rowdy chose not to be with her and Johnny, so be it.

She had too much pride to beg him to stay.

Once Johnny had eaten his fill, she changed his diaper, then tucked him back into the crib that Rowdy had purchased and assembled next to her chaise.

"Come here," she said to Mr. Bojangles, who stared forlornly at her from the foot of the bed. "I'm sorry I haven't been giving you as much attention."

She snatched him up for a cuddle, then exchanged his purple sweater for pink-and-black zebra stripes.

He licked her in appreciation.

"I love you," she said. "You're the most loyal man I've ever had in my life."

He fell asleep in her arms.

She kissed the top of his furry head, then turned out the light and settled for cuddling her dog rather than the big lug who apparently didn't want to be with her and his son enough to risk raising Pearl's and Gigi's hackles.

After a fitful night's sleep, Tiffany yawned her way to the hall bath, then used the time before Johnny woke to grab a quick shower.

Rowdy usually arrived at the house no later than eight. He helped with the chickens, then shoveled the front and back walks if there'd been any overnight snow.

But when she finished her shower, dressed and even towel-dried her hair and he still hadn't shown up, she forced a few deep breaths to fend off a full-blown panic.

What would she do if one day Rowdy just didn't come?

He'd already mentioned that after New Year's he was expected back on base, but until then, there was nothing binding him to her and Johnny. She looked in her vanity mirror. At the dark shadows beneath her bloodshot eyes and the extra weight she carried in her cheeks. She hadn't done her hair since their son's birth, and couldn't even find her makeup amid all of Johnny's baby gear.

She was mired so deep in more reasons why Rowdy no longer seemed attracted to her that when her cell rang, she jumped.

"Hey, sugar." Patsy's cheery tone felt out of tune with Tiffany's gloomy mood. Plus, the jazzy ringtone woke the baby.

"Hey. What's up?" She set her phone on the vanity, put the call on speaker, then lifted Johnny from his crib and into her arms.

Mr. Bojangles, still beneath the covers, stretched and yawned, poking just his head out into the chilly room.

"Uh-oh," Patsy said. "Did an angel wake up on the wrong side of his crib?"

"Not at all." Tiffany cradled him close and he quieted. "He's as sweet as Pearl's apple pie."

"Aw, I miss him. Which is part of the reason I called. First, Rowdy asked me to tell you he won't be by till later. His daddy's got a sick calf, and the only medicine is at a veterinary clinic two hours north. He and Carl volunteered to drive up to get it."

"Of course. I understand." But she didn't. Oh—she would never fault Rowdy for needing to help his family, but it might have been nice to pack up the baby and tag along. Since the girls were in school, Justine could have come, too. Like a double date. But since she and Rowdy weren't a couple, that probably wouldn't work.

"The second reason for my call is that I wanted to invite you, your mom and Pearl over for Christmas Eve. We'll have dinner and sing carols. It'll be fun. I figured for Johnny's first Christmas, we'd do it up real nice."

"Thank you." Tiffany blinked back tears. "That sounds wonderful. What can I do to help? Do you need me to bring anything?"

"Nope. You've got your hands full with Johnny. Plus, I told Rowdy to watch the baby for you all afternoon so you'd have time for a nice soak in the tub and to doll yourself up for pictures."

"You're an angel for thinking of me." Her heart ached that Rowdy's mother had to nudge him to be kind. What had happened between them? Where had she gone wrong?

"My pleasure. Oh—and every year we take family pictures wearing matching sweaters. This year's color is white, so I'll send Rowdy with one for each of you."

"That's not—"

"Don't say another word. I already bought them and can't wait to see how Johnny looks. He'll be like a real live angel."

"Yes, ma'am, he will." Tiffany wished she were close enough to Rowdy's mom to ask her opinion on the awkwardness between them, but she wasn't. The last thing she wanted was for Patsy to find her pushy or demanding.

After a few more minutes' small talk, Tiffany said goodbye, then got on with her day. Whether Rowdy showed up or not, she still had a long morning and afternoon planned of feeding and doing laundry and helping Gigi and Pearl with their myriad of holiday preparations.

Sitting in her room moping wouldn't get anything done.

The sooner she got used to being a single mom, the better off she'd be.

* * *

"Sorry," Rowdy said to Tiffany when he didn't get to Pearl's house until after six that night.

She paced the living room, carrying their screaming, red-faced son in her arms.

Mr. Bojangles sat on the sofa high atop a mountain of pint-size clothes waiting to be folded.

When Tiffany didn't look in his direction, Rowdy added above the wails, "We ended up driving clear to Benson County. Then Dad called and said our family vet had the medicine after all. We drove home, then Mom needed me to run a half-dozen errands for her party—she called you, right?"

Tiffany nodded, then gave the baby a jiggle.

Rowdy tweaked the little guy's sock-covered foot. "Want me to take him?"

She shook her head and kept right on walking.

"I assume you agreed to come—to Mom's party?"

She nodded.

"Thanks. Mom's excited to show off the baby."

"I'll bet."

"Where are Gigi and Pearl?"

"Their garden club is having a holiday dinner at the Sizzler."

"Why didn't you go?"

"Maybe because I'm not a member?"

"What's with the attitude?"

"Gee, could it be because I've been trying to calm our son for the past six hours?"

"Sorry. I never thought all the crap I had to do would take so long."

"It's okay."

"No, it's not. We're in this together, and I want to help." Rowdy settled his hands around Johnny's waist, taking their son. He held him extra close, cupping his hand to the back of Johnny's head. His screams faded to whimpers.

"I hate you." Tiffany collapsed on the sofa with enough force to startle Mr. Bojangles into a barking frenzy, which in turn made Johnny cry. She said to the dog, "Now I hate you, too."

Rowdy soon enough calmed the baby again. "Look, I'm sorry I haven't been here for you today."

"I'm sorry I snapped. Johnny's crying spells make me feel helpless. It's the worst."

She sighed, running her fingers through her messy hair. She looked nothing like the woman he'd slept with last Easter, but she was still every bit as beautiful to him. There was so much he wanted to say, but how did he start? First, he wanted things to change between them—to get better.

He cleared his throat. "You know how I have to be back on base after New Year's?"

She nodded.

"Which would be easier for you? Tagging along with me? Or staying here? You'd have Pearl and Gigi to help. Plus my mom and Justine. I'd miss you something fierce for the eighteen months left on my enlistment, but am I being selfish in wanting you two with me? If you stay, I guess logistically, it makes more sense. To save money, you and Johnny could still live with Pearl and Gigi. What do you think?"

Her gaze shone with tears, but not a single one fell. She stood, scooped up the dog, then said, "I'm taking a bubble bath. Thank you for watching Johnny until I'm done."

Sounds fun. Mind if I join you?

Rowdy squashed his inner horndog. "What about my question? If you are going with me, I'll need to start making plans—unless you wouldn't mind bunking with a few other smelly SEALs?"

She didn't laugh at his joke. In fact, she didn't even pause on her way to the stairs.

What did that mean? What was she thinking? Why wouldn't she talk to him? He was good at a lot of things, but mind reading had never been one of them.

He asked the baby, "Has she been salty all day?"

Rowdy studied the little guy's face. It was crazy how much he'd missed him. Rowdy had been pissed about the wild-goose chase his father had sent him on. It had taken precious time he would have otherwise spent with his son.

And Tiffany...

He sucked in a deep breath.

What did she want from him? What did she need?

The water went on upstairs.

Eyes closed, he thought about her all soap slick and sexy. Lately, she was impossible to read. He couldn't tell if she wanted him closer or to stay the hell away. Who knew, maybe if he went to Virginia without her, the separation might do them good?

The pang in his heart didn't agree.

Chapter 16

"Rowdy, you shouldn't have." *But I'm sure glad you did.* Tiffany's heart swelled with unexpected, much-appreciated joy. It was Christmas Eve and the size and impressive wrapping job on the gift he'd just presented had to be significant.

Pearl and Gigi had long ago left the house to attend an early church service. They'd taken Johnny with them to show him off to their few friends who hadn't already seen him. Meaning she and Rowdy were finally alone.

To talk.

Hold hands.

Kiss.

Her gaze momentarily locked with his. Her cheeks flushed.

For the first time since she couldn't remember when,

she'd had time to curl her long hair and apply makeup and even eyelashes. She'd done her nails and even added a spritz of her favorite floral perfume. Despite the fact that she currently wore her pink bathrobe and slippers, she felt beautiful under his stare.

"I didn't." Still standing in the entry hall, he cleared his throat, then shoved his hands in his jeans pockets.

Mr. Bojangles danced at his feet. She'd dressed him in a Santa suit for the occasion, but he'd already worked off his hat.

"Excuse me?" she asked on her way to the living room sofa. The square box was much too big for her to open while standing. The silver foil paper was embossed with elegant wreathes. Wide white ribbon had been tied into a giant bow.

"You thanked me for giving you the gift, but it's not from me but Mom." He cleared his throat. "I guess she told you about the family sweater thing she puts us through every year?"

"Yes." Her spirit sagged like one of those blow-up lawn ornaments after the holiday season. She should have guessed he didn't care enough about her to give her a gift.

"Don't get too excited. I'm sure it's just your sweater."

"Right. Thanks." She set the unopened box on the sofa beside her. Was now the time to give him her gift? And that other *thing*. She'd planned to wait until closer to his leaving, but she supposed now was as good a time as any. Like ripping a bandage off fast. The pain would be momentarily intense but then gone.

He'd wandered toward the Christmas tree, still holding his hands in his pockets. "Tiff? Can we—"

"Wait here. I'll be right back." She couldn't bear one more second of awkward silence. Whatever magic the two of them had once shared was gone. She needed to get used to that fact.

In her room, she took a legal-sized envelope from her top dresser drawer, as well as a wrapped rectangular package.

Back downstairs, she found him still in front of the tree, head bowed. What was he thinking? Was he as sad about how things had ended between them as she was? The night of Johnny's birth, she'd been convinced the two of them might actually have a bright future, but now? She'd lost hope.

"I got you this." She gave him the box. "It's not much. But I…" She stopped before her raspy voice told her most tightly held secret. That during the time they'd spent together, she'd grown helplessly, ridiculously attracted to not only his stupid-handsome face but the way he so willingly gave of his time to her, Pearl and Gigi. The one thing he didn't seem capable of giving was his heart. But could she blame him? They might have shared a child, but they hadn't shared much else beyond chemistry. She'd been willing to try. But…

"Thanks. I, ah, got you a little something, but it's back at my parents' house."

"It's okay. Besides, the gift really is something small."

He tore off the paper and bow, setting them on the coffee table before opening the box. It held one of her favorite silver frames from her namesake store, Tiffany. It had been a gift to her from her father on her eighteenth birthday. She didn't currently have the money for a new frame but figured this would be infinitely more special. She'd positioned Johnny for an hour to get the perfect pose of him seated under the tree. He'd worn a red onesie. She'd tied a green bow around his waist, then propped him among the prettily wrapped, mostly home-made presents she and Gigi and Pearl would exchange.

"Tiff…" Tears welled in Rowdy's grassy-green eyes. "This is the best gift I ever could have gotten. Thank you. Seriously. He's everything to me."

But not me?

"There's a smaller, laminated photo, too. I thought you might want to keep it with you when you're de-ployed." Her throat ached while handing over the sec-ond part of her gift. "I called in a favor from Daddy's legal team and got them to work this up."

"What is it?" He gave the envelope a funny look, then seemed hesitant to open it, as if it were a prank and worms might fall out.

"Just a formality. Since you're leaving, I wanted there to never be a question regarding the fact that you're Johnny's father, but I thought there should at least be a few guidelines in place."

"Huh?" Brows furrowed, he asked, "Are these cus-tody papers?"

"Yes. Just sign in a few places, and you'll be free to do whatever you want without worrying about Johnny."

"Come again?" He still looked confused.

"Give them a read when you can. The document ba-sically states that I have full legal custody of our son but that you have my blessing to visit him as often as your schedule allows. Oh—and that—"

"Are you shitting me?" For a second, she thought

he might explode, but then he regained his composure. "The fact that you would sink to this level of distrust when our boy is barely over a week old is…" He shook his head, clamped his lips tight. "I can't even begin to put words to what you've done. Get dressed. Let's get my mother's party behind us—then you and I are going to launch the next world war, because, babe, there's no way in hell I'm signing over custody of my son. I'll be waiting in the truck."

What had she done?

While Rowdy exited the house, filling the entry hall with cold night air, Tiffany wished she'd handled this whole thing differently. Why hadn't she come right out and told him she wanted nothing more than to marry him and try giving their little family a chance at a happy ending?

The answer to that question was heartbreakingly simple. She couldn't tell him what she wanted, because she was afraid.

It was bad enough that he was leaving her, but if she handed him the extra rounds of emotional ammunition stemming from her admission? Well, that would be too painful to bear.

For Patsy's sake, she had to paste on a smile and somehow get through this awful night.

Later she and Rowdy could make their final goodbye.

Tiffany opened the oversize gift box, hands trembling from the fight.

The spellbinding beauty of what she found nestled amid silver tissue paper only made her feel worse. A white cashmere sweater with a Peter Pan collar dotted with shimmering crystals and pearls. The garment's opulence took her breath away. Tucked beneath it was a full floor-length white satin skirt with layers of tulle beneath. This was an outfit suitable for a Christmas bride…

No…

Gigi and Patsy and Pearl wouldn't dare?

But when Tiffany added up all of the instances of her grandmother and mother being oddly away from the house and how Rowdy's mom had been running him ragged with either errands or what could have been diversionary goose chases, it all made perfect sense.

What had Gigi and Patsy been thinking?

Obviously, Tiffany and Rowdy were in no shape to get married—they might never be. If her mother thought she could force the issue by literally forcing a wedding, she had another thing coming.

The next time Tiffany married would be the *last* time.

Her broken marriage had been beyond painful and she would never put herself—and now her son— through that again.

Even if Rowdy bowed to pressure and agreed to the ceremony, what then? What good could come of being tied to a man who clearly despised her?

Leaving the outfit in its box, Tiffany marched to the front door, tossed it open, then charged across the front porch and down the steps, where she promptly slipped on an icy patch and fell on her behind.

The pain was considerable, but she knew she'd live.

The shame of walking in on a surprise wedding with a groom who didn't want to be there—now, that would hurt!

"Tiff, what the hell?" Rowdy hopped from his truck to help. "Are you okay?"

"I'm fine. Not that you'd care!"

"What are you talking about? You're the one passing out custody papers like Christmas candy!"

"What else could I do? It's obvious you don't want to be with me."

"Are you mental? How many times have I told you we should be together?"

"We *should* be? I've already had one broken marriage, Rowdy. Now that I have a son to watch after, why in the world would I turn around and hitch my wagon to a man who doesn't even want me? Let alone love me?"

"Woman, now I know you've lost a few brain cells from lack of sleep. Those are your insecurities talking, because when I tell a woman I love her and want to marry her, I mean it."

"But you never said any of that!" she shrieked.

Inside the house, Mr. Bojangles barked.

A light snow began to fall.

"Great." She threw her hands up. "Now my makeup and hair will be ruined. I'm sick of snow!" she shouted to the heavens.

Rowdy knelt, taking her hands to help her to her feet.

He took the liberty of brushing snow from her behind, and she'd be lying if she said his lightest touch wasn't a thrill.

"Let me be real clear." He cupped her cheeks with his hands. "I adore you. I love you. I need you. When I leave for Virginia, more than anything, I want you and Johnny with me. I selfishly want you two seeing me off on every mission, and I want you waiting for me at the base for a kiss the second I get home. You're stubborn and sassy and will probably be the death of me, but until then, I'm never letting you go. How's that for plain talk? Unless you love plaid. If you do, then I'm gone." His hopeful wink told her he remembered their silly conversation on the topic while house hunting.

Was it possible he'd wanted her to be his future wife even back then?

Since the lump in her throat was too big to speak, she nodded and then kissed him so very hard. "Not only do I vow to never buy a plaid sofa, but I love you, too," she admitted when coming up for air. "I was so afraid—of everything. Of becoming a mom and wife and of needing you but you not needing me. Johnny needs his father and I need my man. God help me, but that man is you, Rowdy Jones."

"Damn straight. And don't ever forget it." He wrapped his arms around her, hugging her right off the ground. He pressed his lips to her so softly, so sweetly, if she hadn't been so darned cold, she might have thought she was dreaming. "Want me to make a fire and we'll skip Mom's party?"

"The party—how could I forget what I raced out here to tell you? It's a setup."

"What do you mean?"

She explained her theory, topping it off by describing Patsy's over-the-top gift that wasn't exactly suitable for a family night of a casual dinner and carols.

"You know—" Rowdy scratched his head, then led her inside out of the cold "—that makes a lot of sense. I even tried calling my friend Logan yesterday, but he blew me off. Sounded like he was at an airport. Could he have been headed here?"

"Only one way to find out." She winked. "But first, wanna have a little fun with our matchmaking mothers and grandmother?"

"You know it. But only if I get to help you dress." His slow and sexy wink was back, along with his stupid-handsome grin. He had enough dark stubble to make him look just like the bad-boy cowboy she'd instantly fallen for all those months ago.

On her tiptoes for one more kiss, she whispered, "I think that could be arranged."

Epilogue

Rowdy held Johnny while Tiffany ducked into the bathroom located just off the baggage-claim area at Norfolk International Airport. She was expecting again—this time, a girl. At eight months and three weeks, she was big as a house and prettier than ever. Also sassier than ever, but since their Christmas Eve wedding, he'd had plenty of time to figure out not only her many moods but what flavor of ice cream best soothed them.

"Any sign of our families?" Tiffany asked on her way back to him with an impatient glance toward the passenger entrance.

"Not yet. Relax. Pearl will be fine."

"I know. But this is her first time in a plane. I want everything to be perfect."

"Since your dad got his early release for good behavior and sprang for them all to fly first class, I'm sure she's fine."

Big Daddy's release had come just in time for Valentine's Day. Gigi had been over the moon. An old college buddy back in Dallas had gotten him on board with a new high-paying position, and he and Gigi were back to living their old luxe life. Pearl's second mortgage had been paid in full, and all of that good news was enough to have had the two most important women in her life forgive them for faking a big fight, then calling off the surprise wedding.

After they'd assured their shocked guests and family that the quarrel was a joke, everyone had shared a good laugh and gotten on with the romantic event. Patsy had even arranged for a few of Rowdy's friends and their wives to be there—including Macy, Jessie and Hattie, who had become Tiffany's rocks whenever Rowdy was deployed.

Hattie owned a favorite SEAL hangout and had introduced Tiffany to loads more wives, who formed the best support system she could have wanted—although, she was still awfully excited to see her grandmother and mom.

"There they are." Rowdy pointed to the women accompanied by Tiffany's barrel-chested dad.

Tiffany's eyes welled and as best as she could, she waddled that way for a round of hugs.

Then came the baby cooing…

"Look at Johnny!"

"He's so big!"

"How cute!"

Then complaining…

"I didn't think we'd ever get here," Gigi said.

"Tell me about it." Patsy blew her nose from a tissue she'd taken from her purse. "Pearl and I have been on a plane since Bismarck. You two only had to fly from Dallas."

"True." Gigi smiled. "Maybe next time you'll listen when I invite you to stay with us for a few days before your Norfolk flight?"

On the walk out to the car, Tiffany's dad held her back. "Before we're all settled in for baby watch, I wanted to tell you how proud I am of the woman you've become. You're an amazing mother and wife and real estate agent—the total package. I love you."

"I love you, too, Dad." She stopped for a hug. "When you went away and then Crawford left me, there was a time when I never thought I'd love again. But then Rowdy came along, and..." she grinned "...now I've never been happier."

Two months later, on a Saturday afternoon, Tiffany was breast-feeding Mariah in the ugly yet criminally comfy plaid recliner Rowdy had talked her into buying, when her cell rang. As was usually the case when she was busy with one of the kids, her phone was across the room.

"Rowdy!" she called.

"Got it!" He'd been changing Johnny's diaper but scooped up her cell on his way back into the living room and handed it to her.

"Hello?" she answered without looking at the caller.

"Tiffany?"

The woman sounded all too familiar.

"Susie?" Tiffany straightened with surprise. "H-how are you?"

"Actually, I'm the proud new mother of Cambodian twins. They're only eleven months old, but I can already tell they'll be geniuses."

"Of course they will." Residual pregnancy hormones brought on tears. "I'm so happy for you and Jeb." And she really, truly was. She'd felt awful about the way she'd ended her arrangement with the couple, but it couldn't have been helped. From the moment she'd laid eyes on him, she'd loved her son. Oh, who was she kidding? From the first beat of his heart, she'd been a goner.

Rowdy waved to get her attention. He whispered, "Everything okay?"

Perfect. Seriously, dazzlingly perfect.

While Susie chattered about her precious miracles, Tiffany blew Rowdy a kiss. After all of her years spent living in Dallas, she'd always assumed she'd end up with a Texas cowboy. Never in her wildest dreams would she have thought she'd get hitched to a navy SEAL cowboy from North Dakota.

But she wasn't complaining…

* * * * *

Marin Thomas grew up in the Midwest, then attended college at the U of A in Tucson, Arizona, where she earned a BA in radio-TV and played basketball for the Lady Wildcats. Following graduation, she married her college sweetheart in the historic Little Chapel of the West in Las Vegas, Nevada. Recent empty-nesters, Marin and her husband now live in Texas, where cattle is king, cowboys are plentiful and pickups rule the road. Visit her on the web at marinthomas.com.

Books by Marin Thomas

Harlequin Western Romance

The Cowboys of Stampede, Texas

The Cowboy's Accidental Baby
Twins for the Texas Rancher

Harlequin American Romance

Cowboys of the Rio Grande

A Cowboy's Redemption
The Surgeon's Christmas Baby
A Cowboy's Claim

The Cash Brothers

The Cowboy Next Door
Twins Under the Christmas Tree
Her Secret Cowboy
The Cowboy's Destiny
True Blue Cowboy
A Cowboy of Her Own

Visit the Author Profile page
at Harlequin.com for more titles.

THE SURGEON'S
CHRISTMAS BABY

Marin Thomas

To my great-niece Adley Faith:
You are braver than you believe,
stronger than you seem and smarter than you think.
Follow your dreams and never look back.

Chapter 1

"Quit lookin' at me like that."

Darn Luke's ornery hide. Hannah Buck squeezed the steering wheel, wishing it was her half brother's neck.

Yesterday after lunch Luke had left the ranch to attend a Halloween party with friends. He'd promised to be home by dark, but ten o'clock had come and gone and Hannah had paced the kitchen floor, imagining him lying dead in a ditch somewhere—just as she'd found their father two years ago.

"You could have texted me that you were staying the night at Connor's."

"I left my cell phone at home."

On purpose. When their father died, the court had appointed Hannah Luke's legal guardian—a job she'd gladly accepted. But she hadn't counted on her then fourteen-year-old brother embarking on a mission to make her life miserable.

The recent skipping school, drinking and smoking pot had to stop. She'd attributed Luke's rebellion to grief and in the beginning hadn't demanded too much of him. Even his teachers had gone easy on him. But two years had passed since their father's death and Luke's behavior was getting out of hand. If he didn't settle down and quit running wild, he'd end up in jail, and then she wouldn't be able to save his butt.

"I can't do this anymore, Luke."

"Do what?"

That he had to ask showed how little he cared about the responsibility resting on her shoulders. "I can't take care of the ranch and chase after you. It's time for you to grow up."

"Jeez...not another lecture." He sprawled across the backseat. "You didn't have to come get me. I could have driven home."

If Connor's mother hadn't informed Hannah that she and her husband were leaving town, Luke would have remained at his friend's the entire day and skipped out on doing his chores. She glanced in the rearview mirror. Her brother had turned sixteen five months ago, but his smooth skin and pudgy cheeks reminded her of the little boy who'd followed her everywhere on the ranch. Hannah had been the only one who'd paid attention to him when their father was lost in the bottle or Luke's mother, Ruth, left on one of her weekend getaways.

Hannah and Luke had grown even closer after Ruth died in a car accident right before Luke's tenth birthday. She recalled the afternoon her father broke the news to them—Luke hadn't shed a tear. Instead, he'd asked Hannah to play a video game with him. She hadn't been surprised that her brother had turned to her, since Ruth had assigned all the mothering duties to ten-year-old Hannah when she'd brought Luke home from the hospital.

To be honest, she hadn't been distraught over Ruth's death, either. It was hard to shed a tear for the woman who'd caused her parents' divorce. Hannah hadn't heard from her mother—not even a birthday card—since the day she'd walked out on her family. Hannah wished she could blame Ruth for her mother abandoning her but that wouldn't be fair. The sad truth was that all the adults in her and Luke's life had let them down.

After their father's funeral Hannah had discovered how badly he'd mismanaged the ranch. Instead of spending time with Luke, she'd spent days poring over financial records with an accountant at the bank. He'd set up a payment plan with her creditors and she'd been forced to let their ranch hand go. Keeping the business from going under had fallen on her shoulders, but she'd accepted the responsibility, hoping Luke would help out, but like a typical teenager all he cared about was hanging with his friends.

"How am I supposed to get my car?" he asked.

"We'll pick it up tomorrow." As far as Hannah was concerned, *her* old Civic could sit on the Henderson property a good long while. Without wheels Luke would be stuck at home and maybe out of sheer boredom he'd do his chores. "How much did you and Connor drink last night?"

"Enough."

She still hadn't broken the news to her brother that she'd been asked to keep him away from Connor. Mrs. Henderson believed Luke was a bad influence on her son. The apple didn't fall far from the tree.

She couldn't remember a time her father hadn't reached for a beer when he walked into the house—morning, noon or night. He'd kept his drinking under control until Ruth died. Hannah wasn't sure if her father's depression had been caused by Ruth's death or learning the *girlfriend* in the car with her at the time of the accident had been a man named Stan Smith.

"You can't keep this up, Luke." When he remained silent, she said, "You know Dad was an alcoholic. You carry the gene." If worrying about her brother's drinking wasn't enough stress, yesterday afternoon she'd discovered an acre of fence had been torn down and several of their bison had wandered onto the neighbor's property. Roger Markham hadn't been pleased when he'd had to send his ranch hands to round up her livestock.

She'd reported the vandalism to Sheriff Miller, who'd attributed it to a Halloween prank by local kids. He'd promised to notify his deputies to be on the lookout for any troublemakers in the Paradise area. Then he'd suggested that until they caught the culprits, Hannah should take Luke with her when she checked the herd—as if that was going to happen.

"Not that you care, but some jerk trampled a section of fence and the bison wandered onto the Los Pinos Ranch." Hannah had insurance to cover the cost of repairing the fence, but the deductible was a thousand dollars. There went her Christmas fund.

"Who gives a crap about those stupid animals?" The truck hit a bump and he groaned. "Watch your driving."

She was tempted to slam on the brakes, put the truck into Reverse and drive back and forth over the pothole until Luke puked. "When we get home, I need you to load the hay bales onto the flatbed."

"I'm too tired."

If she gripped the wheel any tighter, she'd rip it from the steering column. Hannah had planned to go to college after she'd graduated from high school, but then Ruth had died and her father had sunk into a deep depression and she'd ended up staying put. Even so, she'd never regret spending those last few years with her father. Helping him run the ranch had given her a deeper appreciation for rural life, and now she couldn't imagine doing anything else. Eventually she was confident Luke's view of the ranch would change, too, and he'd see the value of his inheritance. Right now, she had to worry about weathering this latest storm with him.

"You know that Dad probably wouldn't have died that night if he hadn't been—"

"Drinking. I know."

Hannah didn't like bringing up their father's death, but she never wanted Luke to forget. He needed the reminder, especially now when he was experimenting with alcohol and drugs. She didn't want him to make stupid decisions that would put his life in danger—like going for a horseback ride after drinking a twelve-pack of beer.

Joe Buck hadn't ridden far when he'd lost his balance and had fallen off Buster, cracking his head open. By the time Hannah had noticed the horse wandering aimlessly in the ranch yard, it had been too late. She'd found her father's lifeless body in a ravine behind the house, his hand clutching a beer can.

"You can take a nap after you load the hay," she said. The herd should have been fed this morning, but she'd wasted the past two hours fetching Luke.

"You're not my mom. You can't tell me what to do."

The jab hurt. She'd been more of a mother to Luke than Ruth ever had. Hannah had been the one to make her brother's breakfast before school. Not Ruth. Hannah had done the family's laundry and made sure Luke's Little League uniform had been ready to wear on Saturday morning. Not Ruth. And when Luke had taken Melissa Walter to the school dance this past spring, Hannah had been the one to purchase a box of condoms and give Luke a safe sex lecture. Not Ruth.

"You've been running wild since Dad died and it's got to stop. If you'd help out more, we could expand the herd." *And I could keep an eye on you.* The thought of something terrible happening to Luke terrified Hannah. They might be at odds right now but he was all the family she had left, and she loved her brother.

"Bison suck."

"They're keeping a roof over our heads and food on the table."

"Connor said his father thinks Dad was stupid to buy bison instead of cattle."

Hannah was well aware that their neighbors believed raising bison for specialty meat markets was a waste of good land. "I don't care what Mr. Henderson thinks."

"School's dumb. I wanna drop out."

It took a moment for Hannah's mind to switch gears.

"What do you mean you want to quit school?" At least from six-thirty in the morning until three-thirty in the afternoon, Monday through Friday she knew where her brother was.

"I'm not learning anything."

"You're staying in school, Luke."

"Just 'cause you're my legal guardian doesn't mean I have to listen to you."

Hannah laughed. "Oh, yes, it does. You're not dropping out. End of discussion."

"You can't stop me." Luke was three inches taller and fifty pounds heavier than Hannah. If he didn't want to go to school, there wouldn't be much she could do to make him go.

She opened her mouth to challenge him, then decided no good could come from arguing her point when he was hungover. Hannah had taken care of others most of her life and at times like this she dreamed of only being responsible for herself.

"I bet Connor's mother would let me live with them."

Not on your life. "Mrs. Henderson doesn't even want you hanging out with Connor anymore."

"Liar."

"You can ask her yourself."

"Why would she say that?"

"Maybe because she caught you two drinking and she thinks you're a bad influence on her son."

Luke laughed, then moaned and pressed his hands to his head. "Connor drank before we started doing stuff together."

"Did Connor talk you into drinking?"

"No. Ben Nichols and I got slammed last year."

"Is Ben the one who gave you the pot?"

"Yeah."

She'd found Luke smoking in the hayloft over Christmas break and had flipped out. He'd been so stoned he was lucky he hadn't started a fire in the barn.

"Maybe you should smoke pot, then guys might like you better." Luke could be downright ugly toward her when he wanted to be. "I bet if you weren't such a nag, Seth wouldn't have dumped you."

Hannah gaped at her brother in the rearview mirror. "For your information, *I* broke up with him."

Seth Markham had caught Hannah at a weak moment when he'd proposed to her following her father's funeral. She'd been in a state of panic after learning about the financial mess the ranch was in. When Seth had promised he and his father would pay off the Blue Bison's debts, she'd decided that marrying him was the only sensible thing to do if she didn't want to lose her and Luke's inheritance.

Seth had pressed her to wed right away but Hannah had needed time to grieve. Three months passed, and when she still hadn't set a date, Seth became angry and they'd argued. He'd almost convinced her to go to the courthouse that day before he'd let it slip that he and his father had planned to sell her bison and expand their cattle herd. Hannah had promptly returned his ring.

"Watch it!"

Startled out of her trance, Hannah realized the truck had drifted onto the shoulder and was headed straight toward a hitchhiker. She slammed on the brakes, then swerved back into her lane—right into the path of a shiny metal object lying on the asphalt. The rear tire blew and the truck fishtailed off the road and down an embankment, where it stopped inches from a barbed wire fence.

"Luke, are you all right?" She craned her neck over the backseat.

Her brother crawled up from the floor. "Shit, Hannah. You could have killed us. Didn't you see that guy?"

She looked out the passenger window. The hitchhiker had dropped his duffel bag on the ground and was jogging toward them. He wore military fatigues and a white T-shirt that showed off his powerful arms and an impressive chest. He had short, dark hair, thick beard stubble covered his face and aviator sunglasses hid his eyes. No wonder he hadn't jumped out of the way—he'd been wearing earbuds.

Luke opened the back door and got out of the truck.

"Everyone okay?" the man asked when he reached them. He took off his shades and ran his gaze over Luke.

"We're good," Luke said.

Hannah joined Luke and said, "I'm so sorry. I wasn't paying attention to my driving. I didn't hit you, did I?"

"Not by a long shot. How about you?"

His eyes were a hypnotizing shade of caramel brown. "How about me what?"

"Did you get hurt?" His sexy mouth spread into a grin.

She shook her head. "I'm fine."

He examined the rear wheel. "You've got a flat tire."

Hannah peered over his shoulder. She'd been driving on bald tires for months. It had only been a matter of time before one of them blew.

"If you have a spare, I'll put it on."

Where were her manners? When he stood, she held out her hand. "Hannah Buck." His warm grasp was the nicest thing she'd touched all morning.

"Alonso Marquez."

"This is my brother, Luke," she said.

The males shook hands and Hannah noticed Alonso was only an inch or two taller than Luke's five-ten.

"I have a spare," she said. "Luke, grab the wrench and jack from the toolbox."

Her brother climbed into the truck bed and rummaged through the steel storage compartment, then handed the tools to Alonso.

Hannah closed her eyes and rubbed her brow, where a dull throb beat against her skull. The headache had begun right after she'd picked up Luke from Connor's.

"Hey," a deep voice whispered near her ear, and she jumped. "It's okay." Alonso smiled. "No one got hurt."

Tears stung her eyes at the note of concern in the stranger's voice. When was the last time anyone had been worried about her?

True to his word, Alonso put the spare tire on in record time.

"Thank you," she said. "And I'm really sorry I almost ran over you."

"Be careful." He saluted her before walking back to retrieve his bag.

"Aren't you going to give him a ride?" Luke asked.

"We don't know anything about him," she said.

"Who cares? He helped us, didn't he?"

True, but what if Alonso turned out to be a serial killer or robbed them at gunpoint after she dropped him off farther down the road? Still…this was a lonely stretch of Highway 8 and the town of Paradise was fifteen miles away.

"Hey, mister, you want a ride?" Luke shouted.

Alonso waved Luke off, then put in his earbuds, threw his bag over his shoulder and started walking.

Luke jogged toward Alonso—funny how his hangover prevented him from doing chores but not racing after strangers. Alonso listened to Luke for a minute, then the two walked back to the truck.

"I told him that you were worried he might kill us." Luke nudged Alonso's arm. "Tell her what you said."

Alonso flashed his white teeth. "I don't kill. I save lives."

"He's a doctor, Hannah."

"Trauma surgeon," Alonso said.

Luke nodded to the man's fatigues. "And he was an Army doctor in Afghanistan."

Hannah would never have guessed the sexy, masculine man was a surgeon. "Why are you hitchhiking?"

"I took a personal leave from the University of New Mexico Hospital in Albuquerque." He looked at Luke. "Kid, I appreciate the thought, but your sister's uncomfortable giving me a lift."

Luke jutted his chin. "This truck belonged to our dad, so it's half mine and I say you can have a ride."

Alonso glanced between sister and brother. He didn't care to get involved in their squabble. The teen leaned in close and Alonso caught a whiff of stale alcohol on his breath. "You can ride up front," Luke said.

"Aren't you a little young to be drinking?"

"I'm sixteen."

"Last I heard the drinking age around these parts was twenty-one."

"No one pays attention to that law."

Touché. Alonso had drunk as a teen—not often— but he'd slammed back a few beers once in a while so the homies in the 'hood wouldn't make fun of him. It had been tough enough that the kids had picked on him for getting good grades. If not for his little sister Lea's asthma attacks, forcing Alonso to skip school to care for her while their mother worked, he'd have been a regular Goody Two-shoes. And Goody Two-shoes never made it out of the barrio.

"Stay out of trouble, kid." Alonso left the siblings by their truck and started down the road. He'd walked less than a minute before Hannah pulled up next to him and lowered the passenger-side window. He took out his earbuds but kept walking.

"Where are you headed?" she asked.

"Nowhere in particular." He'd had no plan in mind when he'd left his job—just that he hoped lots of fresh air and escaping the city would restore his faith in humanity. His coworkers thought he'd lost his mind when he'd confessed that he needed a break from the blood and gore. Their disbelief hadn't surprised him. ER doctors and nurses were adrenaline junkies who thrived on chaos. But Alonso's past was catching up to him. He'd grown up in a rough neighborhood, watching bad things happen to good people. His time in Afghanistan was more of the same—good soldiers losing their lives at the hands of the people they were trying to help. Then he'd returned to the States, where he tried to save more lives—kids shot by kids. Women who were beaten by their boyfriends or husbands. Drug overdoses and innocent men, women and children injured by intoxicated drivers. He'd become weary of all the death and destruction and had needed to escape it for a while.

Luke poked his head out the window. "You can stay at our ranch if you want."

"Luke!" Obviously Hannah didn't want Alonso anywhere near her or her brother. *Smart girl.*

"I'm good, thanks." He read the indecision in Hannah's pretty blue eyes and he let his gaze linger on her.

At first glance she came off plain looking, but upon closer inspection he noticed her eyes darkened to indigo when they shone with worry. Her mouth was a little wide and he imagined what it would feel like to kiss her full lips. *Damn.* He'd just met Hannah and already he was thinking of having sex with her. She was smart to be wary of him.

"Luke's right. You deserve a lift after I almost ran you down, and then made you change a flat tire."

"Thanks." The word was out of his mouth before he could stop it—blame it on her baby blues. Once he got situated in the truck bed, the half window in the backseat opened.

"You can sit up front with my sister."

"I'm fine right here." Alonso put in his earbuds but didn't turn on the music. He shouldn't eavesdrop, but he was curious about the siblings.

Hannah guided the pickup onto the road and Alonso closed his eyes against the cool breeze. When he'd begun his journey five days ago the high had been seventy-three. He'd headed southeast and had walked twelve hours a day, covering almost thirty-five miles per day. Each twenty-four-hour period that passed, the temperature had dropped. He guessed the first day in November hovered near sixty-five degrees.

"Why are you so mean?" Luke's accusation drifted through the open window.

"What are you talking about?" Hannah asked.

"Making Alonso sit in the truck bed because you think he's some psycho."

Alonso thought Hannah should be suspicious of him. Not only didn't she know much about him, but he carried a handgun in his duffel bag.

"Leave it be, Luke. I don't want to argue with you."

Luke tapped his shoulder. "Alonso."

"What?"

"You ever rodeo?"

"No, but I've ridden a bucking bronc before." In high school he and his friends, Cruz Rivera and Victor Vicario, had spent time at the Gateway Ranch, where several cowboys had taught them how to bust broncs. It took only a few short seconds in the saddle for Alonso to figure out rodeo wasn't his sport. He'd spent the remainder of his stay at the ranch taking care of the livestock.

"I want to learn how to ride broncs," Luke said.

"Bronc riding can be tricky."

"But rodeo is so cool."

Alonso sensed a wild streak in the teen—no wonder his sister appeared stressed out. "Some high schools have rodeo teams."

"School sucks." Luke lowered his voice. "I'm gonna drop out."

"I doubt your parents would approve of you quitting school."

"My mom and dad are dead." That Luke said it so matter-of-factly left Alonso speechless.

The truck slowed, then turned onto a dirt road and drove beneath a wooden arch with the words *Blue Bison Ranch* painted in white across it. He should remind Hannah to stop and let him out, but the words never came.

She drove a quarter mile before he saw a house, barn and corral. The place could use a little TLC. The adobe-style home needed a fresh coat of beige paint, and the red barn had faded to pink and was missing a few boards. A flatbed trailer half-loaded with hay bales sat beneath the open barn loft. No ranch hand appeared to greet them—maybe the hired help was out with the cattle.

Hannah parked in front of the barn and as soon as she and her brother opened their doors, they started in on each other.

"Finish loading the hay, Luke."

"You load it. I'm going to bed."

Hannah grabbed Luke's shirtsleeve. "If you think you're old enough to stay up all night drinking, then you can do a man's work the next day."

"I'm sick of you bossing me around. Go to hell." Luke stormed into the house.

Alonso waited for Hannah's next move, then his chest tightened when she dabbed her eyes with her fingertips. He couldn't stand to see her cry.

"I'll load the hay." He hopped out of the truck bed.

She slapped a hand against her heart and stared at

him wide-eyed—yep, she'd forgotten about him. A first for Alonso. He was quiet by nature but a decent-looking man, according to the ER nurses, who repeatedly reminded him of their single status.

"I was supposed to let you off by the road."

"Not a big deal. It isn't that far of a walk." He nodded to the trailer. "Loading hay bales is the least I can do to thank you for the lift."

After a second's hesitation she said, "I need twenty-five more."

"Twenty-five bales it is." He waited for Hannah to enter the house, then went into the barn and climbed the ladder to the loft. As he dropped the bales to the ground below, he wondered if the siblings fought like this every day.

Did it matter? As soon as he finished the chore, he'd hit the road again.

Chapter 2

Hannah stood at her bedroom window and watched hay bales sail out of the barn loft. She was grateful that Alonso had offered to help and embarrassed that he'd witnessed the drama between her and Luke.

True to his word, her brother had crawled into bed as soon as he'd gone into the house. Luke was a spoiled brat and she accepted much of the blame for his self-centeredness. She'd always felt sorry for him, because Ruth had neglected him. Then, when Luke was old enough to do guy things with their father, Joe had chosen to spend his free time with a can of beer rather than his son. So Hannah had babied Luke and now she was paying the price.

The tears she'd held back all day dripped down her cheeks. She wiped the moisture away, assuming her weepiness was the result of exhaustion and worry. She returned downstairs, grabbed a water bottle from the fridge and, ignoring the pile of dirty dishes in the sink, she went out to the barn. Halfway there she froze when she caught a glimpse of Alonso's bare chest. He'd taken his shirt off and his skin glistened with sweat, the muscles rippling when he heaved a bale over his head. The sight of all that masculinity set off an explosion of feminine twinges—erotic little aches that she hadn't experienced in a long, long while.

He disappeared from the hayloft window, then a moment later walked out of the barn, his T-shirt hanging from his jeans pocket. "Almost done." He began picking the bales up off the ground and placing them on the flatbed. The words *US Army* were tattooed above an image of eagle wings and a snake coiled around a rod. He hadn't lied about being a military doctor.

She held out the water bottle.

"Thanks." He guzzled the drink, then sucked in a deep breath.

It was none of her business, but she asked, "How long were you in the Army?"

"I did one tour in Afghanistan before I returned to civilian life."

"Are you originally from New Mexico?"

"Born and raised in Albuquerque." He lifted the bottom of his T-shirt and wiped the sweat off his face. "What about you?"

"Born and raised in Paradise." Four generations of Bucks had lived on the ranch outside the small town—population just a little over two thousand. "My great-grandfather bought this land." But it was Hannah's grandfather who had made most of the improvements—digging the water wells and starting up a bison herd. Sadly her father had run it into the ground.

"Anything else I can help with before I take off?"

"No." She motioned to the flatbed. "You've done plenty, thanks."

His eyes shifted to the house. "Is your brother okay?"

She refused to make excuses for Luke. "He's sleeping off his hangover."

"Does he drink often?"

Was Alonso asking as a doctor or just a guy she'd picked up hitchhiking? "He sneaked a can of beer once in a while before our father died. But last night he got caught binge drinking with a friend."

She waited for Alonso to lecture her on the evils of alcohol consumption, which sadly she was all too familiar with. Instead, he said, "Pull your truck over here and I'll hook it up to the trailer, then you drive and I'll cut the bales and drop them where you tell me to."

She wanted to refuse his help but swallowed her pride. Once Alonso hitched the trailer to the pickup, he walked up to the driver's-side window. "Blow the horn when you want me to toss a bale."

She handed him the wire cutters and work gloves she kept in the truck. After he climbed onto the trailer, she drove off, slowing down when she left the dirt road and entered the pasture. She honked every ten yards. Halfway through her route the bison came over a ridge. After Alonso threw the last bale onto the ground she put the truck into Park and got out.

He hopped off the trailer. "I've never seen bison up close. They're pretty impressive animals."

"My great-grandfather raised cattle. It was my grandfather who switched to bison after he lost an entire herd to disease." She smiled. "Have you ever eaten bison meat?"

"Nope."

"We sell our bison to gourmet food markets, but once in a while a dude ranch will ask to buy one of the animals to keep as a pet. Tourists get a kick out of seeing them."

"How many do you have?"

"My grandfather kept a herd of three hundred then my father decreased it to two hundred, and right now I have a hundred and fifty." She'd had to sell thirty head to cover the back taxes. Once the ranch was in better financial shape, she intended to grow the herd again.

"Ready when you are." He got in on the passenger side and the musky scent of male sweat and faded cologne filled the cab. She turned the truck around and drove back through the pasture. "I would have been doing this in the dark tonight if you hadn't offered to help."

"You don't have any ranch hands working for you?"

"I can't afford to pay one. If Luke would stay out of trouble and do his share of the chores, we'd manage fine."

"Luke mentioned both your parents are gone."

Gone sounded temporary, not permanent like *dead*. Maybe that was how soldiers viewed fatalities in the Army. His comrades never died—they were just gone. "Our father passed away in a horseback-riding accident and Luke's mother died in a car crash."

"Must be rough, handling all this on your own."

"It's been challenging." She parked next to the barn. "You should stay for supper." Hannah decided it would be best if she and Luke had a buffer between them for a while—otherwise they might say something they'd regret. "There's a cot in the storage room in the barn. You can sleep in there tonight, then leave in the morning."

Luke would love it if Alonso hung around and did the rest of his chores for him. But that wasn't why Hannah had extended the invite. She hadn't been involved with anyone since Seth, and Alonso reminded her of how lonely she was for male attention.

"I could use a good night's sleep and a warm meal."

She opened her mouth to ask where he was headed then changed her mind. Come morning Alonso would gone.

"My sister said you're staying the night."

"I'll head out in the morning at first light."

"You don't have to clean the horse stalls."

"Someone has to do it." Alonso tossed a clump of soiled hay toward the wheelbarrow.

Luke climbed the ladder to the loft and sat, legs dangling above Alonso's head. Obviously the kid would rather watch than help. No wonder Hannah was miffed at her brother.

"Where will you go when you leave here?" Luke asked.

"I'm not sure. I don't have any place in mind." He pointed to the wheelbarrow. "Lend me a hand, will you?"

"And do what?"

Alonso set the pitchfork aside and dragged a hay bale

over to a stall, then dropped the wire cutters on top of it. "Spread clean hay in the stalls I've already cleaned."

Luke took his time climbing down from the loft. "A marine recruiter came to our school at the beginning of the year," he said, tugging on a pair of work gloves. "He made his job sound like fun. Is it?"

"I wouldn't use the word *fun* to describe my experience."

"Where were you stationed?"

"I spent a month at Fort Hood in Killeen, Texas, before shipping out to Afghanistan."

"Did any of your friends get killed in Afghanistan?"

Man, the kid was nosy. The doctors and nurses at the hospital tiptoed around the subject and pretended he'd spent time on an exotic island, not in a war-ravaged country. "Three of my friends were killed over there."

And the hell of it was Alonso had just saved their lives after a roadside bomb had taken out their Humvee. No one expected them to get blown to pieces in the recovery room when an Afghan medic-in-training detonated a bomb strapped to his chest.

"I thought the war was over."

"It is, but there are still crazies running loose in the country." Alonso didn't want to talk about his military experience. "You almost done with that stall?"

"Yeah."

"Grab another bale and finish this one."

Luke did as he was told. "You got a girlfriend?"

"Don't have time for one." That was what he told his coworkers, but after everything he'd been through, he decided nothing good lasts, so it made no sense wasting his energy on a serious relationship.

"Don't you like girls?"

"I like girls fine." He chuckled. "You always so nosy?"

"I guess. It's just that this place is boring."

"What do you do to keep busy?"

"Not much. My sister doesn't like my friends."

Alonso's mother hadn't approved of his school friends but she hadn't understood that a brainiac kid didn't stand a chance in hell of surviving in the barrio if he didn't have buddies to defend him. Alonso's best friends had made sure he hadn't been picked on or targeted by gangs.

In the end it had been Cruz's rebellious behavior that had got all three kicked out of school and enrolled in a special program to earn their GED. To this day Alonso believed he'd never have become a doctor if he hadn't had the support of their teacher, Maria Alvarez—now Fitzgerald. Things had worked out for him and Vic. Not so much for Cruz—he'd landed in jail. "Maybe you should make new friends."

Luke ignored Alonso's suggestion and asked, "If you're a doctor, why are you hitchhiking? Don't you have a car?"

"I have a pickup back at my apartment in Albuquerque." He pushed the wheelbarrow past Luke. "I guess I didn't feel like driving."

"You're crazy."

Luke wasn't the only one who thought Alonso was an idiot. When he'd told his coworkers he'd needed a break from the ER they hadn't expected him to hitchhike across New Mexico. "Exercise is good for the brain."

"Then, run on a treadmill."

Running in place didn't work. After Alonso left Afghanistan and returned to the States, he'd believed he'd put all the death and destruction behind him. But more of the same had awaited him in the hospital. "You have any hobbies, kid?"

"My dad taught me how to use a shotgun. I like shooting at targets."

Alonso caught Luke staring into space. "It's tough losing both parents."

"It's not that hard. My dad was a drunk."

Alonso had only just met the teen but he felt a special kinship with Luke. Alonso's father had taken off before he'd entered kindergarten, and he wasn't even sure if his old man was still alive. Once in a while he wondered what his life would have been like if his father had stuck around.

Luke leaned against the side of the stall. "What about you? What did you do with your dad?"

"My father wasn't involved in my life."

"Did you do stuff with your mom?"

"Not really. My mom worked two jobs. It was mostly just me and my sisters."

"Did you guys fight all the time?"

"No."

Luke laughed. "Yeah, right. You were best friends."

"There were times when my sisters drove me nuts and I wanted to pick fights with them, but I didn't."

"Why not?"

"One of them has asthma and if she gets upset she can't breathe." Alonso lost count of the times he or his mother had dialed 911 when Lea had trouble breathing. If they'd had health insurance his sister might have gotten the medicine and inhalers she'd needed to stay healthy, but too often her prescriptions went unfilled because there wasn't any money to pay for them.

"That must have sucked," Luke said.

What had sucked was being forced to stay home from school and take care of Lea, because his mother couldn't miss work. After a while the school refused to excuse his absences and had expelled him.

"How old is your sister?" Alonso asked.

"Twenty-six. She thinks she can tell me what to do all the time."

"Are you talking about me?"

Alonso glanced over his shoulder, surprised Hannah had sneaked up on them. He hadn't heard her footsteps on the gravel drive.

"It's true," Luke said. "You bully me all the time."

"Hey, I'm your guardian. I have to ride herd on you, or you'll end up in a heap of trouble one day."

Hoping to prevent an argument, Alonso said, "We're finished with the stalls. What other chores need to be done?"

"Can you drive a tractor?" she asked.

Luke rolled his eyes. "She wants you to cut the hay."

"If it doesn't get cut soon, the cooler night temperatures will cause mold to grow and ruin the crop."

"I can handle a tractor," Alonso said. He'd had the opportunity to drive different military vehicles while stationed in Afghanistan—how hard could a tractor be?

"We've got a couple hours of daylight left. Enough time to cut half the field."

"Sure."

"I'll hook the side rake up to the tractor. I can follow you in the baler." She glanced at her brother. "I need you to stack the bales as they exit the baler."

"Whatever." Luke marched off.

"I can put up with your gnarly attitude any day as long as you're willing to help." Hannah followed her brother out of the barn. Fifteen minutes later, the three of them stood in the driveway next to the equipment.

"I'll ride with Alonso in the tractor," Hannah said. "Luke, you drive the baler out to the field. After I show Alonso which direction to cut the hay, I'll take over driving the baler while Luke stacks the hay."

An hour later, Alonso was making his third turn around the perimeter of the field. Hannah followed at a distance, Luke stacking the square bales in neat sections on the flatbed.

The work was monotonous but peaceful. Out here he didn't have to worry about someone blowing himself up or a young gangbanger staggering into the ER with a bullet in his chest. Alonso checked the side mirrors and saw Luke signaling him. When the baler caught up, Hannah got out from behind the wheel and approached the tractor.

"We're losing daylight, so we'll stop here. Thanks again for helping us out this afternoon."

"I enjoyed it."

"You're telling the truth, aren't you?"

"Why would I lie?"

Hannah shouted over her shoulder, "Hey, Luke! Alonso likes driving the tractor."

"He's crazy!"

She smiled. "Oh, well, it was worth a shot."

Alonso's breath caught in his throat. This was the first time Hannah's eyes sparkled, and he caught himself returning her smile.

"We'll leave the baler out here and take the tractor to the house. Let's head home and eat." Hannah drove while Luke and Alonso crowded in beside her.

"You don't really like cutting hay," Luke said.

"Sure I do."

"I bet it's not as exciting as being in the military."

"Depends on your definition of *excitement*." Alonso despised movies that glorified war and made superheroes out of men and women who were ordinary people marching off to work each day. "But I get where all this might become a little boring if you grew up with it."

Luke poked Hannah's shoulder. "My sister loves working seven days a week all year long. But I don't want to be a rancher."

Hannah kept her eyes on the path. The rigid set of her shoulders told Alonso that she'd had this conversation before with her brother.

Alonso sympathized with the teen. He doubted Luke had had much excitement in his life. His parents were no longer alive and his sister was all work and no play.

Hannah parked the tractor by the barn. "We're having leftovers for supper."

"Your chili's gross." Luke stuck his finger in his mouth and made a gagging noise. "My sister's cooking sucks."

"If you don't like the chili, then make your own meal."

"Why don't I take everyone out to eat?" Alonso said.

There had to be a fast-food restaurant within ten miles of the ranch.

"You're not buying us dinner," Hannah said.

"I don't care what you guys do. I'm microwaving a frozen pizza." Luke hopped down from the tractor.

"Do you like your chili over rice or plain?" she asked Alonso.

"I'd rather take you out to eat. Save the chili for tomorrow."

Hannah fought a smile. "Luke's being a stinker. My cooking isn't that bad."

Alonso laughed. "Let me take you out."

"There's a restaurant down the road with a great view."

"That works for me."

"You're welcome to use the shower in the house." She walked off and it took a whole lot more effort than it should have to pull his gaze from her swaying hips. It was a toss-up as to whether he was more excited about getting clean or sharing dinner with a pretty girl.

Chapter 3

This isn't a date.

No matter how many times the voice in her head repeated the sentence Hannah couldn't stop feeling a little bit excited about going out to dinner with Alonso. She hadn't been on a date since she'd returned Seth's engagement ring two years ago. She'd been so busy with the ranch and chasing after Luke that she hadn't had the time or the energy to care about her love life.

Sadly, she'd enjoyed the three short months she'd been engaged to Seth—before she'd discovered his motive for marrying her. Seth had been her first serious relationship and he'd spoiled her. He'd taken her dancing, to the movies and brought her flowers for no reason, and she'd soaked up the attention. For a brief while she'd believed she'd found the perfect partner to go through life with. But it hadn't been real for Seth. He'd led her on and had made a fool of her. The experience had left a bitter taste in her mouth and Hannah wasn't eager to rush into another relationship. But there was nothing wrong with enjoying an evening with a good-looking man.

It's not smart to go off alone with a man you barely know.

Gut instinct said Alonso was harmless. He was a surgeon—surgeons healed people; they didn't hurt them. Besides, she could take care of herself.

She ran a brush through her long hair, then divided the strands into three sections and braided it. After buttoning her Western blouse and pulling on a pair of fresh jeans, she slipped her feet into cowboy boots, then spritzed perfume on her neck and studied her reflection in the mirror. She looked nice but not desperate. *Good.*

When she entered the kitchen, Luke was eating pizza at the table. "I want to get my car from Connor's."

She thought of reminding her brother that the car belonged to her and she only let him borrow it, but she didn't want to start another fight. "I'll drive you out there tomorrow."

"Can I do something later if I can get a friend to pick me up?"

"No." Was he crazy? "I want you to stay in and go to bed early." He needed a good night's sleep, because tomorrow they had to finish cutting the hay and repair the broken fence.

"Where are you and Alonso going to eat?"

"I'm taking him to the Red Bluff Diner." That Luke gave up arguing with her over going out with his friends was odd, but maybe he was more exhausted than he let on. "Keep your phone handy in case I need to get hold of you."

The creak of the bathroom door drifted down the hallway, then a moment later Alonso entered the kitchen, wearing clean jeans and cowboy boots—not the hiking boots he'd had on earlier. His tight black T-shirt showed off his muscular chest, and a hint of his tattoo peeked below the hem of his sleeve. And the beard was gone. Now he looked more like a medical doctor—the ones you saw in TV shows and movies. The only real-life doctor she knew was seventy-four-year-old Doc Snyder, who ran the clinic in town.

Hannah took the pen and notepad she kept on the counter and handed it to Alonso. "Would you mind writing down your cell phone number in case we have an emergency?" She ignored Luke's snort.

"Sure." He did as she asked, then he removed his wallet from his back pocket. "Keep this business card." He handed it to Hannah.

Juan Alarez Ranch For Boys.

Alonso grinned at Luke. "If we don't come back, call that number. Riley Fitzgerald's been a friend of mine for a long time."

"I told you my sister thinks you're a serial killer," Luke said.

Hannah rolled her eyes. "If you two are finished making fun of me, then—"

Alonso's cell phone rang and he checked the number. "Speak of the devil… Will you excuse me a minute? I have to take this call.

"Hey, Riley." Alonso retreated down the hallway and stopped by the front door.

"Didn't I warn you about ignoring Maria's phone calls?" Riley chuckled.

"I'm sorry. I've been busy."

"Apparently not too busy. Maria phoned the hospital and they said you'd taken a leave of absence. What's going on?"

Alonso swallowed a groan. "Everything's fine. I needed a break from the ER, that's all."

"Why don't you visit the ranch? We could use an extra hand with the boys."

"Thanks for the invite. I'll think about it." With all the bad in the world, Riley's call reminded Alonso that there were a few good people left who gave a damn about helping the less fortunate.

"Don't know if Maria told you or not, but we built a new medical clinic at the ranch."

"Don't tell me she's putting Band-Aids on the kids in addition to teaching school."

"Not anymore. We hired a full-time nurse. As a matter of fact, she's married to Cruz."

"Cruz is out—" Alonso glanced down the hallway, making sure he was alone "—of prison?"

"I would have mentioned it sooner, but I thought Cruz might want to be the one to tell you and Victor."

He wasn't surprised his friend hadn't contacted him to let him know he'd been paroled. Alonso had visited Cruz in prison before he'd headed off to college. He was ashamed to admit that he hadn't thought of Cruz often during the past twelve years—he'd been too wrapped up in his own life and struggles.

"Cruz and Sara married a month ago. He's mentoring the boys and teaching them rodeo."

"Sounds as if things are looking up for him." Alonso wished his life was going as well.

"He'd love to see you."

Alonso wasn't so sure about that. He'd only heard about the night Cruz had been arrested, and he still felt guilty that he hadn't gone along with him and Vic when they'd confronted the gang leader who'd been banging Vic's sister. Maybe if he had been there, he could have done something to defuse the situation and Cruz wouldn't have ended up in prison.

"What are you doing now?" Riley asked.

"Sightseeing." That was the truth. Since leaving Albuquerque he'd seen a lot of *rural* sights.

"You sure everything's all right?"

Riley had the uncanny ability to sense when Alonso or one of his friends was lying. "I'm fine."

"If you say so. Be sure to give Maria a call soon."

"I will. Tell her I said hello."

"Will do. Keep in touch."

Alonso disconnected the call, then returned to the kitchen. "See you later, Luke." He held the door open for Hannah, then they walked to the pickup. "The days are warm but the nights are growing cooler," he said.

"I wonder when we'll get our first dusting of snow?"

That was the extent of their conversation until they reached the highway and curiosity got the best of Alonso. "You and Luke don't have any other siblings or relatives to help with the ranch?"

"It's just the two of us."

"I have two sisters. Carla lives in Phoenix. She's

been divorced twice but doesn't have any kids. Lea's married with two boys. Recently my mother moved to Santa Fe to be closer to Lea and the grandkids."

"And your father?"

"He took off when I was little."

"Do you keep in touch with your sisters?"

"We talk every few months." He'd phoned his sisters when he'd returned from Afghanistan but had passed up their invites to visit. He wasn't ready to answer their questions about his time in the military.

Hannah slowed the truck when she passed a fifty-five-mile-per-hour speed sign. "Red Bluff Diner isn't far from here." The road forked and she drove west. "I recommend the bison steak fajitas."

"What about regular beef?"

"They have that, too, but it's not as tasty." She smiled. "Try the bison."

"I'll think about it."

"Mind if I ask you a personal question?"

"Go ahead," he said.

"What's up with the hitchhiking? It's not every day you come across a trauma surgeon thumbing his way through New Mexico."

"I needed a break from all the chaos in the ER." He winked when she looked at him. "They don't call it *trauma* for nothing."

"I thought all you military guys loved working under pressure. Taking a long walk can't be near as exciting as saving lives."

Saving lives only mattered if the people remained alive. "I like the fast-paced atmosphere of the ER, but the constant stress drains your energy."

"How long do you plan to keep walking?"

"Don't know yet." Long enough to clear his head of all the bad memories stored in his brain.

She flashed a teasing smile. "You should have driven, then you'd see more of the countryside."

"I saw enough countryside in Afghanistan to last me a lifetime." Then he'd returned to the barrio in Albuquerque—another war zone, just different people and different reasons for killing each other. "What about you?" he said. "Did you always want to be a rancher?"

"I wanted to go to college, but things were crazy at home and someone had to be there for Luke."

It occurred to Alonso that Hannah had been taking care of her brother most of her life. "What would you have studied if you'd gone to school?"

"I'm not sure. Maybe history."

"Seriously?"

"Go ahead and laugh. I have no idea what kind of job I would have gotten with a history degree but I would have enjoyed taking all those classes."

"I never pictured a woman being a rancher."

"I never thought I'd be managing a ranch, either. But life throws you curveballs, and when I was forced to assume more and more responsibility, I grew attached to the land and the animals. And now I can't see myself doing anything else."

Hannah steered the pickup into a gravel lot and parked. The diner sat on the edge of a bluff overlooking a valley. Spotlights shone across the landscape, which was made up of broken mesas.

"Nice view," he said.

"We'll ask for a table with a view."

When they entered the establishment, an older woman in Native American clothing greeted them. "Hello, Hannah."

"Betsy." Hannah nodded to her dinner date. "This is my friend Alonso. Betsy's father owns the restaurant."

"You've got a million-dollar view here," he said.

"Follow me." Betsy led the way to a table by the windows.

Alonso held out a chair for Hannah, then sat across from her. Betsy filled their water glasses and asked if they'd like to view the drink menu. Hannah ordered a glass of red wine and Alonso a beer. "It feels as if we're sitting on the edge of a cliff."

"Too bad it's dark," she said. "On a clear day you can see the Sandia Mountains from here." When Betsy delivered their drinks, Hannah raised her wineglass. "To helpful strangers."

He tapped the neck of his beer bottle against her glass. Hannah was the first person in longer than he remembered who he felt relaxed with—unlike his co-workers, who were high-strung and neurotic.

Hannah signaled Betsy over to their table. "Alonso has never eaten bison. I thought we'd try an appetizer first."

"The nachos?" Betsy asked.

Hannah nodded. "I promise," she said to Alonso. "These will be the best nachos you've ever eaten."

Ten minutes later Betsy delivered the appetizer and Alonso experienced his first taste of bison. "This is good."

"Told you so." Hannah licked her fingertip and

Alonso couldn't tear his gaze from her mouth. Her lips spread in a smile.

"You've got a dreamy look on your face," she said. "What are you thinking?"

"I'm thinking that I'd like to—" *kiss you* "—order the bison burger."

"That's what I'm having."

A surge of testosterone swept through Alonso's bloodstream. He hadn't experienced such sharp arousal since he couldn't remember when. He'd gone on a few dates with nurses when he'd joined the hospital staff, but grew tired of always talking about the things that had happened on their shift—none of them had a life outside of the hospital.

"Did you like the nachos?" Betsy asked Alonso when she picked up the empty platter.

"They were fantastic," he said.

"We'll both have the bison burger," Hannah said. "Make mine medium well, please."

"The same for me." Alonso handed Betsy his menu.

The burgers came out a few minutes later along with a special house-made barbecue sauce. After his first bite, he moaned. "I'll never turn my nose up again when anyone mentions bison meat."

Over dinner he and Hannah chatted about places they wanted to visit in the future. Favorite sports teams—Hannah was a big football fan and cheered for the Dallas Cowboys. They chatted about TV shows and movies—even the latest books they'd read. Not one time did the subject of gangs, murder, shootings or rape come up as it did when he socialized with the hospital staff. Hannah was a breath of fresh air.

"I'm glad you almost ran me over today."

Her eyes rounded and he laughed. "It's been a while since I've had such a charming dinner date."

Pink color stained her cheeks. "I haven't been out for supper in way too long."

Over an hour later, Betsy delivered the check to their table. Alonso paid in cash and left a hefty tip. He didn't want to return to the ranch and end the evening—not when he knew he had to leave in the morning. "Is there somewhere we could stop for a nightcap…maybe dance?" he asked when they left the restaurant.

"There's a dive bar up the road."

"Let's go." He held open the truck door for Hannah and they took off.

Dive was too nice a word to describe the double-wide Hannah parked in front of five minutes later. A pair of motorcycles and a 1995 Cadillac Eldorado sat outside Maloney's.

"You sure this is a bar?" he asked.

"I'm sure."

Once they were inside, Alonso was pleasantly surprised. The owner had torn down the interior walls, creating a large open space. The bikers and an older man sat at the five-stool bar to the right of the door. The rest of the room was filled with mismatched tables and chairs. A jukebox sat in the corner and a sign above a door at the opposite end of the trailer advertised a unisex bathroom. Neon beer signs and No Smoking posters decorated the walls.

"What would you like to drink?" he asked.

"Rico only serves beer or whiskey," she said. "I better stick to beer."

Hannah walked off to pick out a place to sit. He paid for their drink order, then carried the beers to the table.

"Thanks." She swallowed a large gulp before setting her bottle down. Her eyes darted around the room. Maybe she was nervous.

"When was the last time you went out for a drink?" He really wanted to know when she'd last been on a date.

"I can't remember. Do you go out often?"

"Sometimes after a long shift, the staff will head over to a bar near the hospital." He'd tagged along the first few times but after that he'd bowed out, preferring to unwind in his quiet apartment in front of the TV.

"Blue Eyes" came on the jukebox, and Alonso said, "Willie's singing your song." He took Hannah by the hand and led her to the dance floor, where he pulled her close. She smelled sweet and fit in his arms perfectly. When she leaned into him, his body hardened at the contact. He thought about putting a few more inches between them, but Hannah snuggled closer, her pelvis brushing against his hardness. He buried his nose in her hair, thinking he could hold her like this for hours— just the two of them with Willie singing in their ears.

"Well, well, well."

Alonso stiffened and Hannah stepped away from him.

"What are you doing here, Seth?" she asked.

"I saw your pickup out front and thought you were drinking alone." He nodded to Alonso. "Who's this guy?"

"Alonso, this is my neighbor Seth Markham. He and his father own the Los Pinos Ranch."

Seth squeezed Alonso's hand. "I'm also Hannah's ex-fiancé."

Interesting that Hannah had left that tidbit of information out during their dinner conversation. "Nice to meet you."

"What business brings you to Paradise?" Markham asked.

"Just passing through." Alonso slid his arm around Hannah's waist. Markham's eyes narrowed—for a guy who no longer had a claim on Hannah, he acted jealous.

Alonso wasn't in the business of provoking people but Markham rubbed him the wrong way. He moved his hand from Hannah's waist to right beneath her breast and swallowed a chuckle when Markham's face grew red.

"How long are you *just passing through* for?" Markham asked.

Alonso stared at Hannah. "Haven't decided yet."

"We were about to call it a night," Hannah said.

Markham followed them out. "Where are you staying, Marquez?"

"At the ranch," Hannah said, then took Alonso's hand in hers and they walked across the parking lot.

"I'll drive," Alonso said. Hannah offered the keys after he helped her into the passenger seat. He slid behind the wheel and took off. When he glanced in the rearview mirror Markham was standing in the parking lot. "Your ex seemed surprised you were with another guy."

"Seth thinks he can change my mind about marrying him."

"You want to talk about it?"

She was embarrassed to admit how naive she'd been to believe Seth had really cared about her. Thank goodness he'd shown his true colors before they'd walked down the aisle.

"A week after I broke off our engagement, I saw Seth with another woman." On the heels of her anger came hurt then relief. In the end she knew she was better off without him, but it stung that Seth had only been using her. "I was on my way to get Luke from school when I saw him walk out of Maloney's with a redhead clinging to his arm. On the drive back through town I spotted his truck at a motel." She shook her head. "I may be a simple country girl, but even I know the only reason you check into a motel at three o'clock in the afternoon is to have sex."

"You're better off without him."

Hannah offered him a smile. "If your medical career doesn't work out, you'd make a good cheerleader."

Conversation ceased when Alonso turned onto the dirt road that led to the ranch. He parked by the house but made no move to get out of the truck. "If my staying tonight is going to cause problems for you…"

"By problems you mean gossip?"

"I don't want people to think badly of you because you allowed a hitchhiker to spend the night on your property."

"You're not a hitchhiker. You're a surgeon." *And a darn good-looking one at that.* "I don't care what anyone says about me." Besides, her family had been the topic of gossip for years in Paradise. Alonso would give them something new to chat about.

She glanced at the dark house. "Luke must be in bed." For once he'd taken her advice.

"Hangovers will do that to you." Seconds ticked by, then Alonso reached across the seat and brushed a strand of loose hair from her face. She didn't want the night to end. Didn't want to leave his side.

"Alonso?"

"What?"

"Do you ever get lonely?" Until she'd sat across the table from him at the restaurant, Hannah hadn't consciously acknowledged the depth of her loneliness.

"Yes." His whispered answer made her heart pound.

This is crazy. You hardly know the man.

She couldn't argue with the voice in her head, but the strength to resist a night in Alonso's arms had fled the instant he'd pulled her close on the dance floor. "I don't want to be alone tonight," she whispered.

He slid his hand around the back of her neck. "I don't want to be alone, either."

And then he kissed her.

Chapter 4

Alonso squeezed Hannah's hand as they walked away from the pickup. A barn wasn't the most romantic place a guy could make love to a woman, but tonight wasn't about romance. When Hannah had looked into his eyes on the dance floor at Maloney's, he'd recognized the pleading glimmer in her gaze. He'd seen the same haunting look in patients who'd stared up at him in pain right before they went into surgery. Hannah didn't want to be alone tonight, and he didn't care to examine why *he* didn't want to be alone, either. He and Hannah were consenting adults and there was nothing wrong in reaching out to each other for comfort.

"There's a cot and blanket back here," she said, leading him past the horse stalls. When they reached the storage room, she flipped on the light.

Alonso took one look at the narrow cot and said, "Not here." He grabbed the blanket and they walked over to the ladder leaning against the hayloft. "You first."

He followed her up, making sure she didn't slip, the swish-sway of her fanny taunting him. They spread the blanket over a soft pallet of hay, then sank to their knees.

The loft was warm and the earthy smell combined with Hannah's sexy perfume made Alonso's head spin. He removed the band at the end of her braid, then loosened the strands until the kinky tresses cascaded over her shoulder. He brought a handful of her hair, still damp from her shower, up to his face and breathed deeply. He had no idea why their paths had crossed, but Hannah was good, kind and sweet, and in her arms he knew he'd forget all the bad in the world that stalked him—at least for a night.

He opened his mouth to tell her how much he wanted her, but she pressed her finger against his lips and shook her head. The silent message in her eyes begged him not to make any promises. Tonight was all she wanted from him.

They undressed each other—one button, one zipper at a time. Her boots and jeans, then his. He slid her shirt off her shoulders, kissing each inch of exposed skin. The material bunched at her wrist and with her arms trapped by her sides, he trailed his finger over the swirls of lace on her bra. Her breath caught, then her eyelids closed. She moaned when he cupped her breast and the sensual sound released a wave of testosterone through his body.

"Wait." Her fingers clamped down on his wrist.

His heart thudded loudly in his ears, and he worried she'd changed her mind. She got to her feet and walked across the loft, then unlatched the door and pushed it open. Light spilled across the blanket, and when she returned and stretched out beside him, her skin shimmered in the sliver glow of the moon.

He removed her bra, tossing it somewhere behind him. He took his time pleasuring her, nibbling, licking the soft mounds. Her fingers sneaked inside the waistband of his briefs, robbing him of what little self-control he possessed.

Hannah might be sweet but she knew what she needed from him and he intended to deliver. They removed the rest of their clothing and he kissed her, deep and slow. Arms and legs became tangled as they lost themselves in the magic of the night.

A dull pain shot up Alonso's arm, dragging him from a deep slumber. He didn't have the energy to open his eyes and his foggy brain struggled to register the weight pressing against him. The heaviness wiggled and a soft sigh reached his ears, then he remembered—Hannah. He slid his arm free from beneath her, his fingers tingling as the circulation returned to his hand. She snuggled closer, sliding her leg between his thighs, and he caressed her back, trailing his fingers over her spine and sexy backside.

He closed his eyes, believing Hannah was a miracle drug. He'd hooked up with a couple of women after he'd returned from Afghanistan and neither one had made him feel renewed. Hannah's touch had flushed out the ugly side of humanity and replaced it with a sense of hope and peace.

He'd become a trauma surgeon because he wanted to save people's lives—but medical school hadn't prepared him for the toll that all the violent injuries would take on his soul. The tragedies followed him home after his shift, sneaking into his bed and haunting his sleep. But tonight, after Hannah had drifted off in his arms, he hadn't dreamed at all.

He closed his eyes, feeling serene. Content. Maybe he hadn't needed to walk a thousand miles to clear his head—maybe he'd just needed to walk until he'd found Hannah.

Nothing good lasts forever.

With that thought in mind, he kissed her temple, hoping to rouse her from sleep. He needed her again.

She scratched her toe against his calf. "You're awake."

"Are you?"

She rolled on top of him, her hair falling across his face. "I am now." She pressed kisses to his nose, forehead and chin. He chuckled.

"What's so funny?"

"I'm not used to a woman taking the lead." He felt her smile against his neck.

"I'm not a woman who waits for a man to rescue her." She playfully bit his shoulder. "I can do anything a man can and then some."

She'd get no argument from him. He held her face and brought her mouth to his. "You can take the lead anytime." He gave himself over to Hannah and her healing touch. This time their lovemaking was slow and gentle. The stars were no longer visible in the sky when he closed his eyes and drifted into another dreamless sleep.

When Hannah woke in the hayloft, she was alone. She stretched on the blanket, twitching at the bits of hay poking her skin. Then she smiled—a smile that blossomed deep inside her.

Alonso had been just what the doctor ordered.

Her smile grew wider. She knew what she'd done with him had been out of character, but if she was going to have a one-night stand, she couldn't have picked a better man. She could justify her actions all she wanted—she was stressed out, lonely, whatever. But the truth was, if she'd met Alonso when her life hadn't been so crazy, she'd still have been wowed by him.

Hannah didn't completely understand the attraction—they had nothing in common. He was city. She was country. He was college educated. She wasn't. He saved lives. She was just trying to save her brother. He led an exciting life. She didn't. But none of that had mattered last night.

All good things had to come to an end, and even though she'd rather spend the day in the loft with Alonso, she had chores to do. She dressed, then hurried from the barn. When she entered the house, the smell of frying bacon greeted her nose. Alonso stood in front of the stove, stirring a mountain of scrambled eggs in her cast-iron skillet. Their gazes clashed, then his brown eyes roamed over her disheveled state and his lips curved in a smile.

"You have a piece of hay stuck in your hair."

She brushed her snarly tresses out of her eyes and searched for something to say.

"I didn't want to wake Luke to take a shower in his bathroom," he said. "So I used yours."

"I'll be right down." She raced upstairs, took a quick shower, then changed clothes. On her way back to the kitchen she stopped outside Luke's door and knocked. She waited for his usual "go away," but this morning she got no response. She opened the door and poked her head inside the room. His bed was still made and his cell phone sat on the dresser. Where had he gone? Better yet, how long had he been gone?

"Did you see Luke this morning?" she asked when she returned to the kitchen.

"Isn't he sleeping?" Alonso divided the eggs between three plates.

"No. It doesn't look as if he slept in his bed." Guilt tore through Hannah. If she hadn't been wrapped up in Alonso last night—literally—she'd have gone into the house and checked on Luke when they'd returned from Maloney's.

"Have you tried his cell phone?"

"He left it on the dresser." A ploy Luke used when he didn't want Hannah knowing where he was. "I bet a friend picked him up last night." She doubted it had been Connor, which left one other suspect—Ben Nichols.

"Have you checked your phone for messages?" Alonso asked.

"Good idea." She took her cell from her purse and entered the pass code, then breathed a sigh of relief. "Someone left a voice mail." As she listened to the recording, her legs grew weak and she sank into the chair at the table.

"Hannah, this is Sheriff Miller. Come into the station when you get this. I have Luke here."

Dear God, what kind of trouble had her brother got into this time? She'd warned him to straighten up, but had he listened to her? *No.* She set the phone down. "That was Sheriff Miller."

Alonso's eyebrows lifted.

"Luke's at the jail."

Alonso moved behind her chair and massaged her shoulders. The tender act brought a lump to her throat. "Is he okay?"

"I assume so, or Sheriff Miller would have said something." If only Alonso's gentle touch could wash away her fears. Fear that she was failing Luke. She wanted so badly for her brother to succeed—why was he rebelling?

"Did the sheriff say what happened?"

"No, but I'll find out soon." The eggs on the plate in front of her began to blur.

Alonso knelt next to her chair and tipped her chin until she looked him in the eye. "If you want, I'll go with you to see the sheriff."

Her gaze shifted to his duffel bag by the door. She was dragging Alonso into her problems again, but she was so tired of handling Luke on her own. "You wouldn't mind?"

"Let's go." He dumped the eggs back into the skillet, then slid the pan into the fridge.

Alonso drove and Hannah sat in the passenger seat, trying not to worry—fat chance. All she'd done the past two years was worry. If she hadn't let her ego get the best of her last night, they'd have stayed home and eaten chili and Luke wouldn't have been able to sneak out of the house.

Alonso parked in front of the jail and they went inside. Sandy—part-time secretary and part-time dispatcher—sat at her desk talking on the phone. She pointed to the sheriff's door, then cupped her hand over the mouthpiece. "He's expecting you."

When Hannah and Alonso entered the office, the sheriff set aside a file he'd been reading and stood. "Hannah." He eyed Alonso. "I don't believe I've seen you around town before."

Alonso shook hands with the lawman. "Alonso Marquez."

The sheriff's gaze swung to Hannah, and when she didn't offer an explanation for Alonso's presence, he said, "Have a seat." He cleared his throat. "Luke's in hot water."

Hannah swallowed hard and prayed her fear that she wouldn't always be able to save Luke's butt hadn't finally come true. "What did he do?"

"He didn't commit the crime but he was with the troublemakers who did."

"Crime?" The word squeaked past Hannah's lips.

"The convenience store was robbed at 2:00 a.m. this morning. Luke sat in the car while the other two boys held the clerk up at gunpoint."

Hannah gasped. She'd been prepared for petty theft or even slashing someone's tires, but not armed robbery. "What are the names of the boys?" And why weren't their parents here?

"The gun belonged to Kenny Potter. He and his buddy T. J. Templeton are both from Cañon City. High school dropouts with rap sheets a mile long."

She'd never met the boys and Luke had never mentioned their names, but she had a feeling they were responsible for her brother suddenly wanting to quit school. "Was anyone hurt?"

The sheriff shook his head. "Maybe it's time to call in social services, Hannah. I know you're trying your best, but Luke may be too much for you to handle alone."

No way would she allow her brother to be put in a group home or sent to live with a stranger.

"I had planned to phone you tomorrow to discuss another situation that came up with him, but now is as good a time as any."

Hannah braced herself for more bad news.

"Matt Connelly stopped by my office to chat on Friday."

Hannah looked at Alonso. "Mr. Connelly is the principal at the high school."

"Luke skipped classes again on Friday," the sheriff said.

She hadn't known. Usually the school sent out automated messages when students didn't show up and their absence hadn't been reported by a parent or guardian. Hannah had never got the message.

"That makes eleven days in two months."

"Eleven?" She only knew about six.

"Matt said the school quit contacting you to schedule conferences, because you never returned their calls."

"I have a ranch to run, but I'm more than happy to speak with someone on the phone."

"That's neither here nor there." The sheriff shrugged. "Matt's hands were tied, Hannah. He had to expel Luke."

Hannah felt nauseous. "Expelled for…a week or two?"

"The remainder of the semester."

"But he'll fall behind the other kids in his grade."

"Some students need more time, Hannah. You and your brother have had a lot to deal with the past few years. People are sympathetic, but if Luke doesn't turn the corner soon, he'll end up in juvenile detention." The sheriff walked out from behind his desk. "I'll get him."

Hannah felt a headache coming on and rubbed her brow. The school and the sheriff blamed her for Luke's wild ways—but that wasn't fair. Luke was sixteen—old enough to know what he was doing. Old enough to know right from wrong. She couldn't beat him into making better choices. He had to do it on his own.

Alonso squeezed her hand. "It'll be okay, Hannah. The main thing is Luke isn't hurt and no one was injured in the robbery."

Hannah clung to his words, wanting with all her heart to believe things would be okay, but she felt as if her world was spinning out of control and she couldn't do anything to stop it.

When Luke walked into the sheriff's office and flashed his I-don't-give-a-crap scowl at Hannah, she had to bite her lip to keep from laying into him. Then he looked at Alonso's sober face and uncertainty filled her brother's eyes. There were a thousand things she wanted to say, but they'd wait until they had more privacy.

"I told Luke that he's used up his last chance. If he gets into trouble again, he'll be processed through the juvenile court system." The sheriff's threat appeared to have little effect on her brother, who stared at the wall, looking bored out of his mind.

"Thank you, Sheriff Miller." Hannah left the office, Luke trailing her and Alonso bringing up the rear. They piled into the pickup, and no one said a word when Hannah drove across the street and parked in front of the convenience store. "Let's go, Luke."

"Go where?"

"Inside to apologize to Mr. Washburn."

Luke grumbled but left the backseat.

Hannah handed Alonso her credit card. "Would you please fill the tank?"

He ignored the card. "I'll take care of it."

She didn't have any fight left in her to argue, so she let him pay for the gas.

"This is stupid," Luke said.

"No. Hanging out with losers and trying to rob a store is stupid!" They entered the business and walked up to the counter. When the manager spotted them, he stiffened. "Mr. Washburn, my brother, Luke, has something he'd like to say to you."

Luke dropped his gaze and shuffled his feet. Hannah set a hand against his back and pushed him closer to the counter. "I'm sorry about last night," he said.

"You're better than those boys you were with, Luke."

Her brother nodded, his face turning red. "I didn't know one of them had a gun."

"Guns kill people," Mr. Washburn said.

"I know."

"I promise you that Luke won't be hanging around those boys anymore." Hannah didn't know how she'd keep that promise but she'd find a way.

"That's good to know." The phone rang. "I need to answer that. Good luck."

Hannah would need all the luck she could get. They left the store, and instead of driving to the ranch, Hannah headed out to the Hendersons' to pick up the Civic. The family wasn't home but the keys had been left in the ignition. When Luke reached for the door handle, she said, "Alonso will drive the car home."

Luke didn't protest while she waited for Alonso to get behind the wheel of the Honda—a gift to Hannah from her father on her sixteenth birthday. She and Luke didn't speak until she parked in front of the house forty minutes later.

"I'll be in my room doing homework." Luke scrambled out of the backseat.

"Don't bother," she said.

His mouth slackened and his jaw dropped open. "You're always telling me to study."

"You were kicked out of school."

"What?"

"Principal Connelly informed the sheriff on Friday that he had to expel you because you've skipped too many days."

"Six is—"

"Try eleven."

Luke scowled.

"The principal will consider allowing you back into

school after the Christmas break. Until then you're a full-time ranch hand."

Luke spat a four-letter word, then rushed into the house, slamming the door behind him.

Alonso parked the car next to the pickup. "The change-oil indicator light is on," he said.

Knowing Luke, the light had been on for weeks. "I'll take care of it." Add an oil change to the list of a millions things to do. She opened the driver's-side door of the pickup.

"Where are you off to?" he asked.

Had he forgotten that he'd planned to leave today? "Don't you want a lift back to the highway?"

Alonso's gaze shifted between the dirt road and Hannah. He should leave—put Hannah, Luke and their problems behind him. So why did he feel such a strong urge to stay?

He wasn't surprised by his desire to help them, but he was surprised by his reluctance to leave Hannah. He'd just got a taste of her goodness, and the last thing he cared to do was hike down the road alone.

"I might have a way to help Luke," he said.

Hannah stood on the running board and stared across the roof of the pickup. "How's that?"

"I have connections with the people who run a ranch for troubled teens."

That sounded an awful lot like a group home for boys. "Where is it?"

"Not too far from here. It's called the Juan Alvarez Ranch for Boys. I gave you their card. The guy who runs the place was a former bronc rider. He and Maria helped me and a couple of friends when we were expelled from school."

Hannah's eyes widened. "You were expelled from school?"

"I had an interesting childhood." He grinned. "I can make a call to see if there's room for Luke."

As tempting as that sounded, Hannah couldn't let her brother go off to some boys' ranch without first checking it out. "Tell me again the name of the couple who run the place."

"Riley and Maria Fitzgerald." Alonso hadn't planned on spilling his whole life story to Hannah but she needed someone to help her with Luke. "When I was seventeen, Fitzgerald helped me and two of my friends by convincing a juvie judge to let us do community service at a ranch. While we were there, my high school teacher homeschooled us, and we earned our GEDs."

"There's a school on this ranch?"

"Yep. If Luke went, he wouldn't fall behind in his classes."

"It sounds perfect except for one thing. I doubt I can afford the cost."

"It's free. They're funded through private donations." Money from the Fitzgerald Kentucky Thoroughbred farm.

Hannah stared at the house and Alonso could almost read her mind. She was thinking she didn't stand at chance at preventing Luke from running off again and getting into trouble.

"I need to see this place first," she said.

"I'll ask if we can drive out there tomorrow."

She shut the truck door, then came around the hood

and stopped in front of him. "If things work out and they accept Luke, I won't have anyone to help me here."

He'd been hoping she'd ask him to stay. The only thing waiting for him at the end of the dirt road was miles of empty highway. "I'll hang around for a while." Her smile reassured him that he'd made the right decision.

"I'll go warm up breakfast," she said, "while you make that call."

Once Hannah disappeared inside the house, Alonso dialed Fitzgerald's number.

"Change your mind about coming for a visit?" Riley said.

"There's a kid who could use your help."

"Who?"

"His name is Luke Buck. Both his parents are deceased. His sister is his legal guardian, but she's having a heck of a time keeping him in line. He was just expelled from school for the rest of the semester."

"You know we never turn away a kid in need. I'll have Maria get a bed ready in the bunkhouse."

"Thanks, Riley."

"Plan on staying for a while when you come. Cruz will want a chance to catch up with you."

"Sure."

"When can we expect you?"

"Tomorrow."

"See you then."

Alonso shoved the phone into the pocket of his cargo pants and climbed the porch steps. Hannah met him in the doorway. "What did Mr. Fitzgerald say?"

"They're expecting Luke tomorrow."

"Thank you." Her voice cracked and he pulled her into his arms. If he wasn't careful he could get used to holding Hannah.

"It'll be okay. I promise that once you see this place you'll know Luke will be in good hands. When he comes home, he'll be a different kid."

"I hope so." She rested her forehead against his chest.

They stood for a long time, holding each other—Alonso needing her hug as much as she needed his.

Chapter 5

"I don't know why I have to go to this stupid ranch." Luke glared out the passenger window.

Hannah had talked at length with Luke the night before and he hadn't protested when she'd informed him that they were visiting the boys' ranch today. "I promised you that if you don't feel comfortable you don't have to stay." She expected an argument, but Luke turned his sullen face back to the window.

Maybe he was as exhausted as she was. They'd put in a full day's work after rising at the crack of dawn. They fed Buster and the bison, finished cutting the hay. And after storing the bales inside the barn they made temporary repairs to the broken fence—at least the bison wouldn't wander onto the Los Pinos Ranch while they were gone. By two in the afternoon, they'd showered and hit the road. They'd been driving a couple of hours when Alonso left the highway and turned onto a rural road.

"Here we are." Alonso pulled up to a massive gate with the words *Juan Alvarez Ranch for Boys* across the front. He rolled his window down and pressed the green talk button on the security box.

Maria Fitzgerald's voice came over the intercom. "Alvarez Ranch."

"Hey, teach, it's Alonso Marquez."

"Alonso! I can't wait to see you. Come up to the main house." The feminine voice sounded pleasant and Hannah was hopeful this place would be a good fit for her brother.

The iron gates swung open and Alonso drove in.

"Is this a boys' prison?"

"No, but many of the kids here have been involved with gangs, and they want to keep the place as secure as possible."

At the mention of gangs Hannah's positive attitude took a nosedive.

"So I'm hanging out with a bunch of gangbangers from the city?"

"Wait and see. You'll like it here."

Luke gripped the back of Hannah's headrest, leaned forward and spoke in her ear. "I'll get beat up."

"That kind of stuff doesn't happen here." Alonso changed the subject. "You said you were interested in rodeo."

"Yeah."

"One of the best saddle-bronc riders in the country works at this ranch."

"Who?"

"Cruz Rivera."

"Never heard of him," Luke said.

"That's because he rode in prison."

"I didn't know prisons had rodeos," Luke said.

Neither did Hannah.

"Rivera set all kinds of records."

The pickup drove along a steep incline, and when they reached the top, Hannah's breath caught at the sight below. A white two-story house with a wrap-around porch sat in the distance. There were three corrals near a large white barn and white fencing sectioned off parcels of land behind several buildings scattered across the property. Even from a distance, the place appeared well maintained. Alonso parked between a brand-new diesel truck and red sports car.

"Nice wheels." Luke got out and walked over to the Mustang.

The front door opened and two boys with dark auburn hair ran outside. They bounded down the steps and took off toward the barn. A woman with dark hair and an exasperated expression on her face stepped onto the porch. As soon as she spotted Alonso, she smiled and hurried toward him. Alonso met her halfway and gave her a bear hug. "It's good to see you, Maria."

"You look great," she said.

"This is Luke." He put his hand on the teen's shoulder. "And his sister, Hannah. They run the Blue Bison Ranch about a hundred and fifty miles southeast of here."

Hannah shook hands with Maria. "You have a lovely home."

"Thank you." Maria's gaze flicked between Hannah and Alonso, then her smile widened.

Hannah worried that Maria believed there was something going on between her and Alonso. There wasn't. Well, there was but it wasn't... *Never mind.*

"Whose car is that?" Luke nodded to the Mustang.

"Mine." Maria winked at Alonso. "Riley thinks I need to let loose once in a while."

"Doesn't surprise me," Alonso said.

"Luke, there are thirty-seven boys here. I'm sure you'll find a few to make friends with."

Luke didn't appear impressed by the information and Hannah worried he wouldn't give the ranch a fair shot.

"Speaking of boys." Alonso nodded to the redheaded kids playing on the swings with a little girl. "The twins are growing up fast."

Twins? Hannah shuddered. She couldn't imagine having a child anytime soon. Her brother was all she could handle at the moment.

"They're a handful," Maria said. "The little girl is Cruz's stepdaughter, Dani. Did Riley tell you that Cruz's wife, Sara, is a pediatric nurse?" Maria turned to Hannah. "We now have an official health clinic on the property."

"That's great." Hannah was relieved to know that if Luke got injured he'd be in good hands.

"I made up a bed for you in the bunkhouse, Luke. You'll find a backpack filled with school supplies on your bunk."

"Luke brought his textbooks with him," Hannah said.

"Great. I'll chat with Luke's teachers and get his assignments for the remainder of the semester."

"School sucks," Luke mumbled.

Hannah held her breath, expecting Maria to reprimand her brother but the older woman spoke in a calm voice that drew Luke's attention. "We don't have a lot of rules here. But the ones we do have are enforced. You have to go to school each day and you have to complete your lessons. After that you're expected to do your assigned chores. Once those are done, you're free to spend the rest of your day however you want."

That didn't seem like such a bad deal, but Luke didn't agree. "There's nothing to do here."

Maria pointed across the property, where a cowboy walked a horse out of the barn. "Most of the boys here learn rodeo in their free time."

"Is that Cruz?" Alonso asked.

"You won't find a better rodeo instructor than Cruz," Maria said.

Hannah was too far away to make out the man's features, but he walked with a confident swagger.

"Alonso, why don't you introduce Luke and Hannah to Mr. Rivera?" Maria checked her watch. "Dinner will be served in an hour."

"I appreciate the offer to stay for dinner but I'm afraid we have to get back to the Blue Buffalo," Hannah said. "There's no one watching the ranch."

"Well, it was nice meeting you. We'll take good care of Luke. Feel free to call anytime to check up on him."

"Thank you," Hannah said.

Maria returned to the house and Hannah and Luke followed Alonso down to the corral. They stopped a few feet from the pen and listened to Cruz give riding instructions to a boy younger than Luke. Hannah noticed her brother paid attention to every word. Luke might pretend he wasn't interested in the ranch, but Hannah could feel his excitement about having an opportunity to practice rodeo.

The boy climbed atop the bronc, then Cruz stepped back and the chute door opened. The horse leaped into action and Luke moved closer to the pen, his eyes glued to the bronc and rider.

Hannah watched her brother soak in the action and her heart hurt for him. They'd been so angry with each other for so long and she hated that they were always at odds. But she didn't know how to help him. He was sixteen—almost a man—but in her heart he'd always be the little boy who'd been overlooked by his parents. Feeling sorry for Luke had only made things worse when he rebelled. Hannah accepted part of the blame for the situation Luke found himself in. She should have been tougher on him. But it was going to hurt her more than Luke to have to leave him here.

"Watch your hips, Joey! Pull back! Pull back!"

Joey managed to hang on even though he was slipping to the side.

"Look for an opening!" Cruz leaned forward, his body strung tight as if he was the one riding the bronc. "There it is!"

The kid launched himself off the horse and landed on his right shoulder, then rolled to his feet and ran for the rails.

"Good job! You rode like crap, but you nailed the dismount."

Joey flashed a cocky grin. "You wanna challenge me to a ride-off, Mr. Rivera?"

"You wish, kid. Go get ready for supper."

"Yes, sir."

As Luke watched the exchange between Cruz and the teen, the cockiness disappeared from his expression. Maybe her brother would return to the Blue Buffalo with more respect for Hannah—wouldn't that be nice?

"Been a long time, amigo," Alonso said.

Cruz jumped off the rails and shook hands with Alonso. "At least a few lifetimes," he said. A stilted silence followed, then he nodded to Luke. "Who've you got here?"

"Luke Buck, Cruz Rivera."

Cruz shook Luke's hand. "Welcome to the ranch."

Hannah stepped forward. "I'm Luke's sister, Hannah."

"Luke's staying here until Christmas," Alonso said.

Cruz nodded to a rectangular structure behind the barn. "My guess is that Maria already has your bed set up in the bunkhouse. Why don't you go check out your new digs?"

"Sure." Luke looked at Hannah, his brown eyes wide. "Am I gonna see you before Christmas?"

Hannah glanced at Cruz. She wasn't sure if the ranch had rules about visitors.

"Maria usually puts on a big Thanksgiving feast and invites the families of all the kids," Cruz said.

Hannah smiled. "It looks as though I'll be back in a few weeks to see how you're doing." If the ranch wasn't helping Luke by then, she'd bring him home with her.

Luke gave Hannah a hug and Hannah felt her eyes tear up. There was so much good left inside her brother—he just had to find his way back to the kid he used to be. "Behave," she said.

Luke turned to Alonso. "Are you gonna be here for Thanksgiving, too?"

"I don't know," Alonso said.

Hannah expected he'd be long gone from the Blue Bison by then.

"Good luck, kid."

After Luke walked off, both men glanced at Hannah and she guessed they wanted to talk in private. "It was nice to meet you, Cruz." She smiled at Alonso. "I'll wait in the pickup."

As soon as Hannah was out of earshot, Alonso spoke. "Maria said you're married now."

Cruz flashed a full-blown grin—Alonso couldn't remember ever seeing a genuine expression of happiness on his friend's face. "I met Sara right after I was released from prison. Her father owns a restaurant in Papago Springs."

"I hear that's her daughter playing with the twins." Alonso nodded to the swings.

"Dani's father was a doctor who worked in a health clinic in the barrio."

"Was?"

"He took a bullet to the chest when he got caught in the middle of a gang fight involving the Los Locos."

The very gang Alonso and his friends had been pledging before they'd been expelled from high school. Alonso had wanted nothing to do with gangs but they were a necessity in the barrio. Gangs provided protection, and for those really bad off, a place to crash and food to eat.

"I work in the ER at the university hospital. I've seen more than my share of gangbangers come in all shot up."

"You made it through med school. Your dream came true."

"I guess it did." Alonso had confided in his friends that he'd wanted to be a doctor, but a dream like that had seemed impossible for an inner-city kid. "Maria convinced Judge Hamel to write a kick-ass letter of recommendation for me. I think the med schools were afraid to turn me down."

"How did you hook up with Luke and his sister?"

"I took a leave of absence from the hospital. I've been doing some sightseeing in the area and met up with them." Sightseeing sounded better than walking aimlessly across the state.

"Why did you take a leave from your job?" Cruz's direct stare unnerved Alonso. He thought of telling a lie, but his friend would see through him.

"I'm burned out. I needed a break from the death and violence."

Cruz stared thoughtfully, seeing past the wall Alonso hid behind. "I get it." After twelve years behind bars, Cruz probably understood better than Alonso's cohorts. Hell, forget about him. Cruz was the one who deserved sympathy. "What about you?"

"What's done is done. I've moved on."

"Have you spoken to Vic since you got out?"

"No." The one-word answer suggested that Cruz might not have let go of the past. Alonso wished he could help his two friends find peace with each other, but he had enough troubles of his own.

"What's Luke's story?" Cruz asked.

"His parents are deceased and Hannah's trying to keep him in line, but the other night he was involved with a couple of punks who tried to rob a convenience store. This is Luke's last chance to shape up. Next time the sheriff of Paradise promised to arrest Luke if he was caught on the wrong side of the law."

"Is he interested in rodeo?"

"He says he is, but he doesn't have any experience."

"I'll work with him." Cruz glanced at Hannah standing by the pickup. "When are you returning to your job at the hospital?"

"I don't have a definite date in mind."

Cruz looked as if he wanted to ask another question but they were interrupted by a group of boys leaving the bunkhouse.

"It's chow time," Cruz said. "You coming?"

He shook his head. "I need to get Hannah back to the ranch."

"Will I see you again?"

"You can count on it." Alonso didn't know when, but one day he'd stay for a longer visit. "Keep a close eye on Luke, will you? He's all Hannah's got now."

The men shook hands, then Alonso returned to the pickup and he and Hannah drove off. It would be dark by the time they returned to the Blue Bison. In the morning he'd help Hannah with chores then tell her it was best if he moved on.

Best for whom?

Definitely not him.

"I'm stumped." Sheriff Miller scratched his head Tuesday afternoon as he stared at the smashed solar panel used to run the water pump on the south side of the Blue Bison.

"At least we know now that my damaged fence wasn't just a Halloween prank."

The sheriff studied the dirt around the fenced-in tank. "The shoe prints look like work boots."

"Does that matter?"

"If the treads came from athletic shoes I'd guess whoever did this was a teenager."

"You don't think the boys who held up the convenience store did this for revenge?"

"Don't see how. They're sitting in the county jail right now." He stared up at the sky as if the clouds held the answers. Then he cleared his throat. "You and Seth getting along?"

Everyone in Paradise believed she'd broken off her engagement to Seth because she'd found out he'd been meeting Mona Montgomery at the El Ray Inn every afternoon. Hannah let them believe what they wanted. "I gave his ring back two years ago. No one holds a grudge that long." Then again, Hannah recalled the mean look on Seth's face when he'd walked in on her and Alonso dancing at Maloney's. The jerk had no right to be jealous. She rubbed her brow, feeling a headache coming on.

"I'll pay a visit to Roger and tell him to be on the lookout for strangers in the area."

"Have you received any other reports of property damage?"

"No. You're the only one."

Hannah didn't like being special.

Back in the patrol car the sheriff asked, "How do you think Luke will do at the boys' ranch?"

"It was tough to leave him there, but it's a nice place and the wife and husband who run it seem to really care about the kids. There's a school on the property and a medical clinic. Luke intends to learn rodeo in his spare time."

"I hope it works out for him." The sheriff slowed the car when the house came into view. "I don't like you being alone out here with vandals running loose."

"I'll be fine."

"I admire you for wanting to keep the ranch going after your father passed away, but it might be too much for you to handle. You and Luke are young. You have your whole lives ahead of you. You should consider selling and starting over somewhere more exciting than Paradise."

This wasn't the first time she'd been urged to sell. After her father's funeral half the land owners in the county had shown up at her door with offers to buy the ranch. Even Luke had urged her to take the highest bid.

Hannah had had ten happy years on the ranch until her father had cheated on her mother. But even though things had changed and Ruth hadn't been much of a stepmother, Hannah had found solace in taking care of the animals and the land. Instead of finding the same comfort, Luke had grown up turning to Hannah for support. She'd hoped Luke's attitude toward the ranch would change, but there was no evidence of that so far.

When they pulled into the yard, Alonso walked out of the barn and waited for them. She'd thought he'd change his mind about staying on to help her, but she was grateful he hadn't.

"I wondered where you were," Alonso said when Hannah stepped from the patrol car. He'd taken the Honda into Cañon City to get the oil changed and had been gone when the sheriff had arrived.

"I took Sheriff Miller out to see the damaged solar panel."

"I'll let you know if I hear anything that might help our case." The lawman closed his window and drove off.

Hannah stubbed the toe of her boot in the dirt. It had been awkward between her and Alonso without Luke around.

"Has the sheriff come up with any leads?"

Hannah shook her head. "I forgot to mention that Maria called yesterday and said Luke's keeping up with his homework."

"That's good."

"I shared with her some of the things Luke and I have been struggling with." Hannah had been embarrassed at how easy it had been to unload on a near stranger, but when she'd hung up the phone, she'd been confident that Maria and her husband would do their best to help her brother.

"Luke's in good hands. You don't have to worry about him." Alonso's gaze strayed to the patrol car in the distance.

He wants to leave, but he doesn't know how to tell you.

She should insist on giving him a lift to the highway.

It was selfish of her to want him to stay, but there was something about Alonso that touched her.

You're feeling vulnerable because you slept with him. You would feel this way about any man you had sex with.

Not true. She hadn't felt this connection with Seth.

"Hannah—"

"It's okay." The least she could do was spare him the ordeal of saying goodbye after all he'd done for her and Luke. "I know you're ready to get back on the road to wherever it is you're going."

The look of relief in his eyes socked her in the gut.

"It's not that I don't want to stay—"

"I'll give you a ride to the highway." She didn't want to drag this out any longer than necessary.

"That's okay. I'd rather walk." He was really going to leave.

She panicked. "It'll be dark soon. Maybe you should wait until tomorrow?" *Give me one more night in your arms.*

"I should really go."

You should really stay.

"I'll get you a water bottle." She hurried into the house and gathered several snacks for him, but when she returned outside he was gone. She checked the storage room in the barn. Empty. She stared down the road—nothing. He would have had to jog to get far enough ahead that she couldn't see him from the house.

It was as if he'd been a figment of her imagination. But he hadn't.

Hannah took the food inside, then returned to the barn and removed Buster from his stall. She walked him out to the corral to exercise him. She'd had to sell the other three horses because she couldn't afford to keep them, but she couldn't get rid of Buster. He'd been her father's favorite. She trotted the horse in circles, changing the pace several times as the sun slowly set.

When Buster had had enough, she let him stay in the corral while she changed his water in the barn and added grain to his feeder. Finished with the chore, she went out to retrieve Buster, but froze when she saw Alonso walking back into the yard, his duffel slung over his shoulder. As he drew closer, she noticed his weary expression. He stopped a few feet from her and dropped the bag on the ground. The muscle bunched along his jaw seconds before he blew out a harsh breath. "I can't leave."

Hannah's heart stopped beating.

"Until the sheriff figures out who's messing with your ranch, you shouldn't be by yourself."

Her heart resumed beating in a dull throb. Alonso hadn't returned because he couldn't stand the idea of saying goodbye to her—he'd come back to protect her.

Chapter 6

The first week of November had come and gone at the Blue Bison and the anxious, unsettled feeling that had driven Alonso to leave the ER was slowly being replaced by a sense of calm and peace. The fresh air, physical labor and Hannah's Crock-Pot suppers went a long way in improving his attitude. He sure hadn't expected rural life to make such an impact on him.

Maybe it's not rural life but Hannah that's got you thinking the world isn't such a bad place after all.

Because the third bedroom in the house was used as a storage room for boxes and old furniture, Hannah had offered him Luke's room while her brother was at the boys' ranch, but Alonso had declined the invitation. If he slept in the house, Hannah would do nothing to stop him from crawling into bed with her. He liked and admired her—she was a gutsy woman who cared deeply about her brother and her family's ranch. He didn't want to be the guy who used her to scratch his itch every night then split when it was convenient for him. He and Hannah lived in different worlds and eventually he'd have to return to his.

"Finished in here?" Hannah walked into the barn late Saturday morning with a smile on her face.

"You're in a good mood," he said. She'd worn her hair loose today instead of in her usual ponytail, and his pulse sped up when an image of those silky strands sliding through his fingers flashed before his eyes.

She stopped a few feet away from him and he caught a whiff of her earthy, sweet perfume. She'd left the first three buttons of her blouse open and he had to force himself to maintain eye contact and not stare at her cleavage.

"I think you've shoveled enough road apples. How would you like an official tour of the ranch?"

He'd tour a sewage treatment plant if Hannah was his guide. "Sure."

"Be ready in ten minutes." Then she was gone, her sashaying hips taunting him as she left the barn.

Alonso washed up at the utility sink, then changed into a clean T-shirt. Maybe he shouldn't fight his attraction to Hannah. It was obvious she wanted him, and he was growing tired of walking around with a hard-on all day. They were both consenting adults—if they wanted to have a fling, why couldn't they? As long as she understood that one of these mornings he and his duffel bag were hitting the road.

Hannah and a wicker basket were waiting for him

when he got into the pickup. "What's this?" He peeked inside the basket.

"Don't tell me you've never been on a picnic with a pretty girl before?" Mischief sparkled in her eyes.

"My picnic experience is eating Army rations on the dirt ground, but never with a pretty girl." He buckled his belt.

"Then, it's time you found out what you've been missing." She lifted her foot off the brake and drove away from the house. "The water wells are this way." She veered south on the dirt frontage road.

Alonso focused on the scenery—or he tried—but he couldn't stop thinking about how... "Hannah?"

"What?"

"Are you still in love with Seth?" Part of him hoped that she still had feelings for the guy—then sleeping with her would be a lot less complicated because anything long-term was out of the question. "Sorry. I know that came out of the blue."

"I'm not in love with Seth."

"The other night when we ran into him at the bar, it seemed as though he might have feelings for you."

"We've known each other all of our lives but he'd always treated me like a sister or cousin. I was stupid to believe his feelings for me had changed."

"He didn't tell you that he loved you when he proposed?"

"Nope."

"But you went ahead and said yes anyway?"

"I thought I needed help. My father had just died and Luke was acting up." She glanced across the seat. "I didn't know how strong I was until I returned Seth's ring." She stopped the pickup next to a chain-link fence with razor wire around the top. "This well is six hundred feet deep and pumps water from an aquifer to the stock tanks on the property."

"Do you share the aquifer with other ranches?"

"No. That's one reason Seth wanted to marry me. His family doesn't have an underground water source beneath their ranch. If there's a drought, they have to haul water in for their livestock, and at ten dollars per five hundred gallons it gets expensive."

"How many of these pumping stations do you have?"

"Two." She drove toward a rocky incline then parked at the bottom. "You'll love the view."

He carried the basket of food and followed Hannah to the top of the hill. "Hey, you can see the herd from up here."

Hannah spread a blanket on the ground. "When I was in high school, I'd come out here to do my homework."

Once they were seated, she handed him a ham sandwich.

"No news from the sheriff on who's targeting your property?" he asked.

"Not yet." She offered him a water bottle. "How did you end up being a doctor in the Army?"

"I didn't plan on enlisting. Maria Fitzgerald called in a few favors and helped me get an academic scholarship to the University of New Mexico. I talked about going to med school, but didn't think it would happen. Then one day Maria took me to see a recruiter. They offered to pay for my med school if I committed to serve in the military afterward. When I graduated, I was commissioned as an officer and began active duty."

"Where did you do your residency?"

"Lackland Air Force base in Texas. Then they shipped me off to an Afghanistan outpost where they were training local soldiers and police." Alonso didn't want to go into detail about his tour of duty in the Army. He wanted to forget that time—one day in particular—in his life. Besides, his stint in the Army had only lasted a year before he'd been given an honorable discharge.

"Don't laugh, but I've never been out of the state of New Mexico."

"The rest of the world isn't all it's cracked up to be." He finished his sandwich, then dug through the basket and found an apple.

"Alonso, do you regret what we did in the hayloft?"

The chunk of apple he'd just bitten off flew to the back of his throat and he coughed. "No."

Her gaze landed everywhere but on him. "Is there someone special waiting for you in Albuquerque?"

"You must not think too highly of me if you believe I'd make love to you when I'm seeing someone else."

"Sorry." Her gaze softened.

"The truth…is that I've never been involved in a serious relationship with a woman."

"I'm not buying that. Women swoon over men in uniform whether it's the military kind or a white lab coat."

"I've had a few hookups with women, but for the most part I remained focused on my goal to get through college then med school. Now my work schedule doesn't allow much time for socializing."

Hannah's stare warmed his blood, reminding him that he wasn't working at the moment. When she licked her lips, he gave in to temptation and kissed her. He tasted a hint of mustard and grew hungry all over again.

Her fingers threaded through his hair and pressed against his scalp, begging him to deepen the embrace. He laid her on the blanket and stretched out on top of her, groaning at the soft feel of her breasts against his chest. He rocked his pelvis against her and her fingers reached beneath his T-shirt to stroke his stomach. Like quicksand, Hannah was slowly sucking him under her spell.

A bang echoed through the air and Alonso popped off Hannah. "Was that a gunshot?"

"That's Seth or his father skeet-shooting on their ranch." Hannah sat up and straightened her clothes. Her hair was mussed, her lips swollen and she looked more beautiful than ever, but the gunshots had broken the romantic spell they'd been under.

"We should head back," she said. He helped her pack up the food. "I need to pick up a roll of fencing wire at the feed store. Do you want to come with me?"

"Sure." They made the drive to the house in silence, Alonso wondering how long before he gave up and caved in to sleeping with Hannah.

When she parked by the back porch, she said, "I'll get my purse and be right back."

While Alonso waited for her, he checked his phone and discovered a voice mail message.

"Dr. Marquez, this is Benson Levanthal. I know we

discussed a three-month leave of absence but I've had two doctors quit and we're going to be short-staffed starting December first. Is there any way you'd consider returning before then? I'll need an answer soon."

Click.

Alonso's first thought was that he didn't want to leave. But if he stayed, the attraction between him and Hannah would grow too strong, and then what? Even short flings became complicated when feelings were involved. His boss's call had come at the perfect time. Alonso could be with Hannah in every way he wanted and still have a legit reason to leave at the end of the month.

He could have his cake and eat it, too.

"Are you supposed to be calling me, Luke?" Hannah had been on her way downstairs after grabbing her purse from her bedroom when her cell phone rang and the number to the boys' ranch came up.

"I get one call a week if I don't have any penalty marks against me," he said.

"What do you mean penalty marks?"

"I get docked if I don't do my homework or I'm late for class and stuff."

He must be toeing the line then if he was contacting her. "I miss you," she said, surprised she really meant it.

He laughed. "You're just saying that."

Hannah couldn't remember the last time she'd heard her brother's lighthearted chuckle, and she smiled. "So tell me all about it."

"I still hate school and doing my homework, but Mrs. Fitzgerald is really nice and she doesn't get upset if you give her the wrong answer. Yesterday we started a chapter in geometry and she let us work in pairs. It's a lot easier when you have someone to help you with the problems."

Hannah sat on the stair step, amazed her brother was chatting about math. He'd never had much to say about school before. "Are you eating?"

"That's going to be the hard part about leaving here," he said.

"What's that?"

"The food's great and I'm gonna have to go back to eating your casseroles."

"Hey, we both know I'm not a great chef. Maybe you can bring your favorite recipes home and we can cook together."

"Cool."

"Have you had any rodeo lessons?"

"Cruz can't let me participate until my first grade report comes out. I have to be passing all my classes."

"When does the report come out?"

"The end of this week. And I made Bs on all my assignments so far."

"Are you excited about riding?"

"Yeah. I get to watch the others and some of them are really good. There's this one guy named Ricky that Cruz says has a shot at making it to the big-time."

The longer Luke rambled on the more Hannah realized how passionate he was about rodeo. When he returned home right before Christmas she'd have to find a way for Luke to remain involved in the sport, especially if it kept him out of trouble.

"Is Alonso still there?" he asked.

"Yes. And I have to say I'm glad. We had another incident on the ranch." Silence greeted her statement. "Someone smashed the solar panel on one of the stock tanks."

"That sucks," he said.

"Tell me about it. Replacing a solar panel isn't cheap. And our property-insurance deductible rose to two thousand dollars."

"What was it?"

"One thousand."

"We should just sell the ranch, Hannah."

"So you've said." She didn't want to end the call rehashing an old argument. "I know you aren't as attached to this place as I am, but we have time to think about our options. You still have two more years of high school."

"Mrs. Fitzgerald said she's going to send you an invitation to spend Thanksgiving Day here. Are you gonna come?"

"Of course. I wouldn't miss it for anything."

"I might get to ride for you."

"Yeah!" Watching her brother on the back of a bronc would be nerve-racking, but she looked forward to seeing him do something that made him happy.

"I gotta go."

"Thanks for calling, and take care of yourself. Be safe and work hard."

"Yeah, I know. Hey, Hannah?"

"What?"

"You be careful, too." Luke ended the call.

Hannah sat for a moment, absorbing the warm feeling filling her. She and Luke had been at odds for so long, and today's call brought back memories of better times between them. Whatever role fate had played in bringing Alonso into her and Luke's lives, she sure owed him a lot. She shuddered when she imagined where things between her and Luke would be right now if he hadn't gone to the boys' ranch.

She heard the back door open and close.

"Hannah?"

She hurried into the kitchen. "Sorry about that. Luke called."

"Everything okay?" he asked.

"Better than okay. He's doing great." She led the way outside and they got into the pickup. "I was worried he phoned to ask me to come get him."

"Glad to hear that wasn't the case."

"For the first time I feel hopeful that Luke's changing for the better." And she prayed the changes would stick once he returned home. She entered the highway and headed toward Paradise.

"I received a call from my boss at the hospital," he said.

"Oh?"

"He wants me to return by the end of the month."

A sharp pain jabbed her chest. If Alonso had to leave so soon then there was even more reason to enjoy what little time they had left together. "Do you miss working in the ER?"

"It never gets boring. Every day is different."

The exact opposite of her life. "As you've seen, here every day's pretty much the same." She flashed a smile. "Except the weather throws a curveball once in a while." Her seven-day week consisted of up at dawn.

Feed the bison. Check the water tanks and fence line. Muck the barn. Load hay on the trailer for the next day. Eat. Then go to bed.

"You might do the same things each day but I wish I could experience that comfortableness associated with a routine. Some days I'm so mentally exhausted, I feel gutted."

If she didn't know better, Hannah would believe country life was growing on Alonso.

Only because it's different from his norm. She doubted he'd be content in the boonies for very long. "Don't you miss the excitement of saving lives?"

"Yes and no."

"I get the yes. Tell me about the no," she said.

"I operate mostly on gangbangers who spend their Saturday nights shooting at each other. And I've saved more drunk drivers than their victims." He blew out a harsh breath. "Everything that's supposed to make sense in the world suddenly doesn't when the paramedics push that gurney through the ER doors."

"I can see where that would be a little depressing. But doesn't the good outweigh the bad? Maybe you're saving a gangbanger but you're giving him a chance to turn his life around."

"That sounds nice in theory but that's not reality."

"What do you mean?"

"You don't want to hear the gory details."

"I do, too." When he frowned, she said, "I'm serious." She admired Alonso for dedicating his life to helping others, which made him all the more special.

"Let's just say I've saved several lives where the people ended up dead a short time later, whether through no fault of their own or because they went right back to getting involved with whatever had brought them to the ER in the first place."

"Maybe you'll feel different after this break from the hospital." Hannah sensed he didn't want to talk about his job anymore so she changed the subject. "The drugstore in town has an old-fashioned soda fountain if you want to wait there while I pick up the fence wire."

"Are you kidding? I've never been in a feed store. I have to see what all the excitement is about."

Hannah parked in front of the store, and a cowbell hanging on the door handle announced their presence when they entered.

"Thought you might come in this week." An older man with droopy shoulders stepped from behind the checkout counter.

"Hey, Mel." Hannah motioned to Alonso. "This is Alonso Marquez. Alonso, this is Mel McGinnis. He manages the store." The men shook hands. "Alonso's helping me out at the ranch while Luke's away."

"Heard about your brother," Mel said. "He's had it rough since your daddy died."

Hannah had had it rough, too, but few acknowledged that. "Luke is fortunate the sheriff is giving him a second chance."

"What brings you in here?"

"Extra fencing wire." She wanted to be prepared if the vandals struck again and tore down a different section of her fence.

"What else do you need?"

"Just the wire. I'll be back in a week or two to buy more horse feed." Unfortunately, she no longer had the money to stock up on supplies. Hannah purchased what she needed when she needed it.

"Be back in a jiffy with the wire." He disappeared inside the storeroom.

"There's some fancy show-horse harnesses in that aisle." Hannah pointed across the store and Alonso went over to examine the tack while she waited at the register. She had opened her mouth to tell him to check out the handmade bird feeders a local resident sold on consignment when the sound of a ladder hitting the floor and a loud thump echoed through the store.

"Mel!" Hannah raced into the storeroom. Mel had fallen off the ladder and lay buried beneath sacks of livestock feed.

"Call 911." Alonso pushed past Hannah and began lifting the feed bags off Mel's chest.

Hannah hoped Mel hadn't broken any bones. She dialed Doc Snyder's number, knowing he could help Mel faster than the paramedics. "It's Hannah, Doc. Are you at the clinic right now?"

"I'm in Albuquerque seeing a doctor about my hip. What happened?"

"Mel fell off a ladder in the storeroom."

"Is he breathing?"

Hannah covered her phone. "Alonso, is Mel breathing?" He nodded.

"Yes, he's breathing," she said.

"Contact the fire department in Cañon City. I'll follow up with him when I return tomorrow."

She disconnected the call then pressed 911 and requested the paramedics.

"How long before they get here?" Alonso asked.

"Cañon City is about forty-five minutes away."

The old man moaned and Alonso placed a hand against his chest. "Don't move, Mel." He didn't want a broken rib to puncture a lung or his heart. He checked for broken bones, starting at the ankle. Everything appeared fine until he touched Mel's shoulder and the man cried out.

"Your shoulder is dislocated." Mel's face turned ashen and his breathing grew rapid and shallow. Alonso worried the old man would go into shock if he didn't get the pain under control. "I need to put your shoulder back in place." Then he could wrap the joint in ice and numb the pain, which hopefully would help Mel's blood pressure return to normal.

Hannah knelt on the other side of the old man. "Alonso's an ER doctor, Mel. You can trust him."

Mel nodded, then closed his eyes.

"Squeeze as hard as you want," Hannah said, holding Mel's hand in both of hers.

Being as gentle as possible, Alonso worked the frail bone back into place, then said to Hannah, "Find some ice and an elastic bandage if you can." After she left the room, Alonso checked Mel's pulse. Slow but steady. He felt the man's rib cage. "Does it hurt to breathe?"

"A little."

"You need to have your ribs X-rayed."

Hannah returned with a bag of ice from the machine outside on the porch and Vetrap horse-bandaging tape. Alonso opened the ice, poured half in the trash can, then tied off the end of the bag. He moved Mel's arm so it rested across his stomach, then secured the bag of ice to his shoulder with the wrap.

"Maybe you can find a blanket and something to use for a pillow," Alonso said.

Hannah grabbed a handful of saddle blankets from the shelf and Alonso made Mel as comfortable as possible, but it was obvious by the old man's grimace that he was in a lot of pain. "How long have we been waiting?"

"Thirty-five minutes."

Alonso heard the faint wail of a siren in the distance. "They're almost here, Mel," he said.

When Fire and Rescue showed up, they took Mel's vitals then started an IV.

"Mel." Hannah spoke close to his ear. "I'll call Harriet and have her meet you at the hospital in Cañon City."

Mel lifted his uninjured arm and Alonso held his hand. "Thank you, young man."

"My pleasure."

"Don't worry about the store. I'll ask Sheriff Miller to lock up," Hannah said.

The paramedics wheeled Mel outside and loaded him into the rescue truck. After they drove off, Alonso helped Hannah straighten the store. "Will you carry this for me?" She handed him the fencing wire. "Sheriff Miller said he'd be here in a few minutes to lock the store. I think it's okay if we leave now."

Alonso put the wire in the truck bed. "You want to drive?"

"Sure." Hannah slid behind the wheel but before she drove out of town she said, "Things could have turned out a lot differently for Mel if you hadn't been here."

"He's a tough old bird. He'll be okay."

"I know, but I still think you saved the day."

"Hey, I'm no superhero."

She clasped his face between her hands and kissed him. "Paradise has its very own Captain America."

Chapter 7

"I need to stop at the convenience mart," Alonso said after Hannah drove away from the feed store.

"Sure."

When she pulled into the parking lot of the store, he asked, "Do you need anything?"

"No, thanks. I'll wait in the truck."

Alonso grabbed a large soda then strolled through the aisles searching for the prophylactics. He had two choices: the date-night size containing three condoms or the stud size thirty-six count. There was only one choice for Captain America—he grabbed the bigger box. After Hannah's kiss a few minutes ago he'd decided he was done fighting the attraction between them. She wanted him in her bed so that was where he intended to sleep until he left at the end of the month. But this time he was taking precautions, unlike the night they'd spent up in the hayloft.

When they arrived back at the ranch, Hannah made supper while Alonso loaded the hay bales onto the flatbed trailer. Afterward he grabbed a clean change of clothes, shoved three condoms into his jeans pocket, then went into the house, where the smell of bacon greeted him. Hannah stood at the sink washing a head of lettuce, her fanny twitching to an oldies tune on the radio.

"Do I have time to shower?" he asked.

She jumped.

"Sorry." He dragged his gaze from her backside. "I didn't mean to startle you."

Her smile more than forgave him. "Supper won't be ready for a half hour."

He lifted the lid on the Crock-Pot. "Smells good."

"Cheesy chicken, bacon and Tater Tots."

"Is this your recipe?"

"Found it on the internet."

He set the lid back in place, then nuzzled her ear. "I think I'll call you my Crock-Pot princess." He left the kitchen, Hannah's stare burning into his back.

He'd just finished shampooing his hair when a cold draft floated across his naked backside. Before he had time to register that he wasn't alone, Hannah's fingers walked down his spine. His breath caught in his chest when she sneaked her hands around his waist then slid her palms down the front of his thighs. When she cupped him intimately, he braced his hands against the shower wall and clenched his teeth. He let her have her fun for a minute, but the need to have her again had been building inside him since the first time they'd made love, and he couldn't wait any longer.

He turned around and reached for her, holding her against him, letting their wet skin rub together in all the right places. "I bought condoms at the store today. They're in my jeans pocket."

"Good." She stood on tiptoe and kissed him.

"Are you sure, Hannah?" He brushed her damp hair away from her eyes.

"Very sure." She pressed tiny kisses across his chest. Her tender caresses made him feel safe. In Hannah's arms he believed he could conquer anything—a heady feeling for a man who'd been fighting a losing battle for a long time.

Hannah pulled her sweater tighter around her as she sat in the rocking chair on the front porch and sipped a glass of wine while she waited for Alonso to return from checking the stock tanks.

Two weeks had passed since she'd joined him in the shower and they'd fallen into a comfortable routine, one Hannah wished could last forever. Alonso woke early and drove the hay out to the herd while she slept in—a luxury she hadn't experienced in years. Then he spent the rest of the day fixing things around the property that she'd neglected because she hadn't had the time or the money to hire someone to make the repairs. And most important, he'd installed the new solar panel she'd ordered for the water station, so now water could be pumped to all the stock tanks on the property.

While Alonso kept busy, Hannah worked inside the house. She'd given the rooms a thorough cleaning, even dusting the baseboards and ceiling lights. Once all the rooms sparkled, she paid bills, balanced the ledger, transferred money from savings to checking, and when the tax bill came in the mail she cashed in the last CD her father had in the bank.

At the end of each day, she and Alonso talked over supper—about everything and anything, except their relationship. After cleaning up the dishes they snuggled on the couch and watched TV until one of them grew bored and began pestering the other. One kiss led to more, and then clothes came off and they made love. Afterward, Alonso carried her to bed, where they fell into an exhausted sleep.

But every morning Hannah woke up in an empty bed—a reminder that their relationship was temporary. After showering she'd fix a fresh pot of coffee, then sit on the porch and wait for Alonso to return from feeding the bison. Some mornings he grabbed a cup of coffee and sat with her, and other times he'd take her by the hand and lead her back up to the bedroom.

The sound of a horn honking drew her attention and she spotted a dust cloud moving along the road. She set her wineglass down and descended the porch steps. As the vehicle sped closer she recognized Seth's pickup. He honked the horn again—this wasn't a social visit.

He stopped the truck in the driveway. "Where's the city slicker?"

Maybe he'd been drinking. "What's wrong?"

"One of our ranch hands tried to rescue a deer caught in the fence and got chewed up pretty bad by barbed wire. He needs a doctor."

"Who?"

"Joseph."

"Why didn't you take him to Doc Snyder or to the emergency room in Cañon City?"

"He's bleeding bad. And since I found him along your property line, I figured it was faster to bring him here and let your *boyfriend* do his magic."

Alonso wasn't her boyfriend, but she didn't bother correcting Seth. She rushed over to the truck bed and winced when she saw the cowboy's bleeding body resting on a blanket.

"I put a tourniquet on his arm, but he'd lost a lot of blood by the time I found him."

"Alonso's out with the herd." As soon as she spoke, her truck crested the ridge and headed toward the house. "Here he comes now."

Alonso parked next to Seth's pickup. "What's going on?"

"One of the Los Pinos ranch hands is injured," she said.

Alonso peered into the truck bed, then hopped over the tailgate and felt for the man's pulse. "Bring me another blanket and a pillow." After Hannah raced into the house, he examined the man's wounds. "What happened to him?"

"Tangled with some barbed wire."

"Where's the nearest trauma center?" Alonso asked.

"Cañon City, but they're doing construction on the road and the detour takes an hour," Seth said.

"He tore the basilica vein on the inside of his arm. It needs to be sutured and he's lost too much blood already."

Hannah returned with the supplies. "Where are we going?" she said.

"Call Doc Snyder and tell him to meet us at the clinic." Alonso covered the man with the blanket and shoved the pillow beneath his head. The cowboy groaned but remained unconscious. Markham hopped back in the cab and took off, and Hannah followed in her pickup.

The sun dipped behind the horizon and a gust of cold wind sent a chill through Alonso. He tucked the blanket tighter around the man. The brisk temperatures reminded him of the night he'd lost three fellow soldiers. Just like the scenarios he faced in the ER, his skill at saving his friends' lives had been wasted that fateful, frigid evening.

The truck hit a pothole and his butt smacked against the bed, jarring his tailbone and his thoughts back to the present. The town lights glowed in the distance as they approached Paradise. Both trucks parked behind the clinic where the back door had been propped open. Alonso checked the patient's pulse—weak but steady.

"What happened?" An elderly man stepped outside, wearing latex gloves.

"Joseph Rodriguez tangled with barbed wire," Markham said, stepping out of the truck. "I had to put a tourniquet on his arm."

Doc Snyder came over to the truck and Alonso got his first good look at the country doctor. The old man's face was as wrinkled as a paper road map—just how old was this guy?

"Doc, this is Alonso Marquez," Hannah said.

"You did a fine job putting Mel's shoulder back in place the other day."

"Thanks." Alonso helped Markham carry Joseph into the clinic and place him on an exam table in one of the patient rooms. Then Doc pressed his stethoscope against Joseph's chest.

"Weak heartbeat. He's lost a lot of blood."

"He tore the basilica vein," Alonso said.

"Hannah said you're an ER doctor."

Alonso nodded.

"Good. I can use your help." He held out a bag of saline and Alonso started an IV in Joseph's uninjured arm. "I'll need you to do the suturing." If Alonso hadn't been staring intently at the old man's hands he might not have noticed the slight tremble. Old age was catching up with the doctor, and it was too risky for him to close the vein—one slight tremor and the doctor would sever the vein wall and the cowboy would bleed out.

Doc nodded to Seth and Hannah. "You two wait in the front room."

Alonso cleaned the blood around the wound so he had a better view of the vein while Doc gave Joseph a shot.

"That'll knock him out for a while." Then Doc handed Alonso a suture kit.

First, Alonso numbed the area with medication, then he worked quickly to stitch the wound closed. He finished in less than a minute.

"Haven't seen anyone close a vein that fast in my entire career."

"I've had plenty of practice. First in the Army and then in Albuquerque at the university hospital."

Doc pressed his fingers against Joseph's wrist. "Pulse is improving. Let's see if any of the other cuts need stitches."

Alonso cleaned and bandaged several wounds on the man's face, neck, arms and hands. Two of the abrasions needed stitches. Then Doc administered a tetanus shot and a round of antibiotics. "He'll sleep for a while." He pulled a chair closer to Joseph and sat.

"Shouldn't he be transported to the hospital?" If the stitches didn't take and the vein opened again, the man would bleed out on the table.

"That's why I'm sitting with him."

Alonso swallowed a curse. What good would it do for Doc to stay by the man's side when he couldn't hold a needle steady? Alonso took a seat in the other chair by the door.

Doc's mouth lifted in a tired smile. "I'm glad you were here, Alonso."

"It's no big deal."

"I couldn't have repaired the vein with my hands. You saved his life tonight."

Alonso had saved a lot of lives, but too many of them hadn't valued their second chance and had ended up dead.

"Joseph's a good man."

"Tell me about him." Alonso was surprised he'd asked the question. He rarely knew anything personal about the patients he worked on.

Doc tapped the gold band on Joseph's right ring finger. "He's the father of five children. His wife died of cancer. Joseph's mother helps care for the kids while he works two jobs."

"That's rough."

"He punches cows during the week for Seth and his father, then on the weekend he's a roughneck for the oil and gas companies." Doc smiled. "His family means everything to him."

Alonso stared at the man's scratched face and the knot in his gut that he'd brought home from Afghanistan with him slowly loosened. It was a good feeling to know that Joseph wouldn't waste his second chance. His gaze wandered around the room. The sparse rural clinic was nothing fancy or as exciting as the hustle and bustle of a hospital ER, yet what he'd done tonight in this small room was on par with what he did every day at the hospital.

Voices sounded in the hallway outside the door.

"Sounds like Sheriff Miller," Doc said.

Knuckles rapped on the door and the sheriff stepped inside the room. "Joseph's kids are here," the sheriff said. "Can they see him?"

Before Doc answered, five youngsters pushed their way past the sheriff and entered the room. The eldest couldn't have been more than twelve or thirteen.

"Be careful," Doc said. "Don't touch your papa. He's sleeping."

The littlest girl climbed into Doc's lap and stared fearfully at her father. "It's okay, Elsa." Doc patted the girl's back. "Your papa is going to be just fine."

An older woman with a long gray braid falling down her back stepped into the room. As soon as she saw her son she began crying.

Hannah hovered in the hallway, staring helplessly at

the sobbing family. The sheriff nudged Alonso in the arm. "Do you speak Spanish?"

Alonso's gaze shifted between Doc, Markham, the sheriff and Hannah—none of them spoke Spanish. So Alonso told Joseph's mother what had happened to him and that he'd be fine once he healed. Mrs. Rodriguez asked how soon he'd be able to return to work, and Alonso advised her that his arm would need to heal for several weeks. The news bought more tears to her eyes.

The sheriff offered to drive Joseph home in the morning, but when Alonso conveyed the message, the older woman asked if she and the children could stay the night at the clinic. Alonso translated their request and Doc agreed then sent the sheriff across the street to pick up snacks for the kids from the convenience store. There was never any mention of who would pay for what.

"Doc, where do you keep the extra blankets and pillows?" Hannah asked. "I'll get them out for the kids."

"The room at the end of the hall," Doc said. "There's a cot in there that I sleep on sometimes."

"Is Joseph going to be okay?" Markham asked.

"He will, but he won't be able to use his arm for a while."

"I'll find him something else to do until you give him the okay to go back to work." Markham glanced at Alonso. "Maybe you can tell him that when he wakes up tomorrow."

"I'll call Alonso in the morning and have him speak to Joseph over the phone before he leaves the clinic."

"Thanks, Doc." Markham left through the back door.

There was no excuse for how the rancher had deceived and hurt Hannah, but at least he wasn't a total ass if he was willing to give his employee a paycheck until the man could work cattle again.

"Would you like me to stay?" Alonso asked Doc.

"We'll be fine," Doc insisted. "Keep your phone by you tonight. I'll call if I need you."

Hannah appeared in the doorway with the bedding. "Tell the kids to come with me and we'll make a fort."

Alonso conveyed the message and the kids followed Hannah back to the front room. Alonso wrote his cell number on a prescription pad and left it on the counter, then went out to the waiting room, where Hannah and the kids were draping blankets over the chairs. The little ones crawled under the covers and Alonso told them to get some rest so their father could sleep, then he told Hannah he'd wait for her outside.

When Alonso left through the back door he noticed Markham's truck still parked in the lot. The driver's side door opened and Markham stepped out. "I've been waiting to have a word with you."

This ought to be good. "Yeah, and what is that word?"

Markham glared. *Too bad.* Alonso had saved a life tonight—that entitled him to be sarcastic.

"I don't know what game you're playing with Hannah, but you'd better not hurt her."

The rancher was one to talk.

"If you try anything with her, I'll—"

Alonso grabbed Markham by his coat collar and shoved him against his truck. The rancher was a few inches taller, but Alonso had been in numerous scuffles during his life and he wasn't intimidated. "What

Hannah and I do is our business. Not yours. You had your chance with her and blew it." He released the coat collar and stepped back.

Markham jabbed his finger at Alonso. "I'm watching you, Marquez."

I'm shaking in my combat boots, buddy.

Markham got into his vehicle and sped off.

"Marlene's bringing Doc and Joseph's family supper, and she said she'd stay at the clinic and help watch the kids so Joseph's mother can sit with Doc in the exam room."

"Who's Marlene?" Alonso held open the driver's side door for Hannah.

"Doc's wife." Hannah slid behind the wheel and Alonso sat on the passenger side. She turned on the radio and neither of them spoke during the drive back to the ranch.

Alonso used the time to mull over the events of the past week. He was surprised that he'd felt the same sense of satisfaction at putting Mel's dislocated shoulder back into place as he did suturing Joseph's torn vein. He wondered if the good feeling inside him was a result of whom he'd helped. Mel and Joseph hadn't just been names on a patient chart—they'd been real people. Good people. People family and friends depended on—not people who hurt others.

"I wonder if my Crock-Pot lasagna is still edible," Hannah said when she parked in front of the house.

"I'm hungry enough to eat anything." Alonso opened the door for Hannah. Once they stepped into the kitchen, she hugged him. "Doc said you were amazing and that you saved Joseph's life."

He relished Hannah's hug, letting her warmth seep into his tired body.

"While you take a shower," she said, "I'm going to salvage supper."

Alonso used the shower in Luke's bedroom and stood under the warm spray, letting the water ease the tension in his shoulders. During all the chaos tonight Hannah had remained calm and steady. She hadn't swooned or panicked at the sight of Joseph's bloody body. She'd make a great doctor's wife.

After his shower he threw on a pair of clean jeans and a T-shirt, then padded barefoot into the kitchen. Hannah stood at the sink shoving food down the garbage disposal. He peered over her shoulder. "That bad?"

She laughed. "That bad." She rinsed out the sink, then shut off the water and dried her hands on a towel.

He should have thought to stop somewhere for fast food on the way home. "Do you have a backup plan?"

"As a matter of fact, I do." She inched closer to him and wrapped her arms around his neck. "I thought we could feast on each other."

He grinned. "I like this plan."

She grabbed his hand and tugged him after her, hitting the light switch on the way out of the room. It took fifteen minutes to climb the stairs—too many stops to kiss and take off their clothes. By the time they tumbled onto Hannah's bed, they were naked and starving.

Hours later, Alonso stared into the darkness, holding Hannah close. He'd never felt more at peace with himself than he did at this moment, and it wasn't because he'd saved a man's life tonight. This feeling of contentment had *Hannah* written all over it, and that scared him to death.

Chapter 8

"Looks as if I arrived just in time," Doc Snyder said when he stopped at the Blue Bison Thursday morning and caught Hannah and Alonso filling the backseat of her pickup with plastic food containers. For the past two days Hannah had been baking up a storm—all of Luke's favorite cookies. Alonso got a kick out of how excited she was to visit her brother.

"We're driving out to the boys' ranch to spend Thanksgiving Day with Luke," Hannah said. "What brings you all the way out here, Doc?"

"Thought I might have a word with Alonso."

"Did something happen to Joseph?" Alonso had called the day following Joseph's injury and Doc had assured him that there had been no complications.

"Joseph's doing fine." Doc motioned to the rockers on the porch. "Mind if I sit a spell?" He hobbled up the steps.

Hannah disappeared into the house and Alonso propped himself against the porch rail. "What can I do for you?"

"I have a favor to ask."

Alonso noticed the way Doc rubbed his thigh. "What's the matter with your leg?"

"You don't miss a thing, do you?"

"Your limp is pretty obvious."

"That's why I'm here. I've got a proposition for you."

A red flag went up inside Alonso's head, but he held his tongue.

"I've been needing hip-replacement surgery for the past three years but there's never been a good time."

Alonso dropped his gaze. *Damn.* He knew what was coming next.

"I was hoping to have the surgery after Thanksgiving, but I need someone to fill in at the clinic for me."

"I can't."

"You have a license to practice, don't you?"

"I do, but the hospital in Albuquerque needs me back by December first." He had three days left before he took off. He and Hannah hadn't discussed his impending departure but it was there in every look and every touch they shared.

He was torn about leaving. He didn't like to think of Hannah alone while Luke was at the boys' ranch. There hadn't been any more mischief but he worried about her safety. And if that wasn't enough reason to call his boss and inform him that he couldn't return just yet, then the fact that he didn't want to go was. Alonso was starting to feel revived, and he attributed his improved attitude to plenty of fresh air and physical labor even though he suspected it had more to do with Hannah.

"I'd be happy to make a call to your boss and explain the situation. Maybe he'd be willing to let you stay."

"I doubt your patients would appreciate an outsider evaluating their health."

"A person in pain doesn't care who helps them."

Couldn't Doc take no for an answer? "I'm a trauma surgeon. I don't have experience with everyday medical ailments. You'd be better off finding a primary-care physician to take over your practice."

Doc looked disappointed but he didn't badger Alonso. He left his chair and limped down the steps. "Who's doing your surgery?" Alonso asked.

"Edward Albertson. His practice is in Albuquerque."

"Hope it goes well."

Doc grumbled something unintelligible, then got into his truck and took off.

"What did he want?" Hannah asked when she stepped outside with more cookie containers.

He rushed over to help her. "Luke is going to get sick eating all these sweets."

"He'll share them with the other boys."

Once they'd stacked the tubs in the backseat, Alonso said, "Doc needs someone to fill in for him while he recovers from his hip-replacement surgery."

Hannah's eyes lit up. "Are you going to help him?" Her excitement made Alonso feel like crap.

"I can't. I leave in three days."

Hannah forced a smile and tossed the keys to him. "You drive." She secured her seat belt. "I'm excited to see Luke. He's sounded so positive when we've talked on the phone."

For Hannah's sake, Alonso hoped Luke had turned a corner. He admired Hannah for not badgering him about his decision not to help Doc. He sensed she wanted him to stay as much as he wanted to stay but they both knew anything long-term was out of the question.

The drive to the ranch should have taken less than two hours but Hannah had needed to stop three times to use a gas-station bathroom. She'd mentioned having an upset stomach when she'd woken in the morning and had skipped breakfast, instead drinking two water bottles on the road. Alonso hoped she wasn't coming down with a virus. Then again, if she was and he caught it, he'd have a valid reason for delaying his departure another week.

When they finally arrived at the entrance to the ranch, Alonso lowered his window and pushed the security button on the gatepost. "Alonso Marquez and Hannah Buck here to see Luke Buck." The lens on the camera attached to the top of the gate swiveled toward them, then a moment later the gate swung open and he drove through.

"How can they afford all this?" Hannah pointed to the holiday plants and decorations adorning the entrance.

"Riley's family makes their money breeding Kentucky Derby horses."

"Wow."

As soon as Alonso navigated the pickup around a

curve in the road, the ranch buildings came into view. "There are a lot of people here," she said.

Several vehicles sat parked in the yard and Hannah's excitement grew. As soon as they got out of the pickup, Maria appeared on the porch and waved. Hannah met her at the bottom of the steps and the women hugged. "Thank you so much for inviting us to spend the day here."

"Luke's doing great. You'll be thrilled with his attitude." Maria smiled. "I promise." She gave Alonso a hug. "Luke and the other boys are getting things ready for the rodeo this afternoon while José and the fathers are cooking the Thanksgiving dinner in the mess hall."

"Guess I better roll up my sleeves then and start peeling a few potatoes." Alonso walked off to join the men.

Maria took Hannah's hand. "The men think us ladies are baking pies in the house." She winked. "But I ordered all the pies from a bakery and had them delivered yesterday. We're playing Bunco and drinking margaritas."

Hannah laughed and followed Maria inside. "Is this the original ranch house on the property?" she asked when she entered the home and noticed the old wood floors.

"It is. Riley and I have spent a lot of money renovating the house. He wanted to tear it down and start over but I hate to destroy someone else's memories, so we added on to the structure."

They walked into a noisy kitchen with a huge farmhouse sink and plenty of counter space. "Ladies," Maria said. "This is Luke's sister. Hannah, this is Cruz Rivera's wife, Sara. Cruz and Alonso were friends in high school. Sara's father, José, is the ranch cook and Sara is a registered nurse. She runs our new health clinic."

Hannah and Sara exchanged greetings. Then Maria introduced Hannah to the mothers of the boys and wives of the ranch hands before sticking a margarita glass in her hand. "Help yourself to any of the appetizers. Dinner won't be served for a while yet." Maria held the cheese-and-cracker tray in front of Hannah and she helped herself to a cracker.

"That's all you're going to eat?"

Hannah didn't want to share that her stomach was upset, so she lied. "We stopped and grabbed a bite to eat on the way here."

Conversation resumed among the ladies and Maria left the room to set up Bunco tables. "I'm so glad you and Alonso came today," Sara said as she helped herself to a piece of cheese. "Alonso and Cruz were best friends growing up in the barrio."

"Barrio?" How come Alonso hadn't told her that?

"Cruz always believed Alonso would make it out and do something important with his life."

"Alonso hasn't talked much about his childhood." Hannah flashed a smile. "We're just friends."

Sara's gaze made Hannah uncomfortable. It was as if the woman sensed Hannah's feelings for Alonso went deeper than friendship. "Cruz and I started out as friends, too." She smiled. "How did you two meet?"

"I almost ran over him." Sara's eyes widened and Hannah laughed. "Luke and I were arguing and I took my eyes off the road for a minute and I didn't see Alonso hitchhiking on the shoulder."

"Hitchhiking?"

"He took a leave of absence from the university hospital in Albuquerque."

"Alonso is staying at your place, then?"

"He's been helping me with ranch chores, but he has to return to the city in a few days." The end of the month was fast approaching, and Hannah tried not to think about how lonely she'd be once he left. "So how did you and Cruz meet?"

"My daughter, Dani, and I were visiting my father-in-law for the summer when Cruz walked into his restaurant in Papago Springs. Lord, he was the most handsome man I'd ever seen." She fanned her face. "At the time I was trying to convince my father-in-law to move to Albuquerque and live with me and my daughter, but he was stubborn. Then Cruz asked about the help-wanted sign in the window and I hired him to fix up the property in hopes of convincing José to put it on the market. It didn't take long for Dani or me to see that Cruz was a special man."

"Did he win over your father-in-law?"

Sara laughed. "It took José a little longer to come around." Her expression sobered. "Dani's father had passed away a few years ago, but José was still having a difficult time letting go of his son."

"I'm sorry about your husband."

"Thanks. Fortunately Cruz came into our lives at the perfect time and helped us all move on."

The love in Sara's voice when she spoke of Cruz tugged at Hannah's heartstrings. If she allowed the affection she already felt for Alonso to have free rein over her heart, it wouldn't be difficult to fall all the way in love with him.

Hannah took a sip of her margarita—a drink she normally enjoyed—but the bitter taste made her stomach churn and she set the glass on the counter.

"What's the matter?" Sara studied her face. "You're perspiring."

The urge to vomit gripped Hannah's stomach and she gasped, "Where's the bathroom?" Sara grabbed her hand and they left the kitchen. At the end of the hall she steered Hannah into a bathroom. There wasn't any time to close the door before Hannah flipped up the toilet lid and tossed her cookies.

She'd barely caught her breath before a second round of heaving hit her. Sara held Hannah's hair off her face until she finished. Then Hannah flushed the toilet and sat on the closed lid. Sara wet the end of a hand towel and mopped Hannah's face.

"I thought you looked a little green in the gills when you walked into the kitchen with Maria."

"I didn't feel well when I woke up this morning but I didn't want to cancel on Luke." Hannah stood up and cupped her hand under the water then rinsed her mouth. "I'm sorry you had to witness that."

"Have you had a flu shot?" Sara asked.

"At the beginning of October."

"What have you eaten lately?"

"Not much. I've woken up with an upset stomach the past three days. But this is the first time I've actually thrown up."

"Don't move." Sara left the bathroom then returned a minute later with a handful of soda crackers and a glass of ginger ale. "Nibble on these and take small sips of the soda."

Hannah did as instructed, surprised when the cracker stayed down. "I guess I shouldn't have gone without breakfast."

"When was the last time you had your period?"

Hannah's mouth dropped open, then she snapped it shut and shook her head. "I'm not pregnant."

"You're sure?"

"Positive." She couldn't be pregnant. She and Alonso always used a condom when they had sex.

Except the first two times.

Hannah counted back the days since she'd picked up Alonso on the side of the road—twenty-six. And she should have had her period last week. So she was a little late. There was a first time for everything. Besides, all the stress she was under was probably messing with her body.

"If you don't feel better in a week, you should see a doctor."

"I will."

"I'd take it easy on the food today," Sara said.

Hannah nodded. Right now, none of the traditional Thanksgiving foods appealed to her.

Sara escorted Hannah into the front parlor. "Sit here for a while and rest. I'll tell Maria you're passing on the first few rounds of Bunco."

"Thanks, Sara." After the nurse left, Hannah closed her eyes. She refused to consider the possibility that she was pregnant with Alonso's baby. Clinging to that stubborn thought, she drifted off.

"C'mon, sleepyhead, we're ready to carry the pies to the bunkhouse and start our Thanksgiving celebration."

Hannah woke with a start and popped off the couch. She rubbed her eyes until Maria came into focus. "I'm sorry. How long have I been sleeping?"

"Not long." Maria's gaze dropped to Hannah's stomach. "The other ladies left already."

Hannah followed Maria out of the house, hoping the older woman wouldn't mention her getting sick to anyone—specifically Alonso. When they entered the dining hall Luke surprised her with a bear hug.

"Wait until you taste José's food, Hannah." He led her to the chow line that consisted of two picnic tables covered with food. She spotted Alonso talking with Sara's husband, and when he noticed her his gaze warmed. Despite still feeling a little nauseous, his stare made her heart beat faster.

She and Luke filled their plates then sat at a table for four in the corner. A few minutes later Alonso joined them. Then Maria walked to the front of the room and gave the blessing. As soon as she finished, the mess hall grew loud with chatter.

Luke entertained Hannah and Alonso with rodeo stories and talked about the boys he'd made friends with. Hannah was relieved that Luke appeared happy and content. "Alonso said you bought a bunch of cookies for me and my friends."

"I did. Remind me to get them out of the truck before we take off later today."

"You're staying for the rodeo, right?"

That Luke wasn't eager for her to leave made Hannah happy. "Of course we're staying."

"I'm getting seconds. Be right back."

After Luke left the table, Alonso set his fork down. "What's the matter?"

"Nothing. Why?"

"You don't look happy."

"I am happy," she said. "I just wish we could stay longer than a few hours." Her eyes followed Luke through the chow line. "He seems content here." She hoped when he returned to the ranch he wouldn't revert back to the moody troublemaker that he'd once been.

Luke came back to the table with a full plate and Hannah watched in amazement as he devoured the food.

"I'll get you a piece of pie." Alonso pushed his chair out but Hannah slapped her hand over his.

"No, thanks. I'm too full."

He eyed all the food still left on her plate but sat down.

"I'll clear the table," Luke said after he chewed his last bite of food. He stacked their plates and utensils then carried them to the plastic tubs set aside for the dirty dishes.

Alonso chuckled.

"What?"

"Your mouth is open."

"He never takes his dishes to the sink at home. This place is magical."

Luke handed Alonso a plate with a huge slice of pumpkin pie on it then sat down and ate his own dessert. "I can't wait to show you how I mark out. I've been working on it all week."

"What's mark out?" Hannah asked.

"Rolling your spurs along the horse's neck." Luke smiled. "It's not easy when the bronc is trying to buck you off."

"How's your schoolwork going?" Hannah asked.

"The same. I'm getting Bs on everything."

"That's great." She nudged his side. "Does Maria have to twist your arm to make you do your homework?"

"No." He glanced around the room.

Hannah suspected he was itching to go off with his friends. "Has there been any trouble between the boys?"

"Everybody here is cool. But this one kid—" Luke lowered his voice "—almost got kicked out."

"Why?"

"Michael ran away and Mr. Fitzgerald spent all day tracking him down."

"Why'd he run?" All sorts of things came to Hannah's mind—too much homework, other boys teasing him, having too many chores to do.

"A social worker had showed up and told Mr. Fitzgerald that they had a spot for Michael in a group home, but Michael said he'd been in one of those places before and he was never gonna go back."

Poor kid.

"Mr. Fitzgerald's gonna work it out so Michael can stay here until he's eighteen."

"That's nice of Mr. Fitzgerald." Hannah's gaze connected with Alonso's. Things might have turned out differently for Luke if they hadn't come upon Alonso walking along the highway a few weeks ago.

"I wouldn't mind staying here until I turned eighteen," Luke said.

"Hey, no way," Hannah said, feeling a little hurt that he was okay living away from her. "I need your help running the ranch."

"I know." The excitement in Luke's eyes dimmed.

Hannah searched for something to say that would bring the smile back to her brother's face, but nothing came to mind. Thankfully Cruz Rivera walked to the front of the room and clanged a spoon against the side of a drinking glass. The crowd quieted. "We have a special treat for all of our guests this afternoon. The boys have been working real hard on their rodeo skills and they'd like to show you what they've learned," he said.

A little girl tugged on his jeans. "What about me, Daddy?"

Cruz smiled. "Excuse me, the boys and girl have worked extra hard." He chuckled. "First up is our mutton bustin' competition. All the little kids are welcome to give it a try. Let's head out to the corral and have some fun."

"See you out there." Luke took off with a group of boys.

"Good luck!" Hannah shouted after him.

The dining hall emptied out and Hannah walked with Alonso to the corral, eager to escape the food smells that had played havoc with her stomach the past hour.

"Did you ever do any mutton bustin' when you were little?" he asked.

"Twice. I was six or seven. If I remember correctly, I fell off pretty quick, but it was fun."

The parents with young children inched closer to the corral, where Cruz and Riley helped the kids put on a protective helmet and a padded vest. Hannah nodded to the metal bleachers. "I'm going to grab a seat."

"Mind if I stay here where the action is?" Alonso squeezed her hand.

"Go ahead." Hannah sat by herself away from the perfume smells of the other women. She enjoyed watching the kids squeal and laugh when they fell off the sheep. Before her father died, Hannah had envisioned herself one day marrying and having a few kids. Her hand automatically went to her stomach. She couldn't be pregnant. Not now. She shoved the thought to the back of her mind and focused on the activity in the corral. She had enough worries; she didn't need to add one more to the list.

After the mutton bustin' contest ended, the older kids lined up for the bronc bustin'. Alonso and Riley encouraged the boys and Cruz coached them through their rides.

Most of the teens ended up in the dirt but a few managed to ride for more than three seconds. Then it was Luke's turn. When he waved to her, she stuck her fingers inside her mouth and let loose a shrill whistle.

Luke lowered himself onto the back of the bronc, and Hannah expected him to fuss with the rope. Instead, he took no time to prepare before nodding to the gateman. The chute opened and the bronc lunged into the arena, throwing Luke's upper body over the horse's head. Luke managed to hold on as the horse spun.

Time slowed to a crawl and just when she thought he'd make it to the buzzer, Luke slid sideways and dropped to the ground. She held her breath, waiting for him to roll away from the horse's hooves, and not until he stood up and ran to the chute did she exhale in relief.

Luke and Alonso exchanged high fives with Cruz, and her brother's goofy grin brought tears to Hannah's eyes. She hadn't seen him this excited since before their father had passed away. Riding broncs made Luke happy, and she hoped that his dream of rodeoing would keep him in school and out of trouble.

After the final ride of the afternoon Riley and Maria thanked everyone for spending the day with them, then the parents began saying their goodbyes. Luke walked her and Alonso back to the pickup so he could get his cookies.

"Thanks for coming," he said.

Hannah hugged him. "I'm glad you're doing well, but I miss you."

Luke laughed. "No, you don't."

She handed him the plastic containers. "They're all your favorites."

"Jeez, Hannah. Did you make, like, five hundred dozen?"

"Just about." She punched his arm playfully. "I'll see you right before Christmas." Only four more weeks until Luke came home for good.

"Keep studying," Alonso said.

"I will."

Hannah couldn't delay the goodbye any longer. "Talk to you next week sometime."

"Okay."

Alonso started the engine and Hannah waved as they

drove away. Luke didn't even glance over his shoulder after he walked off.

When Alonso turned onto the highway, he said, "You're awfully quiet."

"I don't think he missed me."

"He missed you, just not as much as you'd hoped, maybe."

"I'm glad he's having a good time." And she meant it. "I'm tired. Making all those cookies was a lot of work."

"Go to sleep. I'll listen to music."

Hannah leaned her head against the window, closed her eyes and tried not to think about what Sara had asked her in the bathroom earlier that day. Hannah didn't know how much time had passed when Alonso shook her shoulder and woke her.

"I've got to gas up. Wasn't sure if you needed to use the bathroom or not."

"Thanks." Hannah went into the store, used the restroom, then browsed the feminine supplies. *Bingo*. She paid for a pregnancy test kit and a bag of black licorice, then returned to the truck, where Alonso waited.

He nodded to the paper bag. "What did you buy?"

She took out the licorice, careful to conceal the other item from his view. "Want one?"

"No, thanks."

She ate a few pieces then stowed the bag on the floor by her feet and dozed off again. The next time she opened her eyes they were home.

"I'll check on Buster," he said.

Hannah hurried into the house and went straight upstairs to the bathroom, where she locked the door, then sat on the edge of the tub and read the test kit instructions. She followed the directions, then decided to take a shower while she waited for the results. Once she dried off and slipped into her pj's she turned over the stick.

PREGNANT.

It couldn't get any clearer than that. She shoved the stick into the box and the box into the paper bag and the bag into her makeup drawer. Too stunned to process the news, she went into her room and crawled beneath the bedcovers. A few minutes later she heard the shower in Luke's room turn on.

Not long after, Alonso whispered her name when he crawled into her bed and snuggled against her. His warm, naked body pressed into her backside. He slid an arm beneath her pillow and one around her belly—where their baby rested inside her.

This couldn't be happening. To her. *To them.*

Alonso had another life waiting for him in Albuquerque, and her future was right here on the ranch. She turned in his arms and pressed her mouth to his. Whenever Alonso held her, she forgot all her troubles.

Tomorrow morning she'd tell him they were about to become parents, but tonight she wanted to pretend it was just the two of them.

Chapter 9

Startled awake, Hannah stared wide-eyed at the ceiling, her brain registering a sharp pain in her face. Before she understood what had happened, something smacked her in the head and she jumped inside her skin.

"Stop him!"

Alonso's shout cleared Hannah's foggy brain and she rolled to the opposite side of the mattress. She pressed her fingers to her throbbing cheek and watched helplessly as Alonso's arms flailed in the air.

"He's wearing a bomb!"

Dear God. Her own pain forgotten, she attempted to shake him awake, but he was too strong and pulled away. She sprang from the bed and turned on the light. "Wake up, Alonso!"

"Get down!" He flew off the bed, grabbed her

around the waist and threw her to the floor, landing on top of her with his full body weight. The air whooshed from her lungs, and she gasped for breath. Tears of pain filled her eyes and she shoved hard against his chest. "Get off me!"

"Hang on, Tony! Damn it, buddy, hang on!" Alonso squeezed Hannah so hard she couldn't draw a breath.

"Nooo!"

The pain in Alonso's voice brought new tears to her eyes. She hated to hurt him, but he might injure her worse if he didn't wake up from his nightmare. She rammed her knee into his crotch and he released her, then rolled onto his back and moaned.

Hannah scrambled to her feet and grabbed her bathrobe off the back of the bedroom door, then ran downstairs to the kitchen and poured herself a glass of orange juice. Her hands shook as she drank the juice. Once she finished, she poured a glass for Alonso, intending to take it up to him, but she found him sitting at the bottom of the stairs, his bare chest glistening with sweat.

She handed him the drink.

"Hannah." He set the glass on the step and caressed her face. "Did I hurt you?"

Her nose felt a little numb, but she shook her head. "I'm okay."

"Your eye is starting to bruise." He gently pressed his fingers against her cheekbones and nose. "Nothing feels broken." He threaded his fingers through her hair and felt her scalp, then cursed. "You have a bump back here."

"My head clunked against the floor when you fell on top of me."

He took her by the hand and led her to the kitchen, then made her sit at the table. He rummaged through the freezer and pulled out a bag of frozen corn, wrapped it in a dish towel, then sat next to her and held it against the bump. "I'm sorry."

"It's okay. I know you didn't mean to hurt me."

"No, it's not okay." He bowed his head.

"Tell me about it," she said.

"Tell you about what?"

"The nightmare. You shouted something about a bomb."

She watched the struggle in his eyes before he placed her hand on the bag of corn, then stood at the sink with his back to her. "I haven't had that nightmare since I returned to the States."

If it was that painful to talk about she shouldn't make him. "Never mind. You don't have to tell me."

"It was Wednesday. Earlier that morning a Humvee from the base went out to deliver supplies to a village and drove over a roadside bomb. Three of the soldiers suffered severe injuries. I spent hours in surgery, but I saved their lives." He paced between the stove and the fridge. "They were still in recovery when an Afghan medic I was training walked into the recovery room, wearing a bomb strapped to his chest."

"How did you escape injury?"

"I dived through a door into a hallway, but the soldiers I'd just saved were lying in their beds and…"

Hannah pictured the gruesome scene in her head. "I'm so sorry you lost your friends." He didn't say anything. "You called out Tony's name."

"Tony was my best friend. He'd just found out the

day before that his wife had given birth to a son." Alonso closed his eyes. "The Humvee accident blew off his leg, but he'd begged me to save him so he could go home and see his son." Alonso smacked his fist against the fridge. "I saved him, but for what? So he could get blown up all over again?"

Hannah's stomach grew queasy.

"You look as if you're going to faint," Alonso said.

She set the bag of corn on the table and took slow, easy breaths, hoping the morning sickness would pass. Until just now, she'd forgotten about being pregnant. She closed her eyes, willing the tears to go away. Tears of frustration and fear.

Fear of being a mother when she wasn't ready to be one. Fear of assuming more responsibility when she was already up to her eyeballs in running the ranch and making sure her brother toed the line.

And then there was Alonso. He was leaving in three days and she was afraid he'd feel obligated to stick around longer because of the baby—not her.

You knew before you slept with him that nothing permanent would come of your relationship.

But that was before she'd got pregnant.

The tears trapped beneath her eyelids leaked out and slid down her cheeks. Alonso knelt on the floor by her chair and held her hands. "God, Hannah, I'm sorry I hurt you." His tortured gaze held her captive. "I'll help with the chores this morning, then pack my things and hit the road." He pressed a finger against her mouth when she tried to speak. "I had to leave Sunday anyway to report in at the hospital."

Her heart broke. His earnest expression betrayed

how eager he was to leave. "I have something to tell you."

"What?"

She hesitated, knowing the next two words would change his life forever. "I'm pregnant."

Alonso released Hannah's hands and sprang to his feet, then backpedaled until he hit the wall. He stared at her as if he was seeing a ghost.

The word *pregnant* reverberated inside Alonso's head until he thought he'd go deaf. He opened his mouth to speak, but couldn't draw any air into his lungs.

"I think it happened the first time we..."

Of course it had happened then, because he'd made sure he'd used a condom after that night. The nightmare and the shock of discovering that he'd hurt Hannah, and now learning that he was going to be a father...

He couldn't breathe. He lunged for the back door and stumbled out to the porch. The lungful of cold air he sucked in only added to the numbness in his brain. He couldn't think right now and nothing made sense.

He went back into the house, walked right past Hannah without making eye contact, then went into Luke's room and finished dressing. He grabbed the keys to the Civic off the table in the hallway and returned into the kitchen.

"Tell me it's going to be okay." Hannah's whisper reached him before he made it to the door.

"I can't, Hannah. I can't guarantee anything will ever be okay." He closed the door, then hopped into the Civic and sped off, the car bouncing like a rubber ball on the gravel road. When he reached the highway, he turned toward Paradise. He resisted the temptation to stop at Maloney's on the way into town—getting drunk wouldn't make Hannah's pregnancy go away.

A baby. He couldn't wrap his mind around it. He'd never considered becoming a father. Had never been in a relationship long enough with one woman for the subject to even come up.

It was almost 7:00 a.m. when he arrived in town. Nothing but the gas station convenience store was open. He pulled into the parking lot. The blurry-eyed clerk managed a "good morning" when Alonso entered the store. He filled a large foam cup with black coffee, then studied the day-old doughnuts before selecting a package of Twinkies.

Back in the car Alonso choked down the sweet cake. The hit of sugar released his anger and he slammed his fist against the dashboard. The situation he found himself in was no one's fault but his own. He should have kept walking the day Hannah had almost run him off the road. But her sweet smile and pretty blue eyes had sucked him in and now he was paying the price.

A heavy price.

He wasn't ready to be a father. Hell, he'd never planned on having kids.

He'd seen too much during his lifetime—the world chewed up and spit out the innocent.

Maybe Hannah doesn't want to keep the baby.

He hadn't stuck around to ask how she felt about the situation. Shoot, her life was as complicated as his, and raising a child would add to her to-do list every day. And if Luke returned to the ranch at Christmas and reverted to his old ways and didn't help Hannah, then she'd be in a world of hurt.

He drove back to the ranch. Only an hour had passed since he'd left, but when he entered the kitchen Hannah was still sitting at the table, a vacant expression on her face. He felt like crap for running out the way he had. "I'm going to feed the bison."

"You don't have to do that. I know you want to leave."

"I'll stay until you decide what you want to do about the baby."

Her eyes widened. "I'm keeping it."

"You might change your mind." Right now the baby didn't seem real to him.

She got up from the chair and took a box of cornflakes off the pantry shelf. "You don't have to stay, Alonso."

"I'm fifty percent to blame."

She poured a small amount of cereal into a bowl. "I'm not getting an abortion."

"This is a big decision, Hannah. A child is a life-long responsibility." He ought to know. His mother had struggled to keep food on the table and a roof over her kids' heads.

"I helped raise Luke. I realize how much work a baby's going to be." She shoved a spoonful of cornflakes into her mouth and a drop of milk dripped off her chin.

"I don't know if I can always be there for you." There, he'd said it. Put it out in the open instead of beating around the bush.

"I don't expect anything from you."

She damn well should. "You can count on me for financial support." *But anything else...*

She finished her cereal, then set the bowl in the sink and faced him. "I don't think you should stay."

She's giving you an out—take it.

He ignored his conscience. "I don't feel good about leaving you alone when the sheriff hasn't caught those responsible for vandalizing the ranch."

The steely look in Hannah's eyes insisted he wouldn't change her mind. "I'll feed the bison this morning."

"I said I would."

"And I said I don't want you to."

"Hannah."

"What?"

He wanted to tell her that she could try to push him away all she wanted but he wasn't leaving until they discussed the future—more specifically what role she wanted him to play in their child's life. "Mind if I use Luke's car?" He felt stupid for asking when he'd taken off in the Civic a short while ago.

"I don't care what you do."

Alonso read the truth in her eyes—she didn't care whether he stayed or left. She'd given him his walking papers, so why did that make him angry?

Hannah stood in the shadows inside the barn and watched Alonso drive off in the Civic.

I'm going to be okay.

If she repeated the phrase a thousand times over, she might start believing it. Fat chance, when she'd never felt this scared or desperate before. Not even when her mother had walked out years ago and left her behind had she been as frightened when she imagined the future.

Hannah was grateful that Alonso had loaded the hay for the bison before they'd left for the boys' ranch yesterday. She backed the truck up to the trailer and secured the hitch, then drove out to find the herd. The bumpy ride upset her stomach, so she slowed down and tried to make sense of all the thoughts clamoring inside her head.

What kind of a life would this baby have without a stable family?

Hannah had panicked after Alonso had insisted he'd stay—she didn't want to be his responsibility. Even though she'd loved her father and Luke, she understood how tiresome it was to take care of others. Alonso didn't love her, yet he wanted to do right by her. She couldn't do that to him.

Not even for the baby's sake?

Her vision blurred and she cursed. Darn it, she hadn't cried this much in the past five years. He'd promised financial support, but would that be enough? The idea of Alonso not being involved in their child's life didn't sit well with Hannah. She'd grown up believing her mother hadn't loved her. No child should have to live with being abandoned by a parent.

"Oh, no." Hannah hit the brake. The section of fence they'd repaired a short time ago was torn down again. Thank goodness the bison were in the north pasture on the other side of the property. At least she wouldn't have to apologize to the Markhams and ask for help retrieving her animals from their land.

She phoned Sheriff Miller and left a voice mail then drove a half mile until the herd came into view. After dropping the hay from the trailer bed she returned to the house, made herself a cup of tea and sat in the rocker on the porch to wait for the sheriff.

An hour later a plume of dust appeared. The sheriff led a smaller vehicle toward the house. As they drew closer she recognized the Civic. Alonso was back.

The concerned look on Alonso's face tugged at her heartstrings. The poor man had his share of problems—he didn't need to be saddled with hers.

The sheriff stopped the patrol car near the porch and lowered the passenger-side window. "I'll drive out and take a look at the fence. Maybe I'll get lucky and find evidence left behind."

After the sheriff drove off, Alonso spoke. "Are you okay?"

"I'm fine."

"I'll get the fencing wire from the barn and an extra pair of gloves." Halfway to the barn he stopped, then returned to the porch. "If you're not feeling well I can see if Seth Markham will help me repair the fence."

"I'm fine." She had to be fine—what other choice did she have? "And I meant what I said. You don't have to stay."

"And I meant what I said. I'm staying."

But for how long?

"Hannah."

"What?"

"You'll let me know before you decide anything about the baby?"

"I told you, I'm keeping it."

"I know, but I thought you might feel differently knowing I won't be there to help you."

"I won't change my mind." Whether Alonso helped her or not, motherhood still scared her senseless.

Alonso studied her, his brown eyes filling with concern. "Neither one of us is ready for this, but I'm glad you're keeping the baby."

Relief filled her. If he was glad, then maybe after he got used to the idea of being a father, he'd change his mind about wanting to be involved in their child's life.

"You haven't seen a doctor."

Hannah jumped and Alonso regretted startling her. She sat at the desk in the living room, balancing her checkbook and looking sexier than a woman had a right to in jeans and an oversize sweatshirt. She'd been edgy ever since she'd told him about the baby two weeks ago.

To be fair, so had he—ever since he'd informed his boss at the hospital that he wouldn't be returning to the ER until after the first of the year. His boss hadn't been pleased with the news and had told Alonso that if he didn't show up in January he'd no longer have a job. With the baby coming, Hannah knew he was concerned about being fired.

"You're about seven weeks along. You should have a blood test to check your iron levels." And other screens.

She swiveled on the chair and stared at him. "I'll make an appointment."

"With Doc Snyder?"

She shook her head. "I don't want anyone finding out before I tell Luke."

"Are you hungry?"

She glanced at the wall clock. "A little."

"I'll fix supper tonight." Alonso disappeared into the

kitchen and washed up at the sink. A short time later he heard the steps creaking on the staircase, then the bathroom door opening and closing.

There wasn't much in the fridge, but he found a pound of hamburger in the freezer, a bag of noodles and cans of crushed tomatoes in the pantry. He'd make spaghetti. Once he threw all the ingredients for the sauce together, he let it simmer, then he filled a pot with water and set it to boil. By the time he dumped the cooked spaghetti noodles into a colander, an hour had passed.

He went into the front hall and glanced up the staircase. The bathroom door next to the landing stood open. Hannah had finished showering. Maybe she'd fallen asleep in her room. He climbed the stairs and peeked past the partially open door, then almost swallowed his tongue.

Wet hair plastered against her back, Hannah stood naked before the dresser mirror, examining her still-flat belly from different angles. A few more weeks and she'd develop a baby bump. He shifted his gaze to her breasts—those definitely appeared larger. He could have stared at her for hours, but he backed away, not wanting to interrupt the private moment. He tiptoed down to the first floor, then yelled, "Supper's ready!"

"Be right there!"

Back in the kitchen he grabbed a handful of ice cubes from the freezer and pressed them against his forehead, hoping the cold would erase the image of Hannah's naked body from his memory.

"Do you have a headache?" She stood in the doorway, wearing flannel pj's and a bathrobe.

He tossed the ice into the sink and wiped his face

on a paper towel. "What can I get you to drink?" he asked, ignoring her question.

"I'll stick with water." Once Alonso served up the spaghetti and sat across from her, she said, "According to Maria, Luke completed all his class work for this semester."

"That's great. He didn't fall behind." He caught her playing with her food. "What's the matter? You don't like my spaghetti?"

"It's fine." She flashed a smile. "Thanks for making it."

"Why the frown?"

"I'm worried Luke will get into trouble over the winter break."

"I'd offer to stay past Christmas, but if I don't report back to the hospital before the first of the year, I won't have a job." Now that he had a child to provide for, he had to bring in a paycheck.

"Maria and Riley are taking a group of boys to compete in a junior rodeo this weekend. We're invited."

"Where's the rodeo?"

"Los Alamos. I'd like to see Luke."

"Then, we'll go." He twirled the noodles with his fork. "Is Cruz going to be there?"

"Maria didn't say." She sipped her water. "I'll be glad to have Luke back, but I worry that he won't be able to make new friends at school next semester."

"The other kids will notice that he's changed for the better. Don't worry…he'll be fine." Alonso switched the subject. "What about you? You grew up on this ranch. Did you have many friends?"

"I had several friends until high school."

"What happened to them?"

"My father's drinking grew worse and I didn't have time to socialize, because I had to take on more and more responsibility around the ranch. I missed most of the football games and the parties. Eventually my girlfriends quit calling me."

Alonso had made it all the way through high school with two good friends. Actually, they'd been more like brothers. Then Cruz had landed in jail and Vic had gone off the grid for a while. Maria had been so upset over Cruz's situation that she'd focused on Alonso, insisting he go to college. He'd wanted to escape the barrio so he'd allowed Maria to guide him through the college admission process.

"Did Luke play any football?" he asked.

"No, but my father played in high school. He received a scholarship offer from the University of New Mexico."

"He played for the Lobos?"

"No. My grandfather guilted him into staying here and helping him."

"That's too bad."

"Dad didn't talk about the past, but I'm guessing his troubled relationship with my grandfather was one of the reasons he drank."

"Do you think he was happy managing the ranch?"

"I think he wanted to run it into the ground."

It must have been difficult for Hannah to watch her father neglect the property. Alonso's father was no winner but at least he hadn't been around to make his life miserable.

"I can't remember how many times I told my father

that I loved this ranch and I'd take good care of it after he wasn't here anymore."

"What did he say?"

"That I should move to the city and find a man to marry."

Ouch. The man sounded as if he didn't care about his daughter's happiness. "Was your father close to Luke?"

"Not really. Luke looks like his mother and reminded my father of Ruth's infidelity."

Alonso finished his meal in silence. Hannah's father had let her down in the worst way. Then Seth had hurt her when he'd only proposed in hopes of joining their ranches. Luke was all Hannah had left, and he was a handful.

And then Alonso had got her pregnant. He was in the profession of saving lives, not ruining them, so why did he feel as if his baby wasn't a blessing but just another responsibility Hannah had to take on?

Chapter 10

"Hannah? Are you ready?"

"Coming!"

Hannah crawled to her feet and flushed the toilet, then gargled with mouthwash. She hoped her morning sickness would go away so she could make it to the rodeo in Los Alamos without having to ask Alonso to pull off the road. Every morning she was reminded that she carried a baby, and she waited with anticipation for that first feeling of joy to overcome her, but so far nothing. She blamed it on the uncertainty that shrouded her relationship with Alonso.

"You want me to drive?" he asked when she stepped onto the porch.

She held out the keys. "That would be great, thanks." He opened the truck door for her and she noticed his frown.

"What's the matter?"

"Nothing, why?"

"You look miffed."

"I'm fine." He shifted into Drive, then turned on the radio.

He was mad.

She yawned. Her morning date with the toilet had exhausted her. "I hope being away from home improved Luke's attitude about ranch chores." As her pregnancy advanced she'd need his help even more, and she worried that he would grow to resent the baby.

"Try to keep your expectations in check."

"Are you speaking from your experience at the Gateway Ranch?"

"You remembered the name."

She paid attention to everything Alonso said, because she cared about him. More than was good for her heart. "Your time there didn't turn you around immediately?"

"It did and it didn't. I was a different person at the ranch. When I went home to the barrio, I reverted to the old Alonso so I wouldn't get beat up."

"Luke's lost several friends since our father died. If he stays out of trouble, I'm hoping he'll win some of them back." A lull in conversation ensued and Hannah searched for a new topic. He hadn't mentioned the baby since he'd asked if she'd scheduled a doctor's appointment. "Have you been thinking about baby names?" He glanced at her, eyes wide with surprise. "What?" she asked. "Did you not think I'd let you have a say in naming our baby?"

He shrugged, but didn't offer any suggestions. Maybe he didn't care.

"I made an appointment for next week with a doctor in Albuquerque."

"Good."

"Don't mention it to Luke." When he frowned, she said, "I know what you're thinking."

"You do?"

"You think because I want to keep my pregnancy a secret that I'm still not sure about keeping the baby." When he didn't protest, she knew she'd guessed right. "I'm keeping the baby."

His hands tightened on the wheel and his mouth flattened into a firm line. When he didn't immediately respond, Hannah's stomach grew queasy for a second time that morning. "Is it that you don't want to be a father or you don't want to be the father of my baby?"

"It's not that... It's..."

"What?" Why couldn't he just spit it out?

"I've experienced a lot of bad in this world. I grew up around gangs. I've seen what human beings are capable of doing to each other and it's not a good place to raise a child."

Hannah took comfort in learning that it wasn't her being the mother of his child that worried him. She didn't want to make light of Alonso's childhood or the struggles he'd faced growing up in a large city. And after losing his friends in Afghanistan, she couldn't blame him for believing the world was a crappy place.

"There's still plenty of good and kindness out there." Good grief, he was an example of that—he'd saved Joseph's life. And he was helping her with the ranch while

Luke was away. "I haven't seen all the bad you have. Maybe that's the beauty of living a rural life. We see and hear about all the bad in the world on TV but we're mostly removed from it."

"Hannah, you're not removed from it. There's an ugly side of Paradise if you care to look closely."

She opened her mouth to defend her town, then snapped it shut. Her neighbor had tried to take advantage of her. Someone was destroying her property. And two delinquents had held up the convenience store. Okay, so the town of Paradise wasn't a true paradise, but it wasn't a horrible place to live, either.

"If you're tired of city life why don't you move to a smaller town?" *Somewhere closer to Paradise.*

"There aren't many positions for trauma surgeons in smaller hospitals."

Hannah couldn't picture herself living anywhere but the ranch, and Alonso's future would always be in a large hospital where he could help the most people. She'd better wrap her head around the idea that he might only see her and the baby once in a while. Other than a check in the mail every month, she couldn't count on him to help her raise their child.

Alonso switched lanes and took the exit off the highway. Two stoplights later he turned right and a half mile down the road he pulled into the fairgrounds.

"Looks like a big crowd today." He handed the attendant a five-dollar bill, then followed the line of vehicles and parked in the next available space.

"Did Maria say when the boys would arrive?"

"The rodeo starts at one." He hopped out, then came over to her side of the truck and held the door open for her. "They should be here soon." He took her hand and they walked to the entrance. "We have time to kill. Let's check out the livestock barns."

The warmth of Alonso's touch cajoled Hannah into forgetting her worries—at least for now. Time passed quickly as he talked about rodeo and bucking horses. She half listened to his spiel, her focus falling by the wayside when he placed his hand against her back or touched her shoulder. She could get used to this man being in her life every day.

"Hannah!" Luke jogged toward them. Hannah tugged her hand free from Alonso's grip and hugged her brother.

"You look like a real cowboy in that getup," she said.

Luke shook Alonso's hand. "Glad you guys are here. My ride's at one thirty."

"Saddle bronc?" Alonso asked.

Luke nodded. "I drew Midnight Express."

Hannah squeezed his arm. "Are you sure you're ready?"

"Cruz said I'm ready."

"Where is Cruz?" Alonso asked.

"He's not here. He said he didn't want all the attention on him and that we shouldn't let any gossip we hear distract us."

"Did Mr. Fitzgerald come with you?"

"Nope."

Hannah shot Alonso a worried glance.

"Sweet Pete drove the van here." Luke pointed to the older cowboy standing with the other teens. "Cruz said we're supposed to find Victor Vicario. He's competing today and Cruz said he might give us some pointers."

Alonso scanned the crowd but didn't see anyone who resembled his friend.

"Vicario's riding first to help raise money for an inner-city kids' club in Albuquerque. He's doing it as a favor to Mr. Fitzgerald."

Alonso nodded to the stands filling up. "Now I understand why there's a big crowd here."

"And Cruz said Vicario's holding a clinic after the rodeo for any junior cowboys who want pointers. Sweet Pete said we could stay for it."

"How many boys are competing this afternoon?" Hannah asked.

"There's five of us."

"You two visit for a while," Alonso said. "I'll see if I can find Vic."

That Victor had volunteered to ride in a fund-raiser surprised Alonso. Back in high school, his friend had only been interested in making a quick buck for himself. Keeping his eyes peeled for his buddy, Alonso cut across the grounds and made his way to the bucking chutes. The area was crammed with young cowboys and their families.

"You looking for me?"

Alonso pulled up short when Victor cut him off. "Hell, yes, I'm looking for you." He grasped Vic's shoulder and gave him a bro hug. "It's been a few years. You look good."

Vic scowled and Alonso regretted his comment. His friend had always been self-conscious of the thick scar that marred his face. "You have time to talk?" he asked.

"My ride's parked outside." Vic led the way to a

smaller lot behind the arena, then dropped the tailgate on his truck and the two men hopped up.

"It's been a long time, Vic."

"You don't have to tell me how many years have passed since…"

Cruz landed in prison.

"I'm surprised you're riding the circuit." Alonso chuckled. "Last I knew you said it hurt your ass too much to fall off a bronc."

Vic returned Alonso's grin, the gesture stretching the scar, which tugged one side of his mouth down. The mark wasn't pretty, and time had only made it more prominent because Vic had lost all his baby fat, leaving his face lean and chiseled. When they'd hung out together in the 'hood, girls would approach them, but as soon as they saw Vic's face up close, they'd cringe and walk the other way.

"Stuff happens and plans change. Maria said you left the Army."

"How often do you talk to her?"

"Once a month. She's always checking up on me."

"We're lucky that she cares about us."

"So what happened with your Army career?"

"Like you said, stuff happens. It was time to get out. I'm a trauma surgeon at the university hospital in Albuquerque."

"What are you doing down this way?"

"I took some time off from the job."

"Why?"

For a guy who didn't discuss his own life, Vic liked to poke his nose in Alonso's business. "I needed a break. That's all."

"Maria says I'm supposed to take a look at this Luke Buck kid and give him a few pointers. She said you're sweet on his sister." Vic grinned.

"Luke and Hannah's parents are gone and it's just the two of them on their ranch now. They raise bison for specialty meat markets. I've been helping her with chores since Luke went to the boys' ranch."

"How'd you end up meeting them?"

"Hitchhiking."

"Are you and Hannah a couple?"

Not in the way Vic was asking. "We're just friends." *Who are expecting a baby together.*

Alonso nudged Vic's arm. "How about you? You got a wife or girlfriend?"

He shook his head. "Too busy traveling the circuit."

"I don't keep up with rodeo. I found out through Maria that Cruz broke all the rodeo records at White Sands."

"If he hadn't gone to prison he would have won a national title," Vic said.

"Maybe. He seems pretty happy working with the boys at Maria and Riley's ranch."

"That wasn't his destiny."

"Like you riding the circuit now wasn't your destiny?" When Vic didn't answer, Alonso asked, "How long you gonna keep at it?"

Vic slid off the tailgate. "Until I win a national title." He adjusted his Stetson. "I better head back to the chutes and check on the boys." He held out his hand. "Good luck with your job."

Alonso would need more than luck to get out of the situation he found himself in with Hannah.

* * *

"I can't believe you're coming home in another week," Hannah said after she and Luke sat down at a table near the concession stand.

"I kinda wish I didn't have to go back to school next semester."

"It won't be so bad."

"I've made new friends at the ranch." Luke's eyes strayed to the teens signing in at the event table near the entrance.

"Luke." When he didn't acknowledge her, she spoke louder. "Luke."

"Huh?"

"Am I the reason you don't want to come home?" They'd always been close until their father had passed away.

"It's not you. It's just that I hate ranch work. I can do what I want here in my free time. Like learn rodeo."

"I realize you don't love ranching the way I do and I promise I won't stand in your way after you graduate from high school. If you want to leave and go rodeo you can."

"But who's going to help you? You can't stay there by yourself."

She laughed. "Why not? A woman can manage a ranch just as well as a man." *If not better.*

"What if something happens to you? There won't be anyone to call for help."

"We have neighbors, Luke, and I carry a cell phone." She punched him playfully in the shoulder. "And Dad taught us both how to shoot a rifle. I'll use it if I have to."

Her brother didn't look convinced. "If I rodeo I'm going to need money."

Hannah swallowed a sigh. "Maybe I can buy your share of the ranch."

He sat up straighter. "What do you mean?"

She waved her hand. "If rodeo is what you want to do, then I can apply for a bank loan to buy your half of the ranch. You could use the money for a new pickup and to help finance your rodeo career until you start winning."

"You'd do that for me?"

"As long as you graduate from high school I'm willing to do whatever it takes to help you succeed." *Even if I go into debt the rest of my life.*

"You should've married Seth. Then you wouldn't have to be alone."

Hannah pressed her hand against her stomach. Little did Luke know she wouldn't be alone for long. "Hey, don't worry about me. I'll be fine."

Luke dropped the subject and asked, "Has there been any more trouble on the ranch?"

"We had an incident," she said. "Someone broke another section of the fence."

Luke dropped his gaze. Maybe he felt guilty that he was enjoying his time at the boys' ranch while she had to deal with expensive pranks. "Don't worry—it's minor stuff."

"Does the sheriff know who's doing it?"

She shook her head. "New subject. What do you want for Christmas?"

He smiled. "Do you have any money to buy gifts?"

"Something small." She winked. "Maybe underwear or socks."

"That's okay. I don't need anything."

Usually her brother's I-want list was a page long. "What about a gas card for your car?"

"Yeah, that would be good." He squirmed on the seat.

"Are you nervous about your ride this afternoon?"

"Nah."

Right.

"Ladies and gentlemen, can I have your attention, please."

Luke and Hannah glanced at the loudspeaker hanging above their heads.

"All junior rodeo contestants report to the event sign-in table to pick up your numbers."

"I better go." Luke stood.

"Alonso and I will see you after the rodeo, okay?"

"Sure."

He turned away but stopped when she called after him. "Don't get hurt."

"That's the plan."

Hannah finished her water, then chucked the plastic bottle into a recycle bin and went to look for Alonso in the stands. He found her first.

"How was your visit with Luke?"

"He doesn't want to go back to his high school. He'd rather stay at the boys' ranch."

"I didn't want to leave, either. He'll be okay once he's home and gets into a routine." Alonso placed his hand against her lower back and followed her into the bleachers. When they were seated, he asked, "Are you hungry?"

"No, thanks. I ate a soft pretzel while I chatted with Luke."

"What's wrong?" He pressed the tip of his finger against the bridge of her nose. "You're frowning."

"I told Luke that I'd consider buying his half of the ranch once he graduates from high school." She sighed. "He doesn't want to be a rancher." She motioned to the arena. "He wants to rodeo." Maybe she shouldn't have said anything to Alonso. Now he'd worry about her and the baby being by themselves once Luke graduated.

She'd hardly slept the previous night because she fretted over the possibility of Alonso proposing to her—out of guilt. Hannah had seen firsthand the damage an unplanned pregnancy could do to a family. Her father had got Luke's mother pregnant by accident, and then Hannah's mother had filed for divorce.

If she and Alonso married just because of the baby, their relationship would never last. She'd rather raise their child alone with one happy parent than two unhappy parents.

"Ladies and gentlemen, welcome to the eighth annual junior rodeo competition at the Alamosa Fairgrounds!" The fans stomped their boots and whistled. "You'll see we have a few new names in the lineup this afternoon. Let's give a warm Los Alamos welcome to the five buckaroos from the Juan Alvarez Ranch for Boys."

The crowd applauded, and then a teenage girl rode into the arena carrying the American flag. She stopped her horse in front of the grandstand. The National Anthem played over the loudspeakers and the crowd sang along.

"Up first today in the saddle-bronc competition is Michael Foster. Cowboy Michael will do his best to tame Lickety-split, a bronc from the Del Mar Ranch in Las Cruces."

The gate opened and Lickety-split sprang into the arena. Hannah had been to a few rodeos through the years and the horses being used today were smaller and less athletic than the ones ridden by seasoned rodeo veterans. Fine by her. She didn't want Luke getting hurt.

Michael kept his seat until the buzzer, then launched himself into the air and landed on his face in the dirt. He was slow to get up, stopping once on the way back to the chute to spit the dirt out of his mouth.

"Not a bad showing for his first rodeo! Let's see what the judges think."

"The score will flash over there." Alonso leaned close and pointed across the arena. The scent of cologne and warm man surrounded her, and she inhaled, resisting the urge to bury her face in his neck. There were moments like now when the gnawing hunger to kiss him almost overwhelmed her. No matter what path their relationship took, she'd always be attracted to him.

"The judges liked Michael Foster's ride. He earned an eighty-two! Congratulations, cowboy!"

After the applause died down, the announcer introduced Hannah's brother. "Up next is Luke Buck, another contender from the Juan Alvarez Ranch for Boys. This is also Luke's first official go-round."

Hannah crossed her fingers when Luke climbed on top of his bronc.

"Luke will try to tame Midnight Express this afternoon. This is the bronc's first rodeo, too."

The gate opened and Midnight Express jumped out, bucked once, then froze.

"Folks, it looks as if our bronc might be shy today. Let's make a little noise and see if we can rile him." The fans jumped up and down on the aluminum bleachers, creating a deafening din. All of a sudden Midnight Express reared and Luke slid off, landing on his butt in the dirt.

"Well, now, that wasn't fair, was it?" the announcer said. The fans booed the horse.

"Looks as though the judges are going to give Luke and Midnight Express another chance." The rodeo helpers walked the horse back to the chute and Luke climbed the rails and slid onto the horse's back. This time when the gate opened, the bronc bucked.

Hannah held her breath as Luke flopped from side to side. He hung on until the buzzer, then jumped for safety. His landing wasn't much better than Michael's. She mumbled a silent prayer of thanks when Luke waved his hat to the crowd and walked back to the cowboy ready area.

"Not bad," Alonso said.

"Luke Buck earned an eighty-one for his efforts and sits in second place!"

"I have no idea why men believe getting whiplash is exciting," Hannah said.

"Let's congratulate him." Alonso took her hand and they left the stands before the other boys finished riding.

When they arrived behind the chutes, Luke and Michael were high-fiving each other and laughing.

Luke noticed her and Alonso and raced over to them. "Did you see me?"

"We did!" She hugged Luke. "Congratulations on making the buzzer."

"It wasn't a great ride, but it was fun."

"Let's hope you get a better draw next time," Alonso said.

Luke exchanged a private look with Michael, then lowered his voice. "Can Michael come to the ranch for Christmas? All the boys are leaving for the week but Michael has nowhere to go."

"What do you mean he has nowhere to go?" she asked.

"His dad's in prison and no one knows where his mom is."

Hannah felt bad for the teen. And relieved. If Michael kept Luke occupied during the winter break, her brother wouldn't be tempted to get into trouble. "Sure, Michael can stay with us."

"You don't have to buy us any presents. We don't care about that stuff."

Hannah suspected Luke had already invited Michael to join them for the holiday. Luke brought his friend over and introduced him, then Hannah said, "We'd love for you to spend Christmas with us, Michael. I'm sure Alonso will appreciate the extra help with chores."

Luke groaned, and Alonso grasped both boys' shoulders. "I'll keep you busy day and night."

"Maria said you can pick us up next Thursday."

"Okay," she said.

"Thanks, Hannah." Luke and Michael went back to the chute to cheer their friends on.

"I have my doctor's appointment that Thursday," Hannah said.

"I'll get the boys." He nodded to the arena. "You want to stick around for the rest of the rodeo or head back?"

Hannah's gaze swung to Luke and Michael goofing off with the other teens. She wanted Luke to have fun and not worry that he had to spend more time with her. "We can leave."

When they reached the pickup, Alonso said, "How about we look for a Christmas tree today?"

Hannah hadn't planned on spending money on a tree, but now that Luke was bringing a friend home she should at least try to fake a little holiday cheer. "Okay." Hannah squirmed into a comfortable position on the seat. All she'd done today was sit on her keister, but keeping her eyes open any longer was impossible.

Chapter 11

Alonso glanced between Hannah and the road. She'd fallen asleep minutes after leaving the rodeo in Los Alamos. He attributed her sleepiness not only to her pregnancy but to worry. He wanted to reassure her that everything was going to be okay, but it wasn't.

The Blue Bison was struggling financially. Hannah was about to become a single mother. In two years there was a good chance Luke would hit the rodeo circuit and leave all the responsibility for the ranch on Hannah's shoulders. And then there was him—the father of her baby was scared senseless.

No matter which way he twisted his thinking, there was no getting over the fact that they were bringing a baby into a world full of hatred and tragedy. He'd seen too much bad to believe their child could escape every evil. What if something happened to the baby that was beyond their control—an illness or accident?

Granted, he'd seen more bad than good because of his chosen career and time spent in the military. But there was bad everywhere—even Hannah couldn't escape it two hours outside of Albuquerque. Her ranch had been the target of vandals. And no matter where you lived, whether it was a major metropolitan area or a small town like Paradise, people were people and not all of them were good. Their child might be able to avoid inner-city gangs and violence in school but there were rural thugs who preyed on people, too.

As a trauma surgeon he could save victims of violence and tragic accidents, but he couldn't prevent them. There was no running away from life, no matter how far he walked. He had a lot of thinking to do when he returned to the hospital after the holidays. Maybe a break from Hannah would help him see things in a different light.

When he drove into Paradise, he parked next to the Christmas-tree lot adjacent to the gas station. "Wake up, sleepyhead."

Hannah's lashes fluttered open and their gazes clashed. In that unguarded moment she smiled, and his heart melted when he got a taste of what it would be like to see her smile every day. "Sorry." She yawned. "I was more tired than I thought."

"Ready to find a tree?"

She unbuckled her belt and peered through the windshield. "None of them looks very good."

He chuckled. "We can't be picky. We're late getting

into the Christmas game." He walked around the pickup and opened her door.

An older man with a grizzled face greeted them. "Howdy, folks. I'll take ten bucks off the price if you buy one today."

Alonso studied the evergreens and said, "They look like something Charlie Brown would drag home." Hannah's belly laugh lightened the mood. It was amazing how her smiling eyes could improve his outlook. "What about that one?" He walked over to a tree with a gaping hole on one side. "You can face this side toward the living room corner. No one would know half the tree is missing."

"What about the gun closet?"

"I'll move it."

"Seems like a lot of work for half a tree."

"It will look better once it's decorated. And if you have outdoor lights, I'll string them across the porch."

"How much is the tree?"

"I'm buying it," he said.

"You don't have—"

"It's only fair that I pay, because you'll be stuck taking down the decorations."

"Fine. You buy the tree." This time when Hannah smiled her eyes didn't sparkle. "I'll wait in the truck."

Alonso paid for the sickly evergreen, then used the twine the salesman provided to secure it in the truck bed. As soon as they arrived at the ranch, he set the tree on the porch.

"I need to check the herd before it gets dark," Hannah said.

"Want me to tag along?"

"No, I'll be fine. There's a tree stand in the attic."

Alonso watched Hannah drive off, wishing he hadn't mentioned her being stuck taking down the tree. His leaving was going to put a damper on Christmas.

What did you expect? She knows she can't count on you for the long haul.

Maybe so, but he had to find a way to make the holiday special because he wanted to see a smile on Hannah's face when he left her.

And he would leave.

Maybe if he told himself that over and over he'd finally believe it.

Hannah breathed a sigh of relief when Alonso's image grew smaller in the rearview mirror. After he'd unloaded the tree, she'd got behind the wheel and driven off to check on the bison.

Alonso reminded her at every opportunity that he was leaving, but he couldn't hide the truth from her. It was there in his eyes each time he looked at her. He felt obligated to stay—for the baby's sake. When push came to shove, the man was not going to abandon her. As much as she appreciated his sense of duty toward her and the baby, she didn't want to hold him back from being what he needed to be—a trauma surgeon.

She was doing exactly what she wanted to do with her life and it wouldn't be fair if Alonso had to sacrifice his calling because they'd messed up and she'd ended up pregnant. Besides, they'd only been together a month and a half—they hardly knew each other.

You know the important things about Alonso—that's enough to build a relationship on. Maybe so, but staying together because of the baby would only carry the relationship so far—then what? Things would grow awkward between them and Hannah would eventually have to insist that he leave.

Hannah checked all the pastures, relieved when she found no signs of property damage. When she returned to the house she saw Alonso standing on a ladder stringing lights across the overhang. As she drove past the tractor behind the barn she noticed it sat at an odd angle. She parked by the porch, then admired Alonso's handiwork.

"That looks nice," she said.

"I found the lights in the attic when I was looking for the tree stand."

"Is the tree in the living room?"

"Yep, and so are the bins with the ornaments."

"Thanks."

"Hannah?"

"What?"

"There's a baby crib in the attic."

"That's Luke's."

"I can put it together if you want."

"Luke can help me with that later."

A long pause followed, then he said, "Sure."

"Alonso, does the tractor look as though it's sitting at an angle?" Maybe pregnancy hormones were affecting her vision, but she swore the machine leaned toward one side.

He climbed down the ladder and stared across the driveway. "Maybe. Let's go take a look."

When they reached the tractor they both gaped in disbelief. Two of the tires on one side were flat.

Alonso dropped to his knees and examined a wheel. "Looks as if someone shot out the tire."

A new tire cost upward of a thousand dollars. And now with a two-thousand-dollar insurance deductible she was screwed. She didn't have that kind of money lying around. She removed her cell phone from her jeans pocket and contacted the sheriff. He was out on a call so she left a message with Sandy.

"I'm sorry, Hannah."

There was that look in his eyes again—the one that said he couldn't leave her to face her troubles by herself. As much as she wanted to cry right now at this latest turn of events, she had to remain strong. "I wish I knew why I'm being targeted. Good grief, I don't have any enemies."

"You sure Seth Markham and his father aren't behind this? They want your ranch. Maybe they think you'll get fed up and sell out if they keep nickel-and-diming you."

"They'd never do anything illegal and risk losing their own property." As they walked back to the house, Hannah asked, "How would you like homemade hot chocolate while we decorate the tree?"

"I've never had homemade hot chocolate."

"Then, it's about time you tasted the real stuff." They went into the house and he showed her the tree. "You're right. The corner is the perfect spot for it." Too bad she couldn't stand in a corner and make the hole in her heart disappear.

Alonso unhitched the flatbed trailer next to the barn, then parked the pickup by the house. It had been in the low forties when he'd left to feed the herd at dawn. Now the sun was out, but a brisk wind kept the temperature from climbing and made the ache in his back worse. Now that Luke was home from the boys' ranch, he and Michael had set up camp in Luke's bedroom and Alonso slept on the couch. Hannah had offered to clear out some of the junk in the third bedroom and bring in the cot from the barn but he didn't want her to go to all that trouble for a few nights.

When he entered the kitchen, the aroma of fresh-baked cookies filled the air. For an instant he caught a glimpse of what future Christmases would be like for his child—with a single mother struggling to make the day special. Hannah would perform all the holiday duties—baking cookies, decorating the house and helping with school parties and plays. But she'd do it alone.

Didn't he want better for his child than what he'd experienced growing up with a single mother? "I don't think it'll warm up much today," he said, alerting Hannah to his presence.

"The weatherman on the radio said there's a chance of snow flurries tonight." She smiled—that same forced smile she'd given him the day they'd returned from the boys' ranch at Thanksgiving. If he didn't know better, he'd almost believe Hannah was too cheery, especially for a woman in her situation. Then again, maybe she was putting on a front for Luke and Michael because it was Christmas.

"I bet the boys would like it to snow." He glanced down the hallway. "Are they up yet?"

"They're out in the barn, feeding Buster and cleaning his stall."

Alonso was relieved that the teens were following through with their promise to help out with chores. "I bought these for the guys yesterday when I went into town." He removed the iTunes gift cards from his pocket. "Do you have a box for them or wrapping paper?"

"You didn't have to get the boys a gift," she said.

"I wanted to." He suspected Christmas gifts weren't in Hannah's budget this year.

"I know they'll appreciate them." She went back to rolling out the cookie dough on a cutting board.

Today was Sunday—Christmas Eve. Hannah had gone to her medical appointment in Albuquerque three days ago and insisted everything was fine.

"You didn't say much about your doctor visit on Thursday."

"I told you. He said I'm healthy. And the baby's healthy, too."

He gave her a minute to elaborate. When she didn't, he asked, "Did your blood work turn out okay?"

"All good. He wants me to come in for an ultrasound in February."

"I'll go with you if you want."

She stopped rolling the dough. "You'll be working at the hospital by then."

He tried to read between the lines but couldn't figure out if Hannah wanted him to go with her or if she was trying to give him an out. He didn't have time to ask, because the back door opened and the boys joined them in the kitchen.

"It's Christmas Eve," Luke announced.

Hannah laughed. "That's right. Santa Claus is coming tonight."

"Can Michael and I go into town and rent some movies?"

"Sure. Pick out a Christmas movie we can watch later," Hannah said.

Alonso caught the secret look the teens exchanged and worried they had more on their mind than renting movies. "I'll drive you guys into Paradise."

"That's okay. I'm gonna take the Civic," Luke said.

"Don't stay out too long. I'm making a big pot of chili and corn bread for lunch."

"Ms. Hannah, can I have a cookie before we leave?" Michael asked.

She waved the teen over to the counter. "Frosted or unfrosted?"

"Frosted." He picked a snowman then bit its head off. "These are awesome, thanks."

"Take a few for the road," she said.

The boys loaded up on cookies and after they left, Alonso said, "I have an errand to run. Do you mind if I use the pickup?" Alonso wanted to make sure the boys really intended to drive into town. The last thing Hannah needed to deal with was Luke running into an old friend and getting into trouble with him.

"Sure. Take your time."

Alonso gave the Civic a head start before he took off in the pickup. When he arrived in Paradise, he spotted the car at the convenience store. Relieved Luke had kept his word about renting movies, Alonso parked farther down the street in front of the drugstore—far enough away that Luke wouldn't notice the truck when he and Michael got ready to leave town.

Alonso hadn't bought Hannah a present when he'd picked out the gift cards for the boys because he didn't know what to buy her. He stared at the flashing neon sign advertising an ATM inside. She could use extra cash but she'd never accept money from him—not even if he claimed it was for his room and board. He'd lived with her since the beginning of November yet he didn't even know her favorite color.

But you know her dream.

And her dream of keeping the Blue Bison afloat was becoming more iffy with each passing day. As long as he remained on the job as a trauma surgeon he was confident he could help Hannah keep the ranch. He had a nice nest egg saved from his time in the military—she could use the money to pay a hired hand to help her with the herd. And he'd send her generous child-support checks each month. He wasn't worried about her financial situation. And until now it hadn't occurred to him that one day Hannah might meet another man who'd be more than willing to take care of her and his baby. What if she fell in love with the hired help? Did he want another man raising his child?

You don't have the right to be possessive of Hannah or the baby if you turn your back on them.

He wanted to be there for them both, but old fears crept in, undermining his confidence.

He glanced down the street and noticed a sign advertising Puppies 4-Sale with an arrow pointing at the feed store. Alonso went to take a look. The bell on the door announced his arrival. "Hey, Mel. You look a lot better than the last time I saw you."

The store manager grinned. "Shoulder's a little sore if I do too much, but thanks to you, I can move it just fine." He demonstrated by raising his arm in the air. "Gave the missus quite a scare, though."

"I imagine you did." Alonso glanced down the aisles.

"Whatcha looking for?" Mel asked.

"I saw that sign for puppies down the block."

"Burt's dog had another litter. There's one left." Mel pointed behind him. "He's sitting in the storage room, watching the TV."

Alonso poked his head inside the room. An old man sat in a lawn chair puffing on a cigarette. "Howdy."

"I saw your sign across the street."

"I was hoping to find this pup a home before Christmas. You interested?"

"What kind of dog?"

"Bullmastiff. It's a male."

No wonder the man was having trouble finding the puppy a home. "He'll be a big dog once he's full grown." Maybe too big for Hannah to handle.

"His sire is two and a half feet tall at the shoulder and weighs 170 pounds."

"I don't know much about the breed other than its size."

"You won't find a dog more loyal to family than a bullmastiff. They're fearless protectors."

Alonso liked the sound of that. "Are they easy to train?"

"If you work with them. Once you develop a bond, they won't leave your side."

"Any drawbacks?"

The old man chuckled. "They drool a lot."

"What about babies? Are they careful around little people?"

"Kids can tug their ears and crawl on their backs. The dog'll tolerate a lot, but they don't like strangers. Watch 'em when new people come by."

"How are they with horses and other ranch animals?"

"They'll protect them, too."

"Let me take a look at the puppy."

The old man opened the dog crate and removed the puppy. Alonso held the pup and the dog wagged its tail, then licked his face.

"He likes you," Burt said.

The dog had a cream-colored coat, black ears and a black snout. "I'm guessing they eat a lot."

"Yep."

He'd have to make sure his child-support checks covered dog food and vet bills. "How many pups were in the litter?"

"Just three. The other two were females."

"What kind of shots does he need?"

"I had the puppies checked out by a vet a week ago. They've had their first round of vaccinations already and they were dewormed." He reached into his pocket and held out a business card. "Vet's local."

"How much?"

"I got a thousand a piece for the females but I'll take nine hundred for the male."

Nine hundred?

"He's a purebred. His papers are right here." He patted his coat pocket. "You ask any breeder who shows these dogs and they'll tell you I gave you a deal."

"I don't plan to show the dog."

"Guess I could take eight hundred, then."

Alonso stared into the puppy's eyes. *Are you worth eight hundred dollars?* The dog licked Alonso's nose and that sealed the deal. He handed the puppy to the old man. "I'll be back with the money in a minute."

Alonso crossed the street and ducked inside the drugstore. After withdrawing money from the ATM, he asked the clerk for a large empty box. While she searched for him, he perused the Christmas aisle and picked out a red bow. Then he paid for his purchase and left.

"You can take this blanket with you." Burt stuffed the cloth into the cardboard box, then held out a plastic grocery bag. "Puppy food and teething toys."

"Thanks." Alonso took the box with the puppy and set it on the checkout counter. "Looks as if I'll need more puppy food."

"Pet supplies are in the back corner," Mel said.

Two hundred dollars later, Alonso had purchased three large bags of puppy food, a water bowl, food bowl and more chew toys, along with a horse blanket and a sturdy kennel in case Hannah wanted to crate the puppy in the house when she wasn't there.

As soon as he'd loaded the supplies in the truck and set the box with the puppy on the front seat, the boys walked out of the convenience store with sodas and a handful of movies. He felt bad for doubting the boys and waited a few minutes until after they'd left before heading out of town.

When he arrived at the ranch, he parked behind the barn and sneaked the dog inside. He set up the crate in the storage room and gave the puppy food and water before heading inside to eat lunch with Hannah and the boys. After the meal, he excused himself to check on the dog. He went back and forth between the house and the barn all day and evening, checking on the pup. Later when everyone went to bed, he'd bring the dog inside. He wanted Hannah to find the puppy under the tree Christmas morning.

Chapter 12

"Shh..."

Alonso held his breath and kept his eyes closed.

"Be quiet." Luke's voice carried into the living room, where Alonso pretended to sleep.

Two pairs of sock feet crept along the hallway. The back door opened then closed. Alonso sat up and shoved his feet into his boots, then checked on the puppy—fast asleep in the crate hidden behind the couch. By the time he stepped outside, the taillights on the Civic were fading fast.

He grabbed Hannah's keys from the hook by the door, shrugged into his coat, then took off after them. Damn Luke for sneaking out during the wee hours of Christmas morning. With luck he'd catch the teens before they got into trouble.

When Alonso reached the main road there was no sign of the car. His first thought was to drive into town, but his gut insisted the teens were headed west, so he turned right and hit the gas. He'd gone a mile when he noticed a vehicle parked on the shoulder of the road up ahead.

He slowed as he approached, saw it was a pickup, then sped by. But as he passed he caught sight of the Civic parked on the shoulder with its lights off.

Damn it, Luke. The kid better not be buying drugs. He shifted into Reverse and hit the gas. Someone hopped into the truck and sped off, leaving Luke standing alone on the road. Alonso parked in front of the Civic. Michael sat in the front seat of the car and stayed there when he spotted Alonso. Smart kid.

"It's not what you think," Luke said.

"So you weren't buying drugs?"

"No!"

"Then, what the hell are you doing out here at two in the morning?"

"I can't tell you."

"If you can't tell me then that means you were up to no good."

"It's not like that. I'm trying to fix something."

Alonso stared long and hard at the teen, who appeared shaken. "Who was that guy you were talking with?"

"I can't tell you."

"Fine, but you're going to tell your sister. I'll follow you home."

Shoulders slumped, Luke returned to the car, made

a U-turn and drove back to the ranch, Alonso riding his bumper.

When they pulled into the yard it was two thirty. "I'll give you until after opening presents in the morning to talk to Hannah. If you don't, then I'll say something."

The boys went into the house and retreated to Luke's bedroom. Alonso locked up, checked the puppy—still fast asleep—then stretched out on the couch and stared into the dark. Hannah was pregnant with his child. Her brother was still up to no good. And the sheriff had yet to catch the culprits responsible for destroying her property.

There was no way he could leave Hannah in such a mess.

Hannah woke to a quiet house Christmas morning. After taking a quick shower she threw on a pair of jeans, which she discovered pinched her around the waist. She tossed them aside and slipped into her comfy gray sweatpants and a pink sweatshirt. Shoving her feet into her rabbit-ear slippers she went downstairs and put a breakfast casserole and a pan of cinnamon rolls into the oven.

"Need help?"

She glanced over her shoulder, then swallowed a sigh. Alonso's sexy sleepy-eyed stare made her want to forget about food and go back to bed—with him. "No, thanks. Breakfast will be ready as soon as the boys are up."

He sat at the table.

"Orange juice?" she asked.

"Thanks."

She set the glass in front of him, then joined him. "I've decided to wait to tell Luke about the baby until after Michael and you leave."

He swirled the juice in the glass. "Don't you think I should be here when you break the news?"

"No, I'd like to handle this my way." *Because Luke will want you to stay.* She didn't give him a chance to argue with her. "I thought you parked the truck by the barn last night."

"I took a drive earlier this morning."

She quirked an eyebrow, but didn't pry. "Remind me to tell Luke that we need to meet with Principal Connelly over break and get his class schedule for next semester."

The timer on the oven dinged and she removed the rolls, placed one on a plate and handed it to Alonso. "I'll be right back." She was halfway down the hall when the boys stepped from Luke's room.

"What smells so good, Ms. Hannah?" Michael asked.

"Cinnamon rolls. Get 'em while they're warm."

The boys joined Alonso at the table and ate in silence. Ten minutes later the rolls were gone.

"Let's open gifts while the casserole is baking," she said. They all headed to the living room. "Michael, you're our guest. You go first." Hannah handed him an envelope.

Michael gaped. "I didn't expect a gift."

"It's not much," she said, wishing there had been more money in the budget for gifts, but the insurance deductibles had wiped out her savings.

"Wow, thanks a lot!" Michael studied the gift card. "I'm gonna buy a new riding glove with this."

"Here's yours, Luke." Hannah had given the same thing to her brother.

"Thanks," Luke said.

"I got you guys something, too." Alonso reached beneath the couch cushion and handed each teen a smaller envelope.

"iTunes gift cards!" Luke said.

"Cool," Michael said. "Thanks, Mr. Marquez."

"Yeah, thanks, Alonso."

"What did you get—" Luke sniffed the air and made an ugly face. "Did someone fart?"

"Luke!" Hannah rolled her eyes.

"Can't you smell that?" Luke asked.

"I think I know what it is." The three stared at Alonso. "Hannah's Christmas gift." He ducked behind the couch.

"What's back there?" Hannah asked.

"This little guy." He stood with the puppy in his hand.

Hannah gasped.

"You bought my sister a puppy!" Luke shouted.

"I hope no one is allergic to dogs," Alonso said.

"Is it a he or a she?" Luke asked.

"It's a male bullmastiff." He handed the puppy to Hannah and she cuddled it against her.

"How big will he get?" she asked.

"Close to a 150 pounds."

"That's huge," Michael said.

"They're gentle giants and used as guard dogs. He'll

protect his family and his breeder said he'll be good with ba—kids of all ages."

Hannah breathed a sigh of relief when Alonso caught himself before he said *babies*.

"I bought a stockpile of food and the puppy has already had his first round of shots."

Although it was thoughtful of Alonso to want her to have a dog for protection and she appreciated that he'd stocked up on supplies for her, how could she afford to keep the animal once he left? And it wasn't only the financial cost of owning and caring for a pet that worried her—the dog would always be a reminder of Alonso.

"Let me hold him." Luke took the puppy from her. "Can we play with him outside?"

"Sure." Once the boys left the house, Hannah said, "As much as I appreciate the thought, I can't afford a dog." Taking care of the bison cost her plenty already.

"I'll pay for its food and vet bills."

She trusted Alonso to keep his word, but what if his work situation changed and he couldn't follow through on his promise?

"You need a dog, Hannah. It'll be just you and the baby once Luke takes off after he graduates from high school."

A knot formed in her throat when she imagined herself alone with a dog and a child. That was not the future she'd envisioned, but maybe Alonso was right. She would feel safer if she had a dog for protection. "Thank you."

Alonso hugged her and she buried her face in the crook of his neck. Why did he have to be the man she wanted but couldn't have?

"Hannah?"

"Hmm…"

"Luke has something to tell you."

"What?"

He stared into her eyes. "The reason I moved the pickup was because the boys left the house at two in the morning and I followed them."

Her heart dropped into her stomach. "Where did they go?"

"I caught up with them a couple of miles down the road. Luke was talking to a guy on the shoulder, but he took off when I stopped. Luke wouldn't say what he was doing out there but I made him promise to talk to you about it."

And earlier Hannah had woken up believing this Christmas would be a new start for her and Luke, but nothing had changed. Her brother was back to his wild ways. "I better find out what he's up to."

"Send Michael inside with the puppy," Alonso said. "He can help me clean the dog crate while you and Luke chat."

"Thanks." Hannah trudged outside as if the weight of her bison herd rested on her shoulders.

"Michael," Hannah said when she stepped onto the porch, where the boys were playing with the dog. "Would you take the puppy inside and help Alonso clean the crate?"

"Sure." Michael sent Luke a panicked look before disappearing with the dog.

Luke shuffled his feet but wouldn't make eye contact with her. "I hear you and Michael sneaked out of the house earlier this morning," she said.

Her brother's hand shook when he pushed the hair off his forehead. Was it that bad? "You told Alonso you weren't buying drugs. Was that the truth?"

Luke nodded, but remained closemouthed.

"Who was the guy Alonso saw you with?"

Tears welled in her brother's eyes and Hannah's chest grew tight. She hadn't seen her brother cry in forever—he hadn't even shed a tear at his mother's or their father's funeral.

"I did it because I thought you'd make me stay here and help out on the ranch after I graduated."

"But I told you I wouldn't."

"I know that now, but—"

"Hold on." The ranch was her dream—whether she kept it or not had nothing to do with Luke. "I won't lie. It will be tough not having your help, but if rodeo is your future, I won't stand in your way."

"But you kind of are."

"How am I keeping you from following your dream?"

"You won't leave this stupid ranch, so I'm gonna have to stay."

She raised her arms in the air. "Why do you believe you have to stay? I already told you that I'd try to buy out your share if and when you knew for sure you were going to rodeo."

"I can't leave you alone. Something might happen to you."

That Luke worried about her warmed Hannah's heart. "Nothing is going to happen to me. I've been taking care of myself and you for a long time. I'll be fine when you leave."

"But you'll be all alone."

Not for long.

"And you'll be lonely."

Hannah couldn't stand the anguished look on her brother's face. "I don't mind being alone."

"But you've always been there for me. It's my turn to be there for you."

Tears filled Hannah's eyes. To hear Luke acknowledge the sacrifices she'd made for him made her love him all the more.

"If I rodeo, I can't be there for you. That's why I did it."

"Did what?"

"I paid a guy to vandalize the ranch."

Hannah sucked in a quick breath.

"The guys who tried to rob the convenience store hooked me up with this person who does stuff for money."

No. No, Luke. No!

"Where did you get the money to pay him?" Her brother didn't even have a job.

"I've been saving my allowance and I borrowed money from Connor."

Connor worked at a pizza parlor after school and on weekends. "How much did you take from him?"

"A thousand dollars."

Hannah felt faint and sat down in the rocker.

"I had to pay the guy three hundred dollars each time he did something."

Did something? That was how her brother referred

to the vandalism? "Luke, those weren't just pranks. The damage cost me—us—thousands of dollars, not to mention our insurance premium went up as well as the deductible."

Luke paced back and forth. "I thought you'd want to give the ranch up after all that stuff happened." He sniffed. "Then I wouldn't feel guilty when I went on the rodeo circuit."

Her brother really hadn't thought this through. "Where did you think I'd go if I no longer had the ranch?"

He stared at her with wide eyes. "With me. We'd travel the circuit together."

Any anger she felt toward her brother evaporated when she looked into his pleading eyes. It had been just the two of them for so long—even when their father had still been alive, Luke had come to her for everything. "You might feel that way now, but I guarantee by the time you turn eighteen you'll be ready to strike out on your own and you will not want your big sister tagging along." He didn't even protest when she squeezed his hand.

"So you met with that guy last night to tell him to hit us up again?"

"I told him to stop. That I didn't need his help anymore."

"Why?"

"Because I realized something when I was at the boys' ranch."

"What's that?"

"That you've sacrificed a lot for me."

She opened her mouth to protest, but he cut her off.

"I know you wanted to go to college, but then my mom died and you didn't want to leave me all alone with Dad." He sucked in a deep breath. "So I'm not gonna leave you all alone, either. If you don't want to sell the ranch, then I'll stay here after graduation."

She wanted to box his ears for what he'd done, but she couldn't love her brother more than she did right now. "Luke, I love you, and I love you even more for wanting to stay here and protect me, but I'm a grown woman. We each have to live our own lives."

"Are you just saying that or do you really mean it?" he asked.

"I really mean it."

"Then, you won't be mad if I tell you I want to go to a rodeo camp next summer?"

She smiled. "I won't be mad, but we might have a problem paying for the camp."

"I'm sorry, Hannah. I'll get a job and pay back all the money you had to spend to fix stuff."

"That sounds like a fair deal." If she could, Hannah would save the money and give it back to Luke once he graduated, so he'd have cash for the road.

"Are you gonna tell the sheriff what I did?"

"No, you're going to talk to the sheriff."

"But—"

"You have to tell the truth, Luke, or else it will catch up with you someday."

"I don't know the guy's real name. He told me to call him Todd."

"Tell the sheriff what you know and we'll deal with the consequences together."

"Will I go to jail?"

"I hope not." It wouldn't hurt for Luke to worry a little. What he'd done was a serious offense.

"When are we gonna see the sheriff?"

"Tomorrow."

Luke stared at the ground, wiping at his eyes.

"I wish you'd have talked to me and shared your concerns before you went to this extreme."

"I'm sorry." He hugged Hannah.

"Let's go inside. It's freezing out here."

Hannah excused herself to take a nap. Ignoring Alonso's questioning look, she retreated to her bedroom, where she sat on the bed and cried. Cried for herself. For Luke. For the baby. And for Alonso. Her little family was a mess. It didn't matter that Luke would leave one day and Alonso would leave soon. They were still a family.

"Hannah?" Alonso stood outside her bedroom door, a plate of crackers and cheese in one hand, a water bottle in the other.

"I'm sleeping."

Obviously she wasn't if she'd answered him. It had been two hours since Luke and Hannah had talked and she'd retired to her bedroom. Luke and Michael had taken the puppy into Luke's room to watch movies.

"Mind if I come in?" He tested the knob, found it open and entered the room. Hannah sat on the edge of the bed with red-rimmed eyes and her blond hair mussed. She looked like a waif, hardly old enough to be pregnant. "I thought you might be hungry." He sat on the mattress next to her and she helped herself to a piece of cheese.

"Thanks."

He handed her the water bottle. "Did Luke tell you why he sneaked out?"

"Yes."

By the looks of her, whatever Luke had done hadn't been good. "If you don't want to tell me, you don't have to." The pain in her eyes was so raw it stole his breath.

"Luke was paying that guy you saw him with to trash the ranch."

"Why?"

She swiped at the fresh tears that ran down her cheeks. "He feels guilty about leaving me here alone if he joins the rodeo circuit after high school. He was hoping I'd get fed up with the pranks and put the ranch up for sale and tag along with him."

Alonso was dumbfounded. He'd never expected Luke to be involved in the vandalism. No wonder Hannah was a wreck.

"Luke met with that guy last night to tell him to stop."

"Why?"

"Because he realized what he was doing wasn't the right way to pay me back for all the years I've stood by him." She waved a hand in the air. "I'm all the family he has left and he was worried about leaving me alone."

The image of Luke, Hannah and the baby standing together as a family drifted in front of Alonso's eyes, and a strong yearning to be part of that circle gripped his gut.

"We're driving into Paradise tomorrow to talk to the sheriff." She leaned her head against his shoulder and he slid his arm around her. Now that there would be no more threats against the ranch, Alonso felt better about leaving Hannah at the end of the month. "Are you sure this ranch is what you want?"

"This is my home, Alonso. I can't see myself doing anything else."

Maybe if his mother had been around more often, he'd think of the barrio as his home, but it would always be the place he'd wanted to escape from.

"Will you drive Michael back to the boys' ranch before you leave?"

It was the least he could do for her. "Sure. And why don't you make up a list of last-minute things I can help with before I go."

"That would be great, thanks."

He walked to the door. "When you feel up to it, come downstairs. The boys want to know what you're going to name the dog."

"I still can't believe you bought me a Christmas puppy."

"I probably should have asked. If you want, I can find the dog another home."

"We'll keep the puppy. Hopefully Luke will become attached to him and have a reason to come home and visit more often once he starts rodeoing."

Alonso left the room, closing the door behind him. Luke met him at the bottom of the stairs. "Is she okay?"

"She'll be down in a little while."

"Did she tell you?"

"Yes."

The teen dropped his gaze. "I hurt her pretty bad."

"Yes, you did."

Luke looked miserable.

"You can make it up to your sister by doing your chores and helping out more around the ranch."

"I'm going to."

"She loves you, Luke."

"I know." He went back into the kitchen and Alonso heard the boys trying to teach the puppy to sit.

Luke had a lot to make up for, but then so did Alonso—the difference was that Luke would stay and earn Hannah's forgiveness. Alonso intended to run away and pray that one day Hannah might find it in her heart to forgive him for bailing on her and their child.

Chapter 13

"Thank you for seeing us, Sheriff Miller." Hannah sat down and Luke took the chair next to her. "I appreciate you coming in the day after Christmas."

"Not a problem. I had a phone call to make." He smiled at Luke. "Are you ready to return to school next semester?"

"Yes, sir."

"After you phoned, Hannah, I asked Principal Connelly to meet with us, but he's out of town for a few more days."

"We're not here to discuss Luke returning to class after the winter break," Hannah said.

The sheriff's eyebrows rose. "Oh?"

"Luke has something he needs to tell you." Hannah nudged her brother in the arm. Luke was nervous, and to be honest, he should be. She might have let him off the hook for what he'd done, but that didn't mean the sheriff would go as easy on him.

"I'm listening, Luke."

"I know who vandalized our ranch."

The sheriff straightened in his chair. "Who?"

"Me."

The sheriff's eyes widened and his mouth sagged open.

"I mean, not me, but I'm the one who paid a guy to…" Luke dropped his gaze.

Hannah took pity on her brother. "Luke and I had a misunderstanding, Sheriff. And instead of talking to me, Luke took matters into his own hands, hoping he could convince me to sell the ranch. Luke realized his mistake and that he'd handled things badly and has since told this person to stop vandalizing the ranch."

Sheriff Miller rubbed his hands down his face and stared at Luke. "I'm not sure what to say."

"I know what I did was wrong," Luke said. "And I'm gonna pay my sister back for all the damages."

"Who did you hire to do this, Luke?"

"A guy named Todd, but that's not his real name."

"How did you know to get in touch with this… Todd?"

Luke cast a quick glance at Hannah. "The guys who robbed the convenience store gave me his name."

"Kenny Potter and T. J. Templeton were involved in this?" the sheriff asked.

Luke sent Hannah a panic-stricken look.

"Sheriff, the other boys had nothing to do with the vandalism. Luke is taking full responsibility."

"It's not that simple, Hannah, when an insurance company is involved."

"I realize that. I intend to call them and explain the situation. We'll be paying for the damages."

The sheriff stared long and hard at Luke. "I've spent hours working on this case. My time could have been better spent helping someone in real need."

"Yes, sir."

"I don't want to press charges. And I'll settle things with the insurance company," Hannah said.

The sheriff leveled a stern look at her brother. "I better not hear of you becoming involved in anything like this again."

"Never again, sir."

"And I expect you to stay out of trouble in school next semester."

Luke nodded.

"I mean it. No more skipping classes. Not even one," the sheriff said.

"I won't. I'm all caught up with my homework assignments for the first semester."

The sheriff looked at Hannah, and she said, "Maria Fitzgerald has been in contact with Luke's guidance counselor at the high school. Luke won't have to repeat the fall semester."

"That's great news," the sheriff said. "What else did you do at the ranch?"

"Learned how to ride broncs, and I competed in a junior rodeo earlier this month."

"Is that right?"

Luke's face lit up with excitement as he told Sheriff Miller about the riding lessons Cruz Rivera had given him at the boys' ranch. Luke's rebellion had cost them plenty, but in the end they were going to be okay and her brother's future looked brighter than ever. Hannah wished she could say the same thing about her own.

"I appreciate you coming in here, Luke, and telling the truth." His gaze swung to Hannah. "I'd be happy to speak with your insurance company if you need me to."

"Thank you." Hannah stood and Luke shook the sheriff's hand.

"I hope you know what a lucky young man you are to have such an understanding sister."

Luke smiled at Hannah. "I know."

After they left the sheriff's office, Hannah stopped at the convenience store and asked Luke to run in and buy a gallon of milk. Then Luke nodded off during the drive home. When she pulled up to the house, she shook his shoulder and woke him.

"I'm really sorry, Hannah." He reached across the seat and gave her a hug.

"From here on out, things are going to get better." She had to believe that. "What are you and Michael planning to do today?"

"I was gonna ask Alonso if he'd go target shooting with Michael and me."

"I bet he would." She'd prefer that Alonso tag along with the boys. Hannah was confident that Luke knew how to handle a gun safely, but she worried that Michael might get hurt if they goofed off and weren't careful. "There's Alonso." He walked out of the barn.

"Alonso!" Luke called out. "Will you take Michael and me target shooting this afternoon?"

"Sure. As long as it's okay with your sister."

"I'm gonna tell Michael." Luke raced into the house. "How did it go?"

Hannah would miss staring into Alonso's warm brown eyes. "Good. The sheriff isn't pressing charges and Luke gave his word that he'd stay out of trouble."

"I believe him. He's a good kid, Hannah."

"I think he and I have turned a corner," she said.

Alonso dropped his gaze to the ground, then expelled a sharp breath and looked her in the eye. "I've finished all the repairs, unless you have any more to add to the list you gave me."

He was ready to leave. "No, you've done more than enough."

"Maria phoned while you and Luke were in town. She'd like Michael to return tomorrow so she can work with him on his math. He didn't pass his last exam and she wants him to retake it. I told Maria I'd bring him back in the morning. I thought Luke might want to come along."

"Sure." If Michael left, there was no reason for Alonso to stay.

Except that Hannah still wasn't ready to say goodbye.

"Can we stay awhile?" Luke asked when Alonso parked the Civic at the boys' ranch late Wednesday morning. "We want to ask Cruz if he'll let us ride a bronc."

"Sure. I'll walk down to the corral with you."

The ranch appeared empty—most of the boys they'd seen at Thanksgiving wouldn't be returning after the first of the year. Riley and Maria would enjoy a short break before the next group of juveniles descended on the property.

Cruz walked out of the barn and waved. "How was your Christmas?" he asked the boys.

"Good," they answered in unison.

Then Luke spoke. "Can we ride a bronc before Alonso and I have to leave?"

"Go into the barn and ask Nelson to pick out a horse for you." After the teens took off, Cruz asked, "How's Luke doing?"

"A lot better."

"What about Hannah? Is there still trouble at her ranch?"

"Not anymore." Alonso wouldn't share the details—Hannah might not want others to know that her brother had been behind the vandalism.

Cruz glanced over his shoulder when Nelson escorted a horse out of the barn, the teens walking alongside him. "How are you holding up?"

Alonso frowned. "What do you mean?"

"Sara told me about Hannah. Is the baby yours?"

"How did Sara know Hannah was pregnant?"

"She said Hannah got sick when she was here at Thanksgiving."

Alonso thought back on that day. It all made sense now—having to stop on the way to the ranch so Hannah could use the bathroom. Her picking at the food on her plate and passing up dessert. Then her buying licorice and whatever else that had been in the brown paper bag on the way back to Paradise. If he had to guess, Hannah had purchased a pregnancy test at the gas station convenience store. "The baby's mine."

Cruz slapped Alonso on the back. "When's the wedding?"

"There isn't going to be one. And I'd appreciate you not saying anything about the baby to anyone. Hannah hasn't told Luke yet."

"Sure."

"I'm heading back to Albuquerque tomorrow," Alonso said.

Cruz looked at him funny but didn't ask why Alonso was taking off. "You ever run into any of the old gang in the barrio?"

"No." He avoided driving through his stomping grounds. There was nothing left there but bad memories. "Have you been back to Albuquerque since…"

"It's okay to say *prison*. Everyone thinks I'll fly into a rage if they mention I was behind bars."

"I wish that hadn't happened to you, Cruz."

"Me, too. But no matter how many times I go over it in my head, I wouldn't change a thing. If I hadn't gone with Vic that night, he might have gotten himself killed."

"I saw Vic at that youth rodeo in Los Alamos earlier this month. Can't believe he's bustin' broncs."

"Maria's been following his career. Vic sends his trophies to her for safekeeping."

"For a guy who never liked rodeo I'm surprised he's riding."

"He's damn good. Just missed the cut for the National Finals Rodeo in Vegas this year."

"Has he stopped at the ranch since you started working here?" Alonso asked.

"No."

Alonso could understand how it might be awkward for the two men after all that had happened in the past, but he hoped someday they'd be able to hash things out and put it behind them. Cruz and Vic had been friends before Alonso had joined the group. "Maybe I read him wrong," he said, "but Vic seemed as if he was just going through the motions. He didn't act like a cowboy who lived and died rodeo."

"Well, for a guy who doesn't like the sport, he's sure stuck with it long enough."

"Maybe you'll get the chance to see him ride next year," Alonso said.

Cruz remained silent, his gaze focused on the boys. Alonso got the feeling Vic's rodeo career was a touchy subject for Cruz. "I should have been there that night."

Cruz's gaze swung to Alonso. "I don't even remember why you weren't with us."

"I was in the emergency room with my sister. My mom was working and Lea had a bad asthma attack."

"How are your sisters these days?"

"Lea's married with kids. Carla's divorced." Cruz grew quiet again and Alonso decided they'd talked enough about the past. "I was hoping to speak to Maria before I leave."

"She's in the main house."

"Is Riley here?"

"Out of town on business."

"When the boys finish, will you send Luke up to the house?"

"Sure."

Alonso offered his hand. "Take care, Cruz. It was good seeing you again."

"I hope things work out for you, Hannah and the baby."

Alonso wanted that, too, he just wasn't sure how to make it happen. He walked to the house, then rang the bell. No one answered, so he tried the knob and the door swung open. "Maria?"

"In the kitchen!"

He wandered down a hallway that led to the kitchen at the back of the house.

"Alonso!" Maria popped off the bar stool and gave him a hug. "I didn't expect you for another hour." Holding him at arm's length, she studied his face. "What's the matter?"

"Everything." The word slipped from his mouth before he could stop it.

"I made a fresh pot of coffee a few minutes ago. Sit down." She grabbed a mug from the cupboard and filled it with brew. "Are you hungry?" She didn't wait for him to answer before she set a plate of sweets in front of him.

He helped himself to a sugar cookie. "These are good, thanks."

"José made them. We're fortunate to have him cooking for the boys. They don't mind doing the dishes afterward because they want to eat whatever José made for dessert."

Alonso was content to let Maria chatter. She had a way of making people feel good and he could use a shot of self-esteem right now.

"I was just telling a friend of mine from the old neighborhood what a remarkable surgeon you are."

"I don't think I ever thanked you properly for pushing me toward college and med school."

"You always had it in you, Alonso. I just believed in you until you started believing in yourself."

Believe in yourself. He thought back to those days when he feared he wouldn't pass all his classes in college then later in med school. Maria had always been there, never allowing him to give up. And she'd been right—once he'd acknowledged that he was good enough to succeed at whatever he put his mind to, he'd never looked back.

So what the hell had happened to his confidence? How had he allowed himself to nurture such a dismal, dank outlook on life? Not even when he was a boy growing up in poverty had he believed the world was a hopeless place.

"Hannah told you the news, didn't she?" Maria said.

He nodded.

She squeezed his hand. "And you don't believe you're ready to be a father."

"Yes. No." He shook his head. "It's complicated." If things were different—if he was different, he'd be excited about becoming a dad, but the idea of bringing a tiny human into such a crappy world scared him to death. Who in their right mind wanted the lifelong responsibility of keeping another human being safe and healthy when so much of what happened in the world was out of a person's control?

"When are you and Hannah getting married?"

"We're not." He winced at the look of disappointment in Maria's eyes.

"You don't love Hannah?"

Until now, Alonso hadn't allowed himself the luxury of analyzing his feelings for Hannah. He liked her. He admired her and he was attracted to her. He couldn't let his thoughts and feelings go beyond that, because he feared Hannah had the power to make him take a leap of faith and give the world a second chance. And he knew that second chances never worked out. He'd saved his buddies in the Army that fateful day, but their second chance had only lasted hours before it had been stolen from them.

"I won't let myself fall in love with Hannah." At Maria's surprised look he added, "The world sucks. I've witnessed too many horrors to believe in happy-ever-afters."

"Where did this pessimistic attitude come from?" She'd badger him until he spilled his guts.

"I think it's been in me my whole life. I just didn't realize it until I was in the Army. Growing up in the barrio I saw things most kids never see in their entire lives. I thought when I enrolled in college and then med school, I'd escape the doom and gloom of my past, but I didn't."

"I don't understand."

"I experienced some pretty rough stuff in Afghanistan. That's why I left the military early. I thought being back in the States and working in an ER would renew my faith in humanity, but it didn't. Every day at the hospital I see bad things happen to good people—people who are doing what they're supposed to do in life. When good people get killed by drunk drivers or shot standing at bus stops, you start thinking it doesn't matter that you're doing the right thing…the bad always wins over the good in the end."

He shoved a hand through his hair. "I took a leave from the hospital because there was no point in doing my job anymore. I was saving teenagers who went right back out on the streets and got themselves shot up again a week later."

Tears welled in Maria's eyes. Hell, he hadn't meant to make her cry. He gave her a hug. "I'm sorry. I don't mean to be such a downer."

"There are other things a man with a college degree can do." She sniffed.

"I'm good at saving people—it's just too bad the world is better at taking them away."

"It's not like you to turn your back on someone who needs you, Alonso."

"I'm not deserting Hannah. I intend to give her financial support and I'll be there to help out if she needs me." He'd help Hannah as long as he maintained an emotional distance from her. He couldn't afford to lose his heart to her and their child. God help him then if anything horrible happened to them.

"Forget about child-support payments," Maria said. "You never knew your father. Don't you want better for your son or daughter?"

"It's not as if I'm never going to see them." Even as he said the words, he knew they were a lie. He'd only visit Hannah and the baby if she reached out to him, and Hannah was a stubborn, strong woman—she wouldn't need him very often.

"I bet you'll feel differently once you hold the baby in your arms." Maria's cell phone rang and she glanced at the number. "Let me take this call. I'll be right back." As soon as she left the room, Alonso made a dash for the door.

He felt as if he'd gone ten rounds with Maria and she'd barely said a few sentences to him. When he stepped outside, he waved at Luke to meet him at the pickup. The kid talked the entire drive back to the ranch, but Alonso was battling his conscience and barely heard a word.

"Hey, Rambo, I'm home!" Luke raced into the living room, where Hannah was taking down the tree decorations. He dropped to his hands and knees on the floor and the puppy raced toward him, his big paws sliding on the wood.

Rambo was supposed to have been Hannah's dog, but the puppy had latched on to Luke, and the two were becoming best friends.

"Was it tough for Michael to go back to the ranch?" she asked.

"No. He likes it there."

"Good." She sent up a silent prayer of thanks that Maria and Riley Fitzgerald had put her brother on the right path.

Luke lifted Rambo up to his face and nuzzled the dog's nose. "You wanna go for a ride in the truck?" Rambo's little tail wagged. "He's smart, Hannah. He knows what going for a ride means."

"Why don't you grab a snack before you check on the bison?"

"I will." He got to his feet. "C'mon, Rambo." Luke

skidded to a stop when Alonso appeared with his army bag slung over his shoulder. "Are you leaving?"

Alonso nodded. "It's time for me to hit the road again."

"But winter break isn't over yet."

"I have to be back at the hospital by January second." He had three days to make it to Albuquerque.

"I thought you were leaving tomorrow," Hannah said. She hadn't prepared herself for their goodbye.

Alonso shrugged. "There's still a few hours of daylight."

Luke's gaze swiveled between Hannah and Alonso. "But I thought you guys…you know…liked each other."

"We do," Hannah said, forcing a smile. "But Alonso's real job is saving people, not feeding bison." Alonso's gaze met hers, and in the brief instant before he looked away she saw yearning—the same longing she'd buried deep inside her.

"It kind of sucks." Luke smiled sheepishly. "I got used to you being here."

Me, too. Each night when Hannah drifted off to sleep, she imagined her, Alonso and the baby becoming a real family. Then she'd wake in the morning and realize it would never happen.

Luke offered Alonso his hand. "Thank you for everything."

"I'm glad things worked out for you, Luke. Do well in school and don't give your sister any grief."

"I won't. Michael's gonna come visit over my spring break. Maria said she'd drive him up here."

"Good. I'm sure your sister will appreciate the extra help with chores."

"Wait until Michael sees Rambo. He'll be huge by then." Luke stepped past Alonso. "Come back and visit us."

Hannah waited until the back door closed before she spoke. "After all the repairs you did, we should be in good shape for a while."

"Albuquerque isn't that far. If you need help, call me and I'll drive down." His stare pierced her. "I mean it." He removed a business card from his pants pocket and handed it to her. "That's the chief of staff's number. If you can't get hold of me, he'll make sure I get a message from you."

Hannah set the card on the coffee table. "If you wait until tomorrow, I can drive you back to Albuquerque."

His mouth curved in a half grin. "I made it this far hitching rides—I might as well return the same way."

"Let me at least give you a lift to the highway." She swept past him, and walked into the kitchen. Luke had left the keys to the Civic on the counter and she grabbed them on her way out the door. She didn't look over her shoulder for fear she'd cry if she made eye contact with him.

Alonso stowed his duffel in the backseat and they drove in silence. When Hannah reached the highway, she shifted into Park. They both stared out the windshield, neither saying a word.

This is what you want.

Not *want*. This was what had to be. Maybe if she told herself that enough times she'd believe it.

Alonso reached for the door handle. "Call if you need me. For anything."

She wanted to shout that she needed him for everything. "Okay," she whispered, battling tears. Damn it. She could do this alone. She'd taken care of herself and Luke for years before her father and Ruth had passed away. There was no doubt in her mind that she could take care of this baby by herself—it was just that she didn't want to do it alone. She wanted Alonso by her side, raising their child together.

He got out of the car and removed his duffel, then stuck his head back through the open passenger window. Their eyes connected and Hannah's breath caught at the sheen of moisture making his brown eyes sparkle. *You love me, Alonso. I know you do.*

"Be well, Hannah." He walked off before she found the courage to beg him to stay.

She kept her foot on the brake as she watched him stroll down the road. Not until he became a speck on the horizon did she put the car into Reverse and return to the house.

Only then did she realize Alonso had never looked back.

Keep walking. Don't stop.

The urge to check over his shoulder to see if Hannah was still sitting in the car was more powerful than the rage he'd felt when his buddies had died in Afghanistan.

This is what you wanted.

The hell it was. He wanted to be with Hannah. He just couldn't, that was all. A horn honked and he jumped sideways, thinking he'd wandered onto the road. A blue Ford pulled onto the shoulder ahead of him. Doc Snyder. The old man lowered his window when Alonso approached. "Where are you headed?"

"Making my way back to Albuquerque."

The doctor eyed him suspiciously. "Why didn't Hannah give you a ride?"

"I needed time to think."

"About what?"

He didn't care for people poking their nose into his business. "Do me a favor and check on Hannah every now and then."

"Might have a problem with that."

"Why?"

"I put off that hip replacement I was supposed to have after Thanksgiving. I'm scheduled for surgery in three days. I'll be out of commission at least a month."

"Who's filling in for you at the clinic?"

"A doctor friend from Gallup. But he can only visit the clinic one day a week." Doc narrowed his eyes. "You wouldn't by chance know a doctor who'd be willing to help out my friend?"

The temptation to stay near Hannah was powerful, but if he didn't return to the hospital he could kiss his job goodbye. An image of Hannah large with child— his child—flashed before his eyes. He couldn't do it. Couldn't walk away from her and the baby. He didn't know what the hell that meant for his career or for him and Hannah. All he knew was that he couldn't leave.

"I'll take over the clinic while you recover from surgery."

"Hop in."

As soon as Alonso got into the cab and snapped his belt on, Doc peeled away from the side of the road. "There's a cot in the back room you can sleep on, unless you plan to drive back to Hannah's ranch every night."

"I'll take the cot." He'd just as soon Hannah didn't know he'd changed his mind about Albuquerque. Not yet. Not until he had an answer for her when she asked why he'd stayed.

"I'll introduce you to my regular patients who come in once a week for blood-pressure checks and prescription refills. Then I'll fill you in on the house calls you'll have to make while I'm out."

"I don't have a vehicle."

"You can use Bertha."

"Pardon?"

Doc patted the dashboard. "This here is Bertha. She's a little rough around the edges, but she gets the job done. Fill her up at the convenience-store gas station and they'll charge it to my account. I'll let the sheriff know you'll be seeing my patients."

"Are you worried about the hip surgery?"

"I'm looking forward to the time off. Haven't had a vacation in years."

"Hell of a way to spend your vacation."

"I take what I can get."

"Are you sure your patients will see me?"

"Why wouldn't they?"

"They don't know me."

"You won't have any problems. Folks are grateful for my help."

"How do I handle payments?"

Doc waved a hand. "You'll figure it out soon enough."

When they reached town, Doc Snyder removed the clinic key from his truck ring and offered it to Alonso. "Let yourself in. I'll see you in the morning."

Alonso was doing a good thing by remaining in Paradise to help Doc. But he knew from experience that it didn't matter how much good he did—in the end it wouldn't be enough.

Chapter 14

A loud pounding woke Alonso and he checked his watch—eight thirty. The clinic opened at eight. He flew off the cot, shrugged into a fresh T-shirt and tugged on a pair of jeans, then shoved his feet into his hiking boots and hurried down the hall to the waiting room.

"Hold your horses!" He flipped the bolt, opened the door and came face-to-face with a chicken.

"Who are you?"

For a moment he thought the bird had spoken, then a head covered in gray wiry curls peeked around the chicken. "Where's Doc Snyder?"

Good question. "He should be here shortly. I'm Dr. Marquez."

"I've been waitin' outside in the cold for a half hour."

"I'm sorry." He opened the door wider. "Come in."

She stepped past him and sat in a chair. He glanced between the woman and the bird, but both ignored him. He needed a shot of caffeine before he diagnosed the lady and her feathered friend. He returned to the storage room where he'd slept and studied his K-cup coffee choices stacked on the counter next to the Keurig machine. He picked a dark roast, waited two minutes, then, carrying his breakfast, he returned to the front room.

"I didn't get your name," he said.

She set the clucker on the floor. "Gertrude. Friends call me Gertie."

"What can I do for you, Gertie?"

"Doc switched my blood pressure medicine last week and said I had to come in today and have it checked."

"C'mon back."

She scooped the chicken off the floor.

"Leave your pet out here."

"Suit yourself." She followed him into an exam room and sat in the chair next to the door.

"Roll up your sweater sleeve, please."

After a minute she huffed. "How many times are you gonna take my blood pressure? Don't you know how to work that thing?"

Feisty old lady. "Your blood pressure is a little high, but not bad." He pressed two fingers against the dark blue vein on the inside of her wrist. "Pulse is fine." Then he felt her thyroid and lymph nodes. "I want to listen to your heart." When he was finished, he asked, "How old are you, Gertie?"

"Too old for you, young man."

He grinned.

"Eighty-one."

"Your eighty-one-year-old heartbeat is strong."

Her eyes twinkled. "Bob always told me I was too ornery to die."

"How old is Bob?"

"He's dead."

Jeez, his bedside manner needed work. He wasn't used to engaging patients in conversation—most of the time they were in shock or sedated. "I'm sorry to hear your husband passed away."

"Bob was my boyfriend."

He gaped at the old woman.

"My husband died thirty years ago of a heart attack. Fell off the tractor in the middle of the field. That man never missed a meal in his entire life, and when he was late for supper I knew he was gone."

Alonso was a surgeon, not a shrink. Hoping to avoid a therapy session with Gertie, he said, "Stay on your medication." He walked her back to the waiting room.

"Do I need to come in next week and have it checked again?"

"Sure." He noticed the droppings on the floor. "But leave your chicken at home."

"That's your chicken now." She opened the door.

"Hey, you can't leave the bird here."

"Doc and I have an agreement. He takes care of me and I pay him in chickens." She pointed to the clucker. "That there is a prize laying hen."

"Doc's having hip surgery and he won't be back for a few weeks."

"Then, keep the hen for yourself."

Alonso sipped his coffee and stared at his supper. Where the heck was Doc? The clinic phone rang. "Hello?"

"Alonso, I can't make it in today," Doc Snyder said. "I'm just getting home from a house call I went on after midnight. I'm in no shape to drive. Look behind the counter and you'll see a stack of files. Those patients are coming in today. I'll bring Bertha by later."

"But—"

The dial tone sounded in his ear. The chicken forgotten, he perused the files. There were ten people scheduled for the day. He was used to seeing three times that many. This job was going to be a breeze. He walked to the back of the clinic to make a second cup of coffee when the front door banged open and a voice called out. "Doc! Come quick!"

Alonso did an about-face and rushed back down the hallway. A middle-aged man stood in the doorway, holding a young boy with a bleeding head wound.

"He fell off his horse." The man's face was stark white and Alonso worried he'd faint if he didn't set the boy down soon.

"I'm Dr. Marquez. I'm filling in for Doc." He took the boy from the man's arms. "Follow me."

Alonso laid the boy on the table in the exam room, then checked his pupils. "Has he come to at all?"

"No."

The answer sent a cold chill down Alonso's back. "How long has he been unconscious?"

"About thirty minutes. I got here as fast as I could."

Alonso felt the boy's skull and neck, then checked his reflexes before probing the cut on his forehead. "How old is he?"

"Seven."

"Was he wearing a riding helmet?"

"No." The father's voice shook.

Alonso wanted to ask what the hell a seven-year-old was doing riding a horse without wearing the proper head gear, but the father's tormented expression told him the man was already blaming himself for his son's accident. "What's his name?"

"Billy. Billy Johnson. I'm his father, Earl."

Alonso's gut insisted the boy had a severe concussion or a possible brain bleed, but he needed a CT scan to confirm it. The clinic was limited to a single X-ray machine. He grasped Billy's hand. "If you can hear me, Billy, squeeze my hand." *Nothing.*

"Open your eyes, Billy."

The boy's eyes moved beneath his closed lids. The pressure in Alonso's chest intensified until it suffocated him. "Billy!"

The boy opened his eyes and stared unseeingly at Alonso.

"Looks as if he's going to be okay," the father said.

It was a good sign that Billy opened his eyes, but Alonso couldn't shake the feeling that the kid's injury was severe. "He needs a CT scan. If there's bleeding in the brain, he'll have to have surgery."

"Albuquerque and Gallup are about the same distance from here. Which hospital should I take him to?"

Billy might not have two hours. "He needs to be air-lifted." Alonso left the room and made an emergency call to 911, requesting a life-flight helicopter. When he returned to the room, he said, "We're meeting the helicopter outside of town. We'll take your truck."

"I can't afford to pay for a helicopter." The man shoved his hands through his hair. "Billy woke up once." He glanced at his son, who lay motionless.

Alonso second-guessed himself. Was he panicking or had he made a rational, reasonable decision based on his exam and his experience treating trauma patients? "I'm not taking a chance with your son's life. This is more serious than a concussion." He started an IV in Billy's arm, then lifted him off the table. "Are you coming with me, or am I going alone with your son?"

The father led the way outside and Alonso laid Billy down in the backseat of Earl's truck. Earl started the engine and Alonso told him the location where the helicopter intended to set down. Fifteen minutes later Earl parked on the shoulder of the road next to the open field and they waited.

Alonso took Billy's pulse—the boy's breathing was shallow. He'd made the right decision to call 911. Billy's fall had been an accident and he might have hit his head even if he'd worn a riding helmet. He just hoped the kid would make it. His thoughts turned to Hannah and the child she carried. She'd insist that their son or daughter wear a helmet if they rode horses, but she might not be able to prevent an accident from happening. He imagined himself standing in Earl's shoes—it was bound to happen sooner or later because you couldn't protect those you cared about from all harm.

"Billy's been riding since he could sit a horse," Earl said. "Avalanche is almost twenty years old. You won't find a better-behaved horse. Billy was trotting him in the corral when Avalanche stumbled. It happened so fast."

Alonso felt bad for the father, but there was no time to reassure him as the helicopter came into sight.

"I've never been on a helicopter," Earl said.

"I was in the military. It's a breeze." Once the chopper landed, the crew carried a stretcher to the truck and Alonso helped them put Billy on it. While one of the medics strapped him down, Alonso informed them of the boy's condition and the need for a CT scan and possibly surgery to stop any hemorrhaging in the brain.

"Is the father coming?" the medic asked.

"I am." Earl handed his truck keys to Alonso. "Leave the truck at the clinic. I'll pick it up…whenever."

"Good luck." Alonso watched until the helicopter disappeared from sight, then drove back to the clinic, hoping his gut was wrong and the boy didn't have a brain bleed. As he approached town, a silver Civic heading in the opposite direction sped past him on the highway. *Luke.* Sooner or later, Hannah would find out he'd stayed in Paradise. He should tell her that he was taking over for Doc, but then she'd ask why, and to be honest he didn't know yet what his hanging around meant for their relationship.

When he arrived at the clinic, there were several vehicles parked out front, including Bertha. It was about time Doc showed up to help him out. The waiting room looked more like a flea market than a medical office. One woman held a handmade quilt on her lap. Another lady had a plastic cake container. The only man in the room sat with a burlap bag marked "popcorn seed." And Gertrude's damned chicken was waddling all over the place clucking its head off.

"Is Doc Snyder here?" Alonso asked the group.

"He left a few minutes ago."

Great. "Sorry about the wait. There was an emergency this morning."

"Who?" the woman with the cake asked.

"Billy Johnson fell off a horse and hit his head."

"Is he going to be okay?" the older man asked.

If Alonso said he didn't know, then his patients wouldn't have much confidence in his doctoring ability. But if he said yes and Billy took a turn for the worse, they wouldn't trust him. Either way he couldn't win. "Billy needed a CT scan and Doc doesn't have a machine at the clinic, so a life-flight helicopter is flying him to Albuquerque."

The group grew quiet—they knew without being told that Billy's condition was serious. "I'm Dr. Marquez."

"We know. Doc said you were taking over until he recovered from his surgery." The lady with the quilt on her lap spoke. She wore a pinched look on her face and appeared to be in pain.

"What's your name?" Alonso asked.

"Maryellen Trumpet."

He searched through the files but didn't see a Maryellen. "I can't find your paperwork," he said.

"I wasn't supposed to visit Doc until late next week, but…" She set the quilt on the chair next to her, revealing her big belly. "I think the baby's coming now."

Alonso stared in shock. "When's your due date?"

"Three days ago."

"Why haven't you gone to the hospital in Cañon City?"

"I'm using a midwife, but she came down with the

flu this week and she told me to go ahead and let Doc handle the delivery."

Alonso felt a moment of panic. He'd never delivered a baby before. "Is there a backup midwife you can call?"

"It's too late," she said.

"What do you mean, too late?"

"My water broke earlier this morning. The pains are two minutes apart now." As if on cue, Maryellen groaned when a contraction hit her.

"You gonna just stand there, Doc, or help this poor woman?" the man next to her spoke.

"I'm going to help her," Alonso said. As if he had a choice.

"Hey, Hannah, I thought Alonso was going back to Albuquerque?"

As soon as Rambo heard Luke's voice he bolted past Hannah in Buster's stall and raced toward his best friend. She set aside the rake she'd been using to muck the stall. "He did go back. Why?"

"I passed a pickup on the road and it looked like Alonso behind the wheel."

Hannah's heart pounded inside her chest. "You must be mistaken."

"Maybe, but it sure looked like him."

Hannah shoved the pitchfork at him. "You and Rambo finish up." She left the barn and jogged to the house. Once inside she pulled her cell phone from her pocket and dialed Doc's home phone. His wife, Marlene, answered.

"Marlene, this is Hannah Buck."

"Hello, dear. How are you?"

"I'm fine. Is Doc at the clinic right now?"

"Didn't you hear?"

"Hear what?"

"He's taking time off to have that hip replacement done. We're driving to Albuquerque tomorrow."

"Who's running the clinic?"

"Alonso Marquez agreed to see Ed's patients."

Her brother hadn't seen a ghost.

"By the way, how's Luke doing?"

"He's doing much better, thanks for asking."

"I'm glad. Ed's sleeping, but I can wake him up if you need to speak with him right away."

"It's not important. Tell him that I'm thinking of him and wishing him a speedy recovery."

"You and me both. That man gets cranky when he has to sit still for more than a half hour."

"Take care, Marlene." Hannah ended the call and stared into space. What did this mean?

The back door crashed open and Luke walked inside, dragging Rambo behind him. The dog had sunk his teeth into the bottom of Luke's pant leg and wouldn't let go.

"You need to train Rambo to stop doing that. I can't have an ankle biter around when the baby starts crawling." As soon as the words left her mouth, Hannah sucked in a quick breath.

Luke stared at her bug-eyed. "What baby?"

This wasn't how she'd planned to break the news to her brother. "You're going to be an uncle." She forced a smile.

"Whose baby is it? Alonso or Seth?"

She scowled. "I broke up with Seth two years ago."

"Girls sleep with their old boyfriends all the time."

How would he know that? "Alonso is the father."

"I know you get pissed off at me because you say I'm immature and I need to grow up, but I'd never desert a girl if I got her pregnant."

"Alonso didn't desert me."

"Then, why did he say he was going back to Albuquerque?"

"Things are complicated." At her brother's scowl, she added, "But Alonso is taking full responsibility for this baby."

"He doesn't want to be a father."

"It's not that simple, Luke."

Her brother pulled out a chair and sat down at the table. "I'm almost seventeen. I can handle the truth."

"If I knew the truth then I'd share it with you. I don't exactly know why Alonso wants nothing to do with raising our baby."

"Why don't you ask him?"

"What good would it do? We raise bison and Alonso is a trauma surgeon. Our lives are going in different directions."

"Did you ask him to stay?"

She dropped her gaze.

"Are you afraid he'll say no?"

"Maybe. I think I'd rather raise this baby on my own than wake up each morning knowing I guilted Alonso into staying here when he doesn't love me."

"Did he say he didn't love you?"

"He never said he did or didn't."

"Do you love him?"

She felt like a punching bag—each of her brother's questions knocking the air out of her. "Yes, I love him." She sighed. "And you weren't wrong about thinking you saw Alonso earlier. He's filling in at the clinic while Doc has surgery."

"Then, you have time to convince him to stay." When Hannah remained silent, Luke asked, "You gotta tell him that you love him."

"What if it doesn't make a difference?"

"You had your heart broken before. What's the big deal?"

That was the problem—she hadn't been in love with Seth—not the way she'd fallen for Alonso.

Alonso didn't think his day could get any crazier as he helped Maryellen onto the exam table. He offered a smile, hoping to reassure the expectant mother. And maybe himself, too.

"I called the midwife again and told her Doc Snyder wasn't around. She'll get here as soon as she can," Maryellen said.

"Good." Maybe he wouldn't have to deliver the baby.

"Is anyone else coming to be with you?"

"My husband's on his way from North Dakota. He works in the oil fields up there." Maryellen sucked in a breath when another contraction hit her.

He held her hand, all the while thinking of Hannah. Was this how she'd end up giving birth to their child— alone in Doc's clinic? When the contraction passed, he took her blood pressure. "Do you know what you're having?"

"A girl. We're naming her Caroline after my mother."

Alonso's memory raced through the pages of his medical textbooks, trying to recall the chapters on childbirth as he washed his hands and put on a paper gown.

Maryellen groaned loudly and he said, "Practice your breathing." He had no idea what the hell he was talking about and was glad Maryellen wasn't panicking. He opened a cupboard and found several clean towels. A knock on the door caught him by surprise. "Maybe that's the midwife." He opened the door and found Hannah standing in the hallway, looking more beautiful than she had a right to be.

"You didn't leave. Why?" she asked.

For a million and one reasons. Did she want to know them all? Right now?

He glanced at Maryellen, who appeared more interested in his and Hannah's conversation than her labor pains.

"Is it because of the baby?" Hannah asked.

"That, but…mostly it was you," he said.

Hannah smiled.

"Doc," Maryellen said. "I need to push."

"Oh, my God." Hannah stepped into the room. "You're having a baby."

"I'm trying," Maryellen said.

"Have you ever delivered a baby, Alonso?" Hannah asked.

"No."

Maryellen's eyes rounded.

"It's okay," Hannah said, taking the woman's hand in hers. "I've delivered calves before. I can help."

Alonso's patient didn't look reassured. "I'm having a baby, not a calf."

"I'm Hannah."

"Maryellen."

"Nice to meet you, Maryellen. How close are the contractions?"

"About a minute apart."

Hannah looked at Alonso and the confidence in him that shone in her eyes spurred him into action. "Help Maryellen out of her dress and put this sheet over her." Alonso turned his back while Hannah helped undress Maryellen. He found a scissors and thread to tie off the umbilical cord and a suction bulb in case he needed to clear the baby's airway.

"Can I push now?" Maryellen grimaced.

Alonso looked between her legs and saw that the baby's head was crowning. No turning back now. "Slow and easy," he said.

Sweat broke out across his brow as the baby's head came farther out with Maryellen's next push. "Does your husband have hair?" Alonso asked, hoping to distract the mother from the pain she was in.

"No," she gasped. "He shaves his head. Why?"

"Your baby girl is bald, too."

Maryellen laughed, then squeezed Hannah's hand when another contraction hit.

After three pushes, the baby slid into Alonso's hands, and he placed the crying infant on Maryellen's chest. After he tied off and cut the cord, he briskly rubbed the little body and a loud cry escaped her mouth. "Her lungs are working."

"You did it, Maryellen." Hannah smiled at the mother and daughter.

A few minutes later, Alonso delivered the placenta and Hannah helped Maryellen clean up while Alonso weighed the baby. "Seven pounds eleven ounces." He wrapped the little girl in a towel, then listened to her chest. "Caroline's heart and lungs sound fine." He handed the baby to Maryellen just as the exam door burst open, knocking Hannah into Alonso's chest.

A wild-eyed bald man shouted, "Where's Maryellen?"

"I'm right here."

Alonso pulled Hannah aside so the father could see his wife and newborn daughter. He kissed Maryellen, then the baby. "She's as beautiful as you, honey."

Alonso and Hannah left the room, giving the new parents time alone.

"You were wonderful in there." Alonso brushed his fingers across his cheek. He stared into Hannah's baby blues. "I can't go back to Albuquerque."

"Why not?"

"I love you."

Tears spilled down her cheeks.

His heart thudded painfully in his chest. How had he ever believed leaving Hannah was the right thing to do? "I love you and our baby, but loving you both scares me to death."

"Parenthood can be frightening, but we'll help each other through it."

He shook his head. "It's so damned risky, Hannah. What if something happens to the baby?" *Or you.*

"There are no guarantees in life. We do the best we

can, make the best decisions we can and hope in the end everything works out." She went up on tiptoe and kissed his mouth.

He wasn't sure it was as simple as Hannah made it seem, but he didn't want to go back to the ER and get swallowed up by all the darkness again. Hannah had shown him there was still beauty and goodness left in the world—all he had to do was give her his hand and she and the baby would keep him looking forward to a future filled with love and hope, not hate and destruction.

"I've been doing a lot of thinking, and I'd like to try working at the clinic with Doc when he returns from his hip-replacement surgery."

"But you can help more people in a hospital."

"I've had my fill of trauma surgeries."

"Are you sure this town, the ranch, me…are enough for you?"

"More than sure." He threaded his fingers through hers. "I need you, Hannah. I need your strength. Your courage." He sucked in a deep breath and released it slowly. "I love you for wanting to bring my child into the world, knowing that you might have had to do it on your own."

Hannah wrapped her arms around Alonso and hugged him. "And I love you for being brave enough to give you, me and the baby a chance to be a real family."

He stared into her eyes. "You have my word that I'll be by your side every step of the way no matter what life throws at us."

"I don't need your word. I just need your heart."

When Alonso kissed her, Hannah felt a surge of joy

rush through her body. The future suddenly looked brighter than she'd ever dreamed possible. Someone cleared their throat and Hannah broke off the kiss.

"Are you going to be much longer, Dr. Marquez? There's a lady in the waiting room who needs her insulin shot."

"Be right there." He smiled at Hannah. "Looks as if it'll be a long day."

"Will I see you later?"

He nodded. "I'm coming home tonight." Hannah and the baby were home now. Once Hannah left, he entered the waiting room and discovered every chair filled. Baked goods and casseroles were piling up on the counter. "Okay, who needs their insulin shot?"

"Me. I'm Gladys. I can't get the hang of that newfangled meter. It's always telling me my blood sugar is low, but I don't think it is."

Alonso checked Gladys's blood sugar, gave her the insulin shot and sent her on the way. Next, he stitched up Kevin Heppner's finger, which he'd gashed when he'd accidentally grabbed hold of a barbed-wire fence without a glove. Then he clipped and filed Mr. Livingston's toenails and recommended he get a pedicure every two months. The man argued that pedicures were for women, which ignited a discussion in the waiting area about the term *metrosexual*, after which Mr. Livingston loudly denied that he was gay.

Not long after Mr. Livingston left, the midwife arrived with two of her children in tow. The kids played with the chicken while their mother tended to Maryellen. Soon after, the new parents left with their baby.

The day slipped by and finally at six thirty he locked

the front door. Exhausted, he stared at the messy waiting room. He stored the perishable food in the fridge—he wouldn't have to make his lunch for a month. Just when he was ready to turn out the lights he heard a scuffling sound—the chicken stared at him from the end of the hallway. "Where have you been all day?"

The bird waddled up to Alonso, then sat on top of his boots. "Make yourself comfortable, why don't you?"

He scooped up his new feathered friend. "I hope Rambo takes a liking to you." He got into Doc's truck and made a phone call on the way out of town.

"This is Dr. Marquez. A patient of mine was life-flighted to the hospital today and I'm calling to check on him."

"What's the patient's name?"

"Billy Johnson. Head-trauma victim."

"He went into surgery to stop a brain bleed shortly after he arrived. He's still in recovery."

"What's his prognosis?"

"Excellent. Dr. McNamara performed the operation."

Dr. McNamara was a well-respected surgeon. Billy had been in good hands. "Thanks for the update."

After a few miles Alonso glanced across the seat—his copilot had fallen asleep. It was almost eight o'clock when he pulled into the ranch yard. Rambo barked, and a moment later Hannah walked into the kitchen, Luke on her heels holding the puppy.

"Is everything okay?" she asked.

"Sorry I'm so late. The patients left me with a mess in the waiting room." He smiled. "It was a long day but a good day."

"Hannah said you're not going back to Albuquerque."

"I need to talk to you about that, Luke."

The teen glanced between the adults. "Okay."

"I'd like to marry your sister and I was hoping you'd approve."

"What about your job at the hospital?" Luke asked.

"I'm ready to move on to something different. A slower pace." Although today had been anything but slow.

Luke grinned. "Does marrying my sister mean you're going to live here on the ranch with her?"

"Yes."

"Then, heck yeah, you can marry my sister."

Hannah playfully punched Luke in the arm. "I'm seriously going to be outnumbered by males." She placed her hand over her stomach. "Let's hope we're having a girl."

"I want a boy." Luke set Rambo on the floor and the dog raced over to the door. "He's got to go outside."

Alone in the kitchen with Hannah, Alonso pulled her close for a hug. "Are you sure?" Hannah had had several hours to think about marrying him after she'd left the clinic. If she was having second thoughts, he wanted to know now.

"I'm more sure of you than anything else in my life."

"I'll work hard so you never lose faith in me." He kissed her gently, pledging his love to her.

"Hey, did you know there's a chicken out here?" Luke called through the screen door.

Alonso chuckled. "I guess it's a good thing we live

on a ranch. Who knows what I'll be bringing home every night."

"I don't care how many critters you bring home as long as you're the one bringing them." Hannah pressed her mouth against his and Alonso tasted all that was good and beautiful—a future together, a family and a forever love.

Epilogue

"I knew Hannah would get her way." Luke walked into his bedroom, grinning.

Alonso shrugged into his suit jacket. "I underestimated your sister." Alonso had believed he'd have a few months to get used to the idea of becoming a married man but Hannah hadn't been willing to compromise on a wedding date.

"You sure you want to marry her? She can be bossy."

"Your sister's not bossy," he said. "She's persuasive." *And a seductress.* But Alonso couldn't very well admit to his soon-to-be brother-in-law that he hadn't put up much of a fight when Hannah had launched her campaign to move up the wedding date using her wiles in bed against him.

Only two weeks had passed since he'd taken over

the clinic for Doc, but he'd settled into a routine with his patients that felt comfortable and right. And each night he came home to Hannah—the best part of his day. Later in bed, after they made love, he'd rest his hand on her tummy and imagine what their child would be like. What its personality would be.

Some nights Alonso swore it was as if the baby was communicating with him. His palm would heat up against Hannah's belly and the warm sensation would then travel up his arm, into his chest and straight to his heart, bringing him a sense of peace he'd never felt before.

He turned away from the mirror. "Yes, I'm sure I want to marry your sister."

"Cool. I'm glad she won't be all alone after I graduate from high school."

"Don't worry about your sister. I'll take good care of her and your niece or nephew. You just make sure you graduate."

"I will. I promise."

"Is it warming up outside?" Alonso asked.

"No, but the sun is out."

Hannah had enlisted Maria Fitzgerald's help in planning the ceremony at the Blue Bison. Cruz's father-in-law, José, had prepared the food for the guests and Betsy from the Red Bluff Diner had baked the wedding cake. Michael came up the weekend before the wedding and helped Luke build a maze out of hay bales for the kids and Rambo to play in after the ceremony.

"Doc Snyder wants to talk to you before you go outside," Luke said.

"Sure, send him in."

A minute later Doc entered Luke's bedroom and shut the door.

"Hey, Doc."

"Alonso." Doc held out a brand-new black Stetson.

"What's this for?"

"For taking care of my practice while I recuperated."

Doc Snyder had recovered quickly from his hip-replacement surgery and was scheduled to return to work in another week. Alonso wasn't sure what he was going to do about a job, but Hannah didn't seem worried, so he'd taken his cue from her and decided that things would work out the way they were meant to be. "You didn't have to buy me a hat." Alonso examined the Stetson. It wasn't his first cowboy hat but it was his first nice one. He tried it on, surprised it fit well.

"Now you look like a country doctor."

"I guess I do." Alonso stared at his image in the mirror. There was no trace of the soldier that had followed him home from Afghanistan. That part of his life was over now. He'd hold the good memories close—his friendships with his comrades—then let the bad ones go.

"I have a proposition for you," Doc said.

"What's that?"

"I've decided to retire and I want you to take over my practice."

Shocked, Alonso didn't know what to say.

"I've been meaning to retire for a while now, but I didn't want to turn my patients over to just anyone."

"You still have some gas left in you, Doc." He expected a smile or a chuckle but the older man's expression remained sober. "You're serious, aren't you?"

"I'm not getting any younger, and now that I can walk pain-free, Marlene wants to travel. We've never been to Italy, where her great-grandparents are from. We just bought our plane tickets. We're leaving in March."

"But—"

"I don't mind consulting on cases if you need a second opinion, but I'm not coming into the clinic every day." He cleared his throat. "Being a country doctor might not be challenging enough for a man with your talents, but folks like you." He straightened his shoulders. "You think you could be happy taking care of your friends and neighbors instead of strangers?"

Taking care of friends and neighbors... Not bodies without names whom he never saw again after they left the surgery suite. Doc was offering Alonso the opportunity to serve people who would become part of his life. "Are you sure you're ready to hang up your stethoscope?"

"Positive. If I bring home any more chickens, Marlene will pluck me for dinner."

Alonso chuckled. "I'd be honored to take over your practice."

"You won't make as much money as surgeons in Albuquerque."

"Money's overrated."

"You won't think so when you have more kids."

"Whoa, let me get used to having one first."

The doctor offered his hand. "I don't know what brought you to Paradise, Alonso, but I do know you're the best thing that's happened to Hannah and Luke. God knows that girl deserves some happiness in her life. You do right by her and my patients, and I'll be forever in your debt."

Alonso patted Doc on the shoulder. "I'm ready to see my bride." He followed Doc outside to the front porch, where the ceremony would take place. Hannah had insisted on no bridesmaids or groomsmen. Luke was giving Hannah away and the rest of the onlookers had gathered in the front yard.

Alonso had invited his sisters and his mother, and they'd been thrilled for him and Hannah. His mother had been especially excited about another grandchild and had offered to take care of the baby anytime Hannah and Alonso wanted to get away together. He smiled at his mother, who stood by the porch steps, tears of happiness in her eyes.

He hadn't counted on being this nervous before the ceremony, but his knees felt as if they were held together with rubber bands. He searched the crowd and spotted Riley and Cruz. They came forward and joined him on the porch.

"This is a big step," Riley said. "You ready?"

"I thought I was." He looked at Cruz. "I'm afraid I'll screw this up."

"Welcome to my world." Cruz smiled, then winced when Riley elbowed him in the ribs.

"You two haven't had it easy all these years, there's no question about that. But you both beat the odds and found a better life outside of the barrio. Let yourselves believe that you deserve to be happy."

"Easy for the rich guy to say," Alonso said.

Riley fought a grin. "I hope I wasn't just a wallet to you two."

Alonso and Cruz exchanged glances, then Alonso said, "You've been the big brother we always wished we'd had."

"And the father we never had," Cruz said.

"And a mentor we probably didn't deserve," Alonso added.

Cruz cleared his throat. "Not a day goes by that we don't appreciate what you've done for us."

"That's enough of the sentimental crap." Riley clasped both men by the shoulders. "I'm proud of you guys."

Someone turned on the music and the bridal march began to play. Riley and Cruz returned to the lawn and stood by their wives and children. The minister opened the front door and Luke escorted the bride outside.

Hannah was breathtaking in a simple white wedding dress. She carried a bouquet of red roses, and a dark red ribbon held her hair back from her face. The minister asked who gave the bride away, but Alonso didn't hear a word after that as he lost himself in the love for him shining in Hannah's eyes.

* * * * *

SPECIAL EXCERPT FROM

H HARLEQUIN®

SPECIAL EDITION

USA TODAY *bestselling author Judy Duarte's*
The Lawman's Convenient Family
is the story of Julie Chapman, a music therapist who
needs a convenient husband in order to save two
orphans from foster care. Lawman Adam Santiago fits
the bill, but suddenly they both find themselves longing
to become a family—forever!

Read on for a sneak preview of the next great book
in the Rocking Chair Rodeo miniseries.

"Lisa," the man dressed as Zorro said, "I'd heard you were going to be here."

He clearly thought Julie was someone else. She probably ought to say something, but up close, the gorgeous bandito seemed to have stolen both her thoughts and her words.

"It's nice to finally meet you." His deep voice set her senses reeling. "I've never really liked blind dates."

Talk about masquerades and mistaken identities. Before Julie could set him straight, he took her hand in a polished, gentlemanly manner and kissed it. His warm breath lingered on her skin, setting off a bevy of butterflies in her tummy.

"Dance with me," he said.

Her lips parted, but for the life of her, she still couldn't speak, couldn't explain. And she darn sure couldn't object.

Zorro led her away from the buffet tables and to the dance floor. When he opened his arms, she again had the opportunity to tell him who she really was. But instead, she stepped into his embrace, allowing him to take the lead.

His alluring aftershave, something manly, taunted her. As she savored his scent, as well as the warmth of his muscular arms, her pulse soared. She leaned her head on his shoulder as they swayed to a sensual beat, their movements in perfect accord, as though they'd danced together a hundred times before.

Now would be a good time to tell him she wasn't Lisa, but she seemed to have fallen under a spell that grew stronger with every beat of the music. The moment turned surreal, like she'd stepped into a fairy tale with a handsome rogue.

Once again, she pondered revealing his mistake and telling him her name, but there'd be time enough to do that after the song ended. Then she'd return to the kitchen, slipping off like Cinderella. But instead of a glass slipper, she'd leave behind her momentary enchantment.

But several beats later, a cowboy tapped Zorro on the shoulder. "I need you to come outside."

Zorro looked at him and frowned. "Can't you see I'm busy?"

The cowboy, whose outfit was so authentic he seemed to be the real deal, rolled his eyes.

Julie wished she could have worn her street clothes. Would now be a good time to admit that she wasn't an actual attendee but here to work at the gala?

"What's up?" Zorro asked.

The cowboy folded his arms across his chest and shifted his weight to one hip. "Someone just broke into my pickup."

Zorro's gaze returned to Julie. "I'm sorry, Lisa. I'm going to have to morph into cop mode."

Now it was Julie's turn to tense. He was actually a police officer in real life? A slight uneasiness settled over her, an old habit she apparently hadn't outgrown. Not that she had any real reason to fear anyone in law enforcement nowadays.

Don't miss
The Lawman's Convenient Family *by Judy Duarte,*
available January 2019 wherever
Harlequin® *Special Edition books and ebooks are sold.*

www.Harlequin.com

Copyright © 2018 by Judy Duarte

HSEEXP1218

Looking for more satisfying love stories
with community and family at their core?

Check out **Harlequin® Special Edition**
and **Love Inspired®** books!

New books available every month!

CONNECT WITH US AT:

Facebook.com/groups/HarlequinConnection

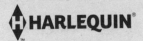 Facebook.com/HarlequinBooks

Twitter.com/HarlequinBooks

Instagram.com/HarlequinBooks

Pinterest.com/HarlequinBooks

ReaderService.com

H HARLEQUIN®

**ROMANCE WHEN
YOU NEED IT**

HFGENRE2018

Need an adrenaline rush from nail-biting tales
(and irresistible males)?

Check out **Harlequin Intrigue®**
and **Harlequin® Romantic Suspense** books!

New books available every month!

CONNECT WITH US AT:

Facebook.com/groups/HarlequinConnection

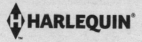

Facebook.com/HarlequinBooks

Twitter.com/HarlequinBooks

Instagram.com/HarlequinBooks

Pinterest.com/HarlequinBooks

ReaderService.com

H HARLEQUIN®

**ROMANCE WHEN
YOU NEED IT**

SGENRE2018

Looking for inspiration in tales
of hope, faith and heartfelt romance?

Check out **Love Inspired**® and
Love Inspired® **Suspense** books!

New books available every month!

CONNECT WITH US AT:

Facebook.com/groups/HarlequinConnection

Facebook.com/HarlequinBooks

Twitter.com/HarlequinBooks

Instagram.com/HarlequinBooks

Pinterest.com/HarlequinBooks

ReaderService.com

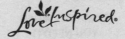

LIGENRE2018R2

Love Harlequin romance?

DISCOVER.

Be the first to find out about promotions, news and exclusive content!

 Facebook.com/HarlequinBooks

 Twitter.com/HarlequinBooks

 Instagram.com/HarlequinBooks

 Pinterest.com/HarlequinBooks

ReaderService.com

EXPLORE.

Sign up for the Harlequin e-newsletter and download a free book from any series at **TryHarlequin.com.**

CONNECT.

Join our Harlequin community to share your thoughts and connect with other romance readers!
Facebook.com/groups/HarlequinConnection

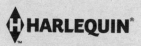

HARLEQUIN®

ROMANCE WHEN
YOU NEED IT

HSOCIAL2018

Reward the book lover in you!

Earn points on your purchase of new Harlequin books from participating retailers.

Turn your points into **FREE BOOKS** of your choice!

Join for FREE today at
www.HarlequinMyRewards.com.

Harlequin My Rewards is a free program (no fees) without any commitments or obligations.

MYR18